W9-BFN-124

The Stewarts
Swept forward by the great events of a new century,
their visions became THE SPIRIT OF AMERICA.

Maurice—His brash independence earned his father's wrath; his steely determination opened the door to fabulous wealth and the love of a beautiful woman.

Casey—Failure almost destroyed his will, until the Rough Riders' bloody charge up San Juan Hill won him a President's admiration and the chance to complete a dream.

Hope—Blond and strikingly lovely, she could not be satisfied by men's admiration. Her own ambitions drove her to the top of the publishing profession, just as her desires drove her to the edge of disaster.

Isaiah—Hope's brother, his genius mapped a new road for a nation; his loneliness pushed him toward a tragic choice.

Van Harrison—Half proud Stewart, half noble Cheyenne Indian, he was handsome enough to attract another man's wife, reckless enough to race the powerful machines his cousins would create.

Willow—A young girl entranced by an older man's charm, she would do anything to marry him, even if it meant traveling half the world to ask him herself.

Bantam Books by Charles Whited
Ask your bookseller for the books you have missed.

CHALLENGE: The Spirit of America, I
DESTINY: The Spirit of America, II
POWER: The Spirit of America, III

The Spirit of America ★ Book III

POWER

CHARLES WHITED

An Arthur Pine Associates Book

BANTAM BOOKS
TORONTO · NEW YORK · LONDON · SYDNEY

POWER

A Bantam Book / May 1983

All rights reserved.
Copyright © 1983 by Charles Whited.
Cover art copyright © 1983 by Lou Glanzman.
This book may not be reproduced in whole or in part, by
mimeograph or any other means, without permission.
For information address: Bantam Books, Inc.

ISBN 0-553-23106-5

Published simultaneously in the United States and Canada

Bantam Books are published by Bantam Books, Inc. Its trade-
mark, consisting of the words ''Bantam Books'' and the por-
trayal of a rooster, is Registered in U.S. Patent and Trademark
Office and in other countries. Marca Registrada. Bantam
Books, Inc., 666 Fifth Avenue, New York, New York 10103.

PRINTED IN THE UNITED STATES OF AMERICA

H   0 9 8 7 6 5 4 3 2 1

I

Laden with snow and gushing billows of steam, the afternoon train from Boston chuffed slowly into Grand Central. Steel doors clanged and passengers poured onto station platforms. Hope Stewart ran down the wrought iron steps from street level, her blond hair flying. She pushed through the crowd, heard male voices singing, and thought: Maurice. She spotted him immediately, standing taller than the rest and peering over the moving sea of heads.

"Maurice! Maurice, here I am!"

He broke into a wide smile and strode through the mass, arms outstretched, to sweep her off her feet with a crushing hug.

"You smell of whiskey and cigars," she said.

"What else is there to do on a train full of college men but drink and smoke?"

She laughed. "Oh, Maurice!"

The others came up behind, eyeing him enviously. All were bundled in greatcoats against the cold. A thin collegian wearing round steel spectacles shouted, "What ho, Stewart, introduce us!"

They crowded around. "Gentlemen," Maurice said with flourish, "may I present my cousin Hope Stewart, the most beautiful female in New York. Hope, these are all disreputable Harvard men, not to be trusted. They haven't seen a woman in months. Allow me to introduce Mr. Grundy, Mr. Poffenbarger, Mr. Pickering, Mr. Lester, Mr. . . . Faraday? Where the hell is Faraday?"

Hope's eyes widened. "What dashing men."

"And I regret to say," Maurice added dolefully, "that they're all on their way home for the spring holidays and must depart on the very next train. Only Mr. Faraday will remain here to entertain you."

There was a chorus of groans.

"Say, where the hell *is* Faraday?"

Maurice's friends accompanied them up the stairs and into the cavernous main waiting room. She held onto Maurice's arm, conscious of the glances from other male passersby.

"Hope, you're irrepressible," Maurice said.

"And you, cousin, are the most talked-about man at Harvard. We've all missed you terribly since Christmas. Women are forever asking me, 'When is your dear cousin coming back to New York?' Brazen hussies. By the time you leave there won't be a virgin left in New York. Incidentally, Aunt Francesca ordered me to bring you straight to Blossom Hill. As usual, she's having a few friends in for the weekend..."

He grimaced. "Oh, Lord."

As the others went off to catch their trains Hope and Maurice walked together toward the carriage park followed by a pale, bespectacled young man burdened down with luggage. Maurice spun around. "Ah, Faraday!" The stranger grinned sheepishly and struggled with his burden. "Hope, this is my roommate Winthrop Faraday. Great bridge player. Also excels at chess, checkers, and cribbage. Honors last term. Faraday, my cousin Hope."

She extended her hand. "Welcome to New York, Mr. Faraday."

He dropped the luggage and took her hand. Bags spilled everywhere and one burst open. His mouth gaped. "Call me W-Winthrop." He stooped clumsily to recover the spillage.

"Come along then, Winthrop."

As they emerged from the station, Hope sensed that Maurice was looking for Aunt Francesca's enclosed victoria drawn by the big matched bays. She led him instead to a gleaming horseless carriage. A clot of admirers gathered around it, staring. The machine was all black metal and brass fittings with rubber tires and high leather seats.

Maurice said, "What on earth?..."

"I knew you'd be excited." Hope climbed behind the wheel. "It's Isaiah's dream machine. He built the engine himself. The chassis is a Winton."

Maurice protested, "Surely we're not riding in *this*!?"

"Put the bags in the back, Winthrop." Manipulating a pair of levers she waved Maurice to the front of the machine. "Cousin, you crank."

On the third crank, the motor coughed, sputtered, and settled into a throaty grumble punctuated by spasmodic explosions and belching a cloud of foul-smelling blue smoke.

The crowd shrank back and gawked, giggling nervously. Maurice and Faraday crowded into the seat beside Hope. She reached into her pocket, drew out a small cigar, and lit it.

Faraday gulped.

Hope patted him gently on the knee. "Relax, Winthrop. You're in for a treat."

With a clash of gears and a head-snapping lurch, they were off.

Faraday, white-faced and clutching his hat, kept muttering, "My word!" Maurice braced against each pitch and lurch, moaning. It was like riding a mechanical bronco, only worse. A bronco one gripped between one's thighs; this beast was beyond control, hurtling into the wind as if launched from a catapult. Maurice shouted, "Jesus Christ!" and looked irritably at their driver. Hope's face and head were encased in a white leather cap and goggles, her body in a canvas coat, her hands—expertly manipulating the steering tiller—in heavy gloves. To add to the sheer madness, the cigar was clenched jauntily between her teeth. She was having an uproariously good time. The monster slewed around a corner, its tires skidding.

"I knew you'd love it!" Hope shouted.

Snowflakes dashed into their faces, as an icy wind cut Maurice's bones to the marrow. Along the streets, pedestrians clutched at heavy coats. White-flanked horses blew steam, as coachmen rode airy perches in suffered silence, gaunt black figures with stovepipe hats and red noses protruding from mufflers. Manhattan sprawled beneath unsightly drapings of ice-encrusted electric wires and sooty icicles. Snow-fringed buildings hunched in cold gray masses. "Sensible people," Maurice muttered, "don't go charging around in such weather. Sensible people stay indoors beside warm fires and drink brandy. Sensible people..."

"What did you say?"

"I said, 'sensible people...'"

"Hold on, cousin. Here we go!"

Hope wrenched at the tiller. They skidded around a corner at Fifth Avenue, passing the great marble pile of the Vanderbilt mansion. A carriage horse reared as a policeman in a blue helmet blew his whistle and a pedestrian narrowly dashed clear and stood at the sidewalk, shaking his fist. On they rocketed, backfiring and belching exhaust. They barreled past Central Park, twisted into the foul-smelling slums of the Lower East Side and rumbled back across town. Joyriding.

3

They were joyriding! Maurice set his jaw grimly. At last he saw the icy sheen of the Hudson River ahead, and the familiar sight of Aunt Francesca's steamers berthed along the quay at Stewart Docks, still weather-locked. They roared northward along the river, twisted up a narrow bricked drive, and came out on a slope below the Stewart mansion, a pile of stone spires and gables crowning the hill. With a final gnashing of gears and screeching of brakes, they shuddered to a halt before a carriage house of brick and marble. The spot commanded a view of an icy river, snowy hills, and a slate-colored sky. Down below, at the river, squatted a brooding masif of dark marble resembling a tomb.

In the sudden silence, a servant hurried down from the main house, followed by a hunchbacked figure in a heavy coat, walking at a curious, foot-dragging gait. At the tiller, Hope Stewart pulled off her goggles and helmet and shook out her blond hair. "Well, cousin, how did you like it?"

"Dreadful." Maurice swung his leg free and vaulted from the machine. He noticed that Faraday still sat in rigid silence, his eyes like marbles. "Absolutely nerve-racking. Remind me never to climb into one of these infernal things again. Faraday, snap out of it!"

The servant arrived, nodded greetings, and, at Hope's command, began grabbing at luggage. The hunchback made his way down the last stone steps, his face twisted in a grotesque smile. "Maurice! By God, how did you like it? Smashing, eh?" He spoke as one imbued with the fervor of creation.

"Isaiah, we could have all been killed. Or worse, arrested. God knows how many laws of the city of New York your sister has broken in the last half hour. There's probably a parade of bicycled policemen behind us."

"Bosh, Maurice. Bosh." Isaiah broke into a wheezing chuckle. He limped to the front of the machine and, with a gnarled hand, lovingly caressed its hood ornament formed of gleaming brass in the shape of a triangle in a circle. He flashed a critical eye at Hope. "You had the fuel mixture a trifle rich. I could hear it as you came up the slope. This engine should never have to labor."

There was a polite cough. They turned to see Faraday looking on. "Ah, Faraday," Maurice said. "Permit me to introduce you. This ugly little man is my cousin Isaiah Stewart, Hope's brother. He is quite addled, poor wretch, especially when it comes to tinkering with his infernal machines."

"Pleased to meet you," Faraday said, without conviction.

4

As they followed the laden servant up the walkway, Isaiah took Faraday's arm. "So you are my cousin's roommate at Harvard. You have my sympathy. As you already know, God has blessed our Maurice with devilishly good looks and the body of a Greek god. Unfortunately, the Almighty was not so generous in other ways..." With a gnomelike grimace, Isaiah tapped at the side of his misshapen head. "But then, Stewarts are a strange lot."

There was a general burst of laughter. Nervously, Faraday joined in.

"Maurice, I love you dearly, but have you gone absolutely insane? Quit Harvard after your junior year? Impossible. Quite out of the question. Your father will have a stroke."

Francesca Stewart Carp, still a powerful figure in the Hudson River steamship and freight business, sat rigidly erect on a Victorian settee. From coiffed white hair to the points of her black shoes, protruding from beneath the hem of a lavender gown, the mistress of Blossom Hill dominated the scene like a bejeweled empress. And all the while this white-haired old woman was paid court by a strange mix of visitors and hangers-on, many of whom seemed to function as a quasi-permanent spectator gallery.

Maurice, Hope, and Faraday balanced cups of hot chocolate on lace knee doilies. Faraday still struggled to get his bearings as one new impressionistic onslaught followed another. Nothing in Stewart family life, it seemed, was beyond open debate, and they carried their family history like so much baggage. Here they sat on a wintry day in a sunroom overlooking the Hudson, surrounded by a clutter of marble, crystal, and jade objets d'art, antique furnishings, Oriental carpeting, brass fixtures, cut glass windows, and endless bric-a-brac, speaking passionately of people·both living and dead.

"Why should I take over things in Pittsburgh?" Maurice was defensive. "I detest the city with its coal smoke and blast furnaces. The sun never even shines anymore. Father is weary of being the industrial mogul, running all those enterprises. He'd rather be drunk. My stepmother sits in front of the mirror all day, preening her fading beauty. Aunt Colette simply endures, married to a weak-willed fraud. Brother Casey, the only sensible one of the lot, fled the scene years ago to go to engineering school in Paris and now sits in the ruins of the French canal fiasco down in Panama, pickling himself in Pernod. And I, Maurice, the youngest and least-interested, am supposed to be the dutiful son, finish Harvard, come home, and take over the goddamned blast furnaces, rolling mill, and riverboats, pour my lifeblood into it as Father did—with all the production headaches, labor brawls, and petty backbiting—and ignore any anarchist thoughts of building a life of my own."

Hope applauded lustily. "Attaboy, cousin!"

The gallery groaned.

Francesca stiffened. "You are a Stewart. You have obligations."

"I have obligations to myself," Maurice said stubbornly.

Hope glanced at Faraday and smiled. Her beauty made his chest ache. She got up from her chair. "Do you ice-skate, Winthrop?"

"Y-yes."

"Good. Let's go ice-skating."

She led him away from the noisy bickering, through a maze of corridors and rooms toward the back of the house. "This family is always battling, Winthrop. They wouldn't be Stewarts if they didn't. Do you like this house? It was built in 1830 by my grandfather Nathan Stewart. He was a fascinating man. He built the Erie Canal and died in drunken confusion, trying to stop a train with his umbrella. That marble monstrosity down by the river is his tomb. It was imported from Italy piece-by-piece and cost him a million dollars. Uncle Nathan was the father of Aunt Francesca and my mother Marguerite. Aunt Francesca was his favorite. After he died, she took over the family business and built it into what it is today. If you find all that confusing, don't despair. So do I."

They found ice skates in a cupboard. Hope led him out into the cold. It was snowing again, the flakes thin and dry. They walked to an icy pond behind the house and sat on a bench strapping on their skates. He breathed her perfumed scent. Her nearness made him giddy. She looked into his eyes and smiled, holding out her hand. "Come on." Her grip was surprisingly strong.

Their skates slashed over the ice, leaving twin cuts on the surface. He followed her across the pond, conscious of her trim waist and firmly rounded hips beneath a short black leather jacket. She skated expertly with powerful leg strokes. His own clumsy efforts—he had never skated well—soon had him puffing. She spun about, eased into a graceful gliding turn, and did several effortless figure eights. Winthrop Faraday was entranced.

They sat together on the bench, warmed from exertion. The gray sky seemed to lower as the cold became more intense. Faraday looked out over the river and the snowy hills fringed with bare dark trees. In the distance behind them rose the city, its facade dark and forbidding.

"Isaiah, the hunchback, is my brother. Our parents died when we were little. Aunt Francesca took us in." Hope's breath was smoky in the cold. "I grew up in this place. I can't remember when I wasn't here."

"It's very beautiful," Faraday said.

"Do you have skeletons in your family closet, Winthrop?"

"Skeletons?"

"You know, scandals. Things that embarrass you and your relatives."

"Not that I know of."

"We do. Stewart closets are filled with skeletons. Would you like to hear about some of them?"

"Well . . ."

"Like, my mother and Aunt Franscesca were sisters, but they didn't get along well. Can you imagine sisters not getting along well? It was all very complicated, including their marriages." She bit at her lip. "I won't bore you with the sordid details. It involved all sorts of nasty things, including a murder. Anyhow, my mother finally wound up marrying her first cousin Thaddeus Stewart. He was the builder of the first transcontinental railroad . . ."

Faraday felt a chill as he listened to her sketchy account of family feuds and bloodlettings. He heard himself saying, "First cousins? Your mother married her first cousin?"

"Yes. Incestuous, isn't it? But those two, Mother and Thaddeus, were in love since they were teenagers. They really couldn't help themselves. We paid a penalty, however. Mother died giving birth to Isaiah. Some people in the family say that Isaiah's deformity is the work of a vengeful God. Do you believe that, Mr. Faraday?"

"Believe what?"

"That God would be so cruel as to do that to Isaiah?"

"I . . . I don't know. I'm not all that religious."

"Neither am I. In fact, I don't believe in God at all. Anyhow, Father could not bear to look at his infant son Isaiah. Too much guilt, I suppose. Father's grief was inconsolable. He died a year after Mother passed away. So Francesca took us in as her wards and brought us here to New York. I was three; Isaiah was one. We've been here ever since."

"What will Maurice's father do?" Faraday asked.

"Maurice's father?"

"When he finds out that he's quitting college."

Hope frowned and shook her head. "There will be hell to pay, Mr. Faraday. There will be hell to pay."

Hope jumped to her feet, skates slung over one shoulder, and moved briskly down the snowy walk toward a large gatehouse. Faraday, trotting, caught up with her as she pushed open a wooden door and stepped inside.

The gatehouse had been converted into a workshop, illuminated by electric lights. Machinery and metal parts were everywhere, gleaming on workbenches and hung from hooks and rafters. The floor was a litter of bolts, screws, steel parts, and metal shavings. There was a strong odor of oil. In one corner, the hunchback Isaiah was busy welding at a heavy metal frame, his eyes encased in smoked goggles. The welding torch emitted a harsh bluish light.

"Don't gaze directly at the light," Hope warned.

Isaiah looked up, grinned crookedly, and shut off the welder. Putting the equipment aside, he removed his gloves and limped toward them. "Welcome to my little shop, Mr. Faraday. Are you interested in the internal combustion engine?"

"I don't know anything about machinery."

"Tut, tut, Mr. Faraday. It's more than machinery; it's a concept." Isaiah rummaged through the litter on a workbench, found a cigar stub, and lit it with a wooden match. Faraday noticed that the hunchback's hands were calloused and smeared with grime, his fingernails black. He wore greasy coveralls and a machinist's cap. "Yes sir, the internal combustion engine is going to revolutionize this world; mark my words. It will give every man complete personal mobility. Just think of that, Mr. Faraday. The time will come when you will own a machine similar to the one you rode in from the train station. Only it will be faster, stronger, more reliable. And you'll drive it yourself, whenever and wherever you please. There'll be decent paved roads, clear across country..."

"Isaiah," Hope said gently.

"... Why, you'll be able to get into your car right there in—where is it you're from, Mr. Faraday?"

"Cleveland, Ohio."

"Right. You'll get into your car right there in Cleveland,

Ohio, and drive all the way to New York City, virtually nonstop. That's eight hundred miles, all the way. In fact, such a motor trip is already being considered by a man named Alexander Winton. Did you ever hear of Alexander Winton, Mr. Faraday?"

"No, I don't think I ever . . ."

"Isaiah," Hope said.

"Marvelous inventor. I've met him personally. Alexander Winton has built a production model horseless carriage, right there in your hometown. It carries six passengers . . ."

"Isaiah," Hope said, "I don't think Mr. Faraday is especially interested in all those aspects of the horseless carriage. We came down here to see your work. Isn't that right, Mr. Faraday?"

"Indeed, it sounds like a fascinating hobby, Mr. Stewart," Faraday said. "Of course, as everybody knows"—he offered a condescending smile—"no machine will ever replace the creature God placed upon this earth as man's primary beast of burden."

"Eh? What animal is that, Mr. Faraday?"

"Why, the horse, Mr. Stewart." Faraday chuckled, confident that Hope would be impressed by the profundity of his logic. "No machine will ever replace the horse."

Isaiah and Hope exchanged glances. The hunchback rolled his eyes toward the ceiling, bit down on his cigar, and limped back to his workbench without another word.

Hope sighed heavily. "Let's go back to the house, Mr. Faraday."

Faraday followed her up the hill, sensing that he had just managed to alienate the most beautiful woman he would ever meet in his lifetime.

"He's an idiot."

"You're being unfair, Hope."

"They're all idiots. They think about themselves, their money, their social position, college life. Good God, Maurice, most of the young men I meet don't even have a career in mind. Ask them what they plan to do and they merely look blank, or talk about polo and trips to Europe."

"Maybe you run with the wrong crowd, Hope."

"It's the same crowd you run with. The Harvard bunch. The Athletic Club bunch. The Pittsburgh Cotillion. The Hunt Club. Newport. The yachting set. I'm so tired of Aunt Francesca's trips to Newport that I could scream. We went to a party last summer, Maurice, that cost ten thousand dollars. Ten thousand dollars! Mrs. Van Bruun hired a theatrical designer to convert her mansion into an Arabian nights setting, complete with papier-mâché minarets and playing fountains filled with champagne. That's obscene."

"Then pull out of it. Nobody's holding you here. I'm going to pull out."

"I don't believe you intend to defy your father."

"I'll do what I have to do."

"It's stupid not to complete your senior year. You've made honors. You've lettered in every major sport. Faraday says you're sure to be elected president of the senior class. Why not wait and make your decision after graduation? There's no hurry."

"I'm making my decision now."

"Bradley Stewart won't allow it. He'll cut you off without a cent."

"I'm aware of that."

Silence. Hope looked across the snow-covered grounds in the morning light to the Hudson, where sunshine struck fire to the ice. She said, "Let's not argue."

"All right."

"Van Harrison has the right idea. He found a career in the Navy. And a good one, too. He's just been promoted lieutenant commander. Isn't that remarkable? He's coming to New York on his next leave. I can't wait to see him. I'm the envy of every debutante in Manhattan, having such handsome cousins. Trouble is, I can't find a man of my own."

"Being a Stewart didn't hurt Van's career."

Hope frowned. Even displeasure did not detract from the beauty of her face. Strange that one so lovely could be so restless, so constantly at odds with life.

"How can you say that?" she said. "Van is brilliant."

"You're naive. Nobody advances to high rank in the Navy or civil service or politics either, without connections. This is reality, Hope. It doesn't change just because Van is a Stewart. How else could a half-breed Cheyenne Indian get ahead?"

Her blue eyes flashed. She stomped her foot. "Ohhhh!" She walked away from him.

Maurice stood looking out the frosted windows into the snow. Tomorrow he would return to Harvard to finish the term. And then, when the semester ended in June, he would go to Pittsburgh and do what had to be done.

For some strange reason he thought of his brother Casey.

What would Casey have done in similar circumstances? And how ironic that their roles were not reversed. Casey would have been in his element, finishing school in anticipation of taking his rightful place of leadership in the family. How strange, the quirks of fate; how bizarre, that life simply dealt the wrong cards to the wrong people.

"Maurice?" Faraday emerged from the breakfast room looking pale and apologetic. For the first time, Maurice noticed that his roommate's neck was scrawny and his face resembled a bespectacled chicken's. "Maurice?"

"Yes, Faraday?"

"Why do you think I made her angry?"

Maurice Stewart shook his head and fished in his pocket for a cigar. "I don't know, Faraday. I don't think Hope really knows, either."

It was raining again. Rain came down in sheets, blasting the metal roof of the cottage. The noise overwhelmed everything and went on for an hour. Then, as abruptly as it began, it stopped. But in his torment, Casey Stewart was only dimly aware of this.

The chill came upon him, as he knew it would. It took him first in the pit of the stomach and shook him like a rag doll. And then it spread into his joints and bones with a consuming ache. No one could adequately describe the ravage of the fever. They had tried, in past years when he was new to Panama. "You haven't felt anything, Stewart, till you've had malaria. It'll make you wish you were dead. Personally, I would just as soon take my chances with yellow jack. At least if you survive that, you're immune."

The fever was followed by the shakes, and the shakes by the sweats. He thrashed in the bed, moaning and grinding his teeth.

A voice murmured out of the brown mist engulfing him. "Casey, *chéri*. Casey, *mon petit*." Cool hands bathed his forehead. A cool cloth fell over his eyes, damp and soothing. "Casey..." The sound was vaporous, coming and going. A dream?

Dream voices whispered to him: "And here you are, old fellow. Divorced, living on wine and quinine in this armpit of the universe with your fever and disillusionment. I pity you, Stewart. I'd say mass for you, but the Lord no longer hears my entreaties."

He opened his eyes. He stared at the high, mahogany-beamed ceiling. He felt the fanning of air upon his face. It was like rousing from a drugged sleep. His hair and pillow were wet, his hearing painfully acute. "Casey, you are awake." He turned his head, saw her face, round and wide-eyed and brownish liquid in the afternoon. Nearby another face swam into focus. It was that of Henri Blanchet, the unfrocked priest, looking sober in the middle of the afternoon. A sudden and inexplicable joy suffused Casey. He wept.

Two hours later he sat in the broken-down wicker chair beside the bed, sipping hot broth from a cracked china cup. The fever was gone, but he was almost too weak to hold the broth. Blanchet smoked a French cigarette clutched delicately between nicotine-stained fingers. "Malaria again. You gave us a start, *mon ami.*"

Casey offered a wry smile. "It was touch and go." He glanced across the room to the sideboard. A bottle of Pernod gleamed dully in the lamplight, still half full. "You're not imbibing, Father? It is late in the day."

"Temporary condition of sobriety." Blanchet's smile accentuated the gaunt leanness of his face. The features were sharp as if cut from wood. The eyes shone with an unhealthy luster. "It is nothing permanent, I assure you. Mlle. Lollie"—he nodded toward the tan-skinned woman moving about the room—"had enough to worry about with you thrashing, sweating, and cursing like a drunken Jack-tar. Such language..."

Casey Stewart's glance strayed back to the bottle on the sideboard, his lips dry and cracked. Lampfire streaked the glass and cast a wavering shadow upon the wall. He put the broth cup aside and said to the woman, "I'll just have a glass of that with quinine, love. Quinine's the only salvation for a man in my condition. And drop in some ice if you've got any."

She poured. There was, of course, no ice. He swallowed, felt the warmth go down his throat and, tasting the bitter quinine mixture, made a face. The alcohol began to spread its lovely numbness. Blanchet went away and Lollie fell asleep in a chair. Casey sat alone with the guttering oil lamp and pondered the twists of fate.

The woman stirred in sleep and her mouth opened slightly, reminding him of the petals of a flower.

Lollie. Lollie DeRange...

"Lollie DeRange," he remembered telling Blanchet months ago, as they drank in a Colón saloon. "Half-breed French and Indian. She came off the island of Martinique with a French

12

sailor. He dumped her in Panama City. She's lived by her wits ever since, singing in some of the less notorious fleshpots. Damned if I can explain how I got tangled up with her, Blanchet. Chemistry, I suppose. I kept remembering Paulette declaring that our marriage was finished and packing off for Paris. One day suddenly there I was, blurting out my troubles to Lollie. God, I wanted to die. She just looked at me with those big brown eyes and said, 'You take Lollie home with you?' I said, 'Hell yes.'"

Life with Lollie eased the pain, but did little else to mend his shattered life. Thank God for the small income from Pittsburgh, for he no longer had any work to do. He wrote letters home to his aunt Colette, spewing it out as a kind of catharsis:

> So I'm adrift in the ruin of this French Canal disaster. It's like living in a graveyard. Gone are all the old friends from those wild days when we were digging and dying like flies. Most of the survivors have fled back to Paris, including the man I respected most and brought down in disgrace, Henri LaVelle. God, how he must despise me! The others lie beneath their gravestones in the jungle. Sometimes I think I ought to be under a stone too. Twelve years, Aunt Colette. They dug twelve years! It cost them twenty-thousand dead and a public treasure of one and a half billion francs . . .

He put aside the empty glass, stumbled back to bed, and slept for twelve more hours. He awoke feeling much stronger, and Blanchet challenged him to another one of their intermidable games of chess. Between moves, as always, the former priest sat back smoking and talking, disrupting Casey's concentration.

"Why do you stay in this pesthole, my friend? Do you like living with ghosts? It is no place for a man of ambition. You are already over thirty. I see no sense in your being here."

"And what about yourself, Blanchet?" He moved his queen bishop.

Blanchet sighed, leaned forward, and studied the board. "With me it is different. I am an outcast of the church and will breathe my last in this jungle." His long fingers pushed forward a pawn. "I committed the unpardonable sin of physically coupling with a lady of the parish. Worse, I made no secret of it. I am also heavily committed"—the Frenchman

13

picked up his wineglass and savored it lovingly—"to the grape. But you have a life and future. Leave Panama, my friend. Leave it to the dead."

Casey could offer no logical rebuttal. He found himself falling back on self-pity and loathing it. "What do I have left, Blanchet? My own father spurned me years ago, denying me my birthright as head of the family. Now I've lost my adopted career, the French Canal. I've lost my wife. My son is a stranger, living at a boarding school in the States. Except for you and a few others, my friends have all gone." He captured the pawn with a knight. "I have Lollie and you, *mon ami*. For now, that seems sufficient."

With a wolfish smile, Blanchet suddenly advanced his queen on a diagonal attack. Casey recognized the move with a stab of dismay.

"Your inattention is costly," Blanchet exulted. "I have you in checkmate!"

"Bastard," Casey said.

The weeks slipped by. He lost track of time. The country simply got drier and drier without rain until roads and trails became powdered dust. By day towering cloud masses rose above the emerald green jungle. One could take a horse and a rifle and go hunting in the hills, riding through clouds of butterflies while monkeys shrieked and chattered overhead. By night the fetid oppression of Panama closed in, smothering a man, magnifying his fears and self-doubts.

As always, clots of humanity moved across the Isthmus in the aging passenger cars of the Panama Railroad. It was an exotic mix of Americans, Europeans, and Orientals, traveling between the ports of Colón and Panama City, peering out dirty windows at heaps of rusted machinery, decaying, abandoned houses, and grassy mounds of overturned earth. He found himself thinking how wonderful it would be if they no longer had to make the crossing by land but could simply remain aboard ship, passing through a Panama Canal. Damn! It must be feasible. It had to be feasible.

He lay in cloying heat beneath the mosquito netting, listening to Lollie's rhythmic breathing by his side. Memories of bygone friends always tormented him in these deep hours of the night. When he could stand it no longer, he got up, found a bottle, and went stumbling down the hill in his underwear to Blanchet's cottage. The former priest got out of bed and sat across the table from him, bleary-eyed, listening to him talk as though taking confession.

"Damn it, Blanchet, what fantastic young men they were. Many were my classmates, you know, at l'Ecole Polytechnique in Paris. Youth is so cocksure. We were absolutely the world's best engineers. They accepted me, an American student from Pittsburgh with a head for mathematics. I was one of their own, Blanchet." He drank the wine from the bottle and felt his head buzzing. "And so we all . . . we all went forth to join the great adventure. Panama! It would be the New Suez, Blanchet. Hadn't Ferdinand de Lesseps himself said so? De Lesseps, the towering genius of all France, the miracle worker. He inspired us to plunge into these stinking jungles of Central America, convinced of Gallic infallibility."

"Ah, yes," Blanchet said. "De Lesseps charmed us all."

"How naive we were," Casey said. "It's so sad, so very, very sad. Sometimes I want to cry, it's so sad. We were like . . . we were like little children, Blanchet. Did you ever think of that?"

His mind groped along, calling up images of rain, mudslides, tropical rot, rust, jungle, puma, mosquitoes, chiggers, spiders, snakes, and, worst of all, disease. How puny were their medicines against the onslaught. He thought of yellow fever. He remembered Carl Rheinhardt, the German engineer who was his friend and how he died: one moment seemingly well and functioning, the next doubled over in a spasm spewing black vomit, his eyes rolling back. The fools. The simple, misguided fools.

It was sad. He wept as Blanchet smoked, his face impassive. Casey felt better. He left the empty wine bottle on the table in front of Blanchet and stumbled back up the dirt path to the cottage and slipped into bed beside the sleeping figure.

"Casey?" She stirred, half awake. The brown eyes were twin pools in the reflected moonlight. He reached across and drew her to him, silken-skinned and firm of breast, young and full of life. She mumbled love words to him in French. He stifled the words with his mouth upon her mouth. Her hand slipped down and closed upon his swelling manhood.

The weeks and months advanced imperceptibly. Four months had slipped past him. Four months! He paced the cottage. It was typically French, one of hundreds built for the white overseers, middle executives, and their families, white with green shutters, wide verandas, and screened porches, all falling into disrepair—the sparsely settled villages, the weed-choked ditches, the abandoned tools, and the giant multi-bucketed Slaven dredges. Rust and rot. Rust and rot. Bah! He could stand no more of this. He left the cottage and took the train to Colón.

He gambled. He drank. He found himself dancing a wild quadrille with a Barbados woman in the smoke-filled gloom of a native bistro. He awoke in a strange empty bed, lying in his own vomit, his money and clothing gone. Wrapping his nakedness in a blanket, he stumbled barefoot into the muddy street, his eyes squinting against the morning.

"*Sacré nom de Dieux!* Stewart, is it you?" The Frenchman who hailed him was an engineer named Claude Etienne, once a classmate in Paris. They had socialized together in the old days, with their wives. Etienne waved down a horse-drawn hack and took Casey to his own lodgings. The inevitable green-and-white cottage stood on the outskirts of Colón and commanded a view of the sea. Etienne's wife Babette, a handsome brunet, heated bathwater on the stove and provided clothing from her husband's wardrobe. That evening, the three of them dined by candlelight on the screened veranda listening to night sounds from the jungle and sipping an excellent Chablis. Etienne was among the last of the administrative staff, finishing up paperwork. They conversed in French.

"Strange country," Etienne said. "A mixture of heaven and hell. The jungle fascinates me, Casey. I can walk out and observe some of the most remarkable flora and fauna on earth. Enchanting. And yet that enchantment masks so many perils: stinging scorpions, deadly plants, deadly snakes. That's what happened to us, you know. We were enchanted, blind to peril. Panama is so different from anything I ever knew before. I spent my childhood in a village called Verdun. There was nothing memorable about Verdun. My whole life changed when I qualified to become an engineer. To attend the Polytechnique was beyond my wildest dreams. Only the very best went there..."

Etienne's wife interrupted gently. "Claude, perhaps Mr. Stewart would rather speak of other things."

"Yes, yes." Etienne dabbed at his mouth with a handkerchief. "Forgive my nostalgia. It's just that those days were so grand at the university, and we were so invincible as Frenchmen and as technical men. Isn't that true, Stewart?"

"What do you hear from Paris?" Casey asked.

Etienne sighed. "It is bad, such a disaster. Charles de

16

Lesseps is going to trial, along with many of the others. Your former father-in-law is a prosecution witness. The country is shaken to its roots. Even Clemenceau, it is rumored, has been touched by the scandals."

"So many payoffs. So much Gallic showmanship." Casey angrily forked a morsel of fish from his plate. "It was all so damned impractical."

Etienne put down his fork. "Do you think the Americans would be interested in taking over the Canal, finishing up what we started?"

"Not much chance of that, Claude."

"Why are you so certain?"

"To begin with, the United States has its own Canal in mind, a sea-level cut. And it would go through Nicaragua, not Panama. The new President, McKinley, is committed to it. There's a study committee at work."

"There are those in Paris who talk of selling out the French interests to the Americans. Your former father-in-law is among them. It is worth thinking about, Casey. Perhaps you could help, by talking to people in Washington."

"Washington? I can't even imagine going there."

"What will you do now?" asked Babette Etienne.

Casey Stewart turned the question in his mind. Somewhere a night bird uttered a raucous call. There were scamperings and chatterings in the darkness. Something screeched and died. "I wish I knew," he said.

The thought hung on the moist night air, Casey's mind plucking at its edges. How much should he reveal to these kind people, casual friends who had brought him in, stinking and naked, without a glance of disapproval? From their aplomb, one would think it commonplace to find a white man stumbling out of a whorehouse in Colón clad in nothing but a blanket and dried puke. What kind of mortals were these French? Dare he bare his soul, tell them the truth? I come from a long and distinguished line of Stewarts. I am a failure. And I despise myself.

"Casey? . . ." Claude Etienne said.

"Maybe I will go back to America," he said. "I am an engineer, after all. Maybe I'll get into something else. Building railroads, perhaps. My cousin Thaddeus Stewart became rather famous in that line of work."

"Ah, yes," Etienne said. "The builder of the transcontinental railroad! We studied his mountain-tunneling techniques at the Polytechnique, remember?"

"I remember."

"You Americans are masters of construction technique. Next to the French, of course."

He chuckled. "Of course."

"*Mon ami*, I would like to propose a toast," the Frenchman said.

"A toast?" Casey picked up his wineglass.

"A toast," Claude Etienne said, "to the American Panama Canal!"

They all laughed. And Casey Stewart drank off his Chablis with flourish.

He took the train back to Gatun and his own cottage. In the stifling air dark clouds massed over the green hills, thunder grumbled, and lightning flickered. It was time for the dry season to end. Night fell as he trudged up the winding path toward the cottage, the first heavy raindrops beginning to fall. She heard his footfall and came running to snatch open the screen door. "Casey! Casey!" She flung her arms about his neck and hung on. "*Mon chéri!* Oh, I missed you so! I thought you were never coming back!..."

He picked her up and carried her to the bed.

Outside, the night exploded in a torrential downpour.

A chill north wind tossed whitecaps upon the oily surge of the estuary. The day was blustery and gray. Shipping moved sluggishly about the harbor, a restless hodgepodge of barges, freighters, full-rigged barks, and schooners, and ocean-going vessels and coastal steamers. Jacob Brynzsky huddled in his old coat on the afterdeck of the Greek freighter *Argosy*, hands thrust in pockets, watching the harbor recede. The scene muddled his senses. He was a landsman, and only a mariner could find order in such a tangle of masts and spars, and derricks, hoists, rigging, and smokestacks, cast in a somber silhouette against the murky horizon that was England in winter. Well, it was good-bye to all that now, and good riddance. Life in England had been less than exhilarating for the Brynzsky family. He had toiled for two years in bondage to Blumenthal, the furrier, and a more irascible and miserly employer never lived. But from that had come their tickets to deliverance on board this vessel, such as it was.

He heard a step behind him. It was old Pyotr, their former neighbor in the Chelsea slum, disheveled, rheumy-eyed, and reeking of stale tobacco smoke. He and his wife Sadie had bought passage on the same ship. God of Abraham, the man was a bore. Pyotr grunted a greeting and sat down heavily upon a coil of rope. "Our journey begins then, Jacob Brynzsky." He spoke in Polish, with an accent of the eastern border people. "And what do you suppose America will be like, eh?" Pyotr fiddled with an ancient pipe, reaming the bowl with a pocketknife, knocking out black residue against an iron cleat, and filling the bowl with strong Bulgarian tobacco. He struck a match, cupping the flame against the wind in hands that were gnarled and work-worn. Pyotr said, "And will you find there the things that you seek?"

Jacob's reply was noncommittal. "There will be work."

Pyotr ignored the implied rebuff. He smoked meditatively, eyeing a flock of seabirds wheeling over the ship's turgid wake. "It is sad that people must leave the homeland of their ancestors," he said. "We were ten generations in Poland on my father's side. But the life is poor in my home village now. People are worked out and bled out. Many have gone to America to make a fresh start. I only wish I were a younger man, like you. If I were a younger man . . ."

It was the same tiresome refrain. Pyotr meant well but had no imagination in conversation. Jacob cut him off sharply, saying, "I have a brother in Michigan, at a town called Fall River. We will settle there, Sara and the children and me. He is a merchant."

"Who is a merchant?"

"My brother in Fall River. You've heard of the place?"

"No." Pyotr blew his nose between his thumb and forefinger and flipped the gob into the sea. He wiped his fingers on his trousers. "There are many towns in America. Many factories too, I've heard. One can find work. I am a shoemaker. It is an old trade in my family. I don't worry. And you, you are a furrier now. No more will you have to subsist on a schoolmaster's salary, as you did back home. Besides, Michigan is a long way from the Hebrew School in Krakow." An old eye glittered from beneath its straggled brow. "I'll wager there are few Jewish boys to be taught the Talmud in Fall River."

"One can teach other subjects. Geography, arithmetic, logic. There is always room for a teacher." Jacob was defensive. "Teaching is my profession."

"I see." The old man watched their progress as the ship steamed out of the estuary and took on the first deeper swells of open sea. He scanned the sky and sniffed the air. "We'll have rain, likely as not. I can feel it and smell it." He looked back at Jacob, studying the threadbare coat, the black cloth

19

cap worn low over the eyes, the thin, pale face, and the worn shoes. Life had not been easy for the schoolmaster in England. When Pyotr spoke again, his tone was subdued. "And the boy Solomon, he is feeling better?"

Jacob sighed. "He still has fever and a cough. He has caught a cold, nothing more. It will pass."

"Please God," Pyotr murmured.

Jacob left the deck and descended into steerage. The air had a penetrating dampness and the light was bad, emitted by a few guttering oil lamps. He moved forward past dark, anonymous forms and found the small pocket of family privacy which several other passengers had helped him to fashion from blankets strung upon clothesline ropes. Sara still sat where he had left her, in a pool of candlelight beside the boy. Nearby, on a mattress on the damp floor, sat his daughter Rachel. Even in the gloom Jacob sensed the classic beauty of the girl. How tragic that she would spend her seventeenth birthday on board this scow of a ship wallowing through the North Atlantic.

"There is no change?" he said.

Sara shrugged wordlessly, removed a cloth from Solomon's forehead, and rinsed it in a basin. The delicate features of Jacob's wife were almost translucent, but her eyes nested in dark hollows. She had not slept for two nights. He had never seen her so exhausted. The boy stirred and coughed lightly. Sara replaced the cloth on his head. "I tried to give him broth, but he refused to eat. My son, my son . . ."

The nameless fear again possessed him as he sat down wearily beside her and stared into the face of his only son. The boy slept too much, and could be roused only with difficulty. Jacob put the back of his hand to Solomon's cheek and caught his breath. The flesh was hot and dry to the touch.

"What do you think?" he said.

"I cannot tell. It might be the grippe. One of the women over there"—she nodded into the shadows beyond the blanket—"said she thought it was the grippe. She said to keep him warm and feed him liquids and broth. This, and prayer, is all we can do." She hesitated. When she spoke again, her throat seemed to have tightened. "I do not see how he would fail to recover, a boy so attentive to his religion, a boy so innocent and pious . . ." Her eyes glittered strangely and Jacob detected hysteria. Gently he drew her to him. "He is only eleven years old," she whispered. "Not even Bar Mitzvahed . . ."

"Nothing can happen," Jacob said. "After all, he is destined to become our family rabbi, just like his grandfather. Have faith. And now you must rest."

He tried to take her to the other mattress, beside Rachel, but she refused to move. The girl got up and came to her side. "Please, Mother." But Sara would not yield. She sat rigidly, her face pale.

"My son," she said. "My son . . ."

And so they hovered over the boy in the lamplight. Around them, the nameless humanity of the steerage compartment moved about and ate and talked and argued in a dozen tongues. Jacob was conscious of them, this human flotsam of Europe. A motley human assortment it was. They were Swedes, Germans, Irish, Lithuanians, and Russians, sharing one common bond: All were bound for the New World, carrying their worldly goods in roped cardboard suitcases and carpetbags.

Time dragged. The ship rolled and creaked. The dampness and cold of the steerage compartment became more pronounced. The rolling motion grew into a series of sickening pitches and yaws. A storm lashed the sea and the ship, and those belowdecks wallowed in misery. Sara and Jacob took turns holding onto their son, to keep him from rolling off the mattress. A night went by and a day and another night. Solomon developed a weak, rattling cough. The last candle burned down. The storm subsided.

A crew member came by. Jacob called out to the man, "Can you give us another candle? We have a sick boy here."

The man poked his head in, between the blankets. "There ain't no more candles." He was an unkempt lout in a tattered uniform with whiskey on his breath. His glance fell upon Rachel and lingered, lusting.

"Is there a ship's doctor?" Jacob said. "My son needs medical attention badly."

"No ship's doctor, neither." The mouth glistened in a frame of black whiskers, lifting into a leering smile. "But I might be agreeable, for a consideration . . ."

"I'll pay you," Jacob said. He groped in his pocket and held out his hand. "Here. Ten shillings."

The seaman merely stared at Rachel. "That ain't exactly what I had in mind."

"Get out!" Sara's voice had the sound of a whiplash. "Get out!" Her face in the dim light was a study in pale fury. She grabbed up a washcloth and hurled it. *"Get out of here!"*

The seaman withdrew.

Finally it was old Pyotr who brought more candles. The act made Jacob feel guilty for thinking ill of him before. The shoemaker glanced at the sick boy, went away again, and returned with a stocky, black-bearded passenger who introduced himself, in English with a heavy German accent, as a physician. The stocky man examined Solomon, checking his pulse, his temperature, his mouth, palpating his chest, and peering into his eyes. The boy did not respond. The stocky man sighed and drew Jacob out into a passageway.

"It is the grippe," he said. "Your son is very sick, *ja*. Nothing more I can do. He is in God's hands now. All you can do is pray."

The following day, their third at sea, Solomon died in Jacob's arms. Someone brought a sheet, and two peasant women washed and wrapped the body. Jacob gathered up the frail form in his arms and bore it to the deck, followed by a solemn crowd of strangers. There was no rabbi on board the *Argosy*, and so he stood in the wind on the afterdeck and recited the Prayer for the Dead. The deck crew and the first mate respectfully removed their caps and stood by until it was done.

And then the weighted body was dropped into the murky deep.

In the steerage compartment, Sara clutched her arms about her chest and rocked, moaning in grief. Rachel stroked her mother's hair and face, murmuring words of endearment. But there was no comforting her. She neither slept nor ate. Finally, unable to bear more, Sara withdrew into herself, dry-eyed and silent.

"Such a tragedy," old Pyotr said, clumsily patting Jacob on the shoulder. "Such a terrible, terrible thing."

Jacob Brynzsky went out and paced the deck for hours as the *Argosy* labored over the rough Atlantic. And those who watched him from a distance observed from time to time that he paused, clenched his fists, and looked at the slate-gray sky, like a man cursing God.

At last, on a wintry morning dusted with snow flurries, the ship arrived at the port of New York. Disheveled, black-garbed men, kerchiefed women, and children, lined the railings to stare in silent wonder at the smoky gray Manhattan skyline. At last the *Argosy* dropped its anchor off the red brickpile of Ellis Island.

In years to come, Rachel Brynzsky would remember this day as utter confusion. As they poured onto the dock, uniformed officials shouted them into line in half a dozen languages. Lugging their cheap suitcases, faces etched in fear, the people of the herd were duly led, grouped, checked, and name-tagged. It was a hurried business, for a large liner had docked but an hour ahead of the *Argosy*, filling the waiting rooms with a crush of humanity.

"Brynzsky? Brynzsky? How do you spell that?"

"Uh, spell?" Jacob Brynzsky stammered in confusion, his mind temporarily losing its grip on English. "Uh..."

The official looked up from the form with annoyance. "Oh, hell, it doesn't matter. B-I-R-N-H-A-M. Birnham. That's close enough. A good, Anglo-Saxon name. Besides, it's only for an identification tag."

And so, by the hurried stroke of a pen, Brynzsky became Birnham and the family name going back through twelve generations of life in Poland and, earlier, western Russia—a name which had produced rabbis and scholars and even the martyred leader of a peasant band that had fought the invading Mongols—ceased to exist.

"Birnham?" Rachel said in disbelief two days later, leading her silent mother by the hand into the teeming babble of the Lower East Side.

Jacob examined their immigration papers and nodded gravely. "That's what it says here. Birnham. From now on, you are Rachel Birnham."

Sidestepping an advancing pushcart, he took Sara by the arm and looked hopefully into her face for some sign of response. There was none. The eyes of Sara Brynzsky refused to see, and the mind refused to comprehend.

The face of his wife reminded Jacob of something chiseled in fine marble.

II

Spring spread greenery over the broad, sweeping grounds. Crocuses raised their yellow blossoms. The great elms were bursting to bud in balmy air. Two of his father's hunting dogs bounded over the crest of the hill, barking in welcome. Up here, in the forested heights, spring worked its verdant magic; but down below the city was a sprawling and unsightly presence. The sight of Pittsburgh—its factories, crowded streets, and jumbled structures, its turgid waterways teeming with boat traffic—was one of sulfurous smells as chimney smoke lay a pall over everything. God, he thought, how had they managed to live here all these years? Small wonder so many Stewarts had sought their fortunes elsewhere.

He dreaded this homecoming. The impending confrontation weighed heavily upon his mind. Even as a smart Stewart carriage bore him and his luggage up the hill from the Pittsburgh railroad depot, and the stately columns of Stewart House came into view, Maurice felt no elation.

"Here we are, sir." Washington, the aged Negro driver and handyman, tied off the reins of the Morgan horses and climbed painfully down to tend to Maurice's luggage. A screen door banged, and his stepmother Rose was there. She wore a frilly costume in pink and lavender. Her long hair was tinted a bright orange, her face blotched with excessive makeup. She descended the steps as if onstage, trailing a large pink handkerchief. "Maurice! Maurice, my dear, dear boy, how deeeelightful to see you!" A quick hug, a peck on the cheek, a scent of rosewater. "My, haven't you filled out handsomely?"

Others were coming out to join the welcome: his aunt Colette, a tall, elegant woman with defined Stewart features; her widowed mother-in-law Matilda Marten, pinch-faced and disapproving; several visiting houseguests and their children, dutifully waxing enthusiastically; and finally Father himself, looking stouter than Maurice had remembered, his face broad and flushed.

"Ah, my boy, welcome, welcome!" Bradley Stewart's big voice boomed through the babble of greetings. He wrapped Maurice's hand in a meaty grip and pounded him on the shoulder. "By God, what a sight for these sore eyes!"

Maurice murmured pleasantries, smiled, and shook hands. And then he was ascending the broad steps, surrounded by the family hubbub, and moving into the familiar shadowy coolness of Stewart House with its smells of cooking and furniture polish. Only here did the sense of homecoming seem real, for this was the house in which he had grown up and where his childhood memories were stored.

"Your room is all ready, Maurice," Rose Stewart said brightly.

"They say you'll be the star halfback of the Crimson Eleven next fall," Bradley Stewart said. "It's high time a Stewart made his niche in athletics."

"Hmmph," said old Mrs. Marten. "Football is a waste of time."

"Always knew you had it in you," his father said.

He went up to settle and unpack. The room was filled with familiar things of the past—the books, pennants, slingshot and marbles, the hoop and riding trophy, the stuffed pheasant he had shot at age nine, the photograph of his school class when he was twelve, another photograph of Celeste Bourne, his childhood sweetheart who had drowned in the Ohio River on a family picnic, and the model train. He opened a bureau drawer and found the picture that had been on his mind during the train journey from Cambridge, the one of his mother. Maude Stewart had died when he was six and Casey sixteen, her pretty face wasting away to the ravages of cancer. Life had been different at Stewart House before that; they had been more of a loving family—Mother, Father, Maurice, and Casey. He could almost hear her voice now, low and confident and warm. "Always be yourself, Maurice. Be your own man first. You are a Stewart. The rest will take care of itself." He thought: Mother, I wish you were here. I wish I had you to confide in now.

He did not have her. What he must do, he would do alone.

Chauncey Marten joined them for dinner. Aunt Colette's husband was portly and baldish, his face as round as a pumpkin. He wore a black vested suit with a heavy golden watchchain draped across his middle. His handshake was moist and virtually boneless. "Well, Maurice, I trust you had a pleasant journey." The voice was deeply resonant, the expression supercilious.

Maurice masked his dislike. "It was uneventful, Uncle Chauncey."

Chauncey drew a pocket handkerchief and wiped his hands. It was an unconscious gesture, borne of long habit. "So here we are, in a family gathering again."

A scraping of chairs, a moment of silence. Bradley Stewart looked at his portly brother-in-law. "Chauncey, would you say the blessings?" Heads bowed and the rich voice of Chauncey Marten beseeched the Almighty for His personal blessing upon this family gathering at Stewart House. Maurice merely listened, eyes open and head erect.

"And we thank thee, O Lord, for bringing home safely to the bosom of the family our own beloved Maurice, whose scholastic accomplishments and great deeds on the fields of sport reflect proudly upon the family. We pray that thou

25

wouldst confer upon Maurice, as indeed upon us all, the blessings of thy grace and make him a believer. For we are washed in the blood of the lamb, and born again in the resurrection of our Savior and Redeemer..."

Maurice thought: Pious sonofabitch.

The prayer went on intermidably. His stepmother Rose glanced up with a quick, apologetic smile. Aunt Colette fanned herself, her eyes dutifully closed. Old Mrs. Marten squirmed in her chair. The several houseguests gamely affected postures of piety. His father was a study in total concentration, eyes clamped shut, fingers clutching at the bridge of his nose, broad face set in an expression of religious intensity.

Finally, it was done. Servants appeared, bearing steaming dishes and bowls. Rose Stewart dabbed at her mouth with a hankie. "Now that was a mighty fine prayer, Chauncey."

Maurice could not resist the opportunity. "A bit long-winded for my taste."

Bradley Stewart's brow darkened. He put down his soupspoon. "We are not going to have disrespect and blasphemy. You are a grown-up young man now. What kind of ideas do they put into your head at Harvard? I think you should apologize to your uncle Chauncey. He is a man of deep conviction. He is also a substantial citizen and business leader."

Maurice looked coolly into the round face across a platter of mashed potatoes. "Uncle Chauncey, I apologize." Chauncey's eyes glittered in triumph.

Talk was carefully turned to other subjects. There were rumors in Pittsburgh that Andrew Carnegie planned to organize a new corporation called United States Steel. "It will be the world's first billion-dollar company," Bradley Stewart said.

"A noble achievement," declared one of the male guests, a manufacturer of wire fencing. "I understand Mr. Carnegie's personal profit from steel is now twenty-three million dollars a year."

"A noble achievement," someone else remarked.

"I wonder how this will affect the locomotive business," said Chauncey Marten. "If Carnegie forces up steel prices, it could have an impact on profits everywhere."

"A simple matter, Chauncey. You'll merely produce your engines at a higher price and pass it along."

26

"The unions are trying to organize. That complicates things. They'll be demanding higher wages, no question about it."

"Hooligans. The courts and police will deal with them."

"We've got to keep these wages down," Chauncey said gravely. "I say a dollar a day is enough for any working man. A day's work for a day's pay; that's what the good Lord intended. If we let unionists and anarchists have their way, they will undermine the very integrity of free enterprise..."

Dinner completed, the men retired to the library for brandy and cigars. Bradley Stewart lit a heavy black Havana and shook out the match. "It's a damn nuisance, with so much business to attend to. Everything demands my personal involvement, the blast furnace, the rolling mill, the damned boatyard." He settled into a leather armchair. "But it won't be forever. Another year and Maurice, here, will step in, start learning the ropes. I'll just ease my way out. Isn't that right, Maurice?"

Maurice felt all the eyes upon him. He smiled self-consciously and lit a cigar.

"Chip off the old block," someone said.

It was an odd mix of people. Of the five adults now dwelling in the Stewart mansion, only two—Bradley and Colette—were Stewarts. The others, Chauncey and his mother and Rose, had simply attached themselves, or been attached, by marital ties.

Chauncey, of course, was a pious fraud. Since his teenage years, Maurice had known of the secret excesses of this Bible-spouting husband of Aunt Colette's: nocturnal visits to the bawdy houses of Pittsburgh, the unsavory associates, the whispers that went on behind the cloak of respectability. Chauncey Marten was cruel as well. Maurice's dislike had been intensified by the man's behavior toward the crippled Isaiah in years gone by. "The lad is a living testament," Chauncey Marten breathed, "to his parents' mortal sin." But most of all, Maurice despised Marten on his own terms, remembering the day when he was twelve and Marten had come to his room, putting his meaty hand on Maurice's private parts and attempting to coerce him into a homosexual act.

The old woman Matilda Marten lived in her own world of quiet hatreds. Convinced of her son's perfection, she had disapproved bitterly of his marriage on any terms and found ample cause to focus criticism upon all things Stewart. "There

is bad blood in this family," she muttered. "And colored, too."
Maurice ignored her; the others—Bradley, Rose, Colette—
seemed simply to abide her as a senile eccentric.

But it was Rose who was unique, and haunted. Rose Trask
Stewart had never been altogether sane. And yet she had a
gentleness about her that generated affection. When Maurice
visited her rooms, as he did now, it was as if he were stepping
into a very personal, very sweet fantasy world, one in which
few other human beings were granted admission.

"Do you think I'm beautiful, Maurice?" She sat before the
mirror as always, brushing her hair. Her eyes wore mascara,
her face was whitely powdered, her cheeks rouged, and her
lips painted a bright scarlet. "Sometimes I feel... I feel as if
my beauty were fading, and that everybody knew it but me."

"You are lovely, Rose. So young, so pretty. Your name
becomes you."

It was a charade, of course. But then, much of life was a
charade. He remembered her arrival at Stewart House barely
a year after his mother's death. She had been truly beautiful
then, and much younger than his father. Maurice remembered
how he had voiced his resentment to Casey, saying: "What
right does she have to be here? What right does Father have,
marrying her?" It was Casey who had managed to put things
into perspective. "Father lives alone in this big house, with
only us two and the servants. He needs somebody, Maurice.
I understand." And so Maurice had adopted his own kind of
charade, affecting a politeness to her, an acceptance of her. In
time, however, the affection became real, and the charade no
longer necessary. Later, with the arrival of Aunt Colette, her
husband, and mother-in-law, things became more complicated. But surprisingly, it was Colette to whom he would
become most strongly attached.

"We are so proud of you, Maurice," Rose said. She put
down the hairbrush and smiled coquettishly. "You've become
quite the handsome young man. You'll be a fine catch for
some deserving girl. But I warn you, beware of actresses."

"But Rose, you're an actress."

"Ah, yes, but that's different. I'm a classical actress, you
see. Yes. Mine is a career that has added enormously to the
cultural uplift of the theater. And"—she giggled, looked
about the airy boudoir as if to be certain they were alone, and
cupped her hand to whisper—"I have a secret to tell you."

"A secret!"

"Promise you won't tell."

"I won't tell a soul."

"Cross your heart and hope to die?"

"Cross my heart." He made the sign with his finger, knowing what would come next. The game was always the same.

"I'm going to have a new part in a play! It will be at the Garden Theater. Oh, very, very elegant. I am to play Portia in *The Merchant of Venice*. Isn't that exciting?"

And so it went. They chuckled and whispered together, making their charade. Finally he got up to leave and her scarlet lips made a pout. But then she recognized that it had to be, for she herself was preparing for a very important visitor. "Your father will be along any minute. He always brings me champagne and red roses. They're my favorites, you know. Oh, he is simply mad about me." She put a finger to her lips. "But don't tell. The house is filled with eyes and ears. Don't breathe a word..."

"I won't."

He hurried out, as if suddenly hearing his father's foot upon the stair, and thus completed the play.

Bradley Stewart, Maurice suspected, had not visited Rose's boudoir for years.

Colette Stewart Marten worked at her desk in a second-floor corner room which she used as a study. The room was a reflection of herself: neat, ordered, and tasteful. A silver tea service dominated the mahogany sideboard. As Maurice entered he could smell the aroma of steeping English tea. She came around the desk and embraced him. He had forgotten that she was so tall.

"I'm delighted that you're home, Maurice. We missed you at Christmas. It has been nearly eight months."

"I had promised Aunt Francesca to spend Christmas in New York, and..."

She smiled. "It's all right. You don't have to explain."

Tea was a ritual. Colette poured tea from a silver pot into delicate china cups that had belonged to her grandmother. They sat in Duncan Phyfe chairs facing each other. Morning sunlight filtered through open windows faced with sheer white curtains, gently lifting with the breeze.

"I love this room," she said. "Mother used to do her ledgers here, at this same desk, when I was a child. Sometimes I can almost feel her presence when the house is quiet and I'm working."

"Catherine Stewart must have been an incredible woman." Maurice sipped tea, sensing the eggshell fragility of the cup in his big hand. He preferred to drink from mugs, not teacups; and his drink was coffee, not amber Pekoe. A teacup was oddly intimidating. "You used to tell us," he said, "that all the world's important decisions were made over cups of tea. Do you remember?"

She laughed, and for an instant her face displayed the beauty of bygone years. "Tea is the drink of the civilized."

Aunt Colette was the twin sister of his father. The two bore an uncanny physical resemblance, but their personalities were remarkably different. Where Bradley Stewart was rough-hewn and bluff, Colette was sophisticated. Where he reacted with temper, she used tactful diplomacy. Where he bullied his way against adversaries, she won them over by her personality. Of the two, Colette had always been Maurice's favorite.

She put down her cup and fixed him with a knowing look. "Now tell me what's bothering you."

He told her, succinctly and without embellishment. Pittsburgh was not for him. He did not wish to live a life following in the footsteps of his father. His older brother Casey had struck out on his own after graduating from the university in Paris, without recriminations. Now Maurice wanted to have his chance. He saw no point in continuing at Harvard. College was boring and pointless. He would simply quit school and go west in search of opportunity. Perhaps in the gold fields of California, or maybe even Alaska. "I'm tired of trying to fit into Father's mold. I want to be my own man."

Colette listened thoughtfully. When he had finished, she let the silence settle between them. Then she said, "Don't expect him to give you his blessing. Bradley Stewart is a headstrong man. Since the day you were born, Maurice, he has planned for you to succeed him as head of the family. In Bradley's mind, that decision is chiseled in stone."

"But Casey . . ."

"You and your brother are different kinds of people. Even though Casey is the eldest, your father regarded him as footloose and adventuresome. He didn't believe that your brother had leadership qualities. It was an instinctive thing. The male heads of the Stewarts have always been strong: your great-grandfather Isaiah, your grandfather Stephen, your father Bradley. Each has taken up the burden and borne it. Bradley didn't want to do it either, incidentally. His heart was set on being a civil engineer. He had no choice. His parents had grown old. The business was in the hands of hired managers..."

"Yes, I've heard all that before. I grew up on Father's lectures about family obligations. But I was not aware of his feelings toward Casey."

"Casey always resented it. As the eldest, he felt that he should have been chosen. That's one of the ironies of all this. Casey *wanted* to be the dominant heir. Instead, your father sent him abroad to study, provided him with an income, and rejected him. It was obvious that Bradley had no further use for Casey." She paused, smoothed her dress, and examined her fingernails. "I've always thought that this was one of his big mistakes."

"But it still isn't too late. Perhaps Casey..."

"It was too late the day your father made his choice, when both of you were still children." Colette hesitated again, as if reflecting upon deeper, more personal things. "He always had a way of making abrupt decisions. Your great-grandfather, the first Isaiah, was the same way. Two of his four children, Stephen and Nathan, were favored, to the lasting detriment of the others. Isaiah Stewart was also biased and willful toward his offspring. And even I, in my younger years, ran afoul of Bradley's judgments."

"You? But you're his sister."

"This is a man's world, Maurice, and the male head of the Stewart family wields great authority, especially over the purse strings. When I was young, I fell in love with a handsome young man and hoped to marry him. Bradley felt he did not measure up to the standards of what a Stewart in-law ought to be. Actually, he was more concerned about picking the right brother-in-law for himself than approving a husband for his sister. I ... I gave in to him."

"But why?"

Colette shook her head. For an instant, the proud face betrayed deep inner distress. He had never seen her so affected. "Bradley intimidated me. How else can I explain it? He called my fiancé a fortune hunter. He threatened to have me cut off without a cent. My young man had no money, and little prospect for earning any. Bradley, as head of the family, controlled everything. I didn't know my legal rights, or that I could challenge him in a court of law and probably win. Anyhow, the decision was made. Later, to appease Bradley and try to fill the emptiness in my own life, I married

Chauncey Marten. And that"—she bit her lip—"was my second big mistake."

"Chauncey Marten was..."

"...a business associate of Bradley's. And, of course, he still is. They are much alike in their thinking: conservative, small-minded, monetary."

Maurice stood up and paced the room. Everything here was so neat, so impeccably arranged, from the highly polished woodwork to the blue-figured carpet and ivory knickknacks on the mantelpiece. Who would think that the occupant of this room, Colette Stewart Marten, could have been so abused by her own twin brother? He stopped at the fireplace and gazed at a tintype photograph of his grandparents Catherine and Stephen Stewart. They were as physically attractive as they had been resourceful even though Stephen had been brutally maimed and disfigured in a steamboat explosion. Why is it, he wondered, that some human beings have all the gifts?

"What do you think I ought to do, Aunt Colette?"

"Each of us makes his own decisions, Maurice," she said quietly. "I think you've already made yours. You must follow your own instincts. There is no other course."

"But what if I'm making a mistake?"

"Only you can be the judge of that. You're young. There's a lot out there to see, and many women for you to love. Take your own chances; follow your own instincts; go your own way. That's my advice."

He kissed her and left the room, descended the back stairs, and went out of the house to the stables. Saddling a spirited black gelding, he mounted and spurred to a gallop along the ridgeline. The spring wind swept his face and his blood quickly warmed to the exertions of the ride. The gelding thundered over a wooden bridge and up a thicketed slope, emerging finally at the crest of a bald hill commanding a panorama of the rolling Alleghenies.

Far below, the Ohio River meandered in its muddy wake, cut by the creamy white line of a steamboat's progress. From here he could see the fork, where the Monongahela and the Allegheny met to form the Ohio. Down there, too, was the Stewart boatyard his grandfather had founded more than a century ago. He had hunted these hills for birds, deer, and bears. Down in that dirty city, he had gone to grammar school and fidgeted on Sundays in the cloying warmth of a Presbyterian church. Up here at Stewart House, the great fieldstone mansion with its white columns and countless Stewart family memories, he had been born and reared and became a man.

But now the restless spirit was upon him. He looked to the west, into the glare of the afternoon sunshine. How many other Stewart men had done the same thing, sitting on a horse upon this hilltop and looking westward while coming to hard decisions? Stephen certainly had done so before joining the Lewis and Clark expedition for a voyage that would have heavy bearing on the expansion of this nation. Nathan, who was Stephen's brother, had done so before setting off for his own destiny, with Robert Fulton's steamboats and the building of the Erie Canal. Cousin Thaddeus must have done so too, before departing in quest of his dream to build the first transcontinental railroad. And now . . .

Maurice turned the gelding and walked it back in the direction they had come. A squirrel chattered at him from a gum tree; a woodpecker rapped at the top of a rotting oak; and a blacksnake snoozed on a sunlit rock. Every living creature had its place in the scheme of things. And now it was time to find his own.

"Hold him, boy! Give him line!"

Maurice's fly rod snapped and bent as the trout broke water. Exhilaration surged through him. Working cautiously waist-deep in the rushing stream, he played the fish's leaps and runs, keeping just enough tension on the line to prevent it from breaking.

"Oh, it's a beauty. It's a real beauty!" Bellowing his exuberance, Bradley Stewart plunged into the stream waving a net, heedless of wet clothes and slippery rocks. Ten feet away, the trout again broke water, sunlight flashing over rainbow-colored scales. Maurice drew it in closer, taking up line onto the fly rod spool. His father sloshed and shouted and finally, unable to contain himself further, made a diving scoop with the net that swept him off his feet and into the water. As his hat flew off and floated away, he came up sputtering and blowing water.

"You missed!" Maurice shouted, laughing.

He concentrated on the fish. Another leap. A run. A rapid succession of powerful tugs on the line. A flash of white water. Sunlight played in Maurice's face, spoiling his vision. The trout reared up in a blinding silhouette against the sunlight. Easy, he told himself. Careful now. He took more line, moved further into the stream. You're mine, fish. You're mine.

Only a foot separated them now. He reached down quickly, caught the fish behind the gills, hoisted it wiggling violently in the sunlight, threw back his head, and shouted in triumph.

"By God, it's a five-pounder if it's an ounce!"

The trout went into his creel with the two others. Maurice and his father sloshed out of the stream together, soaking wet, broke down their rods, encased them, and headed back to the camp. The sun was setting in a burst of bright orange when they trudged past the giant sycamore and saw the other men, Cunningham and Ridley, coming up from the far side of the draw.

"Any luck, Bradley?"

"Maurice got three fine rainbows!"

"We caught perch, a trout, and two smallmouths."

"We'll eat like kings tonight."

They scaled and cleaned the fish, laying out the filets in heavy white stripes onto a metal grill. The aroma of frying fish and boiled beans rose in the blue smoke of the campfire. And then they ate, seated cross-legged together before the fire and swigging down warm beer. The moon had risen by the time the last tin plate was washed clean in the creek and they settled down for a final smoke. The other men rolled in their blankets and dropped off to sleep. Bradley Stewart leaned back against a log, stretching and yawning. "This is the life. Damned if I haven't died and gone to heaven."

"Hope still talks about these fishing trips with you when she came down for summer visits," Maurice said. "She said they made her wish she had been born a man."

"Fine young woman, Hope. Strong temperament and lots of brains. I always figured she would do well."

"She said you taught her to be independent. You told her that a smart woman could hold her own in a man's world."

"My mother was an example of that. Catherine Stewart was the smartest, toughest woman who ever drew breath." Bradley stared into the fire, remembering. "She kept this family's enterprise from going under during the Civil War."

Maurice nodded, thinking: Should I tell him now? Timing was important, now—with their bellies full and minds clear— was a good time. But then he looked at the sleeping forms of his father's friends and thought again. No. What he had to say should be said in private.

He lay down in the blankets near his father. The fire died

34

down; the moon stood high and clear, bathing the hills with its silvery light. An owl hooted from a sumac tree.

The next morning they rode the horses along back trails, skirting the coal mines and grimy rural settlements on the outskirts of the city. This brought them onto Stewart House property from behind, across the bald hill where he had sat on the gelding two days before. Maurice was stiff and saddle-sore. He took a hot bath and dressed in rough clothes with heavy brogan shoes and a pullover sweater. It was early afternoon when he knocked at the door of his father's down-stairs office-study. Three minutes later, they faced each other across a decanter of bourbon while Bradley Stewart poured.

"We'll be seeing a lot of each other after next year, son." His father passed over a half-filled glass and lifted his own in a toast. "I don't mind telling you; I'm looking forward to it. Cheers."

Maurice put his glass aside. "I don't think so, Father. I have other plans in mind."

His father did not drink. The glass remained in his hand, untouched. "What sort of plans?"

Maurice told him.

Bradley Stewart did not respond immediately. His broad face flushed darkly. His lips moved as if to speak, but no sound came out. He stood up, his portly body silhouetted against a window across the room. At last he found his voice. "You . . . ungrateful . . . whelp!"

He threw the drink into his son's face.

"Father, try to understand!"

But there was no understanding. Bradley Stewart hurled abuse at this son in whom he had staked the future of the family. "Understand? Understand what? That you feel no responsibility to your own blood? That you want to go fritter your life away like some damned playboy? I'm damned if I'll understand!"

Bourbon trickled down Maurice's face. He looked into the blazing eyes of Bradley Stewart, he heard his fury, and knew that no quarter would be given.

"All right, then." Maurice turned and walked to the door.

"Go!" Bradley Stewart shouted. "Go! But you'll fail. You'll fall on your ass and wish you had never known this day. And when you do, by God, don't come crawling back to me for help!"

"I won't, Father," he said. "Believe me, I won't."

Maurice Stewart left Stewart House and headed down the

35

winding road on foot, with the clothes on his back and eight dollars in his pocket.

He did not see the flash of orange hair at the upstairs window, nor see the gently waving hand of his stepmother Rose, nor hear her whisper as tears dribbled mascara down her painted face, "Good-bye, sweet prince. Good-bye."

III

He was a tough, weather-beaten old man. His business was fighting, not politicking. But a soldier had to be flexible. In the real world it was as necessary to politick as to engage in battles, especially where Cuba was concerned. And so here he sat, wearing tan riding boots with a black suit, white shirt, and string necktie, his mustache waxed and his hair parted in the middle. How the *compañeros* would snicker at their general: Maximo Gomez, guerrilla fighter, now leading the charge by riding an overstuffed chair in a New York salon, smoking a cheroot, and charming the gringos with loving lies.

"General Gomez, tell us about your aspirations for Cuban liberty." It was a pale, fat journalist who spoke. The man's flesh was the consistency of bread dough and he spoke atrocious Spanish. "Tell us what the American people can do to further the cause of freedom."

The others crowded around, all sweet-smelling and eager. They were a pocket of political humanity stuffed into tuxedos and making talk in the Manhattan townhouse of Señor José Dilava-Ruiz, a wealthy Cuban-American export banker who wished to corner the market on Cuban sugar when General Gomez's rebels drove out the Spaniards. This ambition of Dilava-Ruiz's was not generally known. Ah, mused the general, with what duplicity men worked their wiles. It was a joke, all a joke. At this moment in Cuba his men would be burning the cane fields again, throttling down the economy, driving the peasants into the towns, and making life harder and leaner and hungrier, the better to pressure the Spanish authorities. He looked up and saw the pencils poised over the notebooks and spoke rapidly in Spanish as an interpreter picked up his words. "The Cuban people burn to be free of the oppressor." General Gomez also spoke English, of course, but it was better not to let one's fluency be known. "We look

36

to the great American people, and their Monroe Doctrine, to help us drive from our shores these foreigners, these brutal committers of atrocities, these Spanish thugs and rapists..."

As the pencils danced across the pages, Gomez waited shrewdly, timing his phrases. How easily they were deceived, these Americans. The American press was the best ally that he, Maximo Gomez, could possibly recruit. One sympathetic reporter was worth an army in the field.

"For too long we have endured as pawns of the despots, suffered their assassinations of political prisoners, their ravishment of women." The pencils flew; tongues licked lips; eyes blazed with the righteous fervor of Truth. "We beg the American government in Washington, and your new President McKinley, to be sympathetic to our cause." He drew a bandanna from his coat pocket, dusted a spilled shred of tobacco from his lapel, and mopped sweat from his face. *Madre de Dios*, these gringos lived in stuffy rooms. "We beseech your support, but we want not one sacred drop of American blood to be spilled in the name of Cuban freedom!"

Several Cubans applauded as General Gomez held himself steely eyed and resolute.

In another room, a Cuban band played spirited music. There were bursts of laughter and women's voices. Rum flowed and the crowd was having a good time. General Gomez thought of the bloody business in Cuba and wondered how the women would sound if stood against the *paradon*, under the rifles of his best men. He imagined the laughter turning to screams.

"You are pleased, my general?" It was the host Dilava-Ruiz. He was a fat, oily man bearing an odor of cologne. "The interviews are going well?"

"Muy bien, Jośe. *Gracias."*

"You would like a tequila, perhaps? Another cigar? Anything, my general."

A tall American with steely eyes and the face of a horse joined them. He was introduced as Mr. William Randolph Hearst, the publisher. Searching his mental files, Gomez offered his simple peasant's smile. Hearst, he remembered, was a Harvard dropout. He had turned up in New York two years ago, in 1895, with $7.5 million in cash and bought the New York *Journal*, now locked in a struggle with Pulitzer's *World* for circulation supremacy. Both newspapers were sympathetic to the cause. General Gomez said in very halting, simple English, "I am delighted to make the acquaintance of the great Mr. Hearst. In my country, you are a famous man, standing for justice and fair play. I salute you." General Gomez touched his hand to his forehead.

The publisher beamed. "We stand four-square for Cuban independence," he said pompously.

Others came to shake the hand of General Gomez. Among them was the new assistant secretary of the Navy Theodore Roosevelt. The two exchanged knowing glances. Roosevelt was a man whose influence far outweighed his official station in Washington. He bore himself as an aristocrat and exuded a feral access of energy. Instinct told the general that this was a man worth cultivating. An aide whispered into the ear of Maximo Gomez who then said, "I have heard of your efforts to build up the Navy. That is good. It will strengthen the security of the hemisphere against foreign domination."

Roosevelt was noncommittal. "You are well informed, General Gomez." He gestured toward a tall, handsome American naval officer with blazing blue eyes but with the facial structure of an Indian. "May I present Lieutenant Commander Van Harrison Stewart. Commander Stewart speaks fluent Spanish and has served as a naval attaché to the United States embassy in Madrid. He is acting as my unofficial interpreter this evening."

The general was on his guard. He extended his hand to the officer and greeted him lightly in Spanish. Stewart's reply was indeed fluent. After a brief exchange of pleasantries, the assistant secretary and the lieutenant commander withdrew to join a stunning young blond woman with laughing eyes and a perfect smile. Gomez stared at her. She was a Golden Girl. He spoke again to his aide, who left briefly and then came back.

"Her name is Hope Stewart, General. She is Lieutenant Commander Stewart's cousin."

Maximo Gomez smiled and nodded. He made a soft sucking sound with his lips. The aide nodded in vigorous agreement.

The publisher Hearst, and several friends were discussing the Spanish presence in the hemisphere. "The foreign colonial empires are passé," the publisher said gravely. "They have exploited the hemisphere long enough. Don't you agree, Senator?"

Senator Marsh was eager to please. "Yes, yes, absolutely, Mr. Hearst. I was saying on the floor of the Senate just the other day . . ."

The general was no longer listening. Things were going

well; he had to admit to himself that Dilava-Ruiz knew his business. The exporter's connections were broad and diverse. As new guests arrived, the whispering aide identified two members of Congress, a White House aide, and several high-ranking representatives of the State Department. Yes, things were going well indeed.

"... look to the American flag as the very emblem of liberty," the senator was saying. "Indeed, the Cubans look to it as we look upon the cross as the emblem of Christianity. As your own correspondents on the island have so nobly reported, Mr. Hearst, General Weyeler and his Spanish troops have executed forty-three thousand freedom-loving Cubans in the ten years of strife..."

"Nonsense," a voice said quietly.

Heads turned. The face of William Randolph Hearst seemed to flush. General Gomez's eyebrows lifted in surprise. He watched as a tall distinguished-looking man shouldered through the crowd. The general looked into a pair of eyes that were gray and steady, bracketed by tufts of white at the man's temples. Gomez recognized mental toughness in the gray eyes. When the American spoke again, it was in flawless Castilian Spanish.

"My compliments, General, for your excellent press conference. I suspect that you understand the nature of the American press better than do most of our own politicians."

Hearst and the other Americans were visibly flustered, not understanding a word that was being said. Only the lieutenant commander listened with comprehension.

Gomez switched to English, waving his hand with nonchalance. "I merely try to speak the truth as I see it, in my humble way. I am a *guajiro*, and must be forgiven my shortcomings, Señor...Señor..."

"Howard Langden." The American had the look and bearing of an old Cuban hand, but the language of a diplomat. "I am the publisher of the New York *Enterprise*."

General Gomez sucked in his breath. "Ah, yes, the *Enterprise*."

Hearst glared, but remained silent.

"Most editors," Langden said easily, "do not grasp the realities of your strategy, General. They are bombarded with rebel propaganda and take it as God's truth, passing it along to the readers. Americans are always hostile to European autocracies anyway, always ready to sympathize with patriots struggling to be free. That is the American way, to favor the underdog such as yourself. But then, you and I already know that, don't we?"

Gomez smiled. "Tell me, Mr. Langden, why does your newspaper question our motives in Cuba?" The general stood up briefly and removed the jacket of his tuxedo. Half-moons of sweat saturated the underarms of his white shirt. At his belt hung a small derringer pistol in a black leather holster. He sat down again in the chair. "Why do you oppose us?"

"The *Enterprise* does not oppose you, General. We have no stake in the Cuban fighting. My personal concern is with the accuracy of reporting to the American people. I suggest that they are being deceived. Much of the reporting from Havana is wild, contradictory, and impossible. And yet these... these lies are conditioning our public into a strong anti-Spanish bias. They are creating a deliberate mood for war."

"Just what are you inferring, Langden?" William Randolph Hearst spoke, his words dripping with hostility. Onlookers watched, mesmerized. The lovely blond Hope Stewart was staring at Howard Langden. The general rocked back in his chair, privately amused.

Langden kept his eyes fixed upon General Gomez. "Nothing that I have not said in print already, Mr. Hearst. It is simply that you and Mr. Pulitzer are fighting a circulation war in the streets, using the Cuban situation as sensational bait to capture your readers and not giving a hang for responsible journalism." Langden turned and glared at his rival. "I am inferring that in this era of yellow journalism, Mr. Hearst, you are the yellowest of the yellow!"

A dense crowd had gathered. All stood in shocked silence. Even the music in the next room had stopped. Hearst was white-faced with fury. Langden gave him a mocking smile. On the fringe of the onlookers, Theodore Roosevelt busily wiped his glasses. Senator Marsh looked like a man wishing he could find a hole in which to hide.

General Gomez knew that it was time to break this impasse. He emitted a soft chuckle. The chuckle grew louder. He came forward in the chair and slapped his knee. "Marvelous, gentlemen! Marvelous! If the two of you were in command of my guerrillas, Havana would have fallen years ago!"

Laughter washed through the crowd. It was like the breaking of ice. The musicians suddenly appeared, striking up a sprightly two-step. Even William Randolph Hearst smiled.

"Everybody, let us dance, drink, have a good time!" Their

fat host Dilava-Ruiz pushed happily through the crush. "We have a lovely evening in store for you all." The crowd began to disintegrate.

Howard Langden offered Maximo Gomez a courtly bow. "If I were a Spaniard, General, I would regard you as a truly formidable opponent."

The general smiled. "And I you, señor."

The lean old man watched Langden go, and saw the eyes of Hope Stewart follow the commanding figure as he took his hat and coat and moved out toward the foyer. Maximo Gomez lit a cigar and inhaled deeply.

America was in a mood for war, he reflected, but not all the battles would be fought in the field.

Hope Stewart was exhilarated. The spring days, and Van's leave, were flying by. Everyone talked of a gold strike in the Alaskan Klondike. The news had been telegraphed by wire from Oregon. Even New Yorkers were electrified.

Aunt Francesca sniffed with disapproval. "A handful of miners bring down some gold dust and the press goes wild over Alaska; grown men quit their jobs, abandon homes, mortgages, and families, and dash away to the Klondike. What is this world coming to?"

Hope looked up from her reading. "That was sixty miners and eight hundred thousand dollars worth of gold dust, Aunt Francesca. Besides, it's preferable to this constant talk of war."

Francesca eyed her niece suspiciously. "What newspaper are you reading?"

"The New York *Enterprise*."

"Hummmph. A bit liberal for my taste."

"What do you know about Howard Langden, Aunt Francesca?"

Francesca pursed her lips. "Handsome man. Widower. Has substantial holdings in publishing, but a rather narrow control of the *Enterprise*. Why do you ask?"

"How old is he?"

"That's an impertinent question." Francesca Stewart Carp frowned. "He's old enough to be your father."

"And how old is that?"

"At least forty-four."

A dinner party marked Van's impending return to sea duty on board the battleship *Maine*. Friends applauded and drank

41

toasts. "Here's to the new first officer!" Young women flocked around him. Hope found the table talk banal. People's minds were on the latest episode of the Yellow Kid comics, or nickelodeons and the Floradora Sextette, or the new look in women's fashions (peacock feathers, muttonleg sleeves, and the Gibson Girl hairdo) and dime novels. They prattled about trolley rides, the scandalous new dances, and Mark Twain. She listened, smiled, nodded, and was bored.

There was the usual philosophical claptrap.

"In the East, especially, you have the first generation of the well-to-do, and then a second generation as well. Life in America, as I see it, simply does not provide for careers beyond this point. And so many of the people I know are desperately in search of better ways to spend their money and time. This is why there is such an intense interest in returning to European manners and diversion. The nobility, after all, are the nobility..."

Hope bridled. "How can you sit there and talk like that, Jeffrey? People are needed in government and politics. There is a tremendous demand for change. Do you realize the extent of poverty in this city? My God, some of New York's slums are absolute pestholes. Prostitution and white slavery are rampant; crime is epidemic; people are starving. And women, to avoid having more babies, are sticking their heads into ovens."

"Tut-tut, Hope. Don't get uppity. These are not things to be talking about in mixed company. Really, I had expected better of you, a Radcliffe girl!"

"Jeffrey's right, Hope. Why don't you go back to Europe, take the grand tour, have a good time? Or better yet, accept one of those proposals of marriage that we all know are pouring in. Oh, don't try to pretend. Every unattached male in New York and Newport is dying to be your escort..."

They were dull; they were insipid; they were shallow. Not only was this true of her friends, it was true of the scions of wealthy families who went to the plays and cotillion dances. From Newport to Cambridge to Manhattan, they were of the same breed: stuffy, self-centered, snobbish. Thank God for Van's decision to spend his leave in New York. Even though a cousin, he spiced up the season. Hope smiled at the hidden ironies. Van was also a half-breed Cheyenne Indian, a fact of Stewart family life rarely discussed. And he saw life from the mature age of thirty-one, another plus.

"Cousin, I envy you," Hope said. The last guest had

departed. In the darkness, they strolled the blossom-scented grounds of the mansion overlooking the Hudson. "First in your class at Annapolis, fantastic athlete, a scholar at Oxford, a remarkable naval career, and now..."

"And now sea duty on board a real battleship," he said. "The Navy has been good to me. It was Mother's doing. She demanded justice after my father was murdered by General Heflin in the cavalry attack on the Creek-of-Many-Branches. President Grant saw to it that my birth was legitimatized and that the Indian boy, Spotted Deer, became a full American citizen, Van Harrison Stewart. I had a presidential appointment to Annapolis before I was five years old. That was another of Grant's crafty moves. An Army commission, after all, would have been troublesome. I would have been sent West to command troops against my own Cheyenne half brothers. This I could not have done." He grinned. "Luckily, the Cheyenne don't have a navy." He stooped, plucked a violet, and handed it to her. "And now my concern is you, my lovely and troubled cousin. What can I do to help you?"

She took his arm as they stood by the river, an arm strong as a bar of iron. Van Harrison Stewart exuded a masculinity to women that was undiminished by one's blood relationship. As an adult Hope could understand more clearly the forbidden passions that had overwhelmed her own parents, the first cousins Thaddeus and Marguerite Stewart.

"Would it embarrass you to hear a girl's secrets?" she said.

The night was moonless and filled with stars. The dark Hudson sighed and chuckled at their feet. Hope stared at the blackness of the distant shore as one in search of an obscure destiny. "I don't understand myself, Van. Since childhood I have been taught to think and act like a Stewart. Uncle Bradley used to take me hunting and fishing around Pittsburgh. I adored the man, and I still do despite his conflicts with his own sons Maurice and Casey and the rest of the family. He used to tell me about how his mother Catherine was a crack shot with a rifle, could handle a bullwhip with the best Stewart teamster, succeeded in building her own steamboat dynasty on the Mississippi, and yet was a loving and faithful wife to Stephen Stewart. Aunt Francesca also taught me to be strong, to be resourceful, and to be myself. And these are the things I wish to be."

"We have to be what we are," Van said.

"But I'm out of step with the times, Van. Manners, custom, fashion. A woman today, in 1897, is not supposed to have a brain in her head or a competitive skill of any kind. She can't vote. If married, she can't own property separately or sign contracts or even have a separate banking account. It is shocking if she shows her ankle in public. It's virtually impossible to get a decent education. I wouldn't have had one either if Aunt Francesca hadn't provided tutors and sent me abroad for more schooling. Harvard is for men only. So are Princeton and Yale. So are most institutions of higher learning and technical or scientific schools. It's a man's world, and women who do stick their necks out and try to bring change, who push for the right to vote, the right to work, and even such a simple thing as the right to control birth, are ridiculed and sometimes even jailed."

"I know a little about that," Van said, quietly. "I'm half Indian, remember, a half-breed in a white man's world." His voice had a depth of suppressed anger she had not heard before. "I am Van Harrison Stewart, the son of socialite Vanessa Stewart Harding and her husband Claude, manufacturer of electrical equipment. But I am also Spotted Deer, the son of Vanessa Stewart, once called Sunset Woman, once the lover of my father Standing Bear, warrior chief of his Cheyenne tribe. I have no greater pride than my Cheyenne heritage. And yet if I wish to succeed in the world of white men and white women, I do not speak of these things out loud."

His feelings were a revelation to her. Since childhood Hope had known this darkly handsome part-Indian cousin, so brilliant in scholarship and athletics and yet harboring what she knew were greater depths. Only now did it come out, in response to her own expressions of frustration. How strange the workings of this Stewart breed in which kinship could be so rich and yet so tangled.

Gradually the conversation came back to her own nagging concerns. "I hate this talk of war. The idea of going to war against Spain is unspeakable. Like you, I have been to Spain and made friends there. I wish I could find a way to resist the war."

"If that is what you really want to do . . ."

"You asked awhile ago if you could help me," she said. "Well, there is something. It has been on my mind since the night we saw General Gomez and listened to the talk that went on there."

"Yes?"

"Van, I want you to introduce me to the publisher Howard Langden."

It was a simple thing. They went to Langden's Fifth Avenue townhouse the next afternoon and knocked on the door. The butler took Van's calling card and returned followed by Langden himself, saying, "What a delightful surprise!" They were ushered into the parlor. Hope was not surprised to find that the home of Howard Langden was roomy and masculine, its furnishings tasteful without ostentation, a blending of fine polished woods, conservative fabrics, brass, and potted greenery. The floors were of inlaid mahogany and Oriental carpets. Van, as usual, declined alcohol and settled for a phosphate soda. To Langden's amusement, Hope accepted a bourbon and soda and lit one of his excellent Havana cheroots. They exchanged small talk. Hope finally came to the point.

"You left Señor Dilava-Ruiz's house before we could be introduced."

"Ah, yes. I saw no point in remaining. The atmosphere was less than cordial."

"Why did you go there at all?"

"To say what had to be said, Miss Stewart. Clearly the purpose of these Cuban revolutionaries and their wealthy friends is not to clear the air. They seek to build a strong base of American support. I cannot blame them for that; I would do the same thing. But someone, I felt, had to express the opposition view, unmask their tactics, and put in a word for peace. No one else seemed anxious to take on the chore, so I did it myself. Rude manners, I'll admit, but the situation gave me no choice."

"After you left, Senator Marsh took you apart."

"I'm not surprised."

"He said that liberals of your stripe have no belly for war, that you'd rather appease a foreign power holding dominion over Cuba in defiance of our own Monroe Doctrine."

"And what did Mr. Roosevelt say?"

"Mr. Roosevelt"—Hope sipped at her bourbon—"displayed his toothiest smile, crinkled his eyes behind those gold-rimmed spectacles, and said, 'My compliments to your musicians, General Gomez. They play bully music!'"

Langden laughed. "Theodore Roosevelt is a militarist. He wants to go to war against Spain, if only to build up the American Navy. He sees America as the guardian of the

45

hemisphere, policeman of the world, missionary in behalf of Anglo-Saxon virtues, and defender of the Protestant ethic. And there are many, I'm afraid, who agree with him. What about you, Lieutenant Commander?"

Van Harrison Stewart pondered the question. "My role is to follow orders, Mr. Langden. I am a naval officer, not a politician or newspaper publisher."

"And an excellent naval officer at that, I've heard," Langden said. "You have a magnificent career ahead of you, young man."

Howard Langden was a master conversationalist and convivial host with an easy charm that put his visitors completely at ease. Van was fascinated by the publisher's collection of ship models and prints and his yachtsman's knowledge of the sea. "Stewart is quite a name in sailing craft and coastal boats," Langden said. "In my opinion the finest boatbuilders on the East Coast are old Captain Francis Drake Stewart of Boston and his son Ward."

"Yes," said Hope gaily, "they are cousins of ours."

Langden almost choked on his drink. "But... Francis Drake Stewart is a *black* man. His son passes for white—went through Princeton with flying colors—but he has Negro blood."

"Only a little, on his grandmother's side," Hope said, watching Langden's face carefully. "Does that bother you?"

The publisher smiled. "Absolutely not. I find it fascinating. Besides, Captain Francis Drake and his son are..."

Hope finished the sentence for him. "...the richest niggers in America."

"Absolutely the richest," Langden said. "Those words, by the way, are Francis Drake's very own. He was a great captain of clipper ships in his day, and now the Stewart racing yacht is without equal in the world. It will win the America Cup next year; mark my words." He sat back and gazed at Hope with those bold gray eyes. "Well, I'll be damned."

"And I"—Van rose from his chair—"will be going. It's getting late, and I have a lady companion to escort to the variety show tonight."

"To a variety show?" said Langden. "That sounds like fun."

"Why don't the two of you come along with us?"

The publisher sprang from his chair. "Excellent! And I'll treat for dinner afterward."

Within two hours they were dressed in evening clothes and riding to the Garden Theater in Howard Langden's two-horse phaeton. The opening night crowd glittered in gowns and tuxedos. Celebrities clustered in the brilliantly lit lobbies: Stanford White, the architect, escorting a very young model named Evelyn Nesbitt, the former heavyweight champion prizefighter Gentleman Jim Corbett, J. P. Morgan, the financier, whose private liaisons with several actresses recently had set tongues to wagging, Boss Coker, and Mrs. William K. Vanderbilt.

The curtains swept open with a blast of sound and lights as the crowd responded to colorful costumes and rapid-fire humor. "I've traveled all over this country," shouted the comedian De Wolf Hopper. "Finally came back to New York to get away from one-night stands and railroad sleeping cars. But I couldn't sleep in the hotel. It was too quiet. Finally I hired two men to shake the bed all night and pour cinders down my neck..."

They dined at the new Waldorf-Astoria. Van Harrison's friend of the evening was a beautiful brunet actress named Beatrice who kept staring at her dashing uniformed escort and blushing outrageously. Later they all waltzed to the music of a stringed ensemble. Howard Langden watched Van and the brunet sweep across the floor and asked, "Are all Stewart men and women so remarkable?"

"And are all the Langdens such marvelous company?" Hope replied.

Van and the brunet went their separate ways. Long after midnight, Howard Langden's phaeton moved slowly up the winding drive to Aunt Francesca's house as the two of them sang a duet in harmony: "*East side, west side, all around the town...*" Howard left her at the door, brushing the tips of her fingers with his mustache. She went giggling into the foyer, closed the door gently behind her, and stood listening to her heartbeat.

Aunt Francesca came down the stairs in her nightclothes. "Goodness, child, are you well? You have the strangest look on your face."

"I am well. I am ecstatic. I am walking on air!"

Hope turned slowly, humming and waltzing across the polished floor of the foyer. From outside, she heard the gentle clip-clop of Howard Langden's matched team as they moved away in the darkness.

A westbound train pulling seventy freight cars chuffed slowly out of the Akron Yard, whistle moaning and headlight piercing through the rain. Beyond the yard limits, shadowy figures moved in quick bounds down a weedy slope and crouched at the edge of the tracks.

"All right now, young feller, we're gonna take the twelfth car," a voice said. "When you see that ladder comin' by, you jump up out of these weeds and start runnin'. Grab a handful of iron and she'll yank you right off your feet, but don't let go. There ain't no turnin' back."

Another man snickered in the darkness. "Not unless you want to end up a hunnerd and eighty pounds of ground meat."

Maurice Stewart drew his coat collar higher. He was drenched and cold and afraid. But the multiple miseries faded as he focused his attention upon the oncoming iron monster, clanking and rumbling out of the night. The advancing headlight played over glistening rails and black crossties. Hunkered low, he edged forward, conscious that the others were spreading out along the graveled railbed. The looming iron bulk expanded, ventilators glowing in the firebox, rumbling and clanking, gushing steam.

"There ain't no turning back . . ."

And then the engine was over him, an awesome, black-glistening presence of sound and heat. He looked up at the passing cab and saw the engineer's face glowing in the firelight. The face vanished. The tender passed, iron wheels squealing on iron rails, and then came the freight cars: one, two, three . . . seven . . . twelve . . .

"Go, boy!"

A hand prodded him in the back. He came to his feet running as if in a dream. Time seemed to stop; his reflexes slowed. The soggy coat clutched at his body; soggy trousers tried to drag him down. The train gathered speed. The ladder was a barely discernible break in shades of black. His feet pounded on gravel; his wet hands reached, touched, grabbed. He was yanked forward, off his feet, shoulder sockets shooting pain. His feet scrambled for support as one foot caught the bottom rung and he was secured. The car lurched and swayed as he climbed for an eternity through black slashing rain, found the top of the car, and hauled his body, sprawling, onto the catwalk.

"Jesus Christ!" he said.

He lay facedown on the catwalk, panting for breath and clutching a metal brace. The rain came down in sheets, pelting the steel top of the swaying boxcar. The rhythm of the train began to seep into his bones and as infinite weariness overcame him, he drifted off to sleep as the train thundered westward through the stormy night.

He awoke stiff and sore. A bright morning sun peeped over the horizon. From his airy moving perch, the Ohio countryside spread cleanly as far as he could see. Spring was evident in newly greening fields, budding trees, and splotches of yellow crocuses. Blossoming dogwood made white explosions in the woods. Maurice lay his chin on the crook of his arms and watched, his mood buoyant. The air was balmy and scented, the sky a milky blue. It was good to be alive.

"You hongry, young feller?"

A tattered apparition rose up behind him, climbing the steel ladder at the end of the boxcar. The apparition had a flying gray mane of whiskers and a tattered ensemble of grimy clothing. Maurice recognized the old hobo who had helped him to hop the freight. He shouted back above the noise of the train, "Starving."

The apparition crawled along the catwalk to where Maurice lay. He settled into a sitting position, back to the wind, and rummaged through several side pockets of a heavy, damp overcoat. "There ain't much in the way of vittles, this not bein' the Waldorf-Astoria, but I reckon I can scare us up a morsel or two." The old man's chuckle had the raspy sound of a bemused crow.

From the overcoat he drew out a waterproof rubber sack containing three apples and two fried chicken drumsticks wrapped in brown paper. There was also a half-eaten sandwich containing some unidentifiable meat, but this Maurice's benefactor did not offer to share. Maurice found himself sitting in the wind clutching an apple and a drumstick. His companion bit wordlessly into the remnant of his sandwich.

Maurice's misgivings vanished as he sampled the chicken leg. Flavor flooding his tastebuds, he wolfed down the meager portion in three bites. As he prepared to toss away the chicken bone, the old man grabbed his arm. "Don't do that, young feller." Plucking the bone from Maurice's fingers, he

49

carefully wrapped it in brown paper and returned it to the rubber sack. "That's a stew bone, or mebbe just somethin' to suck the marrow out of. I see you ain't been on the road much. When you don't know where the next meal's comin' from, it don't pay to throw anythin' away. Waste not, want not."

The old man spread his coat to dry in the wind and lay down on the catwalk. "Where you bound, young feller?"

Maurice shook his head. "West, but I don't know just where. I haven't given it much thought."

"This is your first time ridin' freights?"

"Yes."

"I thought you was a greenhorn. Saw it the minute you stumbled into the hobo camp last night." He offered a calloused handshake. "Tom Moneypenny's my name. Got any money on you?"

"No. I spent it all getting from Pittsburgh to Youngstown. Then I caught a wagon ride as far as Akron. But I didn't feel like stopping there."

"Can't say as I blame you. I never cared much for Akron."

They watched the countryside flow past. Ohio was flatly rolling land, with standing cattle and winding creeks. What a contrast, Maurice thought, between this and Pittsburgh, New York, or Cambridge. Looking back, he realized that he had spent most of his life in cities, but that the nation was mostly rural—small towns, farms, open countryside—with room to stretch and grow.

As if reading his thoughts, Tom Moneypenny said, "I've ridden freight trains from one end of this country to the other, and no two parts of it are the same. I been through states like Nebraska and Kansas where there's wheatfields as far as you can see. Down South it's cotton, and niggers bendin' over pickin' from dawn to dark. Up in the Northeast, it's factory towns, with lots of coal smoke and busy mills. I seen children workin' those mills no more than eight, nine years old. It's a crime how they make them young'uns work. It's the same in the mines, around Pennsylvania and West Virginia. They use child labor, too. You ever been to the mines there in Pennsylvania, young feller?"

"I've never been inside a coal mine."

Moneypenny snorted. "It's a poor way to make a livin'. I wouldn't recommend diggin' coal unless you was starvin'."

The miles poured past them. Moneypenny peered ahead into the wind and said, "We'll be stoppin' for water soon. I

50

know this little town ahead, Fostoria. There's likely to be bulls checkin' the train."

"Bulls?"

"Railroad constables. They're a mean lot. A bad-tempered bull with a hickory club can land you in a hospital, or worse. Every once in awhile they take a notion to clean the trains. We'd better climb down to where there's some cover." Putting on his overcoat, Moneypenny crawled back along the catwalk, descended the steel ladder between the cars, and waited until Maurice came down behind him.

As their speed diminished, Maurice peered ahead. Burly men in black suits and derby hats were fanning out along the track at the water tank, each brandishing a heavy club. As the train jerked to a stop, the detectives spread out on both sides of the cars, moving along the train. Clubs banged at the boxcars and voices bawled, "Out! Out, ye scum! Everybody off!"

Men began tumbling from the cars, to the accompaniment of curses, thuds, and groans. A shot cracked across the afternoon and a body plummeted from the top of a car.

"We'll make a break for it," Maurice said.

Moneypenny wagged his head. "You go ahead, young feller. These old legs of mine couldn't outrun a mud turtle."

"But they'll catch you."

"It won't be the first time . . ."

As Moneypenny's voice trailed off, an iron hand seized Maurice by the collar. He was yanked backward off the boxcar coupling and sent sprawling into the gravel trackbed. He came to his knees and saw a heavy brogan shoe aiming a kick at his midsection. Rolling instinctively, he took a glancing kick in the ribs as more detectives rushed forward, encircling him. He struggled to his feet, fists clenched, to face the tightening circle of derby-wearing men. Clubs thudded against the palms of open hands. A voice said, "Now then, my lad . . ."

He offered no resistance.

The jail reeked of sweat and urine. It was a confined world of echoes, of reverberating voices, of crashing and banging, of steel upon steel. There were four of them in this cell. No one had read any charges to him. Maurice felt that suddenly he had descended into a vacuum.

"Where are we, Moneypenny?"

"The county jail at Fostoria. It ain't much, but it's home."

"Why are we here?"

51

"Trespassin' on railroad property. Assault of a railroad officer. Resistin' arrest with violence. Loiterin' and vagrancy. Just about everythin' short of murder. You name the charge, they can slap it on you."

Maurice rolled over on the cot. It was a rude horsehair pad covered by a single dirty blanket. An open pit festered in the corner, serving as a toilet. "How long will we stay?"

"Hard to tell. It could be a few days or a few months, dependin' on how badly they need prisoners."

Maurice drank water from a foul-smelling cracked porcelain ladle. He sighed and drifted off to sleep. He passed the night sleeping, interspersed with brief periods of troubled wakefulness during which he stumbled to the pit to relieve himself. From down a narrow hallway he heard steel doors banging and keys rattling. A beefy guard appeared bearing a tray and five spoons. "Here's food," the man announced. He opened the cell door and deposited the tray. It contained a gruellike porridge and some scraps of moldy biscuits. As he went away, the others fell to noisy eating. Maurice abstained. Night came again. The cell was lit by a meager kerosene lamp set in an open area beyond the door. Old Moneypenny was in a talkative mood. They sat on Maurice's bunk, staring into the lamplight.

"I had me a son once. You sort of favor him, young feller. He'd have been about your age."

"What happened to him?"

"Dead. Pinkertons beat him to death in the steel strike at Homestead in '92. I reckon you know all about that, seein' as how it happened right there at Pittsburgh."

"My father said the strikers were hooligans and anarchists. He thinks labor unions ought to be outlawed."

Moneypenny snorted. "My boy never had no education. He never had nothin'. He went to work when he was eleven years old, same as I did in my time. He was an ore loader at the Carnegie mill by the time he was fourteen. They was strikin' for a new contract and the mill owners decided to destroy the union. The workers and their families tried to stop 'em from bringin' in the Pinkerton strikebreakers. They come down on the crowd swingin' pickhandles. There was blood everywhere and people runnin'—men, women, and children—and next thing you knowed some hotheads started shootin'. It was bad at Homestead. The people didn't have no chance."

The old man fell silent. Maurice tried to digest the infor-

52

mation in some logical order. It was all foreign to him, as foreign as the notion that people really lived in jail cells such as this. It was beginning to dawn on him that he had lived a sheltered life, enjoying all the benefits and suffering none of the privations. He thought of Hope and her disenchantment with the New York rich. At Harvard, he had known a radical student and gone to a street rally with him where the speaker told the crowd, "The capitalists feed upon your toil and sweat, my friends. The only way you're going to change anything is by spilling blood."

He told Moneypenny about the rally and what the speaker had said. Moneypenny nodded. "You got a country here where a laborin' man makes four hundred dollars a year. In big cities—New York and Chicago—the poverty makes you sick. You get masses of people out of work, nothin' to eat, no place to live. Big city slums is like jungles. But the swells don't know about that. I went to Washington with Coxey's army in '94. That was the army of the unemployed. There was five hundred of us marchin' down Pennsylvania Avenue, wantin' relief. Know what they done? They arrested Jacob Coxey for trespassin'. So the army disbanded and left town. I did manage to sneak into Congress, though, just to take a look. I sat up in the visitors' gallery of the House of Representatives listenin' to the speeches. But it seemed like nobody represented the people, leastways not the poor people. The congressmen all wore tailor-made suits and were hustlin' for them who got 'em elected in the first place."

"And who is that?"

"The big shots."

Their three cellmates had been jailed as vagrants. One was a Mexican migrant who spoke little English and sat for hours on his cot staring at the barred window with a strange light in his eyes. Moneypenny managed to communicate briefly in broken Spanish. He shook his head and made a twirling motion with his forefinger. "*Muy loco*. He's stir crazy, that one. Can't stand being penned up." The two others were merely drifters picked up begging on the town's main street. Old Moneypenny expressed outrage at the incarceration of the three. "They didn't trespass on nobody. Their crime was bein' in the wrong place at the wrong time. And the Mexican's crime is not speakin' English."

Two more days went by. Moneypenny's store of small talk was inexhaustible and full of surprises. Maurice discovered that the old man was a carriagemaker by trade and had a keen mind for mechanics, having worked during the Civil War at the Army ordnance depot in Springfield, Missouri. "We was makin' the Springfield rifle. It had interchangin' parts. Smartest thin' the War Department ever done was to build a weapon like that. You could take four rifles apart, mix up the pieces any old way, put 'em back together in whatever order you pleased, and every one would be good as new. I heard tell they're doin' the same thing now with cotton gins, reapers, and plows. There's no end to the possibilities. Matter-of-fact, I've got me a plan for a little horse-drawn buggy with interchangeable parts." Using a scrap of paper and a pencil stub, he painstakingly drew a sketch of the buggy. The vehicle had a light, sporty look unlike anything Maurice had seen before. Its design promised strength and durability. "Instead of buildin' it all at one time, the way they do in most buggyworks nowadays," Moneypenny said, "you could have the wheels built in one plant, the wood framin' in another, the chassis in still another, and assemble the whole thin' wherever you darn well pleased..."

Another night came.

Maurice awoke with a start. The quiet was broken only by the steady breathing of his cellmates. Gray daylight filtered through the barred window. Something told him that all was not right. He glanced over at Moneypenny's bunk. The old man slept deeply, wrapped in a gray blanket. Maurice squeezed his eyes shut and opened them again. It was nothing, he thought, merely a dream. He turned his face to the wall and tried to go back to sleep. He lay with his eyes closed, but the feeling would not go away. There was something terribly wrong in this cell.

He rolled over, sat up, and put his feet on the floor.

Then he saw the body hanging from the cell door.

The Mexican had used his leather belt. Standing on the wooden stool, he had looped the belt around the top steel crossbar, twisted it to fit tightly about his neck, and then kicked away the stool. His feet dangled three inches from the floor. His eyes were locked open, shining in the gray morning light.

Maurice sprang up, shouting for the guard.

They were released that same afternoon. As Maurice signed for his meager belongings he recognized the chief deputy as one of the club-wielding men at the train. The man scrutinized him with hooded eyes set into a piglike face. "You're a lucky boy, Stewart. Not many young fellers attack railroad officers and get off lightly. Next time won't be so easy. But seein' as how it's your first offense..."

The two drifters were already gone by the time Maurice and Moneypenny stepped out into the balmy spring sunshine, coats slung over their arms. They were grubby and jail-rank with nearly a week's growth of whiskers. The deputy's last words had been, "I want you two out of this town just as quick as you can go. And don't let me ever see your faces back here again." Wordlessly, they marched to the town limits and out onto a dirt road heading west. They continued walking through the rest of the afternoon. At dusk, they split a cord of kindling for a farmer in exchange for a small sack of potatoes. A train whistle drew them through the darkness back to the railroad. They made camp and feasted on Moneypenny's potato stew, fortified somewhat by the week-old chicken bones from the rubber sack.

Bellies filled, they spread their coats by the dying fire and lay contentedly on their backs, looking up at a sky spread with stars.

"Why did they let us go, Moneypenny?"

The old man grunted. "You can thank the Mexican."

"The Mexican?"

"Jail suicides ain't to a jailer's likin'. Fostoria's not a bad little town, and the less said about a cell hangin' the better. No witnesses, no talk. They carried out the carcass, buried it, and that was that. So we was lucky, just like the deputy said. A judge would have put a big, strong feller like you on the county farm for six months labor, maybe more."

A shooting star arced across the velvety night. Maurice watched its passage and wondered: good omen or bad?

"Where are you going from here, Moneypenny?"

Moneypenny produced a stub of presmoked cigar, lit it with a glowing stick from the fire, and blew smoke rings. "I figure I'll head for Michigan. I've got a cousin there, in a town called Fall River. It ain't much of a town, but I might park for a while, get me a job in the wagon factory, earn a little money to tide me over next winter. What about yourself?"

"I don't have any destination in mind. Fall River seems as good a place as any. Mind if I tag along?"

"Don't mind a bit, young feller. Glad to have you."

Maurice rolled into his overcoat and thought about the Mexican and his miserable last days in a gringo jail. He had never seen a dead man before. And the irony of it was, one

55

man's hell had made possible another's freedom. "Fall River it is, then," he murmured to himself.

At dawn, they moved to the railroad tracks and hopped on another slow freight.

The envelope arrived by postal messenger from Colón. It was addressed in a flowing feminine hand:

Mrs. Casey B. Stewart,
Gatun,
Isthmus of Panama,
Colombia,
S.A.

Lollie brought it to him with utmost gravity and watched closely as he tore it open and drew out an embossed card.

"What is it, chéri?" she whispered. "Is it writing?"

"Damned if I know. Looks like an invitation."

"Writing," Lollie said. "It is writing. From America."

Casey Stewart glanced at her distractedly, saw the wonder in her lovely face, and for the first time realized that Lollie DeRange could neither read nor write. Gently he drew her down beside him in the big wicker chair.

"Let's see what it says, Lollie. Well, upon my word, it is an invitation." He traced his forefinger across the words, overprinted in Old English script on the formal white card, and translated into French as he read:

Mrs. Francesca Stewart Carp, of Blossom Hill on the Hudson, cordially invites you to attend the wedding of her niece and ward Hope Marguerite Stewart, to Mr. Howard S. Langden of New York City at noon on the twenty-first day of June 1897 . . ."

"A wedding," Lollie breathed. "They send invitations all this distance for a wedding?"

"It is the custom among relatives and close friends."

"This woman Hope, she is a relative of yours?"

"My cousin, yes. And a very beautiful cousin at that. Hope is tall, very blond with blue eyes. She's a stunner."

"And will you go to the wedding, Casey?"

"Go?" He put the card aside and lit a cigar. "Well, I really can't see traveling all the way to New York for a wedding. A gift will do. Yes. I'll just send them a gift."

56

Her face glowed. She kissed him lightly on the cheek. Her scent was an exhilarating mix of woman and wildflowers. "I'm glad you are not going," she said. "I would miss you very much."

Within an hour, the invitation was forgotten.

April passed into May.

Several new cases of yellow fever were reported in the Gatun area, but no one had died. Compared to outbreaks of the past, it was nothing.

The rains were daily occurrences now. Humidity worsened; mildew set in; rust attacked everything rustable—tools, knives, belt buckles, metal fasteners, nails, hinges—and mosquitoes bred in standing water receptacles, rainbarrels, marshes, creekbeds, and puddles. Lollie accidentally broke one of the screens and singing swarms invaded the cottage for several hours before Casey and Blanchet could make repairs. Cursing and swatting, they finally managed to clear the enclosure. "Voracious devils," Casey said. "Lollie was going crazy from the bites, and she's lived with mosquitoes all her life."

Lollie's illness set in slowly, a week later. At first she complained of lassitude and weakness. That night, Casey awoke to find her shivering violently with a raging fever. He rummaged through the cottage for blankets and spread them over her, but it did no good. She begged for water and drank glass after glass. By daybreak, she suffered from severe pains in the back and legs and a savage headache. Casey called down the hill to a passing black man, who ran to notify Blanchet. The gangling Frenchman came up the hill at a loping trot. "What is it, man? What's wrong?"

"Lollie's sick."

Blanchet knelt over the shivering form in the bed. Bony fingers stroked her forehead and touched deftly here, there. He examined her eyes, peered into her mouth, asked questions. Face darkening, he stood up at last and said, "I'm not sure yet We'll have to wait a bit. It could be . . . Well, never mind."

"Shouldn't we get a doctor?"

"If you like, yes. But the nearest doctor is in Colón. I doubt if he can do much more than we can. Keep her warm; give her plenty of fluids; pray."

Even as Casey spoke, Blanchet drew a crucifix from his pocket, kissed it, and knelt by the bed, murmuring softly.

The hours dragged. The shaking subsided at last and the fever seemed to be going down. Lollie opened her eyes and smiled. "You're getting better," Casey said. "You are going to be all right."

But her face had a yellowish tinge, sending a chill down his spine. Blanchet came in with a basin of warm water and touched his arm. "You had better leave us now. I will look after things. You need rest. Go down to my shack."

"No. I will stay here," he said.

"Please. This is no place for you."

"I will remain."

Blanchet looked into his face, saw the resolution there, and sighed. "As you wish."

Five hours later, she began to spit up traces of dark, dried blood. Blanchet caught the shreds in the basin. *"Vomita negro!"* he whispered. The black vomit. More and more she retched until the stygian matter was coming in mouthfuls as she seemed to lapse into a delirium.

Wearily Casey and Blanchet awaited another dawn. They stood smoking on the screened veranda.

"We just don't know yet," the former priest was saying. "Some think it's from the miasma, the night vapors. There is much fear of the dreadful contagion. You saw how things were during the worst of it a few years ago. They died like flies, blacks as well as whites. It is thought that natives of the islands and of Panama itself have an immunity to the yellow fever. But there is no certainty of that. I've known people to come down with it who've lived in this part of the world all their lives."

"What are her chances?" Casey asked.

The Frenchman shrugged. "Fifty-fifty, my friend. Maybe less."

Her body temperature was lowering, the pulse growing weaker. As the morning sun again rose over a jungle washed stunningly clean by night rains, her flesh was cold to the touch. Lollie lay in a state of peaceful composure, a half smile playing at her mouth. And now, for the first time, Casey was struck by her youth; this young woman with whom he had shared nearly two years of intimacy, as the recipient of her quiet, selfless devotion, was barely more than a teenager.

Blanchet read his thoughts. "Yes, she is quite young. And I believe, Stewart, that she loves you more deeply than she ever thought it possible to love."

"How would you know that, Blanchet?"

"She told me so, in her confession last night."

"You can't take confession. You are no longer a priest."

"In man's eyes, no. In my heart I shall always be a priest. And I think God recognizes that, too. Besides, there are no others around and she is Catholic. Who are we to deny her soul the final rites of the church?"

"The final..." Casey Stewart felt suddenly, agonizingly alone.

Lollie DeRange died an hour later, her head cradled in his arms.

In the cottage, before a motley assembly of black laborers, Indians, and passersby summoned for the purpose, Henri Blanchet conducted the Requiem Mass, without surplice or altar boys or assistants. His deep, strong voice beseeched the intercession and mercy of the Almighty in impeccable Latin. Then they bore her body, wrapped in a sheet, to the crest of a hill overlooking the old Culebra Cut—the scene of so many French mudslides and general disasters—and buried her in warm clay soil. Afterward, Stewart and Blanchet stayed drunk for a week.

The despair would not loose its grip upon him. It came again and again, in fresh waves springing from deep within his soul. If only he could cough it up, spit it out, and be done with it. But it would not cough, would not spit. And so he let himself be taken by it and speculated on how he might find a personal release in death. Time and again he trudged up the muddy slope to stand at the earthen mound, deep in thought. "Damn it, Lollie, why did you leave me? What shall I do now?"

And then one day he returned from the grave, rummaged through the wine bottles, and found them all empty. "Good God," he muttered, "this can't be!" He searched the kitchen area, the parlor, the closets. Nothing. He went into the bedroom and began pulling open dresser drawers. At last, in a bottom drawer among her pitifully few articles of clothing, he found a bottle of Bordeaux red and beside it the white envelope bearing the invitation to his cousin's wedding. He uncorked the bottle and drank deeply, half conscious of the bearded apparition reflected in the mirror. The bottle was half empty when he lowered it and studied the ravaged face. That... that wild-eyed scarecrow in the mirror could not be Casey Stewart! The envelope lay on the dresser top, flecked with spilled droplets of wine. He picked it up, idly slipped out the embossed card, focused his eyes with difficulty, and read,

Mrs. Francesca Stewart Carp, of Blossom Hill on the Hudson, cordially invites you ...

Well, why not?

Grasping the invitation in one hand and the bottle in the other, Casey Stewart lurched out onto the screened veranda and shouted at the brooding green hills of Panama. "I am getting out of here. I'm going to a wedding in New York City. Do you hear me? Listen to me, jungle! My name is Casey Stewart. I am a Stewart. I am a man. I am going to a fucking wedding in New York, and you can't stop me. Do you hear? *You can't stop meeeeeeeee!*"

His maniacal laughter caused a flock of parakeets to explode from a nearby thicket.

IV

"Here y'ar, get yer souvenirs! Souvenirs. Balloons, autographed pictures o' baseball stars. I gotta genuine necklace here bearin' a likeness o' President Cleveland hisself. Souvenirs. Get yer souvenirs..."

Crowds had formed early outside the Congregational Church off Madison Avenue. Women stood for hours holding parasols against the spring sunshine. It sprinkled rain at eleven o'clock, but no one gave up favored vantage points. Souvenir vendors plied their wares; an organ grinder appeared with his trained monkey; fruit and vegetable carts parked at the edge of the crowd, selling penny apples. At last the wedding guests began to arrive in front of the church. Fingers pointed at celebrities stepping down from their victorias, broughams, and even a few horseless carriages. The bride's aunt Francesca Stewart Carp, queen of the Hudson River steamship empire, was accompanied by a retinue of friends and relatives. "Oh, my," went the whispers, "there goes Teddy Roosevelt. And isn't that Sarah Bernhardt?"

June of 1897 had been studded with society weddings in New York. The nuptials of socialite Hope Stewart and the publisher Howard Langden, however, captured the public's fancy like no other. For weeks the press had been filled with stories and gossip about the tumultuous Stewart family, its loves and scandals. Colorful stories about the bride herself—ravishingly beautiful Hope Stewart, rebellious and cigar-smoking, given to racing about New York at the wheel of a horseless carriage—captivated readers; the toast of Manhattan's most dashing young blades, she had chosen to marry a widower twenty-three years her senior.

Inside the church, Reverend Danworthy P. Dowd suffered from a nervous stomach. This would be the most momentous ceremony he had ever conducted. Never had the sanctuary been so beautifully decorated. White roses banked the altar; every candlestick holder had been polished, every pew dusted, every inch of exposed wood waxed. How wise of Francesca Stewart Carp to insist—absolutely insist—that her niece marry in the sight of God. The bride was stunning but headstrong. Reverend Dowd did not hold to willful behavior among women; it was un-Christian and dangerous to the fabric of the family. He disapproved that this young woman smoked, flaunted her smoking in public, and drove a horseless carriage. It was said that she even held certain populist ideas. What was the world coming to? Mr. Langdon would have his hands full. Yes, indeed. Reverend Dowd had said as much to Mrs. Dowd that very morning at breakfast. But to make matters worse, Hope had insisted on a change in the wedding ceremony. It was almost like changing God's Word.

The Rich were different, he told himself, and the Very Rich were very different. One made allowances. After all, the prestige of this wedding undoubtedly would help to fulfill Reverend Dowd's heart's desire: a new church, in the classical style with noble pillars and a handsome cupola, designed by Stanford White himself. But changing the ceremony . . .

The pews were filling. Reverend Dowd withdrew to the meditation alcove in order to observe. He saw J. P. Morgan and several of the Goulds and the Fishes; he saw a Vanderbilt and Commissioner Roosevelt, now assistant secretary of the Navy, and young Harry K. Thaw. Splendid, he thought. Splendid. By the time every pew was taken, the church became warm. Paper fans fluttered amid the dressy splendor. Ushers unrolled a white carpet down the center aisle and scattered it with fresh-cut flowers. There was a heavy scent of blossoms and eau de cologne. Sunlight streamed down from the stained glass windows and splashed upon elegant clothing and jewels. Softly the organ music began as singers performed several romantic solos and duets. And then it was time. The members of the wedding took their places. Howard Langdon appeared, resplendent in afternoon formal attire. Langdon was tall, gray-haired, distinguished, and Reverend Dowd saw the eyes of women watching him from behind their fans. The pipe organ swelled in the mighty Lohengrin anthem. In the back of the sanctuary, Hope Stewart appeared on the arm of her cousin Van Harrison Stewart, a naval officer in full-dress uniform. The magnificence of her white wedding gown, with its long train and cloudlike folds of white mesh, sent ripples of excitement through the church.

And then the bridal march was completed. As the couple stood together, facing him and the open Bible, Reverend Dowd's anxiety increased. He fought to keep his voice steady. "Howard Deering Langden, do you take this woman to be..." They were coming to The Change. All his misgivings returned with a rush. He looked into the magnificent blue eyes of Hope Stewart and saw the unspoken demand there. The memory of her shocking protest flicked across his mind. "We will change the part in which the female promises to love, honor, and obey, Reverend Dowd. This is unnecessary and unrealistic. Make it that we both promise to seek mutual happiness and accord..." He had protested, appealed to Francesca Stewart Carp, spoken earnestly to Howard Langden. It was to no avail. The Change remained. And now, it came. His voice wavered slightly. "Do you, Hope Marguerite Stewart, take this man...and promise to...to"—he swallowed—"seek mutual happiness and accord, so long as you both are together in matrimony..." There was a stirring in the pews. The blue eyes glinted with amusement. The voice said softly, "I do."

He pronounced them husband and wife. The couple swept in triumph along the aisle. Press photographers clustered outside the church, snapping their huge cameras. Reporters' pencils scribbled furiously in notebooks; rice showered; the mob filled the street, shouting happily. Hope and Howard waved, smiled, and climbed into a handsome glassed-in victoria drawn by black chargers. The driver cracked his whip and the great vehicle lurched away. Women emerged from the church, mopping their eyes with damp handkerchiefs.

Reverend Dowd rushed to the toilet and vomited.

The party and reception were at the Stuyvesant Bush townhouse on Fifth Avenue. More than two thousand guests were invited. Live music filled the ballroom as guests swirled through half a dozen elegant rooms, nibbling at refreshments and drinking champagne. The receiving line included relatives of the bride, Bradley Stewart of Pittsburgh and his wife Rose; her aunt Francesca Stewart Carp; Ward Stewart, the handsome mulatto boatbuilder from Boston; the Bushes, who were cousins of the groom, and the new Mr. and Mrs. Howard Langden.

Van Harrison Stewart, the dashing lieutenant commander, was the center of feminine attention. They fluttered around him like birds, cooing and preening. Another cousin Casey, a handsome engineer from Panama, seemed somewhat distant. Women perceived the pain in his gray eyes and so kept their flirtations at a discreet level.

"Fascinating man, but there's something about him that's, well..."

"Haunted is the word you're groping for, my dear."

"Yes. Haunted."

"I've seen that look in men whose wives have just died."

"He is divorced, but not recently."

"Strange."

Casey found himself in conversation with several of the men, including his cousin Ward, the young collegian Hamilton Fish, captain of the Columbia rowing team, and Theodore Roosevelt, the former New York police commissioner. Roosevelt, an ardent huntsman, expressed a desire to go after jaguars in the jungles. "I suspect one could use the Krag-Jorgensen army rifle, with an extra load of shots. What do you think, Mr. Stewart?"

"You need stopping power, Mr. Roosevelt," Casey replied. "The jaguar is a very powerful animal at the charge. The Army rifle penetrates but lacks heavy impact."

"Are you a hunter?"

"Not necessarily of exotic big game. Too many organizational and equipment distractions for my taste. I grew up around Pittsburgh. There we hunt game birds, waterfowl, and deer."

"Bully. Ham Fish and I are thinking about some duck hunting this fall in upper Pennsylvania. Would you and Ward like to be included?"

"I'd be delighted. How about you, Ward?"

The Boston cousin shook his head. "Sorry. I'm minding the whole store for Father these days. We're so backlogged on boats that I can never get away. Even coming up to New York for today was a strain."

Howard Langden overheard and joined them long enough to slap Ward affectionately on the shoulder. "I'm grateful that you did come, Ward. And Hope is too."

"Well, Howard, you've always been special."

Isaiah Stewart, the bride's hunchbacked brother, was clearly out of his depth. He hovered at the punch bowl, usually alone. Members of his own family and a few friends stopped to chat from time to time. Not until mid-afternoon, with the surprise arrival of Thomas Edison, a friend of Howard Langden's, did Isaiah's spirits enliven. Guests converged upon the inventor, shaking hands and asking for his autograph. Ironically, it was Edison who recognized the name of Isaiah Stewart.

"I've heard of your work with the internal combustion engine, Mr. Stewart. You've done amazingly well improving the basic horsepower without adding on weight. I'm intrigued."

"It's nothing, really. A few tricks here and there. Larger pistons, an improved combustion chamber, cleaner valve action. There are a lot of things that can be done, Mr. Edison. The Europeans are showing the way, with their new racing cars. But then, who am I to be telling *you* such things?"

"I'm too old to be puttering with engines. I leave that to people like you and my friend Henry Ford out in Michigan. Do you know of him?"

"Only vaguely."

"He came to see me at Menlo Park. He has some brilliant ideas for production. I gave him all the encouragement I could. Mark my words, Ford is going to revolutionize the motor car industry. I predict great things . . ."

"Ah, Mr. Edison!" gushed a female admirer. "You inventors are such brilliant men. I just adore your telephone!"

"Thank you, madame, but I did not invent the telephone. That was Mr. Bell. I shall convey your good wishes, next time I see him."

Hope took Howard's hand. "I didn't know you were friends with Thomas Edison."

"Through my father, actually. Father once helped him to secure some rather critical financing. Mr. Edison never forgot it. He read about our engagement in the newspapers and insisted on coming."

"Where is your adorable cousin Maurice, Hope?" It was one of the young debutantes, a bosomy brunet, scanning the crowd for eligible males. "I was so hoping he would be here."

"Maurice is in Michigan at the moment. Working."

"Working? For heaven's sake, what for?"

Hope smiled thinly. "To earn a living, I believe."

The brunet's eyes widened. "You must be joking. With all those Stewart millions, I can't imagine..."

"Yes. As a matter-of-fact, he has a job in a buggy factory, as a laborer." Hope glanced across the room at Bradley Stewart, who was engaged in deep conversation with several bankers and industrialists. "His father has disowned him."

The poor girl went away, puzzled.

Chauncey Marten had not intended to go near the punch bowl. It was the devil's own brew, and with temptation swirling about him on all sides, a Christian had to be on his guard. For strength, he recited several verses of Scripture in his mind and tried to think of the temptations which had assailed Our Lord, who had told the Devil, "Get thee behind me." But it wasn't enough. The room was filled with women, their laughter and their scents, their bosoms and thighs. He was torn between the rectitude with which he normally bore himself in mixed company and a rising agony of lust. He looked for his wife Colette, and saw that she was occupied in conversation. He eyed the punch bowl thirstily. The crowd around the table ebbed and flowed, until finally there was only one fellow standing nearby, a tall, clumsy-looking oaf in an ill-fitting tuxedo.

"Lovely party, eh?" Chauncey sauntered past the man and casually reached for a glass cup. "Warm, though. Makes a man thirsty." There was no reply. The man's pockets bulged strangely. It occurred to Chauncey that he might be a thief, but he said nothing. It was none of his business. With a quick glance to see that Colette was still preoccupied, he filled the cup, drank it down, filled it again, drank it down, filled it again, and walked away from the bowl.

He felt more relaxed. In fact, after five minutes he felt positively glowing. A bosomy young thing passed close by and Chauncey managed to brush his hand lightly over her thigh. She glared at him. But his blood was up. He moved, smiling, into a tight part of the crowd milling around the inventor Edison, and pushed himself lightly against a comely redhead. She did not notice. Oh, it felt good. Yes, it felt good. Gently he moved himself back and forth across her backside, feeling the hardening down there. She drew away, paying no attention. He quickly drew out of the crowd, sweating.

He went back to the punch table two more times. He watched the crowd, all those butts and all those breasts, and thought: I've got to have some. I've got to get some poontang. God forgive me, but I've got to.

Chauncey Marten, still wearing his formal wedding clothes, slipped out the side door, found a hansom cab, and gave the man a twenty-dollar bill. "Take me to ... to a brothel, driver." The man eyed him strangely, pocketed the bill, and flicked his horse to a trot.

Who would believe it? Certainly not the boys in Block Nine. Here he stood, pockets full of stash and more lying about for the taking. It was too good to be true. He thought: I ought to pinch myself, make sure I ain't dreaming.

Colby Malcolm Stewart was a gangling, big-boned man with black eyes set narrowly in a long, pale face accentuated by a shock of unruly black hair. The loose-jointed frame defied proper fitting of clothes. Even his tuxedo, rented from a funeral parlor, could not conceal a jutting Adam's apple, bony wrists, big knuckles, ungainly knees, and big feet.

An elderly dowager eyed him suspiciously and whispered to her male escort, "Who is that peculiar fellow? Surely he is not an invited guest."

The escort studied Colby through a lorgnette. "He's one of Mrs. Langden's distant cousins. Colby Malcolm's the name. Nobody seems to know much about him." The man sniffed delicately. "But that's not unusual with these Stewarts. Odd lot."

"Very odd."

"With their money, one can allow for eccentricity."

Colby surveyed the scene with a larcenous eye. It was a setting beyond his wildest fantasy. The swells, all done up in their best gowns and monkey suits, hobnobbed in a scene of Byzantine splendor. His glance took in the great vaulted ceiling, gilded and splashed with carved grape clusters, charging horses, and cavorting cherubs. Fluted marble columns supported candelabra dripping in crystal and golden cornucopia filled with ivy and fern. A ten-piece string orchestra played Strauss waltzes from a platform banked with potted palms in massive copper buckets as dancers swirled across the glistening floor of the ballroom. The scent was of fresh flowers and French perfume. Servants in seventeenth-century costumes, complete with ruffled linen, silk knee britches, and buckled shoes, moved through the crowd bearing silver trays filled with snacks and drink. White-clothed side tables bore a mountainous array of buffet delicacies, from smoked halibut and scrod to sliced boiled eggs, oysters on ice, lobster Newburg, and black caviar mounded on delicate wedges of brown bread. But more to Colby's fancy was the silverware; fine, shining, crested tableware, it was, heavy to the heft as bespeaks solid metal.

His gaze swept lovingly over carefully arranged ranks of knives, salad forks, dinner forks, soupspoons, teaspoons, and serving spoons. That swag alone would bring a man a fortune, never mind the jewels decorating all those lovely white throats. He was tempted to go back to the tables for more silverware, but already his pockets bulged and he worried lest he clank when moving about...

"Lovely evening, isn't it?"

The speaker was a ruddy, white-haired man in evening clothes who emerged from behind a potted palm at Colby's left, casually sipping from a glass of champagne. Colby Malcolm felt a stab of anxiety. The man smelled of plainclothes copper. He offered a noncommittal grunt.

"Understand you're a member of the Stewart family. Mrs. Langden's cousin?" Icy blue eyes bore into Colby's. The eyes crinkled, but without mirth. They shifted to the dance floor and locked onto the figure of Hope, turning to the "Emperor's Waltz" in the arms of her tall, distinguished-looking bridegroom. "Stunning lady. Absolutely the cream of New York, if you ask me. But then, you know that already."

"Oh, sure. Hope, she's the berries. My favorite cousin. I mean"—he chuckled nervously and put two fingers together—"we're just like that, me and Hope."

"Good. Then you'll oblige me by putting all the silverware back where you got it. You wouldn't want to embarrass Mrs. Langden now, would you?"

"The silverware..."

"The stash you've got loaded in them pockets." The copper drew from his vest pocket a massive gold watch suspended from a heavy chain. "I'll give you two minutes."

Colby nodded his head briskly, gave a nasal chuckle, and bobbed his Adam's apple. "Two minutes it is, copper. Heh-heh. Two minutes, right enough."

Ten minutes later, Hope Stewart Langden drew Colby onto the dance floor for a waltz. Vastly relieved that he no longer carried all that hardware, he stumbled over his feet. Still, he managed to perform in credible fashion, counting wordlessly to himself.

"You were a dear to come to my party," Hope said brightly. "Cousin Colby, I haven't seen you in ages."

"Well (one-two-three, one-two-three) I been real busy. Business, so to speak. I been in (one-two-three) business for myself."

Hope's blue eyes widened. The full mouth lifted in a smile. Her marvelous scent of perfume caused his senses to whirl. "Business?" she said. Then, without changing expression: "Tell me, Colby, how much time did you pull in the Tombs for that last forgery?"

His face grew a shade paler. The Adam's apple bobbled again. He lost count, stumbled on a turn, and smiled crookedly. "To tell you the truth, cousin, I done four years, with time off for good behavior. I'd just gotten out on parole when your invitation come in the mail. How did you find me, anyhow?"

Hope's smile broadened. She gripped his hand and led him through a nifty turn. "I have a friend on the Parole Board. He gave me your new address." Her face became serious. "Tell me, Colby, are you going to stay out of jail this time?"

Colby Malcolm looked stricken, his face a study in offended piety. "Hope, never again, honest to God. I'm a changed man. May the Almighty strike me where I stand . . ."

This time she laughed out loud.

Five minutes later Hope poked a wedge of buttered bread into Howard Langden's mouth. He chewed thoughtfully, mumbling, "But who is he?"

"Does he bother you?"

"I don't give a damn. Half the men in this room stole their fortunes. The only difference between them and your cousin is that they haven't gone to prison."

"You're a dear man. Colby is the illegitimate son of another cousin of mine, long dead. He really isn't a very good thief. He always seems to get caught. Anyhow, his father was the black sheep of the family. To be more precise, John Colby Stewart was a low-down cutthroat bastard. He once even tried to murder my father out of jealousy."

Howard rolled his eyes and shook his head. "Stewarts!" he said.

She kissed him lightly on the cheek. "Yes. And you've just married one."

They smoked and talked, talked and smoked. Waiters soft-shoed among the tuxedoed men bearing trays of brandies. It was Roosevelt who got onto the subject of Panama, and Casey's experiences with the French. This provoked an outpouring of comment about the Isthmus, its climate, its fevers, its discomforts. For a while, everybody was talking at once.

"Dreadful place. We went through there on our way to California. Anything made of iron rusts right away. Your possessions grow mold; books come unglued; clothes never seem to dry; one constantly sweats. The place is hell."

"The yellow jack must be fearsome."

"Absolutely. It comes in waves, like the plague. And not just in Panama. Havana and Veracruz are pestholes of the stuff. Gruesome way to die."

"They say mortality is as high as seventy percent, especially among newcomers. But blacks seem to adapt. Wouldn't you say so, Mr. Stewart?"

"Well, my word, you don't confine yellow fever to the tropics. Five thousand died in Memphis in '87. Philadelphia had an epidemic in the 1770s. My father survived that. Terrible thing. Doomed the city as the nation's capital."

Anyone who had ever crossed the Isthmus, Casey noticed, had an expert opinion. Even those who had never set foot there had opinions. Truth mixed liberally with fancy.

"What causes yellow fever?"

"Filth, of course. Sewage, rotting animal carcasses. All sorts of matter festers in the streets of Colón and Panama City. Then there is virulent contamination from the patient himself..."

"Bosh. It's the night airs. In Panama City those south winds, off the marshes around Panama Viejo, are deadly."

"I've heard it's the mosquito; any living organism injected by the bite..."

"Tommyrot."

"I'm serious. There was a physician in Havana, Carlos Finlay, who fancied that yellow fever is borne by a specific mosquito, the stegomyia fasciata."

"Utter nonsense. Absurd."

The consensus was that malaria and yellow fever were airborne and spawned in slime pools and filth. For all this, Casey noticed that one point was generally accepted as indisputable. The same logic had prevailed in Panama: Some persons had greater resistance than others. The thought pained him. Lollie. Why would Lollie be stricken, and Casey Stewart escape?

"The trick is to live an upright moral life," the parson

observed. "A blameless life is a long life, especially in the tropics. The sure path to ruin is debauchery, sins of the flesh, moral and physical cowardice. Do you agree, Mr. Stewart?"

"Total abstinence from strong drink never hurt a man," someone else observed.

"The French are morally decadent," said the parson. "That's their weakness. La Grande Tranchée, they called their Canal. The Big Trench. More like a bacchanalian orgy, if you ask me. Panama has been a veritable sink of iniquity." The good man took a pinch of snuff, sneezed, and blessed himself. "Everything that is ghastly and loathsome is to be found there, including many lecherous women. Oh, I've read the press reports. Am I right, Mr. Stewart?"

"Well, a lot of Americans were involved, too," Casey replied defensively.

"But all those people dying." This was Theodore Roosevelt speaking again. "Was it really that bad, Stewart?"

Casey heard himself saying, "It was like a war, you know. The toll was frightful. Whole families perished." The pain of remembrance surprised him. He poured a shot of straight bourbon, drank it down, and patted his mouth with a napkin. "Superintendent Jules Dingler brought from Paris his wife, a son, a daughter, and the daughter's fiancé. He was a righteous man; he believed nothing could harm stoutly moral people. Within two years, he was the only member of the family still alive. Three years after the digging began, forty-eight officers of the Canal company were in their graves. Laborers dropped at a rate of two hundred per month. Often they simply shoveled the bodies under and moved on. But the deaths weren't all from yellow fever and malaria by any means. People died of typhoid fever, smallpox, pneumonia, dysentery, beriberi, food poisoning, snakebites, sunstrokes. Malaria was the deadliest malady, followed perhaps by yellow fever."

Casey hesitated. The room had grown deathly still and everyone seemed to be hanging on his words; voices urged him to continue. It was like a catharsis, cleansing him of these terrible memories.

"I knew one young French engineer who arrived in Colón with a party of seventeen from Le Havre. Within a month he was the sole survivor. That was in '85, the worst year. Twenty-four Daughters of Charity came. They were of a religious order and wore those big-winged white coifs. We called them God's Geese. Two survived. The mortality rate in hospital wards was seventy-five percent. They ran a funeral train every morning to the burial grounds at Monkey Hill..."

At last, Hope came to the rescue, pushing open the double doors with a radiant smile. "Gentlemen, the ladies miss you terribly." Casey followed the hump-shouldered Isaiah into the drawing room, grateful for the respite. He had not even told them of the Culebra Cut, the terrible mudslides, the awesome loss of life there. How could these people comprehend it all? How could anyone comprehend it?

As the party broke up, Theodore Roosevelt invited Casey to share a light supper at his lodgings in the new Waldorf Hotel. They rode in a hansom cab through the blossom-scented June evening. Over chicken and peas, the two men engaged in vigorous small talk. He found the former police commissioner stimulating company, his interests ranging from big game hunting and politics to the tragic lot of young women kidnapped and sold into slavery as New York prostitutes. Roosevelt spoke volubly about the growing troubles between Spain and Cuba, and America's destiny as a naval power. "If we go to war, Stewart—and I hope to God we do—I'm going to form my own regiment of the roughest, toughest fighting men in this land. I'm going to need volunteers, single men eager to go to battle. Shall I call on you?" Casey was mesmerized. "Of course," he said. "Of course." Dinner completed, they moved into the parlor, where a servant served cigars and a dessert wine. He noticed that Roosevelt accepted neither. As Casey lit an excellent Havana cheroot, his host fixed him with a penetrating gaze. "Mr. Stewart, tell me more about the Panama Canal."

Casey was nonplussed. "What more would you like to know?"

Roosevelt sat back and put his fingertips together. "Everything."

Rain spattered the pools, drummed on roofs of corrugated iron, chuckled in downspouts. Murky water collected in the cobbled gutters and ditches of the Tenderloin. Wet rats scurried in narrow streets littered with garbage. Derbied hoodlums squatted on steps, oblivious to the rain, soaking wet and picking their teeth with stiletto knives. Voices quarreled and shrieked; babies cried. Life went on, and so did death. There was little difference between the two.

The round-faced Swell arrived in a hansom cab. He wore striped gray pants, a splittail morning coat, gray waistcoat, winged collar, and cravat with a diamond stickpin. A dozen eyes focused from the shadows on the stickpin as he came out of the cab, mouth hanging slack, eyes wide with fear. The stickpin winked provocatively in the gaslight.

"Driver, I didn't know it was so late. Driver, I will go back now. Driver. Driver!"

The cab lurched into motion and trundled over the stones, rounded a corner, and was gone. It left the Swell alone in a pool of light, looking up helplessly at the moldy gray wooden facades crowding the street.

Merwina Clive came to the upstairs porch and looked down, saw the Swell, and chuckled. "Looks like you lost your way, Mister. This ain't Broadway." He looked up, trying to see into the darkness. She leaned over the balustrade and drew down one shoulder of her dress, exposing half a breast. "Is this what you come to the Tenderloin for?" He removed his top hat and held it to shade his eyes from the gaslight.

"Where am I?"

"Gonkin's Alley. But it don't matter. I got what you want." She lit a rolled smoke and tossed the match into the rain. "Come on up. The stairs are over there." She turned away and went back into the flat. A moment later she heard his slow footfalls on the stair.

Perez came out of the back room. He was an animal with a knife-scarred face and a heart of flint. "What is it?" he said. "Who're you hollering at?"

"Go back in your room. We got business. Get out of here." Perez went away.

Merwina was pregnant by a drunken drifter. The swell was a gift from heaven. Who would have dreamed, when things looked their worst, that Luck would send this to her? She sat on the broken-down settee and hiked up her dress, baring her legs to above the knees. She still had good legs, good boobs, and not a bad face. It was enough.

He was a comic replica of a man. His face resembled a round pie. He had double chins and pasty skin. His body was a glob of flab. It all spoke of too much roast beef, too much pie, too much easy living. His eyes were two marbles stuck in a lump of dough.

"Hello, honey," she said. "You sure are dressed to kill."

"Where am I?" His tongue darted out, licking fat lips.

"I told you, Gonkin's Alley. But it don't matter, love. There's you and me and that's what matters. You got a hard-on love?"

72

He did not speak. She beckoned him forward and stared deliberately at his crotch. Then she reached out and began to massage him. He said, "Oh, Lord, forgive me. Oh, sweet Jesus, what am I doing here?"

"It don't matter, love." She murmured sweet things, drawing him near. He sat down beside her and she put her hand on his chest. She spoke endearments, and dirty things. He seemed not to pay attention, and yet her voice cast a spell upon him. She had seen it happen before, the disembodiment of the act from the individual. Gently, gently she removed his coat, his vest, his diamond stickpin, his cravat. Gently she undid his trousers and took out the poor, small thing. Even when erect, it was pitifully small. Gently she knelt to it.

He groaned with exquisite pleasure.

She drew her dress up higher.

"Now don't you worry. Let Merwina do it. Let Merwina give you relief. Let Merwina..."

They did it three times. The second and third times, he seemed to find himself, to be aggressive and strong. She smiled as his desire was spent for the third time. And then there was no more. She lay naked beneath his pale body.

With the haste of guilt, he put on his clothes. He stammered, "Thank you, thank you." He gave her forty dollars. And then, as she had prearranged, the hansom cab came. Still buttoning his fine clothes, he stumbled down the narrow stairs in the darkness. She heard the door of the cab open and slam shut. The driver whipsnapped his horse and the cab moved away.

"Perez!"

He was already standing in the doorway of the back room. "Yes?"

"Follow the Swell. Go where he goes. Find out exactly who he is."

"I will."

Perez went down the stairs and vanished into the night.

Merwina held up the diamond stickpin in the light. And then she opened a richly leather-grained wallet and took out three hundred dollars cash and an identification card:

Chauncey Marten, Pittsburgh.

She patted her abdomen with a feeling of new contentment. "Well now, Mr. Marten, you and me are going to have ourselves a blessed event."

* * *

"The boy forever dreams of building a flying machine. I fear, Comstock, that you've put this nonsense into his mind."

The headmaster was displeased. And when he was displeased, his blood pressure went up; and when his blood pressure went up, woe betide the faculty member or student of the Briars Preparatory School. It was Comstock again. Always Comstock. The headmaster stood at his office window overlooking the rolling green hills of Albermarle County, Virginia, and wished to God he had employed a more stable individual for the instruction of General Science. This mousy excuse for a professor now occupying the hard wooden chair was nothing but vexation. He was also a smallish, delicate man, and the headmaster—being himself of noble girth—disliked smallish, delicate men.

"Honestly, Comstock, I despair of you sometimes."

"Yes, Headmaster," Comstock said. Even his voice was an irritant, being of soft and nervous timbre, having none of the authority expected of a professor in a boys' school.

"What I don't understand," the headmaster said, "is why you persist in pursuing this notion, knowing that it is patently absurd. I don't mind telling you, Comstock, that you are the laughingstock of this school. There's hardly a boy who believes a word of this claptrap that you keep throwing at your physics classes. Indeed the only student who gives it credence is Stewart. As if the boy didn't have enough problems with his schoolwork, dreaming and doodling as he does all the time, you reinforce his ineptitude by putting harebrained notions into his mind."

"Actually, sir, Nathan is quite a bright..."

"And since when do we call boys by their first names?"

"Uh, sorry. I meant to say Stewart, sir. Stewart is quite a bright lad, all things considered. Marvelous technical mind. Why he..."

"Oh, don't tell me any more about those infernal kites and things, Comstock. Really, I should have sent you back to Ohio last term, but I weakened. It is Ohio that you came from?"

"Yes, Headmaster. Dayton, Ohio."

"I had high hopes for you, however, and I hate to be disappointed. In most respects, I still think that you have great promise. Certainly in Logic and General Science you've done well. I'm not altogether pleased with your Biology, but since you've agreed to soft-pedal that Darwin business, it is working out well. What you fail to understand, Comstock, is

74

that what goes on in the classroom of Briars becomes a matter of general knowledge. Every professor here reflects upon the school in his manner of teaching and his approach to the subject matter. Needless to say, if his approach is of a controversial nature, that will also reflect upon Briars, for the simple reason that boys go home on holidays and discuss such things with their parents. I regret to say that you have been the subject of at least two letters from fathers who consider your scientific opinions illogical, unfounded, and beyond the bounds of common sense."

"Concerning the flying machine, Headmaster?"

"Concerning the flying machine, Comstock."

"But the concept is not at all illogical, Headmaster. Even in mythology man dreamed of flying. Remember the story of Icarus, whose wings melted when he flew too close to the sun . . ."

"Comstock!"

The man swallowed, blinked, and fell silent. He sat on the chair, thin and slope-shouldered, while the headmaster lectured at length about the responsibilities of a professor at the Briars Preparatory School. The headmaster spoke of his own patience—"God knows, Comstock, I am a patient man."—and how it was wearing thin. If there were a suitable replacement, Comstock would be on the next train back to Dayton, Ohio. But he, the headmaster, would give him one more opportunity to teach Physics in a manner appropriate to this respectable institution and therefore to redeem himself. Was that understood?

"Yes, Headmaster."

"Now, as you already know, Stewart's father is due to arrive for a visit the day after tomorrow. The Stewarts are quite a wealthy family and it would not do to antagonize them in any way. And so the less the boy talks about flying machines, Darwinism, and other such nonsense the better. Is that understood?"

"It is understood, Headmaster."

The headmaster pointed to the door. Comstock, looking mousier than ever, obediently went out.

Nathan Stewart was waiting in the hallway, beyond the stairs. He could tell from the professor's face that things had not gone well. As Vernon Comstock came along, Nathan emerged from behind a pillar and fell into step beside him.

"Bad news, huh?"

Comstock shrugged. "It could have been worse. I could have been fired."

"Because of the flying machine?"

"That and other things."

"Well, don't feel too badly. You said yourself that men of vision are seldom honored in their own time."

"A fine lot you know, for an eleven-year-old."

"Come to the library with me. I want to show you something."

Professor Comstock looked down into the bright gray eyes, thinking of how the young mind resembles a blackboard. This boy came to Briars from, of all places, Panama. He thought in French, not English. And he brought with him an active curiosity unimpeded by parental prejudices. "Not another wing design?"

Nathan took his hand. "Come on."

It was, of course, another wing design. This time the boy had fashioned a hingelike arrangement which, by a system of ropes and pulleys attached to pilot controls, could change the configuration of wing surface in flight.

"What do you think?" Nathan studied Comstock's face for a reaction.

The professor inspected the drawing. The hardware appeared to be a bit heavy, the wing rudimentary, the whole oddly out of balance. "I don't know, Nathan. Honestly, I think maybe we ought to just give up the whole thing."

"We could try building another kite."

"I don't dare. The headmaster will have my scalp."

The boy's disappointment was acutely evident. Comstock sighed and shook his head. It would not do to encourage this any further. Soon the father Casey Stewart would arrive. Comstock had never met the man, knew nothing about him, but the last thing his career needed right now was another run-in with the headmaster. "I'm sorry, Stewart," he said. "I must go now. I've got a lot of papers to grade."

He walked out of the library without looking back.

Nathan Stewart awaited the arrival of his father seated alone on a bench on the broad front veranda of the Administration Building of Briars. The day was warm and humid. He was uncomfortable in a dark suit, wide-collared shirt, and necktie. Other boys passed by on their way to classes but paid him little attention. Parental visits were common to them all, and rarely happily anticipated. The headmaster emerged from the building at three o'clock, somber and authoritative in his vested black wool suit.

"Well, well, Stewart, so here we are. Waiting for your father, is it?"

"Yes, sir."

"Good. Very good." The headmaster clasped his hands behind his back, sniffed the air like a large and curious mastiff, and rocked on his heels. "Yes, very good indeed. Well, well."

Nathan stared out at the graveled driveway that came winding over the hill and said nothing.

"Well, well, well." The headmaster drew a heavy gold watch from a vest pocket, snapped open the case, checked the time, closed the watch, and put it back into the pocket. "Yes, indeed." Whereupon he retreated back into the building.

The horse-drawn coach was a speck in the distance, topping a hill, moving slowly down, disappearing, appearing again, and disappearing, as it grew ever larger. At last it was a jingle of harness and clop-clop of heavy hooves and gravel grinding beneath iron-rimmed wheels. "Whoa!" The mouths of the horses foamed as the driver reined them in. The coach door opened and Casey Stewart, tall, dark-suited, and wearing a new derby hat, stepped down. As the driver brought down his valise, Casey walked slowly onto the veranda, looking intently at this handsome boy who had developed so much in three years that he was barely recognizable. The boy rose from his chair and came forward.

"Hello, Father."

"Nathan."

Gravely, they shook hands.

But then Casey grinned, snatched off his derby, and flung it into the air, caught up his son in a powerful hug and swept him aloft. "You manly rascal! How you've grown!"

Nathan gave a startled giggle.

"Well, well, well." The headmaster emerged from his office with a broad smile, fingering his gold watchchain. "Mr. Stewart, I presume." For the first time since Nathan had arrived at Briars, the headmaster chuckled and patted him on the head. "Fine lad. One of our most promising boys. Yes, indeed."

It was strange. Years afterward, Nathan Stewart would remember the sudden outburst of greeting as the strongest display of affection that his father ever gave him. Afterward, they addressed each other in the manner of adults. The tone of careful reserve was set by the brief reception in the headmaster's office. The customary father-son supper at the faculty table in the dining hall did not help matters. The headmaster asked polite questions about life in Panama, but Casey Stewart seemed evasive and ill at ease.

There was, however, one spark of mutual interest.

"A flying machine, you say? Now that's an odd thing to be studying."

"Oh, it's not a school subject. The headmaster would rather we didn't waste our time on such things. He says it's illogical and unfounded."

"He does, does he?"

"Yes, sir. But Professor Comstock, he has always been interested in flying machines. He says the time will come, and not too far in the future, when it will be as real as... as that horse-drawn coach you rode in from the station. He thinks people will travel long distances in flight. The flying machine might even be used as a weapon of war."

"And what do your schoolmates think of all this, Nathan?"

The boy made a face. "They think it's silly."

The meeting of Vernon Comstock and Casey Stewart was much more spirited than Nathan had imagined it would be. Unlike adult members of the faculty, his father seemed genuinely interested in what the professor had to say. In fact, the interest was shared on both sides.

"The Panama Canal!" Comstock said. "You actually worked on the Panama Canal!"

"Yes. I feel like a refugee from a disaster."

"But the project is feasible. More than that, it's damned practical. The Panama route, in my opinion, is greatly preferable to a dig through Nicaragua, the route so many people in Washington seem to favor."

"Why do you say that, Mr. Comstock?"

"The lock Canal is more practical. Nicaragua is volcano country. A dig there would be a much larger undertaking, with greater risks. Besides, the French have already done the advance work in Panama. Nicaragua would be incomparably more expensive."

"We have the disease problem, yellow jack, malaria..."

"Yellow fever can be conquered, Mr. Stewart. It is a mosquito-borne disease. The same is suspected of malaria. And that ought to be the first priority for the United States. Before you turn a spade of dirt, yellow fever must be brought under control."

Casey Stewart stared at Vernon Comstock. "How do you know that?"

"Know what, Mr. Stewart?"

"That it's mosquito-borne."

"Why, I thought everybody knew it. There's been a great deal written on the subject already. Here"—Comstock turned to his cluttered bookshelves, running across the rows of books with a forefinger—"I think I've got something on it." He drew out a fairly new volume, opened it, and adjusted his spectacles. "Yes. Dr. Carlos Finlay in Havana, Cuba, has determined that the carrier of yellow fever is the female mosquito stegomyia fasciata . . ."

Vernon Comstock remained with them after that. He took them on a visit to nearby Charlottesville and the University of Virginia. They talked with a prominent entomologist who had done extensive studies on the disease-bearing mosquito. "No question about it, Mr. Stewart. The control of yellow fever is virtually within our grasp."

On the final evening of Casey Stewart's visit to Briars, he and Comstock were still talking volubly over supper in the professor's rooms. Nathan nodded off to sleep as the subject turned back to flying machines. He did not hear Vernon Comstock propose that the boy accompany him to Washington, D.C., and then to Dayton, Ohio, for the summer vacation. "Dr. Samuel Langley, director of the Smithsonian Institution, has devoted much of his life to aeronautics, Mr. Stewart. I feel that Nathan could learn much from him. And in Dayton, I have some friends—brothers actually—who're also doing interesting work in theories of heavier-than-air flight. Wright's the name. Wilbur and Orville Wright. They have a bicycle shop, where Nathan could tinker to his heart's content. They're very moral fellows and I know they'd love to have him visit. All this would require your approval, of course."

"It's up to Nathan, Mr. Comstock. As far as I'm concerned, permission is granted. I'll leave a note to that effect with the headmaster."

Vernon Comstock eyed his newfound friend carefully. "It's a shame that Nathan doesn't have a family life. Is there no way that you and your wife could be reconciled?"

Casey Stewart lit a cigar and blew smoke rings, gathering his thoughts. "It was very complicated, Vernon. I wish I could explain everything, but I can't. Suffice it to say that my marriage to Nathan's mother was also a casualty of the

Panama Canal disaster. She was French, a stunning woman, and the daughter of a prominent politician who had done a great deal to promote the Canal project. Henri LaVelle is his name. Unfortunately, when the scandal began to break loose— large payoffs, widespread bribery, a general conspiracy to drain the French treasury in the name of the Canal—I discovered that my father-in-law was deeply involved. It devastated me. I had to make a choice. Would I be silent, and thereby condone his misdeeds? Or would I report my information to the authorities who were beginning to investigate the scandal in Paris? I chose to confront my father-in-law and force him to make a full disclosure of what he knew under threat of exposing him myself. It was a bitter episode, and I paid a heavy emotional price in a shattered family and in lost friendships. I wondered, afterward, if my stuffy sense of rectitude was really worth it. I still wonder. Poor Nathan" —he looked at his son with a warmth that stirred Comstock deeply—"wound up in the middle. Paulette and I decided to send him off to boarding school here at Briars, avoid a bitter fight over his custody, and give him an opportunity to become his own man. I don't know if this was the proper thing to do either, and neither does Paulette. But we did it. And we both feel better for not using our son as a pawn between us. Anyhow, Paulette will be coming here from Paris to visit him, too, and I intend to become a closer father in every way that I can. Most important, I want to be assured that his education is strong and basic. I want to challenge him to think for himself..."

Priscilla Pover exerted a natural power over men. It was animal magnetism rather than compelling beauty. No one could say that Priscilla was beautiful. Attractive, yes, with those violet eyes and heavy tumble of black hair. But her teeth were slightly crooked; her nose had a bump on the bridge; her upper lip was a bit too short for such a full mouth. And yet the imperfections added a fetching quality to the whole, augmented by a saucy toss of her head and the smoldering hunger in those eyes. Violet, they were; violet eyes that had a way of enlarging and lusting when fastened upon a handsome man.

The tongues of Fall River could always busy themselves with the carryings-on of Priscilla Pover, real or fancied. It was, after all, a town of Christian moralities where Good People did not flaunt deviant behavior. "Shameful!" breathed the watchful when Priscilla practically threw herself at Dr. Blanton Brinkman, the handsome young physician from Flint whose three-day visit to his sister in Fall River was extended to three months. They went carriage riding practically every day, and Lord only knew what went on in the woods. Priscilla Pover was queen of the fast set. The lights of the mansion burned all night during her soirees. And, of course, everybody *knew* what was going on.

Everybody seemed to know, that is, except Priscilla Pover's burly, middle-aged husband Harry, the most successful wagonmaker in the state of Michigan. Initially, when he had first married this much younger woman from out of town, the matrons of Fall River were simply resentful that Harry, bachelor heir to the Pover fortune, had not chosen one of their own. But as time went on, and her questionable lifestyle became more apparent, resentment changed to wonder. Harry Pover apparently chose to see no evil. He ran his factory as he had always run it, in a tough and practical way, ruthless and contemptuous of inferiors. Except for his cadre of male assistants at the plant, he had no friends.

Gossips, like hungry birds of prey, feed on tidbits. An interesting newcomer had been employed for some months now at the Pover Wagon Works. Maurice Stewart had come west from Pittsburgh, young, tall, and extraordinarily handsome. Mothers of spinster daughters looked at him and drooled. At the works, men said that Stewart and the big Swede Lars Swenson could do more hard labor in a day than two mules. It was Priscilla, ironically, who had ordered that Stewart be hired the first day he turned up in the employment line with old Tom Moneypenny. "You mark my words; that boy will be on her list." The gossips of Fall River settled back to watch and wait ...

"Come on, ye laggards. We ain't got all week to unload this lot. Look alive, now!"

The foreman's voice lashed at the work gang on the railroad siding. In the crowd of sweating men, Maurice Stewart nodded at the big Swede. "Let's shoulder it, Sven." They knelt at each end of the bundle, got their hands beneath the stack, hunched their shoulders, and lifted. As their bodies took the strain, Swenson groaned. These were ask wood slabs, bundled in three-hundred-fifty-pound stacks. Since dawn the work gang had been manhandling them out of boxcars onto heavy freight wagons at the loading dock. It was now noon.

"All right, Sven. Let's go."

Maurice found a surprising amount of pride in labor. Never had he been obliged to rely on body and brawn to earn a living. Performance had also won him a grudging respect. Initially the workmen of Pover's had been cool toward the college boy from back East. But now, after three months, there was a certain curt cordiality. Men spoke of Stewart and Swenson as "the strong boys."

"Now, Sven, once more. Heave!" Muscles bulging, they brought the wood stack to shoulder height and pushed it onto the wagon load. Then both men knelt in the dirt to dash cold water from a bucket over their sweating heads. Maurice sat down on the loading dock, opened his lunch box, and reflected on the strange turn fate had taken. He knew that the other workmen's initial hostility toward him had to do with Priscilla Pover.

A day after their arrival in Fall River, Maurice and old Moneypenny had come to the Pover Wagon Works looking for jobs. They had been interviewed at the main entrance by a thin, ferret-faced assistant foreman named Slade. Moneypenny, an expert wheelwright and woodturner, was hired immediately. Maurice, however, drew a doubtful frown and icy questions. "What can ye do? Ever worked in a wagon factory before?" His response that he had been to college inspired a derisive guffaw. "Sonny boy, we ain't runnin' a schoolroom here."

At that moment, Priscilla Pover had arrived in a gig drawn by a high-stepping Morgan roan. Men turned to watch as she stepped down and walked coolly into the yard, balancing a parasol. She wore a close-fitting skirt and shirtwaist that accentuated full breasts and rounded hips. Hearing the exchange between Maurice and the assistant foreman, she stopped walking. Violet eyes boldly appraised Maurice Stewart up and down.

"What's the trouble, Slade?"

"No trouble, Miss Priscilla. This here's a college boy from back East, wants to take on a man's job. But he ain't never worked in a wagon factory before. He don't even know how to work wood or metal..."

"Hire him," Priscilla Pover said.

Slade's mouth dropped open. "Ma'am?"

"Hire him as a laborer. A fellow with muscles like that

82

ought to be good for something." The violet eyes smiled. "If he's smart, he'll learn the rest." She walked away spinning the parasol and trailing a scent of perfume.

Thus, Maurice Stewart was hired. In the months that followed, he was given the heaviest, dirtiest jobs in the plant. The company, formed by Harry Pover's grandfather, operated three plants in southern Michigan; this was the main headquarters. Each wagon was painstakingly fashioned by hand and every part specially made—wheels, axles, suspension, tongues, everything. "It's the way they always done it," Tom Moneypenny observed ruefully, "and Harry Pover ain't about to change." The subject of their discussion, a thickset, gravel-voiced man with a fondness for brown suits and strong cigars, commanded the enterprise from a glassed office, barking orders to a clutch of tough assistants, two of them former prizefighters. Pover rarely spoke to the ordinary help. But one day he walked out to where Maurice was rolling steel paint drums off the back of a wagon.

"You, there, Stewart."

"Yes, sir?"

Pover's pale blue eyes squinted from a meaty face. Maurice stood before him, his face streaming sweat. The wagonmaker coolly spat a gob of tobacco juice that just missed Maurice's right boot. "Just wanted to see what kinda' horse turd my wife's dragged in this time." He turned and walked away.

Fall River was a bustling town on a placid stream in wooded hill country west of Detroit. One of its major enterprises was the Pover Works.

Maurice and Tom Moneypenny had lived temporarily with the latter's cousin Hiram, a crotchety old bachelor who owned several buildings in the business district. Eventually Maurice found a rooming house on a tree-shaded back street and moved there. The place was clean, reasonable, and offered excellent meals. His landlady was the widow Hankin, a pale, pious woman who worried about his lack of religion and implored him to attend services at the Methodist Church. "A young man, Mr. Stewart, must look to his immortal soul. The Devil waits to ensnare us with his temptations." The eyes of the good woman played over Maurice's face and shoulders as she spoke, and she cooled herself vigorously with a folding hand fan. "Temptation is everywhere, Mr. Stewart. Everywhere."

September came. Cool Canadian air poured into Michigan.

Life for Maurice Stewart consisted of long workdays and little social diversion. He evaded Mrs. Hankins's efforts to introduce him to "proper Christian young ladies" and spent Sundays tramping in the woods and bird-hunting. Letters from Hope in New York were filled with concern over the possibility of a war with Spain. She also worried about her husband's health.

> Howard is working too hard. He is so outraged that Hearst would deliberately provoke a war that it has become an obsession with him. He says it would be a conflict without honor, a cheap ploy to boost newspaper circulation.

Indeed, a kind of war mania seemed to be sweeping the country. Even the local newspapers were dominated by stories of worsening relations with Spain, and hardly a Sunday went by in the Fall River Park when men did not engage in heated discussions about American expansionism in the Caribbean. "President McKinley needs to be more forceful. He's letting the Spaniards kick us around!" Maurice read and listened without comment. A war with Spain was of no concern to him.

"Stewart, here's a special job for you." The speaker was the ferret-faced Slade, flushed with self-importance after being promoted to full foreman. "You're to go over to the Pover mansion for some odd jobs. Mrs. Pover'll tell you what to do." The lean face seemed to leer. "Take along a horse and wagon."

It was a windy gray day in November. Each gust sent dry leaves spilling from the trees. Fall River seemed to withdraw into itself against the coming winter. He drove the wagon through quiet streets and up Telegraph Hill from the river. Pover Mansion was a Tudor-style brick complex commanding a stunning view of the surrounding countryside. As he topped the winding driveway, Maurice stopped the horse and looked down upon the tree-shrouded town studded with church steeples. The sun emerged briefly from its cloud cover, spreading golden light over the scene. He unhitched the horse and let it graze before walking to the front veranda.

"Beautiful, isn't it?" Her voice startled him. Priscilla Pover walked slowly across the veranda. She wore an off-white ensemble with a sweater, its snug fit accentuating her bosom. A small egret feather had been worked into her upswept hair. The violet eyes scrutinized him playfully. "I saw you stop and inspect the scenery." The eyes swept the sunlit panorama. "There is no view like it, anywhere." It sounded like a statement of personal possession.

He suffered a moment's confusion, groping for what to say. "Yes, it is beautiful. It reminds me a little of my fath..." He hesitated. "That is, of a place I knew in Pittsburgh." He smiled. "But the air is much cleaner here. Fall River doesn't have blast furnaces."

"Thank God." She turned away. "Follow me."

The storeroom occupied an outbuilding behind the main house. Inside, all was a jumble of discarded furniture, equipment, tools, and junk. Maurice pushed open the exterior double doors, raising a fine cloud of dust. Shafts of sunlight stabbed through the dust particles and illuminated networks of spider webs and shadowy furnishings covered with ancient dustcloths.

"I want it cleared out and hauled to the dump, every last piece," she said. "Then you are to do a thorough job of cleaning, painting, and repairs." The full mouth lifted. "I intend to convert this into a playroom."

"It'll take time. Maybe I ought to bring Sven..."

"That won't be necessary." She was looking at him with a strange intensity again. "You are quite capable of doing it alone, I'm sure. There's a cot in the back and some blankets. You can sleep there if you like and take your meals with the kitchen help." Then, with a toss of her shiny black hair, she was gone.

The days passed slowly, bringing a glorious Indian summer. Maurice went about his chore in virtual solitude and spent his nights in the small sleeping quarters behind the storeroom with a coffeepot and a wood-burning grate. Thoughts of Priscilla Pover hovered in the back of his mind. The eyes had a special haunting quality. He tried to discard the whole thing as fantasy, but isolation thwarted the effort. He was left completely alone. Even the servants at the house seemed strangely detached. A black Jamaican woman put out his meals but avoided conversation.

On sunny mornings he would occasionally see Priscilla leave the main house in the jig, the Morgan roan highstepping down the winding driveway, and hours would pass before she returned. Repeatedly he loaded the wagon and drove it down the hill, for emptying at a secluded dump, half hoping to meet her on the road. It did not happen. He was busy for a week hauling and cleaning. It was Monday afternoon of the second week before he took the final load. He returned from the dump sweaty and covered with grime. It seemed that half the dirt from the storeroom clung to his body. As he stopped the team beside the outbuilding, she stepped from the shadows of the doorway.

"You've done well," she said.

He wrapped the reins around the brake handle and climbed down, drawing out a pocket bandanna to wipe sweat from his face. Abruptly she took the bandanna from him. "Let me . . ." Because of his height, she had to reach high to wipe his face. He was conscious of the breasts straining inside her thin shirtwaist. Her perfume scent was exotic. She rested her free hand on his shoulder. "What a mess." The violet eyes seemed to smolder. "You're dirty and sweaty all over." She stopped wiping and took his hand. "Come with me."

They went into the main house. He was conscious of fine woods, tapestries, and expensive overstuffed furnishings. Servants worked in the kitchen, but ignored them. He followed Priscilla Power up the sweeping main stairway to the second floor. She led him to a bedroom with an adjoining tub bath. A new set of men's clothing lay across the bed. "I want you to bathe and put on those things," she said. "This evening, you are to escort me to a party."

Maurice swallowed his astonishment. "A party?"

"That is, if you're free."

"Oh, I'm free. My social calendar these days is, to put it mildly, very flexible."

The violet eyes warmed again. "Good." She left him.

The bathroom was of marble, the tub gleaming white with elaborate fixtures. He soaked and soaped lavishly, thinking of what an improvement it was over Mrs. Hankins's metal tub with hand-pumped cold water. This water was actually hot, a luxury he had not enjoyed since leaving Pittsburgh. After the bath, he found a straight razor and comb. Finally, he put on the clothing, a new dark suit and vest, white shirt with celluloid collar, a cravat with a gold stickpin, and new shoes. Everything fit well except the shoes, which were too tight. He put on the coat and surveyed the result in a full-length mirror.

"Not bad." Her voice startled him. She stood in the doorway, smiling. She had changed into a dark green gown with a high neckline and a single pearl necklace. The effect was compelling and sensual. "There is something irresistible about the right man in the right clothes."

A question had been nagging at his mind. Now, he reasoned, was the time to ask. "But what about Mr. Pover?"

Her expression was noncommittal. "My husband has other plans for the evening."

Dusk gathered around the hilltop house. They stepped into the broad upper hallway. She took his arm and they descended the stairway. Unexpectedly, from below, he heard happy voices and musical instruments.

"Here she comes," someone shouted. "Hurrah for Priscilla!"

They turned at the landing and Maurice looked down into smiling upturned faces. More guests were arriving at the front door, depositing hats and coats with the butler and exchanging handshakes. He saw two well-dressed midgets and a tall, tattooed woman. About her neck was draped a live boa constrictor. A voice said, "Priscilla has a new escort." The word rippled through the foyer and parlor. By the time they reached the bottom step, Maurice found all eyes upon him. A giggly young blond on the arm of a much older man started blowing kisses. "He's beautiful! Priscilla, he's the most beautiful man I've ever seen!"

The following three hours were a strange mix of the banal and the bizarre. Parties and small talk had never been his strong point, especially with such an odd human assortment, but it seemed to make no difference. "Come over here, darling, and kiss me." The speaker was a huge woman, dripping white flesh and seated on a couch in danger of imminent collapse. One of the midgets planted a kiss on her cheek.

Maurice resolved to observe the social forms: to smile, to listen, and to offer witty comments. He would remember, afterward, a bewildering succession of women with knowing eyes, extended gloved hands, mingled scents, and well-dressed men looking intense and talking about Gentleman Jim Corbett's defeat in the prize ring. ("Fitzsimmons ain't half the fighter Corbett used to be. Too much high life and easy living; that's what done Corbett in.") The parlor was modish and cluttered, with velvet print wall coverings, marble-topped tables, plaster casts of the "Venus de Milo" and "Winged Victory," wax flowers in cut crystal vases, and a stereopticon with slide photos of the Rocky Mountains. Whiskey was served from decanters, and Maurice noticed that both men and women drank, and some of the women—Priscilla included—even smoked.

"So you're Priscilla's latest? Welcome to the merry-go-round." She was young and very pretty, with a pouty mouth and upswept brown hair in the new Gibson Girl style. Her eyes were thickly lashed and striking. Boldly she took his hand and held it in her own. "I must say you are an improvement over some of the others. That Dr. Brinkman, for instance. Nice-looking, but terribly stuffy. I hope you're not stuffy, Mr. . . . Mr. . . ."

"Maurice Stewart." He smiled, suddenly aware that up to now he had not been introduced, nor had anyone asked his name.

"I'm Helen DeMare." The eyes widened expectantly. There was a pause, as if waiting for him to respond. "Helen DeMare. Does that mean anything to you?"

"Should it?"

She laughed nervously. "Touché. I really asked for that, didn't I? Helen DeMare—that's me—is an actress of sorts. I'm just starting, really. Comedy parts and all that. Our company is playing this week at the Bijou downtown. I do a comedy skit with Joey, over there." She nodded toward a roundish man with big ears and a toupee. "A lot of the people here are in show business. That's what Priscilla did, you know, before she married Pover. She was Priscilla Gayle, one of the Floradora Girls." She looked at him oddly. "You didn't know that either?"

"No." He was beginning to feel foolish. "I'm a bit out of touch."

She put her hand on his arm. "Hey, you really are. You poor boob; you don't know anything. What do you do around here? I mean, when you're not being Priscilla's latest."

"I do odd jobs at the wagon plant."

The eyes crinkled with sudden mirth. She cupped her hand over her mouth. "At the wagon plant?" She giggled behind the hand. Maurice felt a flush of consternation. She said, "Oh, dear!" and struggled to regain her composure.

"No wonder that suit looks so new, and those shoes so tight . . ." The hand came up again.

The whole ridiculous scene struck him. Angrily he tried to draw away from her, but she took his arm and held on. "Hey . . ."

"I'm sorry," he said. "I don't . . ."

"Hey," she whispered, coming close. "I'm not making fun of you. Relax. It's all right. Don't be upset." Her touch seemed to pleasantly penetrate his arm. The eyes looked at him without guile. He thought: How young must she be?

Sixteen? Seventeen? "Any man as handsome as you, Maurice Stewart," she said, "has no apologies to make."

A servant stepped into the middle of the room and announced gravely, "Dinner is served."

Dinner was a formal affair of gleaming tableware and snowy linens. Food was served to thirty-six seated guests by waiters in starched white jackets. Priscilla Pover was everywhere, smiling, laughing, talking, touching. She seemed to bathe in people and her guests responded in kind.

Maurice sat near the foot of the table beside an elderly man who had had too many whiskeys. He was, of all things, a retired banker from Detroit. "It takes all kinds to make a world, my lad." He held forth at length on the curse of money, to which no one but Maurice paid attention. "Everybody wants to be rich as J. P. Morgan, young man. Riches are the key to happiness, right? Carnegie said so, in his *Gospel of Wealth*. Even our Mr. Mark Twain admitted that his ambition was to get rich and live like his millionaire friends. But what on earth makes you think the rich are any happier than the poor?" The banker blew his nose noisily on a napkin, drank, wiped his mouth with the back of his hand, and leaned close. "I'm gonna let you in on a little secret, young man. They ain't one bit happier. The rich suffer from vexations of the spirit." He belched softly. "Vexxxations of the spirit. D'you want to know why? Because the rich have made it; that's why. They've made it, and if they're rich enough they don't have to make any more. And if they don't have to make no more, there's nothing left for them to do with their miserable idle lives but lay around fornicating and getting drunk." He leaned back, the better to savor Maurice's amazement at such profundity. "What d'you think of that, young man?"

Maurice said, "I think it's a terrible waste."

Things got even livelier after dinner, with drinks, cigars, tipsy giggles, and impromptu performances. Two muscular women stripped off their clothing and did a juggling act in the nude with six expensive cut glass bowls, two of which were smashed. The tattooed lady lapsed into an alcoholic stupor and her snake went gliding away across the floor. A strong man insisted on trying to lift the Fat Lady, couch and all, and wound up in a shuddering heap on the floor complaining that he had ruptured himself. The banker from Detroit was stroking the thighs of a comely redhead, who finally took him by the hand and led him upstairs. Maurice drank whiskey in a mad swirl of giggles and chatterings and shrieks, while a trio of musicians played ragtime tunes with piano, tenor banjo, and cornet. ("I was in love with a cornet player once," a mannish-looking woman was saying, "and my dear, you haven't *lived* until you've tried it....")

"Are you having a good time, Mr. Stewart?" It was the girl Helen DeMare, dancing past with one of the actors. She left her partner on the floor and came over to him, giggling. Plucking a glass of wine from a passing tray, she removed a small medicine box from her purse and dropped in a dash of white powder. "Have you tried this?" She giggled again, sipping the wine. "It's cocaine, the Heavenly Powder. Sheer ambrosia. That fictional English detective Sherlock Holmes has made it enormously popular. Even President McKinley likes a few grains of coke in his wine. Try some." She mixed a bit of powder into Maurice's whiskey.

The hours poured past on a liquid tide of pleasure.

Priscilla Pover found him later with his coat off, arm wrestling the circus strongman. She invited him to dance.

"I don't dance very well," he said.

"Nonsense. Everybody dances. This is a slow waltz. You'll enjoy yourself."

"I don't dance very well..."

But already she had him on his feet and was steering him across the parlor toward the French doors leading out to the veranda. The cold air braced him. She closed the doors behind them, so that the music could be only faintly heard. A bright November moon coasted through a wispy cloud bank, casting the scene in a shimmering silvery glow with deep shadows.

Priscilla Pover pressed against him and began slowly to move. To his surprise she came only to his shoulder and had to dance on tiptoes. He let his body follow, conscious of her hand upon the back of his neck. It was a gradual, undulating thing. He breathed her scent as she flowed with his body, breathing as he breathed. There was a delightful tightness in his groin, a stirring and rising. Her hand tightened at his neck, and the other undid his shirt and slipped inside, caressing his bare flesh. His mouth found hers, and the kiss poured through him like molten fire. The moment was ethereal, overwhelming. She murmured to him almost as if speaking to herself. "You are a beautiful man. Priscilla's new beautiful man." He drew her in more tightly, pressing against her. She moaned softly.

The French doors opened behind them, spilling out music

and voices. She pushed back from him and turned, pale face drawn with anger. A familiar rasping voice spoke drunkenly above the party noises. "So, Priscilla, here you are." Harry Pover, thickset and menacing, stood framed in the light.

She stepped away from Maurice. "Harry, what do you want?"

Pover drank from a bottle, lowered it, and swayed slightly. "A little company, that's all. Jus' a little company from my wife."

She glanced at Maurice. He waited, uncertain and wary. Priscilla's voice was suddenly cold. "You may go now, Stewart." The dismissal struck him like a slap.

He looked at Pover. The eyes of the wagonmaker seemed to glitter in triumph. Or was it a trick of the light? Suddenly sober, Maurice Stewart left the veranda and walked over the dew-covered grass to the storeroom. An infinite weariness overcame him. He went to his cot, took off the new clothes, and threw them across the lone wooden chair. Then he lay down naked and watched the moonlight from the window spatter silver rectangles over the dusty floor.

His thoughts were in a torment. Had the cocaine addled his senses? Why had she enticed him? Had she known that Pover would come? Was it the deliberate act of a scheming woman? No. Those sighs and whispers on the veranda had been too real, those kisses too filled with heat. He groaned in self-torment. Finally he drifted into a fitful sleep.

When he awoke, the moon was down, the room in darkness. His subconscious mind had detected a squeak of the door. He lay still, aware that someone stood over him in the darkness. He heard the breathing. And then he became conscious of her scent, a powerful play of musk upon his senses.

With a whisper of cloth, her gown fell free. She came into his arms, naked and trembling, hands groping for his manhood.

He entered her. She cried out with ecstasy.

Sunlight stood on the rim of the hills when at last they rested, entwined in each other's arms. Maurice told her that he had never known such splendors. He poured out a rambling torrent of love words.

She kept looking into his face, the violet eyes large and almost childlike. "My God, what a stud you are." Her hands played over the member that had brought her such delight.

"How magnificently you're endowed. Do you have any idea of what an instrument this is?"

"And what," he asked guardedly, "about Pover?"

She shrugged, with a look of distaste.

"My husband is quite impotent."

Two days later, Maurice Stewart went back to the wagon factory. Old Tom Moneypenny was bursting with news. "I had a talk with the superintendent Curry. He'll bring you inside the factory on my say-so. No more manual labor; this is journeyman's work. I need an assistant with a mind for learnin'. I think it's time you made a move. What do you say?"

And so Maurice went inside.

Moneypenny was a taskmaster and a superb craftsman. It was a meticulous skill, involving woods, metals, balance, and suspension. A Pover Wagon—or a Studebaker or a Conestoga— was not simply hammered together. It was created by artisans whose watchwords were strength and durability. "But a wagon ain't nothin' next to a carriage," Old Moneypenny muttered. He fashioned iron cornerstraps at the charcoal bellows, drew them red-hot with the tongs, hammered the last essence of shape on the anvil, and plunged them into cold water with a gush of steam. "Now carriage work and coachwork, that's a real art. You got to know your business, know your woods..."

Rigorously he schooled Maurice in the shaping and turning of woods, the differences in weight, flexibility, and strength of ash, hickory, and hardrock maple. A Pover Wagon was a sturdy, no-frills vehicle, and many still trundled over the freight roads of America after thirty years of service.

"Young feller, there's many a teamster puts his life and fortune in your hands and don't even know it. I've built wagons for haulers that wasn't even born when I shaped the iron. That's a fact."

Maurice saw that the old man put extra touches into the basic Pover design. His knowledge of woods was equaled only by his knack with metals. Moneypenny understood metal. Other shopworkers talked of this. "Old Moneypenny, he can tell if a strap's got a fault just in the way she hammers. He can sniff the smoke from a forge and tell ye if the temperature's right. Damndest feller I ever seen with metal." He was especially expert at working brass, a finer craft which some men lacked the patience to master. Brass fittings and corner straps were lightweight and durable, and weight was always on Moneypenny's mind.

"Every pound on that wagon means more mulepower and less payload, young feller. As for brass, it's got more give to it, pound for pound, than iron." Maurice watched, listened, and learned. He also wondered aloud what inspired Moneypenny, knowing that his efforts were unappreciated.

"Ah, that's our little secret." The ancient face lifted in a mass of wrinkles. "All in good time, young feller. All in good time."

Maurice was warmed by the memory of Priscilla Pover. It gave him an inner glow. Moneypenny, hearing the whispers among the men and eyeing him quizzically, commented, "That woman's a bad 'un, young feller. She's trouble for sure." Maurice ignored him, concentrating on the business of fabricating wagon beds, bending, and warping wooden parts and fitting wheel rims from red-hot iron bands.

Weeks crawled by. She did not come to the wagon works and made no attempt to contact him at his rooms. There was one perfumed note which said simply,

Love, P.

His desire kindled again. He rented a horse at the livery stable and took solitary rides up to the mansion, leaving notes for her in the mail slot. They were not answered. And yet on rare occasions he caught distant glimpses of her, shopping in town or driving her trotting gig down a wooded lane.

Christmas brought snow. Ponds froze over and the river had a fringe of ice. He gave Tom Moneypenny a briar pipe and Mrs. Hankins a lace handkerchief. He sent gifts to the family in Pittsburgh and to Hope in New York. Gifts arrived from Hope and his brother Casey. His stepmother wrote about her aches and pains. There was no word from his father.

There was no word from Priscilla Pover, either.

"Hey, there, Stewart! I'll be darned; it's really you!" Helen DeMare stood on the sidewalk of Main Street, her face glowing in the cold. Maurice did not recognize her at first, for she seemed to have matured in the month since the party. She wore a fur wrap and muff and matching hat that came down around her ears. Her eyes sparkled. She was quite beautiful.

They had hot chocolate in a soda shop. Helen brimmed

with news of her acting, her travels, her plans. "I've been to Chicago since we met. There's an opportunity at the theater there. But we're still playing the Bijou here. I'm so excited. I'd love to play Chicago!"

He talked about the plant, old Moneypenny, and the things he was learning. It seemed terribly humdrum, compared to her glamorous life. Impulsively she took his hand and felt its calloused hardness. "These are a laboring man's hands. My father had hands like that. He was a blacksmith."

The subject turned to Priscilla Pover. Helen's face clouded. "Maurice, I'd be careful if I were you." She looked at him with a lingering warmth. He noticed for the first time that her eyes were hazel and flecked with gold. Tufts of brown hair protruded from beneath the fur hat. She had a pert oval face, the nose uptilted and lightly dusted with freckles.

"I haven't seen her," he said carefully. "I wondered if you might know anything." He was uncertain and groping. The hazel eyes watched him steadily.

"You're not falling in love with her, are you?"

The directness of her question was like a blow. Lamely, he denied it, but she persisted. "Yes you are; you're hooked by Priscilla Pover. She has seduced you and entrapped you and made you miserable." Helen frowned and pursed her mouth. "Ah, Priscilla and her wiles. I wish..." The hazel eyes flicked to his, widened, and looked away. "Oh, never mind."

"What are you trying to say, Helen?"

Abruptly she got up from the table and began gathering her things. "Don't ask me, Stewart. You're not the first man to get caught in Priscilla's web, and you won't be the last. My advice is to forget about her; put her out of your mind. My God, are you so blind?"

She stalked out of the soda shop.

Priscilla's note arrived during the afternoon of New Year's Eve. His excitement surged. Joyously he put on the good suit and hired a horse and buggy. It was eight o'clock and snowing when he arrived at the hilltop mansion. She was alone, wearing a lavender evening gown with a plunging bodice. Her black hair tumbled in soft waves over snow-white skin. The violet eyes seemed to light up with lascivious pleasure as she greeted him. "Maurice, how good of you to come." A tight-lipped servant served them a candlelit supper of roast pheasant and white wine. The wine was an exquisite Bordeaux, smoky to the taste and warming to his insides. Afterward they sat before the fire in the parlor. She mentioned lightly that

Harry Pover was spending the holiday with his mother in Detroit. The violet eyes flashed over a brandy goblet. "I am not welcome there. Harry's mother and I do not get along well."

She arched her neck and stretched languidly. The curve of her throat was like alabaster in the firelight. He moved to her, put his mouth to that white neck, caressed the swell of her breast. The house was silent but for the measured ticking of a clock. Time hung suspended. Gradually the gown came free of her body. He wallowed in the delicious warmth of her, touching and tasting and breathing her scent.

"Priscilla's beautiful man. Let me touch it. Ohhhhhh, how exciting it is, how big and luscious and full..."

She was panting. She was insatiable.

They rested as the clock struck twelve.

"Happy New Year, darling," she murmured against his naked chest. "Happy 1898..."

He left her in the snowy dawn, driving the buggy through a hushed world of falling white flakes.

"Moneypenny, you're a genius. That's a fantastic vehicle!"

The old face beamed. "I been a'workin' on it for three months now, gettin' everythin' just right. Look at these sketches. See how the design is light and airy? Ain't that a sight, Stewart? Look at the curves here along the front. Them's good light lines. Strong, too. This thin woodwork is pure hickory, but reinforced underneath with lightweight alloy steel. Same way with these wheels. Did you ever see lighter spokes in your life? They're wooden, with steel-reinforcin' rods. A class buggy this is, with a sportin' flair. The ladies'll love it."

Moneypenny's words came in a rush. His gnarled hands swept over the unrolled drawings, his fingers jabbing at details. The weathered face was flushed, the eyes glistening.

They were at Hiram's house in Fall River. The taciturn cousin stood at Moneypenny's elbow smoking his pipe with feigned indifference. "It don't look like much to me," Hiram observed laconically. "The world's full of buggies."

"Ah, but that's where you miss the point, Hiram," Maurice said. "This one has got style. It's going to be lighter and stronger than anything ever hitched to a horse. And we'll build it cheaper than any competitor. The trick will be assembly line production. Right, Moneypenny?"

Moneypenny grinned. "We build interchangeable parts

then put the whole thin' together piece by piece, same as we did them Springfield rifles durin' the war. Remember the Springfields, Hiram?"

Hiram grunted. "And who's going to manufacture and sell this marvel?"

It was Maurice who answered. "The Pover Wagon Works, that's who."

Tom Moneypenny's eyes lit up. "The young feller's got the right idea!"

"Do you mean to say Harry Pover's agreed to it already?"

The old face lost its luster. "Well, we ain't talked to him yet. But I know he's goin' to like it. This here buggy will make a fortune."

"When will you talk to Pover?" Hiram said.

"First chance we get."

Maurice and Moneypenny walked out into the snowy night. The old man's enthusiasm drained. They trudged along side by side, boots crunching in dry snow. "I can't talk to Pover," Moneypenny said mournfully. "I ain't good with words. I wouldn't know what to say."

"Then I'll talk to him." Maurice's tone expressed a confidence he did not feel. The thought of going to Priscilla Pover's husband was not pleasant. "It'll be a cinch; you'll see."

Moneypenny eyed him ruefully. "I'm glad one of us has got confidence."

The last two weeks of January passed in a howling blizzard. Old Tom and Maurice devised a scale model of the buggy, whittling and tooling the parts, and redid Moneypenny's rough sketches. Maurice's impatience grew. They asked to meet with Harry Pover, but could not get a definite word. There were rumblings of war with Spain and Pover was meeting with military brass over wagon orders for the Army. Another week went by. Tired of waiting, Maurice finally marched into the office of the superintendent accompanied by the nervous Moneypenny. Spreading out the plans, Maurice told Curry about the buggy, expanding upon its virtues of weight, durability, design, and cost. The superintendent, a pale, dyspeptic man who seemed to carry the world on his thin shoulders, listened with interest, scanned the blueprints, and furrowed his brow thoughtfully. "I just don't know, Stewart. It's a good plan, all right. I'll mention it to Mr. Pover, but don't get your hopes up."

"Mention it to him when?"

"This month, maybe next." Curry twisted uncomfortably in his chair. "Mr. Pover's a busy man."

Moneypenny started to speak, but Maurice cut him off. "Curry, this is special. It won't wait a month or two. We've got other offers to consider. You must talk to Pover right away."

"It can't be done right away, Stewart."

"Then I'll talk to him."

"You'll talk to him?"

"I will."

"Mr. Pover, he don't talk to the help, Stewart. You know that. You've got to go through channels."

"Channels my eye." Maurice angrily grabbed up the plans. Leaving Moneypenny behind, he went straight to Pover's office, swept past two startled assistants, pushed open the door, and went in. The door slammed shut behind him and he heard the lock click.

"What the hell? . . ." The stocky wagonmaker rose out of his chair.

"Pover, I'm about to give you the money-making opportunity of a lifetime. If you're as smart as I think you are, you'll listen."

"You can't just barge in here like this! Get out of my office, boy!"

"Now this"—ignoring the protests, Maurice cleared a space on the desk and unrolled Moneypenny's blueprints—"is a set of plans for the damndest buggy you've ever seen. We've already got a prototype model in the works, and I guarantee you every prosperous farmer and smalltown businessman in this country will buy it. We'll sell it cheap, on advance orders, provide customer financing, and ship it in boxes broken down for easy assembly. It's a whole new concept in . . ."

He gave it his best. Maurice was surprised at his own fervor. Under any other circumstances, he would have made his point. But Harry Pover was not a man to be convinced. The more Maurice talked, the higher grew the obstacles between himself and the wagonmaker. Pover not only was unyielding, his intransigence quickly turned to wrath.

"Now you listen to me, fella," he stormed at last. "Just because you're a college boy from back East, you've got no call to barge into my private office trying to tell me how to run my business! I don't intend to waste my time with scum from the back shop." Pover's face was beet-red, his eyes bulged, and his big fists pounded the desk like hammers. Other fists also pounded on the locked office door behind Maurice and voices were shouting for it to be opened.

Pover and Maurice glared at each other across the paper-strewn desk.

"Now get the hell out of here," the wagonmaker said.

Maurice saw that further argument was useless. He gathered up the plans, folded them under his arm, and withdrew. Pover's last words were, "And get the hell out of my factory and my life. You're fired!" Maurice opened the door, shouldered past the crowd of assistants, and went to his locker in the factory.

"What happened?" It was old Moneypenny, ashen-faced.

"Nothing happened."

"What did you tell the man?"

"I said I was offering him the money-making opportunity of a lifetime."

"What did he say?"

"He said to get out of his office and his factory; I was fired."

"You were fired?"

Maurice put on his cap and coat and picked up his lunch bucket. "That's right, fired." He slammed the locker door. As other employees looked up from their work, he walked to the factory exit.

Moneypenny trotted along beside him. The old man suddenly burst into a loud guffaw and clapped Maurice on the back. "That was the damndest thin' I ever seen, young feller. By God, it was the absolute damndest! What d'you figure on doin' now?"

Maurice stopped walking and faced the old man.

"How much will you sell it for?"

"Sell it?"

"The buggy. I'll buy it from you." He glared back toward Pover's office. "This has become personal. I want to give it the Stewart name; form a company. Then I'll finish our scale model, get a brochure made up, take it on the road, and sell it."

"Sell it? We ain't even built the first one yet. We've got no parts, no wood, no machinery. How can you sell somethin' you ain't even got?"

"Leave that to me. Two thousand dollars, Moneypenny. Is it a deal?"

"One thousand and we're partners, fifty-fifty. And you can name it any damn thing you like."

Maurice put out his hand. Moneypenny, with an expression of sudden awe, took it. "Hell," he said, "what have I got to lose?"

They shook on it.

* * *

Maurice sat in the barber chair listening to the talk of the locals. His mind focused upon the task at hand: finishing the model and brochure of the Stewart Continental and getting it financed. That was the rub, financing. He had already visited the two banks in Fall River and been rejected by both. "Sorry, Mr. Stewart, but it's just too chancy. Besides, with the country about to go to war..."

They were talking about the Cuban problem again. What did that have to do with getting a loan? The fact was, nobody wanted to take a chance. Even Hiram Moneypenny was wary. Old Tom's cousin could afford it—he still had the first dime he ever made—but his stingy soul could not be swayed. It was enough, however, that Hiram now provided a workshop to complete the buggy model and free bed and board for Maurice.

"Trim the sideburns, Maurice?" The young barber's name was Jeffrey Straight, and he was one of a growing number of people in Fall River with whom Maurice had developed a casual acquaintance. Jeff owned the shop and didn't seem to mind putting Maurice's haircuts on the tab now that he was temporarily unemployed. It was one of the small advantages of living in a town where people knew each other.

"Lightly, Jeff, if you please."

He could ask the family for help. It was always a final resource, and certainly he was entitled to a share in the Stewart fortune. Even his brother Casey drew a regular stipend from the Pittsburgh accounts. Lord knows, there were millions there. But the thought of asking his father for a penny was repugnant. Even now, as he thought of it, the words of Bradley Stewart echoed in his memory: "You'll fall on your ass, by God. And when you do, don't come crawling back to me for help!" Well, he would not. So strong, indeed, was his commitment that he would not even seek help from other family sources, including his cousin Hope. If he was a stubborn fool, then so be it.

He got out of the chair, surveyed the haircut in the mirror, and nodded approval. "Jeff," he said with a knowing grin, "I don't suppose you'd like to invest in a..."

"In Stewart Continental?" The barber chuckled. "Not today, Maurice. Thanks all the same."

Stewart Continental. Maurice put on his hat and coat and walked into the snowy afternoon, aware of the grandiose title of a company and a product that didn't even exist. He knew that barbershop idlers snickered about the young "tycoon" who took his haircuts on the cuff. Some even made snide remarks to his face. "Well, an' how's things on Wall Street today, Mister J. P. Morgan? Har-har-har." Icy wind cut at him, a reminder that his coat was cheap and thin. God, it was cold in Michigan! A recent thaw and freeze had draped buildings and utility poles with gigantic icicles. Watery sunlight sifted down through a gray overcast sky. The thermometer was plunging again. On Main Street, horses stamped and blew their foggy breaths as pedestrians hurried along, huddled in greatcoats.

Stewart Continental, indeed! He had even asked Priscilla to invest, following one of their infrequent but fervid lovemakings. Her laughter had stabbed at his pride like a knife. "Invest in your harebrained buggy scheme? You must be mad, Maurice. Adorable, but mad. No, dear, it's quite out of the question. Besides, I get all my money from Harry, and that wouldn't do at all, would it? I mean, for me to invest his money in a potential competitor." Her laughter pealed through the refurbished storeroom, now handsomely carpeted and decorated in a French provincial style complete with parlor, sewing room, marbled bath, and boudoir. "It wouldn't be sporting!"

But three evenings after the haircut he arrived at Hiram Moneypenny's house to find a visitor waiting. It was Ruggles, the retired Detroit banker he had met at Priscilla's party in November. Over coffee and cigars, Ruggles said, "Stewart, I am prepared to negotiate a loan for your buggy project. I am doing this not out of any great faith in what you've got to offer—God knows, you have no background in business that I know of—but at the behest of a very dear friend who seems to have enormous belief in you. How much do you think you will need?"

Maurice was hard put to contain his joy. "Mr. Ruggles, I need enough to pay Tom Moneypenny, enough for printing sales brochures and handbills, enough for my personal travel expenses while on a sales trip in the spring, and enough to set up a small shop, so that my partner can produce a couple of full-scale models. Three thousand dollars will do nicely."

The banker made a face, mashed his cigar into an ashtray, and stood up. "Very well, then, three thousand it is. But I shall demand payment in full, with interest, in one year. Otherwise, your, um, advocate will be obliged to pay the debt. Do you understand?"

"I understand. But Mr. Ruggles, one question . . ."

"Yes?"

"Who asked you to help me?"

100

The banker shook his head. "I'm not at liberty to say."

He saw Ruggles off in his carriage and walked back into the house exhilarated. Hiram Moneypenny appeared in the parlor, filled with unspoken curiosity.

"We've done it, Hiram! We're on our way!"

Later, he tossed on his cot unable to sleep. It was actually happening! And now there was just time to get everything ready. How lucky could one man be? Ruggles's words kept tumbling through his mind. ". . . at the behest of a friend . . . enormous belief in you." Was it Priscilla? Of course it was Priscilla. Priscilla had come through for him after all. How strangely things worked out. But how could he possibly express his appreciation?

Maurice Stewart drifted off to sleep, resolved that her faith in him would be more than justified.

V

Commands barked across the morning. The gray bulk of the battleship *Maine* stood off the Navy docks, shedding herself of mooring lines, cable, gangways, and other impediments of the land. A bo'sun's whistle piped shrilly, sending white-uniformed sailors scurrying across the decks.

"All squared away and ready for sailing, sir." Lieutenant Commander Van Harrison Stewart saluted in the bright sunlight of the bridge.

Captain Sigsbee, commander of the dreadnought, nodded amiably and returned the salute. "Very well, Number One. All engines forward, flank speed."

"Engines forward, flank speed, sir."

"Two points to starboard and steady as she goes."

"Steady as she goes, sir."

The ritual of departure was always bittersweet. From his position on the bridge Van could see the tall, clapboard mansion rising from its grove of trees in the town of Key West. The reminder brought a rush of heavy nostalgia. She would be there soon, Pauline, looking out from the upstairs window of the room in which they had lain together through his last night on shore. They had parted on the dock, and a difficult parting it had been; he to board his ship for Havana, she to step into her smart, yellow-wheeled buggy and return to Duval House to await her husband. The idyll of love thus ended, Van mused, and reality returned. The fact that she was married added a delicious forbidden element to it all. Good-bye, Pauline.

The great ship slid out upon turquoise waters sparkling in sunlight. From the shore, wives, sweethearts, and friends waved farewell, their white handkerchiefs fluttering in the distance. After a quarter of an hour the *Maine* rounded the point and Key West vanished from sight. Signal bells quickened the ship's speed. The great prow cut a rising froth as she nosed into the Caribbean, heading south.

Night closed over the tropic waters, bringing an incredible display of stars and an iridescent wake. Officers gathered in the wardroom where Captain Sigsbee, a pleasant, quiet commander with long service on board United States ships, introduced several new officers who had joined them at Key West. The commander then withdrew, leaving the wardroom talk to younger men.

"Everybody in Key West was talking about war," said young Honacker, a gunnery officer. "They're betting we see action before this voyage is over."

"Nonsense. This is a peaceful mission. President McKinley himself said as much. We make a courtesy call to Havana, nothing more."

"Call it courtesy if you wish, but we're carrying an awful lot of extra ammunition for a friendly inspection of Morro Castle."

The battleship plowed southward on a glassy sea.

At eleven o'clock on the morning of January 25, 1898, all flags flying and the ship's company arrayed on the decks in tiers of dazzling white, the *Maine* slid into Havana harbor beneath the brooding hulk of Morro Castle and dropped anchor.

Captain Sigsbee focused his binoculars on the stone quay and announced gravely, "Prepare for distinguished visitors, Number One." Van looked over the commander's shoulder and saw an official motor launch setting out on the sunlit harbor. She flew the flag of Spain. Within fifteen minutes the Spanish acting captain-general was piped aboard, accompanied by a retinue of ranking officials and the United States representative in Havana, Consul-General Lee. There followed an hour-long exchange of formalities, including an officers' reception on the afterdeck overshadowed by the guns of the dreadnought. Tensions were masked by a veneer of impeccable cordiality. Van Stewart was kept busy in his role as

Captain Sigsbee's official interpreter, carefully mouthing the stiff Castilian phraseology demanded of the event. Finally the officials made their departure, extending invitations to the *Maine*'s officers for a formal reception that evening at the castle of the captain-general.

"Order ship's company to stand down, Number One."

"Aye, sir. Bo'sun, pipe crew to stand down."

As the pipe shrilled, the *Maine* let out a collective breath. Sailors broke ranks and filed belowdecks.

Captain Sigsbee offered a thin smile, in the manner of a commander having absolute trust in his subordinate. He knew of this fine officer's strange mingling of white and Indian blood, of course; the information was in Stewart's confidential personnel file, and bore a White House stamp. If it took half-breeding to mold such men as this, however, then one might wish for an entire Navy of half-breeds. "So far, so good, Number One," he said. "We will depart ship at oh-seven-hundred hours in formal dress uniform. Bring all officers except the normal watch . . ."

Day after day the *Maine* swung at anchor in the bright Caribbean sunshine. Quiet prevailed in the city of Havana. Captain Sigsbee posted extra guards at night and ordered that the armory watch be prepared instantly to break out arms. Since nothing occurred officers were allowed to go ashore; Van and several others accepted an invitation to a Sunday bullfight. Aside from hostile glances from Army troops and civilians, their hosts were the souls of propriety.

And yet a nameless anxiety continued to make its presence felt.

"It don't feel right to me, Number One." The watch officer Lieutenant Muldoon stood looking out over the Havana waterfront under the stars. He sniffed the air like an old salt testing for rough weather. "I get a queasy feeling. It's like campin' in somebody's front yard, knowin' you're not welcome."

"You're a fussbudget, Muldoon. Haven't the Spaniards treated us like amiable hosts? I seem to remember that you put away quite a lot of their wine the other night."

"They're good hosts, right enough. But I can't seem to shake this creepy feelin' that somethin' is about to happen."

There was no practical reason for such apprehension. Even Consul-General Lee, a man of caution borne of long service as a career diplomat, saw nothing to ruffle the placid relations between the Spanish authorities in Havana and the officers and crew of the *Maine*. As evidence of this, Lee sent off regular dispatches informing Washington

Peace and quiet reign. Visit a success.

Three weeks went by. Gradually things were changing. Under subtle American pressures, Spanish authorities had acquiesced to greater autonomy for the Cuban nation. Food was in critically short supply, largely due to rebel attacks in the countryside. From his own conversations with Spanish officers, it was clear to Van that since the authorities from Madrid were anxious to avoid open conflict with the United States, they were distributing American food shipments to the population. He became friends with a young Spanish nobleman, Dupuy de Sagasta, who expressed the Spanish sentiment. "It would be tragic, Van, if our two countries went to war. I feel that the basic misunderstanding between us could easily be worked out, if only we communicated in a common language."

Language. Van's fluency in Spanish was both a blessing and a curse. It was a blessing in that he could speak and understand the people of this hot, passionate country. It was a curse in that he saw the seething frustrations of his own countrymen aboard ship, American sailors having no command of Spanish and therefore seeing animosity where none existed. The sailors called the locals *garlics,* and made rude jokes about their manners, language, customs, and women. It troubled Van to see strangers in a straitlaced Catholic country regarding all women as hot-blooded Cuban whores, waiting to be ravished by the first American sailor to come along.

"If we stay here much longer," he cautioned Captain Sigsbee, "there will be incidents. The men are restless."

The *Maine*'s commander placed tighter restrictions on shore liberty for the crew.

February 15. The evening was hot and oppressive, the air remarkably still. Van set the watch and stood on the poop deck. Except for the hum of electrical dynamos belowdecks, the ship was deathly still. Two officers smoked under the after turret, their voices a gentle murmur. Over the side, the chop of the harbor was so light that it washed the great steel hull without a sound. Van thought: How remarkable. This is a ship carrying a complement of three hundred fifty officers and men, but at this moment in time and space I am virtually alone.

It was time for lights out. From the forward deck there came the gentle bugle sound of "Taps." The bugler was in good form tonight, inspired no doubt by the quiet, the sea, the stars, and his own sense of isolation in the velvety darkness. Van lit a cigar and listened, leaning his elbows at the railing and staring out at the star-studded horizon. He thought of the women he had known in a dozen years of Navy life. So many ports, so many women, so many goodbyes. It was a good life, but no life for a married man. And thus he remained single at the age of thirty-two. One was married to the sea and ships and command. In time, he hoped to command a vessel such as this one, a great sturdy ship with gunpower and a steel plate, a ship built for battle, the embodiment of American seapower. He thought of Hope.

"I will worry about you, Van," she had said. "War is no longer a valid solution to international quarrels. Surely man has advanced beyond that by now." Hope, the beautiful and willful idealist, determined to change the nature of man. It was an impossible dream, Van reflected. Man did not change. Only his weapons of war changed, becoming more sophisticated, more technologically advanced. And now he stood on the deck of the most supreme weapon of warfare known to the world, the battleship. The battleship was the queen of the seas, and he who ruled the seas ruled the world.

Another twenty minutes went by. Van glanced at his watch. It was 9:40 P.M.

And then the *Maine* exploded.

The blast erupted in a fiery column that lit up the night. The ship lurched heavily from bow to stern. Van braced himself at the rail as deck lights flickered and went out. From amidships came the clanging of alarm bells. He rushed forward, colliding with other officers and men.

"What is it, sir?"

"Explosion!"

"What the hell? . . ."

As Number One, his duty was to immediately assess damage and form rescue parties. Van moved toward a companionway amidships. Shadowy figures were coming up from below. The deck seemed to tilt beneath his feet, as if the whole ship were pitching downward at the bow. He ducked into a passageway and descended a ladder. There was a crashing and splintering from below as bulkheads gave way. Men screamed and water rushed underfoot. He was in the pitch-black main corridor, feeling his way. Someone bumped into him.

"What's happening up there, sailor?"

"It's terrible, terrible! They're dying. They're drowning!"

More men pounded past him in the darkness. He seemed to be groping his way forward for an eternity. A flashlight flickered, briefly illuminating scenes of grisly wreckage in one of the crew compartments. He glimpsed a young sailor, no more than a boy, writhing on the floor in his skivvies, impaled through the body by a jagged steel beam. Van rounded a corner and stopped. There was no more corridor. Above him portions of the deck itself had been blown out and he could see the stars. Flames licked at shattered woodwork and tangled wreckage. Bodies were flung everywhere, the dead and the dying. From the fire area he could hear the sporadic popping of small-caliber ammunition as flames licked at weapons lockers.

"Poor devils, they never had a chance." It was a young Marine guard speaking. He stood swaying in the wreckage, his uniform in tatters and blood streaming from a head wound. His eyes were glazed and his face was the color of chalk. "The forward magazines went up. The men, sir, they was blown right out of their bunks."

"Come on, then. Let's move aft." Van gently took the young Marine's arm and led him, shuffling like an old man, back into the corridor.

They were halfway to the exit hatch when a nearby ammunition locker exploded. The hot blast pitched Van off his feet and slammed him headlong against a steel bulkhead. A torrent of water came gushing from a split in the steel hull. Blinded, fighting for consciousness, he felt himself rushing along the black tunnel, his arms flailing. A searing pain shot through his left leg. A light! Grabbing with one hand, he hauled his body into the exit hatch.

"Here's one!"

Hands grabbed him beneath the arms, pulled him out onto the deck. He was half carried, half dragged toward the poop deck.

"It's Number One. Good Lord, his leg is half gone!"

They tried to tend to his leg, clumsily wrapping it in lengths of torn sheeting. Pain smashed at him in waves. Someone knelt beside him. "Number One?" He recognized the voice of Captain Sigsbee. The voice sounded strangely calm in the midst of all this havoc. "What has happened, Number One? The crew quarters, could you reach them?"

"Dead," he mumbled. "Didn't have a chance. Died in their bunks. Drowned. Smashed. Awful. The Marine. What happened to the Marine?"

Sigsbee turned briefly, asked a question, and spoke to him again. "There was nobody with you, Number One. Evidently he's still down there..."

"She's down by the bow, Captain," an officer said. "We've still got a quarter-boat here on the poop davits. Will you abandon ship?"

"You officers, take the quarter-boat and row around the ship. Pick up anybody you can find in the water."

"Aye, aye, sir."

Floodlights from ashore now played over the stricken battleship, casting the scene in a macabre glow. Life stirred frantically in the harbor. Boats from the Spanish cruiser *Alfonso XII*, moored at the next buoy, already were advancing, their oars rising and falling in the eerie light. Other boats were coming from the civilian Ward Line steamer, *City of Washington*, anchored somewhat farther away. Shouts of rescuers, in English and Spanish, punctuated the night. Van was aware of crowds gathering on the distant quay, as people poured from their homes and rushed to the waterfront.

A needle stabbed at his arm, injecting morphine. But he remained conscious as the *Maine* continued to settle until only the poop deck where he lay remained above water. They picked him up and prepared to lower him over the side. Captain Sigsbee gripped his hand. "Good luck, Number One." Van was placed in the quarter-boat. As oarsmen pulled away, water rose swiftly around the battleship. In the floodlights Van saw Captain Sigsbee step from the flooding poop into another boat. The captain saluted and was rowed free of the great gray bulk of the battleship as it settled onto the bottom of the harbor, the superstructure jutting into the night sky.

Van and the other wounded were taken to the *City of Washington*. The liner's deck swarmed with an excited mob of Spanish officials, Americans, Cubans, and newspaper correspondents. "What happened, Lieutenant Commander?" shouted an American journalist, scribbling feverishly into a notebook. "What did you see?" Through the misty consciousness of morphine Van was unable to give a coherent reply. They briefly lowered him to the deck. Someone shouted in

Spanish, "Praise be to God, Van. You are alive!" Dupuy de Sagasta knelt at his side. Tears streamed down the Spaniard's handsome face. "What a terrible thing has happened. A terrible thing!"

Van was placed aboard a litter and taken into the main dining saloon of the steamship, where the wounded and dying were lain on mattresses on the floor. He drifted off to sleep despite the moans and babbling of a young sailor by his side, dying of massive burns.

The following morning they took Van off the ship to a hospital in Havana, where Spanish surgeons amputated the remnant of his shattered leg just below the knee.

He lay drugged for the remainder of that day, but then was able to sit up and take notice of life again. On the next day, the seventeenth, all Havana turned out for a massive state funeral for the dead of the battleship *Maine*. Captain Sigsbee visited him in the late afternoon. The commander was visibly exhausted, but insisted on giving his first officer a review of the momentous events.

"We lost two hundred fifty-two men on board, including Officers Jenkins and Merritt. Eight more are dead of wounds. Only sixteen sailors came off unscathed. The ship is beyond hope of salvage. She lies on the mud of the bottom with nothing above water but twisted wreckage and the mainmast. The treatment of you wounded personnel by the Spaniards has been most considerate and humane. The entire city is dressed in mourning, with flags at half-mast. Today the bishop of Havana presided over the state funeral and burial of our men in the Colón Cemetery." Sigsbee sighed and looked wearily out the window. "Two hundred sixty dead."

"What happened, Captain? What caused the explosion?"

The *Maine*'s commander shook his head. "I wish to heaven I knew. We have gone over the wreckage and sent down divers. There is no evidence of a mine or other explosive device. It could have been entirely accidental. There is no indication of foul play by the Spaniards. It could even . . ." He hesitated, glancing around the room as if to be absolutely certain they were alone. "It could even have been the work of the rebels, to bring us into the war. In my message to Washington, I urged that public opinion be suspended until we know more. But that is a vain hope. The nation is in an uproar. For three years Cuba has been a sputtering powder train, and here at last is the explosion. The militants are clamoring for war."

Van nodded grimly, thinking of the night he had met the rebel general Maximo Gomez and the publisher William Randolph Hearst. "Yes, they would be doing that."

"I understand by cable that Mr. Hearst's newspapers are already on the streets of New York with lurid headlines and drawings purporting to reveal how a bomb was planted beneath the ship, wired and detonated from shore. I must assume," Sigsbee mused dryly, "that the *Journal* has sources of information denied to the United States Navy. President McKinley is in a dreadful bind. The clamorous American press is fighting a war already..."

The captain of the *Maine* slumped in his chair, as if bearing an enormous weight upon his shoulders.

Van thought of his Spanish friends in Havana and remembered the tears on the face of Dupuy de Sagasta. What irony that due to journalists and politicians, military men were swept up in the onrushing avalanche of war.

"Well, you're out of it now, Number One." Captain Sigsbee glanced down at the lump on the bed, formed by the heavily bandaged stump of Van's leg. "And out of the Navy too, I'm afraid." He said it very gently, as one man to another cushioning the blow. "Thank God, it could have been worse."

The suddenly terrible reality struck Van Stewart like a blow. Out of the Navy! He had not thought; he had not dreamed... He had never even considered such a possibility. His career was ended, at the age of thirty-two. In a world of strong and resourceful men, he would be a cripple. As if to emphasize the irony of that, he felt a tickling sensation in the area where his left foot used to be. A one-legged half-breed Indian in a world of strong white men...

He had never had a drink of whiskey in his life, knowing how it might stir his Indian blood, but he wanted one now.

"God of my father," he muttered.

Captain Sigsbee walked out of the room, wiping his eyes.

"Sure, young fella, I'll buy one. We need a light buggy, something with a little style to drive the missus to church. Everything they make out here is too heavy, and if you order a buggy from back East it costs a fortune. What are those terms again?... Well, that sounds reasonable enough."

He was selling. The sky was blue, the weather blessedly warm, the fields of Michigan green with garden crops, corn, and wheat, and the Stewart Continental was selling! Undeniably he had a knack for it. Numerous people had told him as much. "Young fella, you're a natural-born salesman. I congratulate you." The key to it was the women. This Maurice had learned early in this first swing through Michigan, Illinois, and Indiana. Women, especially farm women, exerted profound influences upon their husbands. And the place to meet such women was in church.

A formal introduction was unnecessary. The important thing was to be noticed. By attending the largest church in town, a handsome young stranger driving a spanking new buggy with a black top and yellow wheels was bound to be noticed. Maurice also made a point of attending Wednesday night prayer meetings. These events not only reinforced the previous Sunday's recognition; they also gave him an opportunity to meet individuals.

"Welcome, Mr. Stewart, to Grand Rapids. This your first visit to our town?"

"My very first visit, Parson. But I don't intend for it to be my last."

"Is your visit business or personal?"

"Business. I'm a field representative for Stewart Continental."

"Stewart Continental. Hum. Is that a family operation?"

"You might say so. The Stewarts have been in business since 1792, when my grandfather started the Stewart Line in Pittsburgh. That was riverboats and freight hauling."

"Ah, the Stewart Line. Of course. Amanda, this here's Mr. Stewart. He's in Grand Rapids on business..."

And so it went. One influential person referred you to another and another and another. The quickest and surest way was to find common ground, and the stranger's common ground was also the lodge or the brotherhood.

"Knights of Pythias, you say? Are you a member, Mr. Stewart?"

"No, sir, but my partner is. His name is Tom Moneypenny, and he's a member of the Fall River lodge."

"Moneypenny, eh? Moneypenny. Can't rightly place him, but it don't matter. A lodge brother's a lodge brother. What can we do for you, Mr. Stewart?"

And thus he worked his way from town to town. Women remembered him as the young man they had seen in church. Farmers responded to talk of the Odd Fellows, the Elks, and the Granges. One avoided high-pressure selling. His object was to make friends, not necessarily a sale. Often he split a cord of kindling wood, shared the evening meal, and helped to slop hogs after supper before a potential customer finally sat down, lit a pipeful of tobacco, and said, "What's your business, Mr. Stewart?"

Women, especially middle-aged farm wives, could be a problem. They lived hard, boring lives stuck out in the middle of nowhere. A handsome young stranger on the premises drew openly lustful stares at the dinner table, and occasional nocturnal visits to his bed or cot or hayloft. And thus he contrived the fiction that he was engaged to be married as soon as he returned to Fall River. It disappointed his hostesses, but seemed to suffice. One needed to instill a high degree of confidence, after all, in order to persuade a buyer to pay ten percent down for a piece of merchandise on the mere strength of a salesman's promise that it would be delivered at all. With the Stewart Continental priced at two hundred dollars, that meant twenty dollars cash in Maurice's pocket with every signature on the sales contract. "Mr. Herman, you can pay for it over a period of two years if you like. Your credit is good with Stewart Continental."

Six weeks from the day he had left Fall River, Maurice was back carrying one hundred fifty orders in his pocket, along with three hundred dollars in cash down payments.

Moneypenny almost had a stroke. "My God, young feller, that's twenty thousand dollars worth of buggies! And you're guaranteein' delivery in a hundred and twenty days? We ain't even got a workshop, much less a factory!"

"But you've got the detailed blueprints ready, right?" he retorted. "And the new prototype model's built! So we're ready to get cracking on financing and production contracts."

It was easier said, however, than done. Even with the orders in his pocket, bankers were not rushing to back the venture. Maurice remained a newcomer to Fall River and had no family ties there. "We'll have to study this, Mr. Stewart." And, "A venture of this type will have to be approved by the board." Banker Ruggles had gone East and was not expected back in Detroit for six weeks. It was Jeffrey Straight who came unexpectedly to his aid. Poring over the plans, the models, and the sales contracts, the young barber rubbed his hands excitedly.

"I like it, Maurice. I think we can get some investors together, form a corporation. My dad's got a pretty good head for this sort of thing. Let's go have a talk with him."

A week later, at a crowded meeting in a small room behind Straight's Barber Shop, Stewart Continental, Inc., was born. With financial pledges secured, Maurice and Moneypenny now went to every job shop and small buggy works in southern Michigan and northern Indiana to negotiate for production. Now it was Moneypenny's turn to shine, and the old carriagemaker proved a formidable persuader on technical matters. "Sure, you can turn fifty sets of wheels in sixty days. This design ain't nearly as complicated as it looks. Here, let me show you . . ." And so they contracted out each component of the Stewart Continental, wheels, axles, body panels, tongue assemblies, leather tops, leather cushioned seats, leaf springs, bolts and pins, and braces. In the meantime, on the outskirts of Fall River, Jeffrey Straight found an empty millhouse that would serve as a temporary assembly plant and the word went out that Stewart Continental was hiring a few good hands . . .

It was a damn fool thing to be doing. The work was piled up awaiting his attention virtually around-the-clock. There were orders pouring in and production troubles to attend to and God knew what else. But here he was dressed in his Sunday best driving one of his buggies through the warm July evening to meet Priscilla Pover at a secluded wooded spot by the river. He had almost fancied himself free of her, so compelling had the work become. The arrival of her perfumed note proved otherwise.

Meet me at the falls, nine o'clock.

His heart seemed to expand in his chest and he dropped everything to do her bidding. Now the soft sounds of a summer night came from the dark woods and fields as the horse trotted softly over a winding dirt road lit by splashes of moonlight. The scent of her letter mingled with the smells of earth and the dewy air. His excitement surged as the road dipped toward the river and the sound of the rapids could be heard.

"Maurice?"

At her soft call, he reined in quickly and scanned the shadows. From a dark copse of oak she emerged into the moonlight riding the gig, the Morgan roan dancing nervously. He parked his buggy and went to her. She came down into his arms, her kiss warm and lingering. From the gig she drew a heavy comforter and they strolled arm-in-arm to the grassy riverbank. White water gleamed in the moonlight, chuckling and dancing over the rocks. There was a heavy bed of moss on the bank. They lay down together on the moss and he took her gently. Her moans blended with the sound of rushing water.

Afterward they lay together naked looking up through the trees at the drifting moon. It was a dreamlike interlude, so beautiful that Maurice's heart ached with longing. Why could they not be together always, instead of at stolen interludes? Maurice Stewart had to acknowledge at last what Helen DeMare had told him so bluntly that day in the soda shop. He was in love with Priscilla Pover.

"I'm tired of these games," he said. "I want you to be with me all the time."

He looked at her face in the shadows. She was smiling, saying nothing. The eyes were lynxlike. He told her about himself, his ambitions, his past. He spoke of the crisis with his father and his determination to make good.

From the woods came a whippoorwill's call.

"Do you love me?" he said.

She chuckled softly. "What a funny thing to ask. Why do you ask that?"

"Well, do you?"

"Of course I love you, silly. Do you think I'd give myself to a man I didn't love?" She yawned, stretching her body like a cat. "Do you have to be so serious about it?"

He swallowed hard, felt himself at the brink of decision, tried to ignore a stab of anxiety. He said, "Marry me, Priscilla. Leave Pover. You don't love him. Leave him and marry me."

Her smile seemed to congeal in the moonlight. The mouth became a dark slash. There was glint of malice in the eyes. "Marry you?"

"Yes. Leave Pover now, tonight. Don't go back. Come with he, and we'll go away. You can get your divorce. We'll be together all the time . . ."

The whippoorwill stopped calling. Even the chuckle of the rapids seemed to subside. The forest waited, hushed. A wisp of cloud slipped over the moon, casting her face in shadow. A new sound came from her, a nasal, brittle sound. Confused, he rose up on one elbow.

She was laughing.

"Marry you? Hah-hah-hah. Leave Pover and go away with you? That's rich. That's really rich!"

He felt a surge of anger. His mind tried to control its sudden confusion. "Priscilla . . ."

She rolled over, came to her knees, and stood up. Her

body in the shadows was like white marble. He had never seen anything so beautiful. "Marry a grease monkey like you? You're out of your mind." She found her clothes and began to dress.

He came to his feet. "I don't understand. If we love each other, why can't we be together? It doesn't make sense for you to live with a man you don't love. How can that be?"

"Ah, Maurice, what a simpleton you are. Pover gives me more than physical intimacy. Besides, I don't wish to be possessed by any man." She drew the gown over her head. For the first time he noticed that she had worn no underclothing. "Love? Love, my dear, is where you find it."

"But if you feel that way, why did you help me?"

"Help you?" She had put on her shoes, found a brush in her things, and passed it through her long hair with vigorous strokes. "What do you mean, help you? You needed a job, and I liked the way you looked . . ."

"Not the job at the plant. I mean Ruggles. Why did you ask Ruggles to finance my buggy if you felt this way? He said you had expressed a lot of belief in me . . ."

"Oh, I do have belief in you, Maurice. You're a very smart, very attractive young man." The dark eyes swept him up and down. "You're also hung like a stallion and built like a Greek statue. But you're mistaken about Mr. Ruggles. I don't know in what way he financed you, but I had nothing to do with it. And now, I'm afraid I must be off." She glanced up at the racing moon. "It's getting late."

Priscilla Pover gathered up the comforter and walked to her gig without looking back. He was still putting on his clothes, cursing himself as she drove away.

Idiots. They were all idiots. She had never known a male who could not be manipulated by a clever woman. If you didn't lead him by the nose, you led him by the balls. It really mattered little. Truth to tell, Priscilla rather despised all of them, but found them necessary. If she went for too long without a man, she got horny and out of sorts. That made life unpleasant. She despised being frustrated more than she despised men.

There were, of course, other objects of interest to add spice to one's existence. If there was no immediate male satisfaction to be had, then she could find the company of an exciting female. Priscilla had had several affairs with females over the years, typically actresses. The theater often attracted persons of flexible intimacies. The bull dykes were to be avoided at all costs; Priscilla found them coarse, unattractive, and as jealously possessive as any man. But on occasion she had found physical pleasures in comely young things, starstruck and susceptible to the soft wiles of an older woman. Never had Priscilla felt anything for them beyond a quick lust. Never had she experienced a truly powerful and possessive desire...

Not until she met Helen DeMare.

Helen was different: still very young, just turned sixteen, but wise beyond her years; still blessed with the look of innocence, but seemingly experienced at subcurrents of passion. From their first meeting at a theater party eight months before, Priscilla Pover had been alternately intrigued and captivated. Helen was an angel with bold eyes, a tart in virgin's clothes. Their glances had met and held, their words exchanged hidden meanings; and to Priscilla's enticement and chagrin, the implied pleasures remained always just beyond reach. The closest she had come was during a brief visit to Helen's dressing room at the Bijou when the girl, changing between acts, had permitted her to help her dress. Priscilla's hands touched lightly that velvety skin; her eyes stared hungrily at those forbidden places; her chest constricted with desire. But then Helen, with an impish smile, had stepped behind the screen. That's when Priscilla, inflamed, had had the riverside rendezvous with that beautiful stud Maurice Stewart. His incredible virility temporarily banked the fires within her. And then, mumbling like a schoolboy, he had asked her to marry him. She still laughed out loud at the memory. What fools they were!

"Fool!" she said aloud, glaring at her reflection in the boudoir mirror. She had completed her loveliest costume—a soft rose gown with a high neck that complemented her coloring—upswept her hair in the Gibson Girl fashion, and applied just a hint of makeup to accentuate her eyes and mouth. Her tummy was nervous, her skin prickly with anticipation. Tonight, Helen DeMare at last was coming to the mansion alone. All day Priscilla had planned for their evening together: a light wine, a light supper, a bit of cocaine, soft lighting and music from the Victrola, and then...

For the first time in her thirty-two years, it was Priscilla who felt the ecstatic agony of love.

She arrived just after sunset, driving a light trap. The evening was warm. She wore a gown of light green and her hair fell in an auburn ponytail from beneath a flowered bonnet. The ensemble was springish, and the effect caused Priscilla to catch her breath. Priscilla put her arm around Helen's waist as they walked into the house, chatting lightly. How trim that waist was beneath her hand. Almost trembling, she took the bonnet and breathed the fragrance of that auburn hair as Helen turned away. The girl was magnificent.

"I am so glad you came, Helen. It does get lonely in this house. Harry is away so much of the time." How banal it sounded. Why must they mask their feelings behind meaningless woman-chatter? Didn't Helen know by now how passionately she was desired? Surely she knew! "Come into the parlor, where it's comfortable. Or would you prefer to sit out on the veranda?" It was the parlor. Priscilla poured a light wine. Their fingers brushed in passing it, the touch sending electricity through her.

"You are lovely," Priscilla said. "That gown fits you perfectly."

Helen seemed preoccupied, evasive. She had not planned to stay. There was something she wished to discuss with Priscilla, woman to woman.

"Why, of course, dear. We can discuss anything. I have planned a light supper, nothing fancy. It's a fish recipe we brought back from Paris. I think you will enjoy it . . ."

The girl was quiet, barely tasting her wine, refusing to smoke, letting Priscilla do the talking. They ate by candlelight in the sunroom, where Priscilla had arranged fresh flowers. Helen had been in Chicago, playing a week's run in a comedy that had folded. But she had to come back to Fall River. Something new and compelling had come into her life. To be perfectly honest, she could not be happy anywhere else and yet was miserable here, too. It was a dilemma for which she was unprepared.

"There, there, my dear." Priscilla smiled. The girl's eyes were hazel, flecked with gold. It was too good to be true! Helen DeMare was feeling the same thing, the same marvelous, headlong, insane joy and groping for the words to express it. The prospect of the night ahead almost made Priscilla swoon. She resisted an impulse to reach across the table and take her hand. "Life is strange and its pleasures full of mystery. Sometimes we have to take it as it comes; there is no other way. Sometimes, we simply have to drop our restraints and let go. Whatever will be, will be."

"I came here," Helen said softly, "to ask you to leave him alone."

Priscilla's smile faded. Her sense of almost-giddy anticipation began to evaporate in confusion.

"I don't understand, dear."

"Maurice Stewart. I'm asking you to leave him alone." The hazel eyes gazed at her levelly. "You don't love him. You entice him, use him. There is nothing in your heart for him. But while you keep Maurice on the string, he can't think clearly. His emotions are a muddle. He cannot find happiness of his own. And neither"—the eyes faltered and looked down at the table—"neither can I."

The anger came in a rush. Why this little snip! "You've got a lot of nerve! The very idea, coming to my house, accepting my hospitality, and telling me that you're mooning over that . . . that grease monkey. Really, girl, you're quite out of your mind." Priscilla stood up so abruptly that the table tilted, sending cups and glasses crashing to the marble floor. Red wine splashed on the front of Helen DeMare's dress, making an angry, spreading stain. "You're saying that you want him for yourself; is that it?"

"Yes. I want him for myself. I love him, and . . ."

"Well, let me tell you something. Maurice Stewart loves me. He is madly in love with me, and has told me so. That is his affair; he's a grown man and doesn't need a wet nurse. And what you are saying is that I should somehow let him go, give him his freedom, tell him to turn it all off and go play with Helen, because Helen loves him. How naive you are! Life does not work that way, my fine little strumpet. Love isn't something that people turn on and off like a water tap."

"You're cold and selfish, Priscilla. You've got a husband, wealth, servants, a life of ease, and money. You're ten years older than Maurice . . ."

"A husband?" Her face suddenly mirrored her disgust. "Do you call Harry Pover a husband? He is a eunuch, a momma's boy. He is incapable of being aroused by anyone. Harry has never in his life performed the act of sex with another human being. On our wedding night, he wept like a child. That was five years ago, and he has never once touched me. We have separate bedrooms, separate lives. He wants me because . . . because it was considered unmanly for him not to have a wife, a pretty wife who could entertain and keep his home and maintain the pretence of his virility. And while we live our separate lives, and he chooses to ignore my adventures,

117

Harry is insanely possessive of me. For all our differences, I am his one link with stability."

"That is all the more reason that you should leave Maurice alone. You put him in a terrible position, loving a woman he can't possibly have..."

"*Stop it!*" The pain lashed at her now. The pain was worse than the fury, because it struck in the vitals of pride and passion. My God, the cruel irony of it. She, Priscilla Pover, loved this girl, loved her and wanted her and would surrender anything to her. Now, in rejection, she wanted her more than ever; rejection had sharpened and intensified both the hurt and the want. With a surge of despair, she stepped around the table and slapped Helen savagely across the face.

"What do you know about love? You've had no experience beyond an occasional romp in the hay. Some man shows you a hard-on and you take that for love. How utterly childish and ridiculous you are. I could give you everything, Helen. Don't you know how I feel? You flaunt your pretty little body at me and then take it away. Do you think I'm made of stone?"

Priscilla fell to her knees beside the girl. She moistened a napkin and dabbed it upon that adorable face, where the mark of the slap was a spreading redness. Helen's startled expression redoubled her own anguish. "Look at me, Helen. Darling, I adore you. I want you terribly. Listen, I am rich. I can give you everything your heart desires. Do you want a real stage career? We can get the right producers, arrange great parts, make you a star! Helen, don't you understand. Darling"—frantically, her hands caressed Helen's thigh, her hips, her back—"I'm offering you the whole world!"

"I don't believe it," Helen murmured.

"What don't you believe, darling."

"You're one of those... women."

"What do you mean?"

"One of those women who like women."

"I like *you*, darling. Can't you see? There is happiness for us. What does it matter if a person is male or female? Love is all that matters. I can give you what you want. I want to love you, protect you. I want..."

But Helen was standing now, standing and staring at her with those big hazel eyes, staring in silent disbelief. Helen turned away, walked slowly to the door, opened it, and went out. Priscilla rushed to the door. "Please! Please don't leave me!" The girl did not look back. She walked across the veranda in the moonlight, unhitched the horse, climbed into the buggy, and drove away.

"Helen, pleeeease! . . ."

The horse's hooves thudded away into the night. Horse and buggy turned a bend in the road and vanished from sight.

Priscilla stood in shock, staring at the empty road in the moonlight. Humiliation was an acid dripping into her soul. At last she went back into the house, found a bottle of rum in the liquor cabinet, and took it to the parlor. From a drawer she drew a small vial of the white powder. Pouring a tumbler half full of rum, she mixed in a few pinches of cocaine and added water. Then, alone, she drank and listened to the ticking of the grandfather clock. The drink filled her with warmth. Her head began to buzz and her lips to numb. It was an escape to nirvana. Piss on little Helen and her lover. Piss on them.

She belched softly and giggled. The clock struck twelve. The bongs went on and on and on. But finally they stopped. She found a cheroot on a side table and lit it, watching the blue smoke drift into the light of the electric lamp. Drink and drug brought an amazing clarity to the mind. Suddenly she was acutely more alert than ordinary beings. Now she understood fully all that had happened. Helen did this deliberately. Priscilla had allowed herself to be entrapped. The girl had led her to the brink of desire—desire so fervid that she momentarily lost her senses—and then turned away. In fact, the two of them had plotted Priscilla's undoing; Helen and the stud Stewart, scheming to bring her to her knees. To her knees! Even now, in her agony, they were probably screwing and laughing.

The thought of Helen giving that luscious body to Maurice Stewart inflamed her. They would not get away with it. No one could treat Priscilla Pover in such cavalier fashion. She would have her revenge.

The empty glass fell from her hand and rolled into a corner. The stub of cheroot smoldered on the side table, burning a deep black gash into the polished inlaid mahogany. The clock struck two.

Priscilla Pover slept.

It was three weeks before her plan fully materialized. She waited deliberately, savoring it all. If one was to exact revenge, one needed time to plan and the proper instrument. And what better instrument than Harry Pover? Dull, impotent, brooding Harry Pover. She waited for the right time and the right setting. When the time came, she dressed carefully, so as to be her most attractive self. Harry drank through a tedious, rainy Sunday afternoon and then faced a Sunday supper of cold leftovers. Heavy drinking and cold suppers always put him in a bellicose mood. Priscilla broached the subject over the table in the sunroom.

"That former hired hand of yours needs to be brought down a peg, Harry. You know, the college boy who tried to sell you his buggy idea."

"What do you mean, brought down a peg?"

"I've been worrying about this for several weeks now, wondering how to tell you..."

Pover had speared a cold green bean with his fork and lifted it from the plate. "Tell me what?"

She looked distraught, dabbing at her eye with a white napkin. "Oh, never mind. Forget I said anything, Harry."

Pover frowned. The fork descended back to the plate. His eyes were bloodshot from drinking. His meaty face glistened. He reeked of sweat, cigars, and liquor. His big hands closed into hamlike fists. Priscilla felt the edge of his temper sharpening. "What'd the college boy say, Priscilla?"

Her violet eyes welled. She let herself seem distraught. "He... he asked me to go away with him, Harry. He said I ought to leave you and get a divorce and marry him. He said..." She sniffed, looking down meekly at her plate.

The fists tightened. The knuckles grew white. "Go on. What'd he say?"

"He said you weren't good enough for me." She looked up, caught his bloodshot gaze. "What do you think about that, Harry?"

Pover's mouth worked. A flush was spreading over his face. "What am I supposed to think about it?"

She leaned across the table, exposing a generous cleavage. The violet eyes flamed and she licked her lips lightly, so that they glistened in the lamplight. Her voice was very quiet when she spoke again. "Do you want another man to take what's yours, Harry?"

Harry reached for a wine goblet, lifted it, and drank. Red wine dribbled down his chin when he lowered the glass. "Nobody's going to take what's mine."

"They say that buggy is going to make him rich, Harry. Folks are laughing because Harry Pover passed up a chance like that. They say Stewart's new assembly shop is open, and he's putting together buggies like crazy. The Stewart Continental, they call it. Everybody's buying one. He's got investors now. Jeff Straight and his friends have bought stock, Dr. Snyder, the Branch brothers..."

"Is that so?"

"I've been doing some snooping, Harry. Give that boy time, he could be a real problem. If he wants to take me away from you, who knows what else he might try to take away? He might even start building heavy wagons, like the Pover."

"Wagons?"

"He might, Harry."

Harry Pover had lost his appetite. He lit a cigar and brooded. He poured himself another goblet of red wine. He muttered, half to himself, "Take him down a peg." Priscilla watched the effect of her words sink deeper and deeper, causing powerful subcurrents of anger to play across the meaty face.

Priscilla Pover smiled.

It was a good shop. Jeff Straight had acquired a lease on an abandoned mill and storage house served by a railroad spur track at the edge of town. Weeks of hard work achieved miracles of cleaning and refurbishment. While carpenters still hammered at an addition to the main structure, railroad shipments of buggy parts began to arrive. The plan was to unpack individual components as they came in from job shops—buggy bodies, collapsible tops, wheels, spring assemblies—and partially assemble each vehicle for repacking and shipment to customers. Already Maurice had arranged with livery stables, warehouses, even a church men's group in area communities, to serve as receivers and distributors. But for now everything was arriving and nothing going out, so that Stewart Continental was a growing hodgepodge of parts in various stages of storage and assembly.

"We're gettin' too many goods under one roof, Maurice. A fire'd clean us out for sure. What did the railroad say about shippin'?"

"They say we'll start getting boxcars for loading first thing Monday morning. I wouldn't worry about it, Moneypenny. You've got things well organized, and the hands are catching on to the assembly work very fast."

Old Moneypenny proudly surveyed the workroom. Hiring had been slow and highly selective. Half a dozen employees worked at uncrating and assembling. "They're just country boys," the carriagemaker said, "but they'll get the hang of it, soon enough."

"I don't doubt that a bit."

Maurice was ecstatic. At last it was really happening! Stewart Continental was coming together like a dream. Already the first shipments of buggies he had sold in the spring were on their way. New orders poured in, the result of Maurice's new idea for direct mail advertising and also from the hiring of two full-time traveling salesmen. But the real spur to sales was the product itself. Stewart Continentals, with their distinctive yellow wheels, glistening black bodies, convertible tops, and bright red tongues, were becoming more popular each day. Letters arrived from potential customers in every mail delivery. The typical query was from a young man or woman.

Dear Sir: I seen one of yur buggies in town today and I would like more informasion about the prices and finansing of same. Yours very truly . . .

"We've got a winner, Maurice. This thing is taking the country by storm!"

"Keep your fingers crossed, Jeff. We're not out of the woods yet."

"Oh, I've got 'em crossed, all right. Toes too."

He had made a conscious effort to drive thoughts of Priscilla Pover from his mind. The episode on the riverbank had left him frustrated and angry. But he seemed to be developing a thicker skin. It was Helen DeMare who brought the warning. She arrived at the assembly shop in the company of several other members of the Bijou theatrical troupe. Maurice was surprised and delighted. She looked especially fetching in a blue frock with gray trimming and a powder-blue hat. Her touch upon his arm was electric. They chatted amiably as he conducted a guided tour. "Now, this is where we do the assembly work. Eventually this area will be a regular production line, with each worker performing a specific task. The time savings is tremendous, and the costs . . ."

She drew him aside. "Maurice, there's something you must know. I've got friends who know Harry Pover. He has vowed to put you out of business, by fair means or foul."

Maurice was not surprised. One did not dally with another man's wife without consequences. He sighed. "I suppose we must pay the piper. What does he intend to do?"

"I don't know. But you must be on your guard. Pover and his thugs are not above violence." She hesitated. "I worry about you, Maurice."

He took her hands and held them. They were strong hands. "Thank you for telling me."

She smiled quickly. "I must go now." She stood on tiptoes and kissed his cheek.

He could feel the kiss long after Helen and her friends had left.

They came in the night. Maurice was working late in the office. Lamplight cast the shop in deep shadow. He heard a creak of the door, a heavy step on the stair.

"Moneypenny?"

There was no answer. A casual nocturnal visitor, he thought, a distraction. Irritated, he bent to a column of figures. They would have to wait. The presence at the door caused him to look up. The man wore dark, heavy clothing and his face was masked.

"What is it? Who the devil are you?"

The rush took him unprepared. Maurice was rising from his chair when three masked men burst into the small office. A gloved fist shot across the desk and struck him in the side of the face. He crashed heavily onto a pile of boxes under a rain of kicks and blows. The air went out of him. He lashed out with a kick, struck flesh, and heard a groan. But the assault was a savage, headlong thing. From the corner of his eye he glimpsed another fist smashing down. And then the night rushed over him like a shower of stars.

He went swirling down, down, down into the depths. His body was formless, floating through a gray haze. Pain licked at him with tongues of fire, across the body, in the joints, in the face. He awoke in the shambles of the office, blinking against the harsh light of a naked, swinging light fixture. Struggling to his feet, he stepped out to the stairs and immediately sat down again.

The place was a wreck. Chunks of broken and battered merchandise were strewn everywhere. Packing crates had been burst open and scattered asunder, tools smashed, windows shattered. A spasm of pain shot through him again and Maurice groaned. He knew that his jaw was broken. His left arm was giving him trouble. There was something wrong with his leg. He remained sitting on the stairs, unable to move farther. It was morning when the first workmen arrived and found him.

"We'd best get him to town to Doc Snyder. Don't try to talk, Mr. Stewart; you've been beat up pretty bad."

"They did a job on this place. Look at that mess."

"Easy now. Take him under the arms. That's it. We'll get him to the wagon."

The ride seemed to take forever. Each bump and lurch brought fresh agony. They carried him into the doctor's small home and to an examining room in the back. Dr. Snyder went over him, making small noises in his throat. A probe here, a touch there...

"Ouch!"

"You've got a fracture of the left leg. That left wrist is broken, for sure. So's your nose. It'll have a hump on it when it's healed, but that can't be helped. Your jaw is in bad shape; I'll have to wire it shut. You're battered and broken, Maurice, but you're alive and that's what matters."

Three hours later he lay in splints with a wired jaw and assorted mustard plasters. Dr. Snyder had given him morphine against the pain and ordered that he remain on a cot in the clinic for several days...

Old Moneypenny shook his head. "Boy, you sure as hell ain't much of a fighter."

"The shop..." Maurice grunted through clenched teeth.

"It's a mess. There ain't a piece of stock worth salvagin'. That little night's work will cost us a pretty penny. But don't worry none. Jeff and his friends are out there now, tryin' to get organized. Banker Ruggles, he showed up too. Just happened to be in town. He'll be comin' to pay you a visit, I expect. And that little girl Helen, she's all shook up." The old eyes gave him a searching glance. "I never seen a young woman take on so. You'd think... Well, never mind. She's on her way over now."

Helen arrived five minutes after Moneypenny had left. She took one look at the bandaged, splinted man on the cot and burst into tears. She fell on her knees beside him and lightly touched his face. "You poor dear. You poor, poor dear." She kissed his forehead and he felt her warmth. He tried to say something but could not. With his good arm, he hugged her clumsily. She lay her head upon his chest.

Ruggles came in the afternoon. The banker seemed genuinely concerned. Helen sat quietly nearby as Ruggles talked. "You were doing well, Stewart. I've been meaning to come around earlier and congratulate you. This is a terrible thing, terrible. But rest assured, our agreement is still valid. In fact"—he turned to Helen—"I'll consider that loan a three-thousand-dollar investment in the company, if you like. Your instincts were absolutely correct, Miss DeMare. This young fellow is going places."

Helen was shaking her head. Too late, Ruggles realized he had spoken excessively. Maurice's eyes widened as he looked at her. He murmured through the wired jaw: "You?" She nodded and looked away.

She came every day to the clinic, sometimes bringing her lively friends from the theater. She fed him broth through a straw, soothed him, helped to bathe him. Maurice began to look forward to her chatty, lively presence. Helen's small talk was larded with backstage gossip and happenings in the community. Her circle of friends was very wide; she knew everybody who was anybody, and relished discussing them.

"Do you have someone to look after you?" Dr. Snyder asked one day in Helen's presence. "When you leave here, Maurice, you'll still need regular attention."

"He can stay with us," Helen said.

"Well..."

"I live in a theatrical boardinghouse. There's plenty of room and lots of company. He'll be treated like a king."

And so it was decided. Six days after the attack, Maurice hobbled on one leg and a crutch to a waiting carriage and was whisked away to the Twelfth Street Thespian Boardinghouse, a rambling three-story structure of white clapboard owned by a retired circus juggler. There he was surrounded by an exotic assortment of humanity in all sizes and carried bodily to a large sunny room on the second floor adjoining Helen DeMare's own bedroom. He could not go down to join the crowd at dinner, so the dinner crowd came up to him. It was a jolly scene of wine and song and good humor. Many of the people he recognized from Priscilla's first party and from casual meetings around town. They served him wine through a straw and quickly made his wired jaws ache from suppressed laughter.

On his second night there, Helen did not go to her room at all.

"I love you, Maurice," she whispered, lying naked beside him in the darkness. "You're the first man I've ever loved."

His senses were a tangle of mixed emotions.

Helen DeMare had been a virgin.

*   *   *

"They've done it. And now there's hell to pay."

Howard Langden's face flushed with indignation. Hope, startled by her husband's intensity, reached across the breakfast table and took his hand. He sat rigidly, staring at the two-line, eight-column headline spattered across the front page of Hearst's *Journal:* THE WAR SHIP *MAINE* WAS SPLIT IN TWO BY AN ENEMY'S SECRET INFERNAL MACHINE. Accompanying the lurid report were imaginative diagrams purporting to show how the Spaniards had clamped a mine to the hull of the battleship and blown it up from shore.

"And look at this trash in Pulitzer's *World.* WHOLE COUNTRY THRILLS WITH WAR FEVER, YET THE PRESIDENT SAYS, 'IT WAS AN ACCIDENT!' This is trash, riddled with supposition and rumor. THE CRUISER *NEW YORK* ORDERED TO HAVANA. CONSUL-GENERAL LEE ASSASSINATED. THE CABINET IN EMERGENCY CONFERENCE. CONGRESS IN SPECIAL SESSION, PRESIDENT MCKINLEY RUSHES TO CAPITOL. Humbug! Not a word of it is true." Langden flung away the newspapers in disgust. "Flagrant distortion of the lowest sort, all to sell newspapers."

"What will you do about it?" she asked quietly.

"Do? My God, we've been doing everything possible. The *Enterprise* has tried to be a voice of reason and fact. Every item that our correspondent reports out of Havana is doublechecked for accuracy. He is the best man I could find for the job, an old pro, knows his way around Cuba, speaks Spanish like a native. We've also printed some dispatches from a young English chap down there, name of Winston Churchill. We'll wind up refuting every word in both the *Journal* and the *World.*" Langden threw up his hands. "But what good does it do? The public wants cheap sensationalism. Hearst's *Journal* sales are soaring to a million copies per day. Pulitzer's *World* has sold five million copies this week! And what's our reward for honesty and integrity? Nothing. Nobody wants to read truth. The public doesn't buy the *Enterprise*."

"That's not true, Howard. People who make decisions buy it. Those who wish to be informed..."

"Informed!" He snorted. "Informed people are a minority, Hope." He rose from the table and stalked to the window commanding a view of midtown Manhattan. "Momentous decisions are being made out of context with reality. They are reinforced by the gullibility of the man on the street. The public is enraged. It doesn't matter that that rage is deliberately provoked by venal and irresponsible men. What matters is that Americans are angry, and becoming more so. They're fed constant distortions about Spain. The *World* runs a series called THE HIDEOUS HISTORY OF SPAIN, complete with illustrated accounts of men and women being massacred in the streets by roving bands of Spanish soldiers. The *World's* man in Havana writes,

> *American citizens are imprisoned or slain without cause.*
> *Blood on the roadsides, blood in the fields, blood on the*
> *doosteps, blood, blood, blood!*

Ye Gods, the man never left his hotel bar!"

"Howard..."

"But I can't blame the man on the street. If I didn't know any more about newspapers than he does, I'd be mad as hell too."

"What you're saying, Howard, is that you are wasting your time, that your efforts are useless, that what the *Enterprise* prints doesn't matter. Am I right?"

He glowered defensively. "How can you even think such a thing?"

"I merely asked a question."

"Of course I'm not wasting..." Howard Langden hesitated, recognizing the baited question. He smiled. "Touché."

"I repeat," she said. "What do you plan to do?"

"I plan..." He walked across the parlor, thrust his hands into his pockets, and stared at the floor. "I plan to see President McKinley."

"Good." Hope caught his eye and smiled mischievously.

"You are amazing," he said.

The White House exuded an air of gravity. William McKinley was an island of calm in the storm. A pleasant, grayish man, he also had the wistful, anxious-to-please manner of a smalltown politician. Such gentle humility, Hope recognized, was the key to his political strength. "Howard, I am flattered that you would come to see me," McKinley said. "And this is your lovely wife Hope. May I express my condolences, Mrs. Langden, over the wounding of your kinsman Lieutenant Commander Stewart. A fine officer. The Navy will sorely miss him."

After several minutes of small talk, there came a lull.

McKinley lifted his eyebrows expectantly. Howard Langden came to the point. "Mr. President, we must not go to war with Spain. This would be a senseless and pointless venture. The nation is being stampeded..."

McKinley listened intently. Howard Langden spoke of the circulation battles between the *Journal* and the *World*. He recounted the incidents of false and inflammatory reporting from Cuba, the linguistic handicaps of American journalists in Havana, their exploitation by rebel emissaries who frequented the hotels and bars of the Cuban capital, and the glaring distortions surrounding the sinking of the *Maine*. "Mr. President, I implore you not to let hotheads influence American foreign policy."

Hope watched the President's face as her husband spoke. Despite his brief tenure in office, William McKinley already bore its heavy burdens. And now he grappled with the terrible complexities of peace and war.

"Mr. Langden, I'm aware of your sincerity." The President's voice had the gentle quality of a Methodist Sunday School teacher. "But permit me, if I may, to try to describe the scope of what we face. The American people, I fear, are terribly desirous of having a war. Rightly or wrongly, a kind of belligerent enthusiasm is sweeping this country. For example, when the *Maine* was sunk, a group of Methodist laymen were meeting in Mexico City. They sent me a cablegram admitting their ignorance of the cause of the disaster, but nevertheless regarding it as—and I quote—

a sacred and significant sacrifice on the altar of humanity.

They offered themselves to the flag. Let me also quote an editorial from the New Orleans *Times-Democrat*, which is far removed from your journalistic competitors in New York. The New Orleans editorialist wrote,

No explanation by the Spanish government, no offer to make reparations, could prevent a declaration of war.

Even Mr. Theodore Roosevelt, who I understand is a personal friend of yours, feels that war is necessary to build up the Navy and establish a base in the Caribbean to protect the building of a canal across Central America. Senator Cabot Lodge is demanding that we go to war immediately..."

"But Mr. President..."

McKinley lifted his hand. "Let me finish. These realities, Mr. Langden, are merely fragments of the whole. America is inflamed with jingoism, and frankly I am at my wits' end trying to come to grips with it. Mr. Hearst and Mr. Pulitzer are not the fundamental instigators of this. However much I deplore irresponsible journalism, I submit that the warmongering publishers are giving the public what it wants. I know that you are an exception, impelled by what you feel are the best interests of the nation. I applaud you, and thank God for your decency. In a democracy, however, the presidency is an instrument of the whole, and the whole is not dictated necessarily by reason. The power to declare war rests with the Congress. And the Congress, Mr. Langden, will ultimately decide whether we shed the blood of American boys in Cuba."

"The Spaniards don't want a war, Mr. President. It is the last thing they want. My word, virtually on the eve of the *Maine* disaster they announced a new policy of self-government for the Cubans. A complete withdrawal from the island could be negotiated. What more evidence of goodwill do we need? A war with the United States would be suicide for Spain."

"Yes, I am aware of that." William McKinley wearily passed a hand over his eyes. "As you know, Mr. Langden, I have urged that Spain be given every reasonable chance. In response to this, Mr. Roosevelt declared that I have the backbone of an éclair."

The interview was terminated. McKinley bowed them out. Langden insisted that they take the evening train back to New York. His face had a gray pallor; Hope tried to make him comfortable with pillows and a glass of warm milk. "Darling, you must rest. Let's go to the seashore for a few days."

Langden shook his head. "This week, we must face the lions."

"Face the lions?"

"The board of directors of the *Enterprise*, my dear. I have enemies within my own house who wish to see me deposed. I inherited the paper from my father, as you know, but did not inherit complete control. My authority as publisher hinges on but two votes." He sat quietly in his nest of pillows, rocking to the movement of the car. "The directors are displeased with our street sales. Not that we have lost any ground— actually, we've gained a bit of circulation lately—but compared to the successes of Hearst and Pulitzer, the *Enterprise* has taken a terrible beating."

"I'm sorry. I didn't know . . ."

Langden sat quietly for a while. When he spoke again, it was in the manner of a man stepping across an invisible line.

"Hope, I wish you would become involved in the operations of the *Enterprise.*"

"Become involved? In what way?"

"In every way. I'd like for you to begin learning administrative details, the very basics of how a newspaper is put together. You should familiarize yourself with advertising, circulation, printing, reporting, everything. We can begin tomorrow in the boardroom."

A stab of anxiety went through her. "But Howard, I know nothing of a newspaper."

He smiled. "You'll learn, my dear. You'll learn."

"Women are not accepted in such work. There would be resentment."

"I'll match your intelligence with that of any man."

"But why?" She searched the gray face for answers that she dreaded. "Why should it be necessary at all?"

He took her hand. "I won't burden you with maudlin speculation. Suffice it to say that if anything should happen to me, I fear that the *Enterprise* could fall into the wrong hands. I could not tolerate that, Hope. And so I need to train an assistant, so to speak, someone in whom I have implicit faith. I've given it a lot of thought. You are the logical person."

Hope Stewart Langden lay her head upon his shoulder. "I will do anything you say." She loved this man with a depth that astonished her.

But suddenly she was filled with a nameless dread.

The meeting of the board of directors of the New York *Enterprise* took place at noon the following day in the executive suite of the hulking newspaper building on Forty-second Street. The room was totally representative of male occupancy, from its leather chairs and polished woods to the heavy ashtrays and brass spittoons positioned at strategic locations. Dominating all was a life-size oil painting of the founder Earl H. Langden, grandfather of the present publisher. Even two secretaries, serving the dozen directors gathered around the conference table, were male.

"Gentlemen, you all know Mrs. Langden." Heads swiveled; eyes blinked. The presence of a woman, even for the preliminaries of a board meeting, was unheard-of. Hope felt smothered. She smiled lightly and looked into the faces, resisting an impulse to drop her eyes. Howard continued, "I have appointed Mrs. Langden as my executive assistant. Henceforth, she will be privy to all business of the *Enterprise* and attend board meetings in her official capacity . . ."

"This is highly irregular, Langden." The speaker was a thin, pale man of seventy, totally bald and wearing round steel spectacles. His vested black suit was devoid of embellishment, lacking even a pocket handkerchief or gold watchchain. He reminded Hope of a mortician. "We have not been consulted. I'm afraid I must take strong exception to this."

"Your exceptions are duly noted, Mr. Camp." Langden turned to a male secretary. "Please record that the director Manley Burton Camp registers objection. Anyone else?"

"I do."

"And I."

"I'm afraid so, Langden."

"Yes, I object most strenuously."

"It is not done, Langden."

The accord was unanimous. Hope looked to Howard, expecting to see his resolve crumble. It did not. He struck the table lightly with a gavel. "Objections are duly recorded. My decision as chairman stands."

The air seemed to thicken. Hope tried to fix her attention to the dull recital of reports from the treasurer, the secretary, the vice chairman, the chairman of the operations committee. All was steeped in detail, numbers, percentages, management jargon. As things droned on, eyes flicked periodically toward her. The hostility was as heavy as the cigar smoke. In a moment of intense silence, she sneezed into a handkerchief. The sound seemed to ricochet. "Oh, dear," she said.

Two hours crept past. The stern visage of the founder looked down upon their deliberations. Even the damned portrait seemed to stand in silent rebuke. What in God's name was she doing here?

The debate over circulation began quietly enough, an offshoot of a report by the management committee. Manley Burton Camp fixed the publisher with a challenging eye. "I don't mind saying, Howard, that the *Enterprise* is not measuring up in the fight for readers. Hearst and Pulitzer are making us look like schoolboys. Their street sales are overwhelming, compared to ours. I am acutely disappointed. Can't you kick those editors of yours in the butts; get a little excitement into this newspaper?"

"Manley's right, Howard." This was the Director Crandon

Lakehorn, a ponderous man with a walrus mustache. "They're making us look like damn fools."

The debate rapidly caught fire. One by one, the board members expressed dissatisfaction with editorial policies that were causing the *Enterprise* to take such a beating from its rivals. Hope felt the seething undercurrents of male competition and marveled as her husband clung tenaciously to principle, refusing to yield.

"The New York *Enterprise* is dedicated to honest journalism. We are committed to giving the public truth, gentlemen, not cheap sensationalism. I have said this before and I'll say it again: The day this newspaper must play to the crowd for its readership is the day I am no longer publisher..."

And there it was. Howard Langden's control hung by a slender thread. In the face of crisis an unhappy board of directors was subjected to a take-it-or-leave-it mandate. Despite this, he also forced upon them the unwelcome presence of his wife. Hope thought: How can he possibly survive?

It ended in the third hour. Sullenly, the directors gathered up their papers and filed out of the boardroom. Few bothered to even acknowledge Hope. Only Manley Camp offered a frosty smile and a word of parting. "Perhaps we shall meet again, Mrs. Langden. Say, at a garden party or some other more appropriate setting."

She replied with equal coolness. "I intend to be too busy, Mr. Camp, for garden parties."

As he closed the door behind him, Hope fought down an impulse to hurl a spittoon.

The standoff stirred a sensation. In the cubicles and clutter of the *Enterprise*, gossip moved like a flash fire. Hope's arrival in the newsroom the following morning brought ripples of excited comment among reporters and clerks. "Damned if she ain't going through with it." "What a looker! Even more smashing than her pictures!" "It won't last. That dame will be back with her lah-te-dah socialites within a week." "Can you fancy giving up all that lap of leisure for *this*?"

Jack Slade, managing editor, was a tobacco-chewing bear of a man who ruled his domain by growls, grunts, and glares. His displeasure struck terror in the hearts of the most seasoned reporters. He gazed at his newest cub journalist with eyes like marble chips. "So you want to learn the ropes, eh? Just because you're Mrs. Howard Langden, don't look for any favors from me."

"I don't expect any favors, thank you."

"All right, then." He turned in his battered swivel chair and shouted across the unbelievable clutter of the newsroom. "Fat John! Get over here! I'm sendin' this cub to the street beat with you." The summons brought a corpulent, black-haired apparition named Fat John Korpan. His crumpled clothes were spotted with food stains. His bloodshot eyes looked her up and down insolently over the stub of a dead cigar as he grunted a greeting. Slade smiled thinly. "See that she stays outta trouble."

Hope followed Korpan out of the *Enterprise* offices and into Forty-second Street. "Just stick with me, Missy," he said, "and keep your nose clean."

"My name is not Missy. It's Hope."

"Sure, Missy. Look out! Don't step into that pile o'horse shit."

She almost fell down, sidestepping the brown mound. Her escort laughed uproariously.

Hope Stewart would never forget her three weeks in the company of Fat John Korpan. A wild, unruly character, he seemed to know every bartender, thug, policeman, and prostitute in the city of New York. In quest of news, they prowled police precincts, jails, and back alleys, ambled through the squalor of tenement rows and the Tenderloin District, where derby-hatted hoodlums watched their passing with icy eyes. "Them's the dudes," Korpan growled with a jerk of his thumb. "Cut your heart out quick as look at ya." He giggled wetly and wiped his nose on his sleeve.

In the company of Korpan, she covered a murder at a house of prostitution, where young teenage girls stared at her as a police detective examined the body of one of their co-workers, stabbed in the throat by a drunken sailor. It was the first dead body Hope had ever seen. She swallowed down nausea and grimly took notes.

"But prostitution is against the law. Why don't they send them to jail?"

Korpan laughed raucously. "They do, Missy. Every once in awhile a politician gets a burr up his ass and the cops make a roundup of all the whores. They take 'em by wagonloads into court and then to Blackwell's Island."

"Blackwell's Island?"

"Penitentiary. It blows your mind. A lot of them girls is kidnapped into prostitution, see, then hooked on narcotics. They get cut off the dope cold, not even a cigarette. They stand in the cells screamin' and shakin' the bars and cussin' a blue streak. They go bananas."

"And what happens to the men who patronize them?"

"The men? Uh, nothin' happens to the men. They ain't arrested."

"But that's unfair!"

"Life is unfair, Missy. Look around here." They were in a neighborhood of wooden tenements, jammed together on both sides of an alley. The corpse was being loaded into a police morgue wagon. The stench was sickening. Garbage festered in the alley and in dark spaces between the buildings. Open sewage ran in ditches. Children screamed. Adults quarreled in a dozen languages. "You got five hunnerd people packed in a city block. You got young people, old people, starvin' to death without even a crust of bread. You got disease and murder and rape and violence. Life ain't worth a plug nickel down here. It ain't like Fifth Avenue."

They covered a protest demonstration in Union Square. The crowd consisted of men and women with threadbare clothing and pinched faces, bearing the odor of poverty. A husky, handsome man in work clothes harangued them from a makeshift platform. "Men and women, do you know that the state government is your worst enemy? It is a machine that crushes you down in order to sustain the ruling class, your masters. Fifth Avenue is laid in gold, every mansion and townhouse a citadel of money and power. And yet here you stand, a giant public, starved and fettered and shorn of strength. There is strength in union, strength in the strike! I say, demonstrate before the palaces of the rich. Demand bread. If they deny you, take the bread. It is your sacred right!"

The crowd burst into cheers. The handsome speaker looked down upon them with the bearing of a vagabond king. As the crowd broke up, Hope said, "Who *is* that man?"

"Silas Proctor, Missy." Then Korpan gave her a knowing grin. "Labor organizer, when he ain't in jail."

"Is he a criminal, too?"

"Nope. But makin' speeches in some quarters is against the law. Especially when you're tryin' to organize a labor union."

At the end of the third week, Hope Stewart Langden came in off the street and was assigned to a desk to edit copy and write headlines. Already she had had several byline stories in the *Enterprise*, including an account of the prostitute's mur-

134

der in the Tenderloin District. She went home each evening talking incessantly of her experiences.

Hope did not hear the brief exchange between the managing editor Jack Slade and his star reporter Fat John Korpan.

"What d'you think, Fat John? Will she make the grade?"

"Missy'll make the grade. That broad is tough as nails."

Slade spat tobacco juice into a brown-splashed spittoon beside his desk. "Good. Because one of these days, I figure she's gonna be runnin' this goddamned newspaper. And then she'll need all the grit she's got."

A month later, on April 25, Congress declared war on Spain.

And the following day, Fat John Korpan dropped onto Hope's desk an interesting morsel of news, a copy of a message that had been received by the men's clothing firm of Brooks Brothers in New York:

Can you make me so I shall have it by next Saturday a blue cravenet regular lieutenant colonel's uniform without yellow on the collar and with leggings? If so, make it.

It was signed, *Theodore Roosevelt*.

"Bastard," Hope said.

Marten, Fernwythe, and Marten was an old and venerable firm, conducting a variety of businesses from its offices on Market Street in Pittsburgh. The first Marten had been Chauncey's grandfather Melvin, a softgoods wholesaler and founder of the enterprise in 1782. Fernwythe, his unmarried young business partner, had died unexpectedly at the age of thirty-two, run over by a brewery wagon. The second Marten was Melvin's son Robert, a deacon of the Presbyterian Church who had raised his son and sole heir Chauncey in an atmosphere of business conservatism and stern moral rectitude. Chauncey had not been permitted to smoke, go to dances, or keep company with young females until he was twenty-one years of age, at which time it was assumed that he would carry on in the family tradition; that is, conduct business in a conservative way, become a pillar of the church, and marry a respectable girl from a good family who conducted herself properly and did not use rouge or lipstick.

Chauncey was twenty-seven when his father unexpectly contracted typhoid fever and died. He took over the business, which now consisted of wholesale dry goods and hardware. Unlike his father and grandfather, the round-faced young man had certain unconservative characteristics of which neither would have approved. He suffered from deep sexual frustrations, aggravated by severe repression. He also harbored restless material ambitions. While the former was something one endured and attempted to contain, at least here in Pittsburgh, the latter could be achieved by dint of shrewd business dealings and sound connections. The truly wealthy men of Pittsburgh were in iron, steel, coal, and heavy manufacturing. To widen his circle of acquaintances Chauncey joined the newly formed Tuesday Club, which consisted of activists in community and business affairs. It was there that he met Bradley Stewart.

The master of Stewart enterprises had expanded his family business from general freight, land, and river shipping, into ownership of a blast furnace, a steel rolling mill, and several lesser manufacturing interests, including a small but thriving locomotive works. "Picked it up at distress prices, you might say. The previous owners owed us a great deal of money and we simply took in the Spartan plant to help settle the debt." Chauncey, who could function quite well with men of kindred business interests, set out deliberately to cultivate the friendship of Bradley Stewart, an unhappy man whose wife was said to be dying of cancer and who had two sons and a spinster twin sister Colette. Bradley was not aware that the moonfaced Chauncey often visited houses of ill fame and was known in certain quarters of Pittsburgh for his lecherous appetites, including a hidden penchant for homosexuality. In time the two became friends.

Chauncey was a frequent visitor at Stewart House, the hilltop mansion which was one of the landmarks of Pittsburgh. Within a year it was announced that he was engaged to marry Colette Stewart, a handsome woman some years older than he. The wedding was conducted quietly and without fanfare.

For several years Chauncey managed to give up his old ways and live as a dutiful husband. His business burgeoned handsomely. By arrangement with Bradley, he took over the locomotive works and expanded it into the construction of heavy-duty engines. Stewart connections in railroading, a legacy of the famous construction engineer Thaddeus Stewart, brought a heavy backlog of orders as the nation's rail business continued to expand westward.

The marriage to Colette was cordial but lacking in fire. She simply overpowered him in intellect and force of personality. She did not love Chauncey. It was as simple as that. Their wedding night was an embarrassment for both, and they made no further attempts to achieve marital intimacy—although for appearance's sake they shared adjoining bedrooms. As time went on, Chauncey was drawn more and more frequently to certain fleshpots of Pittsburgh, where for a price one's impulse could be indulged and his secrets kept.

He lived in mortal terror of being found out.

Nearly a year had passed since the New York wedding of Hope and Howard Langden. Chauncey Marten had forced from his conscious mind the memory of that night in Gonkin's Alley. One did not dwell on the unpleasant or the unseemly, and the few moments of sexual debauchery with Merwina Clive had been both. He felt himself lucky not to have contracted a loathsome disease.

It was an evening in late spring. A heavy mist wafted up from the rivers and mixed with coal smoke to envelop Pittsburgh in heavy fog. At eleven o'clock, slightly tipsy and flushed from exertion, Chauncey emerged from the Silk Stocking, a house of leisure near the Allegheny River. He had parked his horse and enclosed buggy at the alley, where it stood in a mist-shrouded pool of light reflected from a streetlamp. As he unhitched the reins and prepared to climb up, a movement inside the vehicle startled him. A woman leaned forward and said, "Well, well, if it ain't the Swell. How are you feelin', Mr. Marten? Remember me?"

She was thinner than he remembered, her mousy blond hair cut short. She wore a nondescript dark wrapper against the night. Beside her on the seat, he could discern a small bundle. Chauncey quickly removed his foot from the step and backed away. "What are *you* doing here?"

Melwina Clive offered a throaty chuckle. "Now that depends, doesn't it?"

"D-depends?"

"On how much of a gent you are, so to speak. From the moment I first laid eyes on you, Mr. Marten, I took you for a class customer. You see, I pride myself as a judge of people; and I says to myself that evenin'—that heavenly evenin', when we was together at my place—Merwina, this is a gentleman of the first water." She giggled softly. "That's what I said."

137

The bundle on the seat stirred and emitted a soft gurgling sound. Chauncey's eyes widened. "What is that?"

"Oh, that?" She gathered up the bundle in her arms and drew back a fold of blanket. Chauncey could just make out a small bald head and two dark eyes studying him. It was a baby. "Mr. Chauncey Marten," Melwina announced, "meet baby Colette."

"Baby Colette?"

"Your daughter."

"My...daughter!..." He was confused. Perspiration broke out on his face and trickled down his neck. There was a heavy feeling in his chest. "My daughter? There must be some mistake." He wanted to flee. "My daughter?..."

Merwina Clive held the bundle out toward him. She looked down at the tiny wizened face. "Say hello to Daddykins, Colette."

"Colette?"

"A nice touch, don't you think? Colette. It's a fine name for a young woman. It's got class."

"But my wife is... How did you know my wife's name was Colette?"

"Oh, I've got ways. A girl lives by her wits." She put the bundle back on the seat and slid over to make room for him. "Now, then. Where are you going to take us?"

Chauncey was shivering now. He thought he was having a nightmare. He was in his bed and having a nightmare and would wake up very soon. Oh, Lord, please let it be a nightmare.

"You can't be serious," he said. "What kind of an ugly joke is this?"

"It's no joke, Mr. Marten." Her voice was suddenly hard and flat. "You've got yourself a little family now. Colette and me come all the way from New York to this"—she sniffed the smoke-laden air—"this pigsty of a town. Now I expect you to do right by us." She chuckled. "As they say, you pays the price of pleasure."

Moving as if in a dream, he climbed into the buggy, took the reins, and snicked at the horses. They moved out at a steady clip-clop along the cobbled old streets. What would he do now? Where would he go? Chauncey tried to ignore the woman at his side. How in God's name could he have done such a stupid thing? She was not even clean. But that name, Colette, was a diabolically clever stroke, shocking him to the very core. How had she discovered his identity? He almost asked the question aloud when suddenly he remembered. The wallet. He had lost his wallet in New York. She must had taken it from his trouser pocket after they had finished . . .

Merwina seemed to read his thoughts. She reached into her bodice and drew out a fold of leather. "You ought to be more careful with your belongings." She handed him the wallet. He looked at it dully in the glow of a passing streetlamp. He put it into his coat pocket.

What should he do? Take her to the police station? Take her to a hotel? Order her and the baby out of his buggy this minute? The thought of the police—of questions and exposure and scandal—chilled him.

Pittsburgh was a city of transients. Since the days when the western wildness first opened, the restless human tide had flowed through it bound for the great Ohio River and the West. River travel had given way to rail, but still the flow continued. Business establishments in Pittsburgh depended on providing board and lodgings for travelers.

Chauncey took Merwina and Colette to a small hotel, one that he had used on prior occasions. He roused the proprietor and checked them in as "Mr. and Mrs. Jones and Infant." While Merwina stood smirking, he made an elaborate charade explaining her presence in Pittsburgh, none of which the proprietor believed. Merwina complained that she was hungry, and so he took them to a small café for a greasy fish supper. As she wiped her plate clean with a chunk of brown bread, Merwina said quietly, "You'll have to do better than this, Mr. Marten. A lot better . . ." He gave her what cash he had, forty-two dollars and change, and left them promising to return the next day.

The week that followed was sheer torment for Chauncey Marten. There was no one to whom he could turn for help. At home, his mood of preoccupation and despair caused Colette to eye him suspiciously. For a moment he even thought of blurting out the whole thing to her, but then stifled the impulse as sheer madness. Bradley Stewart would kill him. No one could share this. No one could understand it. He must work things out for himself, alone.

At Merwina's insistence, he drew a large amount of cash from the bank—over a thousand dollars—and gave it to her. She bought new clothes for herself and the baby and moved into a much finer hotel downtown. It was a place where Chauncey Marten was well-known as a businessman, and his visits to the woman in room 312 quickly became a topic of whispered speculation among the staff.

"You can't stay here," Chauncey said in despair. "They know me here. You've got to move."

"All in good time, lover. All in good time." Merwina busied herself changing the baby's diapers. "This sure is a far cry from Gonkin's Alley." On the tenth day after Merwina's sudden reappearance in his life, Chauncey Marten made his decision. He walked into a small shop near the riverfront and bought a pistol and ammunition. Carrying it in his pocket, he went to the musty offices of Marten, Fernwythe, and Marten and sat at his desk all afternoon, thinking. While the life of Market Street poured past his window, he considered the irony that a man could live all these years and not have a single close friend with whom to confide at a time like this. Chauncey Marten suddenly realized that it was not really the threat of exposure that made it so hellish—although certainly that was bad enough—it was the fact that nobody, nobody in this entire city in which he had been born and raised, really cared.

At nightfall, he drew out a sheet of note paper and wrote on it the words:

I'm sorry.

He put the note into an envelope, unsigned, and wrote Colette Stewart Marten's name on the outside. Then he went out onto the street and walked for three hours, aimlessly. His walk took him through some of the meanest parts of Pittsburgh. But no one bothered him. No one seemed to see him. No one cared.

Shortly after midnight, he arrived at the riverfront where the Monongahela joins the Allegheny to form the Ohio. Black water lapped sluggishly at the stones at his feet. A smoky fog shrouded the city. He could barely make out the ghostly forms of river vessels and the reflections of running lights.

And then he drew the pistol from his pocket, loaded it with ammunition, put the barrel into his mouth, and pulled the trigger.

The following day, as Pittsburgh reverberated to the suicide of such a prominent citizen—a pillar of the church, the newspapers said, a respected third-generation business-man and devoted husband—the strange woman in room 312 checked out with her baby and boarded a train for New York.

VI

"Forward, *ho!*"

Casey Stewart touched his spurs to the black gelding's flanks. The big horse broke into a trot, instinctively keeping the pace of K Troop. Around him the unit became a jingling mass of horses and sweating cavalrymen riding in the straight-backed manner of disciplined troops. Hoofbeats stirred the ever-active San Antonio dust, quickly enveloping the formation in a brown cloud. He concentrated on the sweaty backs of the men in front of him, each uniformed in a blue tunic and khaki trousers, each wearing his dusty gray campaign hat forward at a rakish tilt. The reviewing stand came into view ahead. It was a crude wooden platform on which the regimental officers were arrayed in stiff formality. He recognized Theodore Roosevelt, stocky and mustachioed in the tan uniform of a lieutenant colonel.

"*Hands . . . salute!*"

Fingers snapped to hat brims. They sat on their saddles rigidly, holding the salutes and reining mounts one-handed. The reviewing officers saluted back, the lieutenant colonel standing in front and squinting in the sunny glare.

"*Front!*

K Troop rode to the end of the long parade ground. The Texas sunshine beat down and wind gusts sent dust devils swiveling along the bare ground. Six weeks of marching feet and thudding hooves had left the field dried and mulched. K Troop followed its yellow guidon in a column and drew up facing the distant reviewing stand to watch the remainder of the regiment come through. A thousand horsemen made a splendid spectacle of flags, polished brass, and accoutrements. Casey Stewart felt a twinge of pride. He was a long way from Panama. And for weeks a fresh excitement had been rising in the encampment of the First U.S. Volunteer Cavalry. Beside him, the tough little broncobuster from Oklahoma Territory, McGinty, spat a discrete stream of tobacco juice. "Cuba, Stewart," he muttered. "We're a'goin' to Cuba!"

When the last horseman passed the stand, fresh commands

keened across the parade ground. The regiment moved again, this time forming a solid mass in front of the lieutenant colonel. Horses stamped and blew; harnesses creaked. Sun-blasted faces streamed sweat. Casey sat on his black gelding conscious of the close odors of men, chewing tobacco, and horseflesh. The high-pitched voice of Lieutenant Colonel Roosevelt carried with astonishing clarity over the mass.

"Rough Riders! You have come through your training in bully fashion. In a few short weeks, you have developed from a thousand highly resourceful individuals into a formidable force ready to do battle. We shall test our mettle against the foe with great fighting spirit!" It was the vice commander's typical speech, larded with expletives and zeal. Casey thought: Does the man never run down? Their mission, Roosevelt said, was to free the suffering Cuban nation and also to expand American enlightenment into the southern part of the hemisphere. "It is fitting that the Rough Riders should lead the way, for this regiment is unique in the history of warfare. You men bring together a combined experience unequaled anywhere on earth. You are a mixture of warriors and sportsmen. Some of you have fought the fierce Apache, served as peace officers, sailed around the Horn, and mined the gold fields. Many have achieved excellence in the college classroom or on the playing grounds. I am proud of every man jack of you . . ."

Roosevelt paused for effect. Satisfied that every eye was upon him, he took a step forward, mopped his face with a red bandanna, drew the familiar black-ribboned pince-nez from his breast pocket, and clamped it to his nose to scrutinize them.

"But it is not going to be easy." His voice became more subdued. In the rear ranks, men leaned forward in their saddles to hear. "As Colonel Wood and I have told you from the beginning, it'll be hard work, rough fare, and the possibili-ty of death. Some of us will not come back alive." In remembering the scene later, men would insist that Roosevelt's gaze flicked to Allyn Capron, the tall, yellow-haired horse soldier commanding one of the companies from the Indian Territory, and to Hamilton Fish, the burly former collegiate rower from New York who had just been promoted to ser-geant. "But I expect every man to do his duty."

As he stepped back, smiling, the Rough Riders burst into cheers.

They broke ranks, disintegrating into a wild, yelping gallop back to the tenting area. Orders barked across the afternoon;

horses were unsaddled, watered, rubbed down, and herded into troop corrals. Tents were struck, baggage packed. The bugler sounded chow call, setting off a dash for the steaming soup kettles and stew pots. Mess pans rattling, the men formed lines and took their food.

"We're going, Stewart. We're really going."

Big Hamilton Fish eased his muscular bulk down to share Casey's seat on a flat boulder near the horse troughs. Around them, men bent intently to the business of eating beans and fried pork, sopping up the juices with torn chunks of brown bread. Teddy Gilmore, a former gambler and cardsharper, ate with noisy gusto. Squatting in the dust beside him were McGinty, the broncobuster, and Delvin Baker. The latter was a pale, bespectacled former high school teacher from Pittsburgh who professed to be, at heart, a pacifist.

"McGinty, I hear we might go as infantry." Gilmore spoke excitedly between mouthfuls. "If you ain't got no horse, how are you gonna manage with them little bandy legs?"

Another soldier snickered. "McGinty never walked more'n a hundred yards in his life."

The diminutive Oklahoman, perennially a butt of humor, wiped his mess plate clean with the last of his bread. "I'll manage; just don't you fellers worry none." With delicate flourish, he popped the bread into his mouth, licked his fingers, and belched. "Ole McGinty ain't going to be left behind."

Casey congratulated Hamilton Fish on his promotion to sergeant.

Fish smiled gently. "I don't feel qualified, not with this sort of men around me. Many of these fellows would be officers in any other command. You're a good example, Stewart. Why didn't you put in for a commission?"

"I'm an engineer, not a cavalry leader." Casey chewed thoughtfully. "Besides, I'm not sure I'd be up to the responsibility of command. Roosevelt himself didn't accept it because he lacked experience. So Leonard Wood is the colonel and T.R. is the lieutenant colonel."

Fish chuckled. "I'll grant you one thing. Teddy Roosevelt will be right up front, especially if there's a newspaper correspondent around. He's a glory-hunter. He wants to be President someday, and I wouldn't be at all surprised to see him make it."

Casey put down his fork and looked across the campground to the regimental commander's mess table, where Roosevelt was holding forth in the company of Colonel Wood and several civilian visitors. "Neither would I," he said.

Packing and loading the trains was grueling work. They had to deal with twelve hundred animals, including a hundred fifty pack mules. Casey and McGinty drew mule duty and labored half the night cursing and prodding the brutes into boxcars. "Ain't nothing more stubborn on earth," brooded McGinty, "than an Army mule." They marked and stowed duffel, stacked wooden ammunition boxes for the Krag-Jorgensen carbines, and filled whole cars with horsefodder. As dawn streaked the sky over the town of San Antonio, Casey flexed muscles that were stiff and sore. In the distance he could see the silhouetted roofline of the Alamo. Captain Allyn Capron joined him and offered a plug of chewing tobacco. Casey sliced off a chunk with his bowie knife and studied the old fortress. "What d'you suppose it is, Captain, that inspires men to die for nothing more tangible than an idea? You're fifth-generation Army. You ought to know."

Capron spat into the dust. "Darned if I can answer that, Stewart. I doubt if anybody really knows. The hell of it is, brave men perish on both sides of a fight. The rightness or wrongness of the cause doesn't seem to have a whole lot to do with it. Men get their blood up, that's all. I've seen a lone Apache ride straight into a hornet's nest of rifle fire waving nothin' but a spear."

"Do you think those men in the Alamo figured they were dying for Texas independence?"

"Frankly, no. They were Tennesseans, mostly—Crockett and that bunch—and I doubt if they had any high-flown notions about Texas. That makes for inspirational readin' in the history books, but it ain't necessarily so. They probably weren't much different from us Rough Riders. None of our men have ever been to Cuba. Some of 'em never saw a body of water bigger than the Pecos River in flood. They don't even know who the President of the United States is, much less understand foreign affairs. They couldn't tell you where to find Cuba on a map. These fellows are in it for the adventure. But when it comes to fightin', they'll do well enough. Territorial men have been fightin' all their lives."

At dusk the troops took their final rations and marched in long, dusty files to the train, ancient wooden coaches with hard seats and filthy floors. Kerosene lamps, slung from overhead racks, emitted sooty fumes. At last, around midnight, Casey felt his coach lurch forward. The aged locomotive spun its wheels with a spasm of chuffing, gushed steam, and labored into the night. As they gathered speed, he peered out at the drab moonlit landscape of Texas. He was heading again into the unknown.

Before drifting off to sleep, he thought of Lollie.

It was four days' travel to Tampa, Florida, port of embarkation for the Cuban expeditionary force. The train rattled out of Texas and across Louisiana, Mississippi, Alabama, and into Georgia. In towns and crossroads settlements, clots of humanity gathered beside the track to wave at the passing troops. There were stops to take on water and fuel and feed the animals. Cheering townsfolk gathered around the soldiers; pretty young girls offered flowers, fruits, watermelon, and buckets of milk. Roosevelt was in his element, making fiery war speeches from station platforms, shaking hands, kissing babies. Delvin Baker shook his head in amazement. "If I didn't know better, I'd swear he was on an election campaign." And then the train rolled on, bearing its cargo of womenless men remembering wistfully these brief brushes with paradise.

Tampa was a sprawl of sun-drenched sandy flats studded with pine trees and anchored to a natural bay at the terminus of a one-track railroad. The troops shuffled off the train under a barrage of commands from sergeants and lieutenants. Hamilton Fish squinted into the glare and said, "I don't believe it."

Casey nodded wordlessly. It was a scene of mass confusion. Lieutenant Colonel Roosevelt stalked up and down, furiously slapping his boot with a riding crop. "This is unconscionable, absolutely unconscionable." No one met the regiment. There were no bivouac instructions, no arrangements for food. Tenting areas and parade grounds spread as far as the eye could see, all in ankle-deep sand. The only orders were delivered by a trainman: "This is where you unload." The troops milled about in the heat while Roosevelt called a meeting of officers. It ended with lieutenants and captains riding back to their units, looking resolute.

"Unload. And then wait."

So they unloaded. They waited. And while they waited, the resourceful Roosevelt ordered Captain Capron to hand-pick a squad for special duty. Casey and Sergeant Fish were selected for the squad. As afternoon waned and a blood-red sun settled over copses of pine and live oak, the detail commandeered another division's wagon train at gunpoint and brought it back to the railhead. The Rough Riders cheered.

The days went by in heat and work details and drills. Water was bad, the food miserable, supply chaotic. In the off-hours, Casey and Delvin Baker took long walks to look around the town. Here, the war was almost a comic opera.

Tampa was ill suited to be transformed suddenly into a military cantonment. Aside from its derelict houses, the one notable feature of the place was a single huge hotel built of brick in the Arabian nights style complete with silver minarets, ornamental brickwork, vast piazzas equipped with rocking chairs, and spacious lobbies featuring marbled stairways, columns, statuary, and potted palms. The structure was the brainchild of railroad magnate Morton F. Plant, who now added to the hubbub by running tourist excursion trains in from Jacksonville to gawk at the Cuban invasion force.

Finally, after six weeks, sail they did. But not in the manner they had anticipated. First came the order to leave the horses behind. McGinty expressed the cavalry's outrage. "My gawd, Stewart. How're we goin' to fight without horses?"

Then came the order to sharply reduce the manpower of the invasion force. The Rough Riders were to be trimmed from a thousand men to five hundred sixty. Roosevelt, flushed with anger, stalked to the division command post and lodged a noisy protest. The orders stood. And so on the eighth of June, after a wild night of false starts, the vice commander led his depleted force into a pier at the Port of Tampa to board the rusty coastal freighter *Yucatán*. Orders from Washington then stayed the sailing of the fleet. For a week, thirty-two crowded transports swung at anchor while sweating troops whiled away the days at deck drill in the manual of arms.

Finally the anchors were weighed. Flags flying, bands playing, and decks black with cheering troops, the convoy steamed out of harbor.

The transports moved through sapphire seas, shepherded by an escort of gray gunboats and destroyers. The latter dashed about like terriers, raising bow spray and plumes of black smoke. On the evening of the fourth day, Casey Stewart stood at the railing studying the flat calm of the Caribbean while the first stars dusted a darkening sky. Trooper Gilmore joined him, offered a chew of cut plug, and stared at the horizon toward Cuba.

"What do you reckon's waitin' fer us out there, Stewart?"

The question also nagged at Casey's mind. "It's anybody's guess, Gilmore. I don't even think the commanders know."

They lapsed into silence, feeling the warm air against their faces. Gilmore spat into the dark ocean. "Stewart, did you ever have a premonition that you were goin' to die?"

Casey shrugged. "I'm sure the notion crosses everybody's mind. But I can't say that I've had any strong feelings about it. The way my life's gone these past few years, it wouldn't matter much one way or the other. Why do you ask?"

Gilmore was silent again. For the first time, Casey was struck by the westerner's youth. He could not have been more than twenty-three. Gilmore pushed back from the railing. "I just wondered, that's all." He turned and walked away.

Casey felt a sense of onrushing events.

The guns of the heavy cruiser spoke again, spouting smoke and flame in the crisp morning light. Shells fluttered overhead and descended onto the distant shore, and burst like black mushrooms at the base of the green hills. Beyond rose the serene peaks of the Sierra Maestra, majestically disdaining the petty skirmishes of mortals.

Captain Allyn Capron, surrounded by noncommissioned officers and troopers who would make up the first landing party, bent over a map. Casey, McGinty, Baker, and Gilmore were included in the group.

"Our maps ain't the best, but we know that this here is the town of Daiquirí." Capron's blunt finger jabbed at a spot on the map. "The Cubans tell us there's a broken-down pier and some fishing shacks, a railway, and an abandoned ironworks. Our ultimate destination is Santiago"—the finger swept across the map—"over here. The Spaniards are said to have a garrison of twelve thousand troops in Santiago. The city is surrounded by trenches protected by barbed wire. We've got a hard march ahead. From Daiquirí we take this wagon road westward through the jungle along the beach to Siboney. At Siboney, here"—the finger traced the route—"we turn inland, pass over this gap, and into rollin' hill country. The ground between Siboney and Santiago is cut by the San Juan River, which winds back and forth across the wagon road. The land is interspersed with jungles, thickets, and broad savannas. The Spaniards have got a great field of fire..." The captain paused, stuffed tobacco into a handsome briar pipe, lit it, and blew smoke into the sea breeze. "We go in on the boats as soon as the guns finish their work. I want every man's rifle loaded and bayonet fixed. Understood?"

The guns pounded the coastline for another quarter of an hour, setting a few fires in the village. Stomach churning, Casey found himself crouched down in one of a line of lifeboats loaded with soldiers. They were being towed by a motor launch through overhanging smoke toward the beach. Little McGinty knelt beside him, holding his rifle in a white-knuckled grip.

"Do you think them Spaniards will give us a hot reception, Stewart?"

Casey fought down nausea. "I wouldn't be at all surprised, McGinty."

Gusts of sea breeze tore away the smoke like a ragged curtain. Beyond the town, Casey saw a line of armed men climbing the steep hillside. They wore tan uniforms and wide-brimmed straw hats. The smoke returned, blotting the men from sight. The boats pitched in heavy surf as they approached the ruined dock. Casey's boat managed to unload, and then he was running clumsily under the weight of equipment toward a burned-out shack. Troopers fired their weapons into the village but received no answering shots. Behind them, men began to shout and Casey turned to see two boats capsize in the surf. Soldiers thrashed in the water and several sank from sight.

A lieutenant went running back to the beach past Casey, shouting, "Jesus Christ!"

There was no fight at Daiquirí. The smoke blew away. A detail ran up the stars and stripes on the village flagpole. From the transports, pack horses and mules were pushed overboard to swim to shore. The Rough Riders mustered on the sandy beach in midday heat. Casey adjusted his blanket roll, the heavy Krag-Jorgensen carbine, ammunition pouches, pistol, rubber poncho, and haversack. Captain Capron emerged from the mass of sweating troops. "Stewart, we lost a corporal in the surf. I want you to be actin' corporal."

He nodded and swallowed hard. "Very well, sir."

"There'll be no more unloading of transports at Daiquirí. It's too rough. The convoy will move to Siboney. We're the rear guard, protectin' the landin' force from an attack up this road."

Casey peered toward the head of the column. He saw Lieutenant Colonel Roosevelt mount his horse Texas, and move out onto the wagon road. "Does that mean, sir, that we might not see action at all?"

Capron smiled thinly. "Not if the colonel's got any say-so."

They moved along the road for about a mile and then took positions at the edge of the jungle. Roosevelt chafed from inactivity, riding up and down on his nervous horse. The hours dragged into afternoon, with frequent meetings of the officers. Gnats and sandflies tormented the troops.

"Who is the little general talking to Roosevelt?"

"That's Fightin' Joe Wheeler, late of the Confederate cavalry. He's as feisty a devil as they come."

"I heard him say we was goin' to be in a fight. He'd see to it personally. He wants the Rough Riders up front."

"So does the lieutenant colonel."

"Dollar to a dime says we won't stay long in rear guard."

"Them ain't no odds."

Evening came. Again the officers met. At nightfall orders passed down the line. "Prepare for forced march!"

"I told you so."

"Now, boys, we'll play like we're dog-faced infantry."

Within half an hour they were on the march beneath a rising tropic moon. Belts creaked, mess pans clanked, and blanket rolls glistened in the silvery light.

"Where the hell are we going, Corporal Stewart?"

"To Siboney, Gilmore. And keep your rifle dry."

It was a punishing pace. Hourly ten-minute breaks did nothing to relieve aching feet and throbbing muscles. Never had Casey driven his body to such extremes of effort, not even on the long mounted patrols out of San Antonio. The men sweated and slapped mosquitoes and cursed.

Siboney was a clutch of run-down houses facing the beach. As the regiment arrived, other troops of the expeditionary force were noisily unloading by floodlight from the transports. The exhausted Rough Riders stumbled into a coconut grove. "Colonel Roosevelt says to spread your ponchos and get some rest." Laying their bodies down, they fell into fitful slumber amid scuttling land crabs. Above them brooded the dark ridges of a hostile land.

Before dawn, thunder rolled over the ridges and a rainstorm broke.

Sergeant Hamilton Fish shook Casey awake. "On your feet, Stewart."

Casey rolled free of his soggy blanket, every muscle protesting. "Fish, what time is it?"

"Time to stir the troops. We'll breakfast and move out. The First and Tenth squadrons are already gone. General Wheeler reconnoitered last night and found the Spaniards' positions. They're dug in a few miles inland."

The Rough Riders awoke reluctantly, musclesore, wet, and cold. Casey prodded his grumbling squad to the cookfires. They wolfed down black coffee and fried pork, and then broke camp. Wet blankets and ponchos were difficult to roll.

The soldiers were led by a tall officer with the rugged leanness of an outdoorsman. He approached Casey and smiled. "Corporal, I'm Captain Gorgas. Where is your commanding officer?"

Casey nodded toward the east. "Already moved out, Captain. The sergeant is over there."

"Thank you." Gorgas went to Sergeant Fish, spoke briefly, and then rejoined his own men.

"What was that about?" Casey asked a short time later.

"Medical detail. They're setting up a yellow fever clinic here at Siboney. He wanted to know when we would be moving out."

Involuntarily Casey shivered. "They're expecting a lot of sickness?"

"It looks like that," Fish said.

By six o'clock the ranks were ready to march. Sergeant Fish moved ahead with four troopers, taking the regiment's point. Casey was summoned to join the headquarters group on the rutted dirt road.

Theodore Roosevelt sat on his horse, scanning the terrain ahead with field glasses. Captain Allyn Capron nodded to Casey. "You'll join the lead party, Stewart. Lieutenant Oker is in command with twenty men behind the point. His sergeant is sick. You're his replacement."

Casey moved ahead, aware of the unwelcome stares of men whom he barely knew by sight, much less by name. An army consisted of small pockets of comrades, cool to strange corporals. Midway along the line he encountered Gilmore. The familiar face put him more at ease. Lieutenant Oker, a tall, saturnine backwoodsman from Kentucky, acknowledged Casey's presence by spitting a stream of tobacco juice.

Captain Capron shouted, "Move 'em out!"

They advanced in single file along a narrowing wagon road bordered by heavy undergrowth. Birds shrieked overhead. Sunlight filtered down in dappled shade. After an hour's march, every man's shirt was sopped with sweat. Dense jungle made it impossible to put out flank guards.

The road cut northward up a broad valley. A trail forked off to the right, climbing a ridgeline along the western crest. The Cuban guide swung off onto this trail, paralleling the main route. They took a ten-minute break, and Capron explained to the sergeants and corporals that the two advance squadrons of Regular Army troopers had continued on along the wagon road. They were nearing a point on the map called Las Guásimas. "If you hear movement down there, don't start shooting. You might hit our own men." The big westerner paused, scanning their faces. "And one other thing: If we go into attack, no man stops to help the wounded. Them's orders from on high." He took a swig from his canteen, capped it, and stood up. "Time to march again."

Casey's blanket roll, overcoat, and pack grew heavier. Other men began to cast off such burdens and soon the line of march was littered with the droppings of an army on the move. Sergeant Fish fell back to join Casey briefly. The big New Yorker eyed the discarded litter with disapproval. "Men won't carry what they think they can do without." He shared a chew of Casey's tobacco and moved into the lead once more, disappearing around a bend in the trail.

Casey did not recognize the gunfire at first. From the valley it sounded like distant fireworks. "The Regulars have run into trouble," muttered an older trooper. "That's Fightin' Joe's men. Sounds like he's deployin' them into in a skirmish line."

Something rustled in the leaves over their heads. The sound went *whit-whit-whit*. Several men dove for cover. "Mausers!"

"On your feet," Casey snapped.

From behind, he heard advancing horses. Colonels Wood and Roosevelt rode into view, followed by Captain Capron. The officers dismounted and Leonard Wood began shouting commands. "Form a skirmish line here. You men, get into a skirmish line right and left!" The orders sent troopers plunging off the trail into the jungle. Casey heard his name called. "You go forward, Stewart," said Captain Capron. "Find Sergeant Fish. We've got to determine where that fire is coming from. I'll be right behind you."

Casey's stomach tightened. Clutching his carbine, he moved forward at a trot. The whisper of Mauser bullets was closer now, lower down in the trees. *Whit-whit-whit*. Two men fell heavily in front of him. He bent over a very young trooper lying partially on his back, a hole gaping obscenely in the boy's forehead as his brown eyes were locked open. Casey's voice rasped, "Jesus." He went ahead, taking a bend in the trail and descending slightly. There was a sharp odor of gunsmoke. More men lay about, hit. A voice cried, "Help me. Help me." Wounded men removed their shirts to press field dressings to torn flesh. Their skin gleamed whitely in the jungle light.

He almost fell over Hamilton Fish. The big sergeant lay in the trail at the very point of the regiment, shot through the heart. Casey wanted to vomit. He picked up Fish's carbine, the barrel still hot to the touch. From behind him a voice said, "Get down, Stewart!" He ducked as a fresh fusillade of gunfire rattled from a hillside thicket on the other side of a ravine. Bullets raked the leaves and thudded into the ground. He lay still, heart hammering, sheltered by the body of his dead friend. The firing subsided and he lifted his head cautiously, trying to see through the heavy growth. Nothing. At his feet the green jungle sloped away and the tangle was impenetrable. Crouching, he moved back toward the voice that had warned him. He found Captain Capron, lying in a weedpatch.

"Captain, what happened? Are you hit?"

The lean face was the color of chalk. With one hand, Capron clutched at a spreading crimson splotch in his abdomen. "Report back to Colonel Roosevelt. Tell him we're shot up bad. Can't get a fix on the Spaniards. Get some troops up here."

He tried to comfort the troop commander. Capron groaned and fell back. "Don't . . . stop for . . . the wounded . . ."

Casey crawled rapidly back down the trail.

A fly buzzed somewhere. Voices murmured in the near jungle.

"Where's them shots coming from?"

"Can't tell. Don't see nothin'."

"Over there. They're over beyond the draw."

Casey found Roosevelt at a temporary command post fifty yards back from where Capron had fallen. The lieutenant colonel was on foot now. More wounded men sprawled in the jungle and along the trail. The air was hot, damp, electric. The deputy commander took his report without speaking, squinted up the trail, and drew a revolver. "Very well," Roosevelt said. "Let's move out." His voice called into the woods, thin and clear. "On your feet, Rough Riders! Move out!" And then they were charging pell-mell up the rise, yelling like banshees and firing into the trees. The Krag-Jorgensens had a deep, flat report. Answering Mauser bullets clipped and whined about them, filling the air like killer bees. Casey noticed that several of the civilian correspondents followed on Roosevelt's heels, charging unarmed. A spurt of dirt at his feet gave him an extra burst of speed.

All was confusion. The Mauser fire intensified. In midstride, men jerked and fell, ugly wounds opening in faces and bodies. The attackers broke into the clear on a brow of land and hesitated, breathing hard. Richard Harding Davis studied an opposite slope through binoculars. "There they are, Colonel. Over there!" Casey brought up his Krag-Jorgensen and squeezed off shots into a clump of thicket, the stock slamming against his shoulder. A tan shape tumbled from the underbrush. "Good shooting, Stewart!" And then they were charging again, a howling mass thundering down one slope and up another, firing as they went.

The Spaniards broke cover and fled up the slope. Carbines barked frantically. Several Spaniards fell before the main body vanished over the hill.

As suddenly as it had begun, it was ended. Gunsmoke hung in the fetid air. A heavy quiet descended over the battleground, broken by the moans of injured men. A terrible weariness poured over Casey and his brain seemed to cease functioning. A squad climbed the hill and formed a defense line at the top, overlooking a broad savanna that rolled away toward the north. Lieutenant Oker put Casey in charge of a detail to bring up ammunition from the rear. He took Delvin Baker with him. The schoolmaster was even more white-faced than usual. Retracing their steps along the trail, they found the body of Captain Capron, still clutching his abdominal wound. A few yards beyond lay Trooper Gilmore, shirtless in the sunshine. A vulture descended from a gumbo-limbo tree and perched on the body. The bird plucked at Gilmore's open blue eyes. With a curse, Casey drove the bird away.

That evening, by order of Lieutenant Oker, Casey Stewart was promoted to sergeant.

They buried the dead in a common grave.

"Yeeee haw!"

The guns came up at the rush, the horses straining under the whipcracks of mounted artillerymen. Iron-shod wheels of the gun carriages rumbled heavily on the muddy slope. Marching troops gave way, cursing. "Move, there!" bawled a lieutenant on horseback. "Clear the road!" The big horses thundered past, slapping leather and flinging sweat.

"Damned gunners," muttered a trooper. "Think they own the road."

"You'll be glad we've got 'em, up ahead," another man said. "Ain't that right, Sergeant Stewart?"

Casey's attention was distracted by a high, fluttering sound. "Down!" he shouted. The troopers dove for cover as the Spanish shell exploded above the road, raining fragments. The burst was followed by two more in quick succession. Ahead, one of the artillery horses screamed and went down in a tangle of harness, its hindquarters shot away. The artillery lieutenant swayed in his saddle and fell into the road.

"Chaos," Lieutenant Oker grumbled. "Bloody chaos."

The Fifth Corps was a shambles of ten thousand troops on the road to Santiago. They had advanced less than three miles through a broad rolling valley cut by the twisting San Juan River. In years to come, Casey would remember the march as an unending series of discomforts: broiling heat, suffering troops, the ugly crack of enemy fire, torrential rains, the chaotic lack of organization. The mass of troops slogged forward, alternately sweating and chilling. Those who had discarded their blankets and coats paid dearly now, sleeping miserably on the open ground. Life had lost all semblance of order. All they knew was that the Spaniards held a series of heights called San Juan Hill, protecting the town of Santiago, and somehow they must take it.

On the fateful morning of July 1, Casey awoke in a field of rising mists. As the sun rose, hordes of infantry and dismounted cavalry struggled under fire through a bottleneck river crossing, hemmed in by jungle. Hundreds fell under fire. But at last the terrain opened onto a series of broad, grassy fields ascending six hundred yards to the fortifications protecting Santiago. Casey shaded his eyes from the glare and made out a white line of entrenchments at the top, dominated by a dun-colored fort.

"That," muttered Delvin Blake at his side, "is San Juan Hill."

More horse-drawn artillery splashed through the ford and swung away onto distant slopes. Within half an hour they were in position and had opened fire, each burst marked by billowing smoke. Spanish guns replied from the heights, quickly finding the range. As answering shells burst onto the batteries, the Americans quickly harnessed up surviving horse teams and withdrew.

Mauser bullets whipped the high grass. Casey's throat tightened with tension and thirst. The troops were bunched up and milling aimlessly, Rough Riders mixed in with regular infantry and National Guard units. An entire regiment of New York troops, many of whom had never fired their rifles, simply lay down and refused to move. The result was a jostling, struggling mass. Men were falling everywhere, their wounds gushing bright scarlet.

"We can't stay here!" Casey heard himself shouting. "You men, let's move! Get forward onto the slopes. Rough Riders, follow me!" Gripping their carbines, they strode forward through knee-deep grass, aware of the deadly bursts peppering the earth around them. Casey spotted a broad depression in the ground, forming a brow in the hill. He headed for it, and thus brought the troops—some three hundred strong—to temporary shelter from the withering gunfire.

A major joined them, breathing hard. "Sergeant, who the hell do you think you are, moving these troops without orders?"

"Stewart, sir. Headquarters detachment, Rough Riders."

The major, a florid-faced National Guardsman, spat into the grass. He had been drinking. "Roosevelt's bunch, eh? Grandstanders. Well, no pissant of a sergeant is taking over my troops. I'm putting you on report."

"Yes, sir."

The major crawled away to a rock outcropping and took a long pull at his canteen. He stood up as if to issue a command. Casey started to call out a warning, but was too late. The top of the officer's head exploded and fell facedown in the grass.

"Best shot the Spaniards have got off all day," a private muttered.

"Well, we've come this far. What next, Sergeant?"

Casey did not offer a reply. He wished that he knew. They were cut off from officers and command, at least temporarily. The sun climbed higher and the heat intensified. Canteens ran dry and thirst tortured the men. An officer came bounding up the slope and tumbled into the depression. It was Lieutenant Oker. The lanky Kentuckian wrung Casey's hand. "Damn fine thing you did back there, Stewart." He offered a chew of tobacco, which was accepted gratefully.

"What's the situation, Lieutenant?"

155

"As best I can tell, our main body of Rough Riders is over there on the right with Colonel Roosevelt," Oker replied. "It's called Kettle Hill. Down there"—he waved toward the ford and the road—"things are still a mess, with troops coming up and trying to fan out into skirmish lines. This is the goddamndest situation I've ever seen. Wherever we try to move, the Garlics have got us in their sights. We ain't got enough ammo or hospital attendants for the wounded, and no ambulance wagons." Oker studied Casey's face. "What do you think?"

"I think we ought to get an attack going, and the sooner the better. We can't stay here and be picked off piecemeal. They'll have the artillery on us next thing you know." He thought of Ham Fish, dead on the trail six days ago. "I'd rather die on my feet than on my butt."

Oker grinned. "All right, then. Let's do it."

Casey lifted his voice and briefly addressed the men. He and Lieutenant Oker intended to lead them up the slope, all the way to the Spanish positions. He searched the faces and found Delvin Baker's. One lens of the schoolmaster's glasses was shattered and he stared back at Casey without seeming to recognize him. "This is strictly a volunteer effort," he said. "Nobody is forced to go. I don't have the authority to give such orders." The weary faces offered no response. He told them to check their ammunition, fix bayonets, and share what they had, starting with water. Then he turned away from them, resolved to do what he had to do.

His stomach contracted with nervous tension. He smiled grimly. Who would have imagined the drunken Casey Stewart, staggering out of a Colón whorehouse, someday getting himself into a fix like this?

He turned to Lieutenant Oker. "Ready?"

"Ready."

"Here we go."

He got to his feet and began to climb; the slope was endless, and steepening. Bullets whispered in the grass, singing their deadly refrain, *whit-whit-whit*. Behind him every man rose to his feet, but many quickly fell as Spanish fire ripped into their ranks. Casey's boots seemed made of lead, his hip joints frozen. He fired the carbine from the waist, aiming at the ugly white scar crowning the hill and shouting, "We're coming, you sons of bitches!"

From nearby Kettle Hill, Colonel Theodore Roosevelt,

dismounted and under fire, lifted his binoculars and trained them on the main slope. "Those men are attacking. Bully! What a bully show!" He drew his revolver and waved to his Rough Riders. "Let's go. Follow me!"

San Juan Hill steepened just beneath the gunpits, giving Casey Stewart's force another short space of cover from the dreaded Mausers. Every muscle of his body shrieked from the effort; his breath came in wheezing gasps. The fury of battle engulfed his consciousness. But there was no stopping now. If they stopped they would never make it. Fifty yards, he told himself. Another fifty yards to the gunpits. He threw a glance over his shoulder. The ragged line of blue weaved and stumbled. Farther behind, the panorama opened like a vast grassy bowl swarming with advancing troops, the most distant reduced to the size of ants. Bayonets flashed; shellfire burst among the tiny figures like terrible mushrooms; rifle volleys had the sound of tearing cloth.

A hot blast threw him off his feet. Chunks of raw earth rained down. He rolled to his knees. Several men had been hit and the hillside erupted in smoke and flame and flying metal. How could the Spanish guns hit them at such close range? Wounded men were screaming. Abruptly a sickening realization came to him. Casey turned his head and looked into the valley behind him. American artillerymen were toiling at a battery on a distant slope, each firing marked by a gush of smoke. They were being hit by their own guns! Farther down the slope, an officer on horseback was galloping madly toward the guns to warn them. But another blob of smoke gushed from the battery and Casey buried his face into the earth. The explosion hit above him and to the right.

The cannonade ceased. Loose clods of dirt trickled down the slope. Men stirred, checking their bodies for wounds. There were shrieks and groans. Casey closed his mind to the new sounds. He rolled over and retrieved the carbine. Without a backward glance he moved slowly again toward the summit. Abruptly he stopped, turned back to the others, shook the carbine over his head, and shouted, "Come on, you bastards! Let's go!" And then he whirled around and started running.

The charge carried him over the brow of the hill. Before him, dun-colored figures were still emerging from the gunpits and bounding toward the rear. They were retreating. The

Garlics were retreating! His boots left the grass and crunched onto bare earth. He lowered the carbine to bayonet level, trampled down a line of barbed wire, and vaulted the parapet. He looked down into the startled face of a Spanish officer. The officer raised a pistol. The muzzle of the weapon coughed once, twice. Something bit at the side of Casey's face. He plunged down, following the bayonet, and drove the blade into the man's chest. From the throat of Casey Stewart there came a bellow of animal rage.

They poured into the trench behind him, left and right. Blue-clad attackers mixed with the remaining defenders in a fury of thuds, screams, and shots. In the suffocating dust and heat, they fought with fists, knives, and rifle butts.

And then it was quiet again, rifle shots popping after the retreating troops. They climbed out of gunpits littered with bodies. Casey stumbled through the glare, dimly aware of men in dusty blue crowding around him shouting in exultation and slapping him on the back.

"You did it, Stewart!" Lieutenant Oker emerged through shimmering heat waves, reaching for his hand. "Goddamnit, that was magnificent!" Casey shouldered past him, blood trickling from where the bullet had creased his face, and walked a few paces back down the grassy slope. He still carried the carbine, its stubby bayonet streaked with red.

He found Delvin Blake lying beside a small crater where the last shell had landed. The schoolmaster was on his back, looking up at the blue sky. His shattered glasses gleamed in the grass nearby. His breathing was shallow and his skin the texture of white putty. Both legs were blown off at the hips.

"Casey, is that you?" Blake whispered.

"Yes, Delvin." He knelt beside the shattered body. "It's me."

"What a beautiful sky. Just look up there. How blue. And the clouds, they're coasting like gigantic blobs of cotton. We never had a sky like that in Pittsburgh. Look, Casey. Isn't that beautiful?"

He looked. "Yes. Yes, it's beautiful."

When he turned back to the stricken man, the breathing had stopped. He felt numb and hollow inside. A middle-aged newspaper correspondent came trudging up, notebook in hand, spied Casey, and quickened his step. "Were you in the fight, Sergeant?" The man's eyes glittered, greedy for verbal scraps from the carnage. A pencil poised over the notebook, ready to strike. "Tell me what it was like!" the correspondent said.

Casey glared at the thin face. It was bastards like these who had started this senseless business in the first place. Delvin Blake had been right all along.

"Go to hell, he said, and walked away.

The war news was dreadful. Hope worried about Casey and wrote to him often. She was elated by the news of his heroism on San Juan Hill and hoped it would mark a quick end to the campaign. But then her spirits sagged as the stalemate in Cuba wore into August and troops began to sicken and die of malaria and yellow fever. The impact of war on Howard Langden was even more profound. "Cuba, the Philippines, this whole thing is ludicrous," he chafed. "And now the expansionists are dominating everything coming out of Congress. They seem compelled to turn America into a world power."

"Your problem, Howard," said an old friend at a dinner party, "is that you are an isolationist."

"An *isolationist*?" he snorted. "I'm not even familiar with the term."

The anticipated showdown over control of the *Enterprise* did not materialize. Howard's health improved somewhat, but not decisively. He was tired. His doctor recommended a month's rest on the beach at Newport or at Saratoga Springs for the mineral water.

"The man's insane," Howard grumbled. "I can't leave New York now. There is too much happening, too much at stake."

Hope's career intensified. She spent her days in the various business departments of the *Enterprise*, immersed in details of circulation, advertising, accounting, and payroll. At night she toted home textbooks on business procedures and read them in bed until long after midnight. By six in the morning she was on her way back to the office in a chauffeur-driven electric car.

Some *Enterprise* employees resented her presence, especially in the traditionally male domain of management. Surprisingly, however, men overcame their bias more quickly than did women. Nonetheless, the atmosphere was often strained. And among social peers, it could be openly hostile.

"Frankly, Hope, I think it's outrageous for Howard to expect you to do all those things. The very idea, a woman in

159

the business world. Surely you must know that your friends consider it scandalous."

"For heaven's sake, Maude, what's scandalous about work? I'm stimulated. I've got a career, a future, a purpose in life. Howard happens to be a man who regards a woman as more than a mere possession. We're not only lovers"—she smiled at her friend's shocked reaction to the word—"we are also very good friends, because we have things in common. I'm learning something new every day."

"But, my dear, it isn't as if you can't afford to live in a genteel way. Howard Langden is a millionaire. You could be one of the most socially prominent women in New York, giving delightful parties and having a wonderful time. As it is, you've declined so many invitations that even your best friends despair of you. Soon, people just won't invite you at all."

"Good. I don't have time for their parties."

Career even took priority over Aunt Francesca's little notes mentioning this tea or that dinner party. Only Howard mattered, Howard and the *Enterprise*. And he gave her absolute freedom to advance at her own pace. They never discussed where that advancement eventually might lead.

"What do you think I should do next, darling?"

"Have you been out on the circulation trucks?"

"No."

"Then I suggest that you go. That's where the real competition is, on the street. You also ought to acquaint yourself with the printing presses and the composing room. It's not necessary to run a Linotype machine, but you certainly ought to know what a Linotype machine does and the problems its breakdown can create. In fact, there's a whole range of production problems worth knowing about." He gazed at her in the special way that warmed her. "That is, unless you're tired of being a career woman."

"I'm ecstatic about being a career woman. It's the most interesting thing I've ever done, except for marrying you."

One evening as she rode a horse-drawn circulation wagon through lower Manhattan, Hope saw street ruffians attempting to snatch a carpetbag from an elderly, shabbily dressed woman. Grabbing her umbrella and shouting to the wagon driver, Hope leaped down and rushed to the woman's aid, swinging the umbrella like a club. Several bystanders, inspired by her fury, joined into the affray. The young footpads ran off, leaving the old woman shaken and angry but unhurt.

Her small, flowered hat was askew and she had dropped her purse.

"You poor dear." Hope picked up the purse and brushed it off. She tried to straighten the woman's hat. She patted her arm. "You poor, poor dear."

"I'm quite all right, thank you." The voice was low, the eyes a steely blue.

"Let me help you," Hope insisted. "What a terrible experience. Bernie, call a hansom cab and I'll take this lady to my house. Some food, some rest."

The old woman stood proudly erect. The eyes had a glint of amusement. "I'm quite all right; I assure you. I've had robbery attempts before. It is nothing to be concerned about."

"Then I'll see you to your home. I insist. Where do you live?"

"I live across the river in Hoboken. I ride the ferry."

"All right, then." Hope turned to the wagon driver. "Take us to the ferry, Bernie."

They rode the ferry to Hoboken. The old woman got off clutching her carpetbag and purse. Hope accompanied her along a cobbled street to a modest row of brick flats. The card on the door read, C. Dewey. It was already long after dark. The old woman was greeted excitedly by a gray-and-white miniature sheepdog. The animal accepted Hope's pat of friendship. Tea was prepared on an old wooden stove and leftovers were warmed for supper.

"Are you Mrs. Dewey?"

"That's the name on the front door," the woman replied.

"Do you go into the city often?"

"Every day, to my job." As they ate the frugal meal, the old woman became more relaxed. At Hope's gentle prodding, she talked about herself in the rambling, evasive manner of a recluse. "I leave here very early every morning. By taking the ferry, I escape the crowds that might stare at me. Anyway, I always have enough business in town to keep me busy all day. And I always like to ride on the water. That's one reason why I live in Hoboken. But the rents are cheaper here, too, and it's quiet. I must say, Hoboken is one of the cheapest places I know to live."

The mood relaxed even more. Hope felt comfortable. She talked about herself, too. The old woman seemed surprised. "Oh, yes, I've heard of Mr. Langden. I read the *Enterprise*, but not every day. Things are so expensive, you know. A newspaper costs a penny. I usually manage to find one that somebody has thrown away. But if you're the wife of the publisher, my dear, why are you riding on a circulation wagon?"

The steely eyes brightened as Hope explained. And in bits and pieces, more of the old woman's story came out. She had never married. Her father had died while she was very young. Lawyers and plotters took away much of his fortune, leaving very little for her. She did not trust lawyers, because they were thieves at heart.

Hope nodded. Clearly the old soul was eccentric. A charwoman no doubt, part of the vast army of anonymous poor who each poured in and out of Manhattan.

Nearly two hours had gone by. It was almost time for the last ferry back to Manhattan. The old woman asked a neighbor to find Hope a hansom cab. The vehicle drew up outside, its horse blowing steam in the misty night.

"You're absolutely certain that you are all right?" Hope asked.

The old woman nodded. "I'm perfectly all right, thank you."

Fifteen minutes later Hope stood on the ferry watching the dark water flow past. She thought of the old woman living alone with her dog and the fantasy about a rich father. She smiled to herself. There was certainly nothing harmful about fantasizing.

Months went by. The American fleet was victorious at Manila. The war ended. Church bells peeled in New York. Autumn came, touching the city with its leafy splendors and bringing a cool, sunny nostalgia to the afternoons. From time to time Mrs. Dewey would appear outside the *Enterprise* and send a message in to Hope, who would then come out and treat her to lunch and a carriage ride in Central Park. The old woman never came inside the newspaper office. "People," she explained, "would stare at me."

Howard finally took a month off. They went to Newport. His spirits revived and he grew stronger. Within two weeks it was hard to imagine that he had been ill. The change was remarkable.

The day was breezy, clear, and fine. Hope spurred the chestnut mare to the crest of a grassy sand dune and looked out over the panorama. On the horizon to the north lay the village of Newport. At her feet, the sea was a wash of brilliant blue, crested near the shore by froth-topped breakers and dotted in the distance with sailboats.

"Hullo there!" The shout came from behind her. It was Howard astride his black quarterhorse, galloping across the field from the road. The stallion thundered up the dune and then her husband was beside her again, looking tanned and fit.

She leaned over and kissed him. "You're a handsome devil."

He laughed. "It's the gray hair. Gets 'em every time."

"Very distinguished."

"Old, you mean."

"Distinguished."

"I'm almost fifty, nearly twice your age."

"You're only forty-six."

"Old."

"Distinguished. And brilliant. And very, very brave."

"Race you down to the beach."

"Done!" The mare skirted a bend in the beach, and then the smooth undisturbed surface stretched ahead for miles until the vista was lost in smoky salt spray, on and on and on into infinity. Hope laughed with the wind in her face. The mare set a steady rhythm between Hope's thighs, mane flying, hooves splashing as the surf washed up in glittering patches of white froth. Behind her, the heavy beat of the stallion drew nearer. The stallion was a strong mount, Excalibar, the pride of Langden Stable. And then he was beside her, matching stride for stride.

"Hah!" Howard shouted.

Suddenly the stallion crowded close. Howard's arm encircled her waist. He drew her from the sidesaddle of the mare. She shouted and kicked in surprise. He reined in the stallion, circling. The mare pounded ahead, saddle empty. The stallion stopped in the surf and the two of them slid down, to roll together laughing in the water. His mouth found hers, and she lay back into the sliding froth as his playful kiss softened and warmed.

"Hope," he murmured.

His lips found her throat. His hands explored the curves of her breasts and thighs.

"Hope."

His fingers undid her bodice and his kisses followed the gentle swell of breast and nipple, rising in the sunlight. "So damned pink and proud," he said. There was an interval of loving and taking off things and loving and taking off things, until finally they were together naked in shallow water and he rose up and gently mounted her.

The sun beat down.

"Hope," he said. "Hope. Hope. Hope. Hope... Hope!... Hope!... *Hope!*"

It all merged together: sun, sea, surf, sand, and her own spasms of sheer joy.

They lay in the water, their breaths subsiding and the gentle curls and eddies lapping, swirling, caressing.

"Distinguished," she said with a giggle. "And hung like a stud."

"Such language from a lady."

The telephone was ringing when they returned to their cottage. It was Benson, one of the male secretaries in New York. "Mr. Langden, there's trouble. You had better return immediately."

The board was forcing a showdown vote. A strong movement had been building to name Manley Camp as chairman of the board. Another director, Curtis Lively, was designated as publisher. "Hell," Howard fumed, "Lively's a banker, not a newspaperman. He doesn't know a printing press from a three-legged stool."

They arrived in Manhattan on the evening train. Hope accompanied Howard to the office, where he began immediately making telephone calls to various members of the board. His support had been eroded by the defection of a weak-willed director named Thomas whose daughter had married Camp's grandson. During Langden's absence other opposition members had persuaded Thomas to sign over his proxy votes. "I'm sorry, Howard; I really am," he mumbled. "I didn't know. I didn't realize."

Howard Langden fought back. It was a persistent, deeply personal battle utilizing all his persuasion, pressure, and personal appeal. It went on through the night and into the next day, but to no avail. Not one vote could be changed nor a share of stock bought. Howard and Hope walked into the boardroom facing the inevitable.

Manley Camp basked in his triumph. "If you had not been so hard-headed, Langden..." Camp's eyes flicked to Hope. The thin lips lifted in a mirthless smile. "You have only yourself to blame"

"I'll buy you out, Camp," Langden said. "Name your price."

"I'm sorry, Mr. Langden, but my shares are not available."

"Damn it, every man has his price!"

"Not in this case."

The matter was settled. Manley Camp offered a motion that they consider reorganizing the *Enterprise*. The male secretary called the name of each director in order to record his vote. "Mr. Driscoll. Mr. Gage. Mr. Holloway, Mr. O'Neal..." It was a measured series of responses. Howard Langden's two-vote control evaporated. It ended with him one vote short.

"I move," said Manley Camp, "for Mr. Langden's discharge as publisher." The roll was called again. "And now I move that Mr. Lively be designated as publisher." The roll was called...

The directors filed out, avoiding Howard Langden's eyes. He sat, pale and unspeaking, in the chair at the head of the conference table. Hope watched his face with rising anxiety. A clock ticked in the corner.

"Howard?"

He did not reply. His eyes blinked. The left side of his face sagged strangely.

"Darling, let's go home now."

She got up and went to him. He did not move his head to look at her. His left hand trembled on the leather arm of the chair.

"Howard?"

She put her hand to his face. His forehead bore a soft sheen of cold sweat. His eyes shifted in their sockets. His mouth jerked and a strangely mumbling sound came out.

"*Howard!*"

An ambulance arrived. Hope's mind was a wild tangle of impressions: white-clad attendants bearing the silent figure of her husband down on a stretcher, the crowd gathering to watch and the sounds of women sobbing, the ambulance wagon rushing along Forty-second Street drawn by two galloping horses, the hurry into the hospital...

"Your husband appears to have suffered a stroke, Mrs. Langden." The physician was a pale, bespectacled man with a wad of fountain pens in his coat pocket. "He might have a good bit of recovery. They often do. A great deal depends on the next twenty-four to forty-eight hours."

She sat all night at his bedside in the private room. Aunt Francesca came in and out. Friends appeared, said comforting things, and disappeared. Someone handed her a copy of the *Enterprise*. The small front-page headline caught her eye: PUBLISHER SUFFERS STROKE. There was no word of the vote by the board of directors. She slept in the chair. A nurse woke her, bringing food but she did not eat. The night passed, another day, another night. Jack Slade came; Fat John Korpan came.

"There's a woman here to see you, Mrs. Langden. I told her it was out of the question, but she insists. She's sitting in the waiting room."

It was Mrs. Dewey. She had brought food in a paper sack. She had read about Howard in a day-old newspaper on the ferry. "I'm sorry, my dear."

Hope ate the food and talked. She talked about the events leading up to the stroke. She told Mrs. Dewey of the directors' rebellion and the vote to oust Howard Langden. "It was unfair," she said. "And I think it was mainly because of me. They resented my presence at the board meetings."

Mrs. Dewey pursed her lips thoughtfully. The steely eyes had a glitter. She patted Hope's hand. She asked questions about Manley Camp. How many shares of *Enterprise* stock did he hold? In what other companies did he have a financial interest? What was the basis of his wealth? Was there, perhaps, a special stock holding that was close to his heart? In finance, Mrs. Dewey reflected, it was not impossible to find an Achilles' heel. Hope had studied Camp's file. She gave very precise replies. Later she would recall the astuteness of the questions. Mrs. Dewey said, "You really should get some rest, my dear." She gathered up her carpetbag, purse, and a sack of dog bones and left to catch the Hoboken ferry. Hope watched the dowdy departing figure, thinking that when Howard got better she would buy the old soul a new coat. Fat John Korpan was just arriving as the old woman shuffled away down the corridor. The reporter looked back at her curiously.

"Who was that?"

"Mrs. Dewey," Hope replied listlessly. "She's a friend of mine. She lives in Hoboken."

"I've seen her someplace. I never forget a face. But it didn't have nothing to do with Hoboken." Fat John scratched his head.

It was night again. She sat in the chair beside her silent husband. A lamp spilled its faint glow over the room. Howard Langden stirred. And then he whispered, "Hope?"

She jumped up from the chair and went to him. "Howard? Howard, did you speak? Darling, here I am!"

"Hope." It was slurred, and barely above a whisper. Only one side of his mouth worked. But very slowly, very decisively, he lifted his right arm and touched her face with the tips of his fingers. The right side of his mouth twisted in a grotesque smile. "Hope."

In two more days, Howard Langden could speak whole sentences and push himself to a sitting position. His left side remained paralyzed, but the doctors were astonished by his progress. "Mrs. Langden, your husband is a very determined man."

She was feeding him porridge with a spoon when Manley Camp walked into the hospital room. "Mrs. Langden?" He clutched at a briefcase with both hands. The skull-like face was even paler than usual. The eyes moved from Hope to Howard and back again. The man was terribly ill at ease.

"Please, Mr. Camp. Sit down. It is nice of you to come."

"This is not exactly a social call." He hesitated, cleared his throat. "I . . . I understand that Howard is improving." The eyes shifted again to the patient. "Is that true, Howard? You're getting better?"

"Ish true, M-Manley," Howard Langden replied. His mouth drooled slightly.

"Good. Our disagreement was nothing personal; I think you know that. Business is business. I mean to say, your sudden seizure was not really my intention. I had no idea . . ."

"Of course you didn't, Mr. Camp," Hope said. "Howard realizes that, and so do I."

"But I must admit, Mrs. Langden, that your counterattack was brilliantly executed. I've seen a lot of stock manipulations and boardroom battles in my time, but nothing quite so swift and decisive as this."

"My counterattack, Mr. Camp? I'm not sure I know what you mean."

"Your friend Hetty Green has staged a one-woman raid on my most important holdings outside the *Enterprise*, Mrs. Langden. I knew she was an eccentric old bird, and rich as Croesus, but this has been positively ruthless. She simply bought up control of my common stock in Ohio Tool and Die, which my family founded a hundred years ago, and threatens to destroy the company unless I turn over every share of *Enterprise* that I own at current market value . . . That is, if you wish to buy them." He opened the briefcase and drew out a sheaf of papers with a trembling hand. "And I'm instructed to sign them over to you personally, Mrs. Langden."

"Mr. Camp, I really don't underst . . ."

In a moment, it was done. Manley Camp sat in the chair beside Howard Langden's hospital bed and signed over his entire bloc of *Enterprise* voting stock, in exchange for which Hope promised that her check would be in the mail the following day. Camp then tucked the briefcase under his arm, nodded to Langden, and went away.

Fat John Korpan arrived the next morning bursting with excitement. "I remember!" he shouted.

Both Hope and Howard smiled. "What do you remember, Fat John?"

"That old woman, the one you called Mrs. Dewey. That's Hetty Green! Hetty Green, in the flesh. Richest goddamn woman in the world. Crazy as a bedbug, but worth sixty million dollars and one of the sharpest traders on Wall Street. Son of a gun! And you knew it all the time."

Hope smiled. "Howard would like to have a cigar, Fat John. Would you light one for him?"

She drove to Hoboken in Howard's Winton automobile and arrived after dark. The dog barked as she knocked on the door marked C. Dewey. The old woman peered out through a slat in the door before opening it. She greeted Hope with a warm smile. Hope walked in with her arms filled with presents—a new dress, new hat, new coat, shoes. They were all serviceable, conservative things, designed to wear well. The shoes, of course, were sturdy black walkers. "I just hope that everything fits," she said.

The dog wagged its tail and put his forepaws on Hope's knee.

"Down, Mr. Dewey," Hetty Green said.

"I was a bit confused on names," Hope said, looking at the animal. "Is *that* 'C. Dewey'?"

"Yes. He's my most loyal and trusted friend. He keeps watch on things when I'm gone. This place is as much his as mine."

"Why didn't you tell me?"

"It was just a whim. I never know who my real friends are. I never know if they're nice to me because I'm me, or because I'm Hetty Green. Some people are always after my money. And besides, I'm a very private person."

Hope smiled and patted her hand. "I can't thank you

enough for what you did. Howard has asked me to take over as acting publisher until he's fit again. It scares me to death, but I'll try. How did you work this miracle, anyhow?"

"It was nothing. Actually, I made a rather nice profit on Ohio Tool and Die. I bought a rather large bloc of shares. The sharks on the exchange smelled blood, a takeover in the works. Word got around that I was buying, so they bought too. When I gained control I gave Manley Camp my ultimatum. He burst into tears. In the meantime, the price had jumped a point. Camp signed over the *Enterprise*. I sold. The speculators were left holding the bag." She chuckled. "I enjoyed that."

Hope shook her head. "Hetty Green, you're a wonder."

Hetty stood up, smoothed her frayed dress, and went to the wood stove to poke up the fire. "All I've got is leftovers for supper. Would you care to join me?"

"I'd love to. I'm famished."

She got up from the sofa, and Hetty handed her an apron.

"The President's train! Here comes the President's train!"

People jostled on the station platform beneath pillars wrapped in red, white, and blue bunting. All Buffalo was spruced up and decorated on this September day for the great 1901 Pan American Exposition. It was an event of magnitude, the biggest thing ever to happen in the city.

Howard Langden leaned forward in his wheelchair. Hope still ached to see her man so afflicted. He had insisted on making the trip from New York. The presidential invitation, after all, had come in McKinley's own strong hand, written on the face of the card:

Please join us, old friend.

The trip had done wonders for Langden's spirits. More than two years of illness had worn him down. And yet he never complained or indulged in self-pity; he always looked forward to a complete recovery. "I'm going to take you back to Newport one day," he said. "We'll make love again in the surf."

Hope's eyes glistened. "I'll be there."

The *Presidential Special* arrived on the main line, gleaming black with great silver driving wheels, tooting its whistle, and flying its flags. Hope steadied Howard's wheelchair, feeling the rising excitement. "Here he comes!"

169

"I hope Mrs. McKinley is feeling better," Howard said. His speech was still slurred. "She has not been well."

The train ground to a stop, gushing steam. Officials scurried about for the welcome. The band, resplendent in uniform, struck up a new Sousa march. Artillery pieces were poised in a nearby clearing, charged with powder.

A young lieutenant shouted, "Fire!"

There began a twenty-one-gun salute. *Blam! Blam! Blam! Blam!*

Dignitaries began to emerge from the train. Howard recognized the presidential secretary George B. Cortelyou. "George!" he shouted. "Over here."

Cortelyou joined them, looking concerned. "Damn it, Howard, I'm sorry about your illness."

Langden's face lifted in a twisted smile. "It could have been worse."

The secretary looked admiringly at Hope. "This wife of yours is doing a terrific job running the *Enterprise*."

"No one could do it better," Langden said.

The President appeared with Mrs. McKinley on his arm. Tall, gray, and smiling, he waved to the crowd. Two Secret Service men took up positions. A cheer went up. "Hurrah for McKinley! Hurrah!" Hope and George Cortelyou wheeled Howard to the line of carriages awaiting the fifty-member reception committee. The McKinleys were escorted to a stately black victoria drawn by the sleekest matched team in Buffalo. When all the dignitaries were loaded into their vehicles, the procession clipclopped up Delaware Avenue to Milburn House, flag-draped in somber Victorian splendor. Fifteen minutes later Hope and her husband were sipping punch from glass cups at the official reception.

"I hate these affairs," Cortelyou grumbled. "So many things can go wrong."

Langden chuckled. "Why should you be concerned, George?" He glanced across the room at the President, who stood in a circle of admirers. "You know how he loves to be adored by the crowd."

"We've got one of those dreadful handshaking ceremonies the day after tomorrow." Cortelyou fretted. "You never know who's going to turn up. It will be advertised in advance, of course, and open to all. I've tried to get him to cancel, but he won't."

"Can't you add more guards?"

"He doesn't like that. McKinley feels that the President

should be accessible to all. He thinks no human being would have cause to harm him." Cortelyou shook his head morosely. "I wish I were as optimistic." He left them, pensive, and preoccupied.

The exposition was gaudy and tacky but fun. Hope wheeled Howard over the thirty acres of grounds, sometimes in the company of friends and sometimes by themselves. The displays depicted the Latin American theme, with pastel replicas of missions, belfries, arches, and arcades. Plaster statues stood everywhere. When darkness fell they watched enthralled from a balcony as the electric lights came on. Virtually every building was outlined in lights, but the most spectacular display was the four-hundred-foot Electric Tower, ablaze with thirty-five thousand bulbs powered from the great dynamos at Niagara Falls. The evening ended with a massive fireworks display, titled "Our Empire" and featuring fiery pyrotechnic representations of Cuba, Puerto Rico, and the Philippines.

"Glorious!" Hope exclaimed as they returned to their hotel. "How lucky we are to be alive at a time like this."

Howard patted her hand. "With you, any time is great to be alive."

The afternoon of September 6 was sunny and very warm. They passed the day with more sightseeing and arrived at the Temple of Music in late afternoon just in time for the public reception. Displaying a pass signed by Cortelyou, they entered by a side door to join several local dignitaries in shaking McKinley's hand.

"I'm glad you could come, Howard," McKinley said with his fatherly smile. "Perhaps you'll be out of that wheelchair soon. Hasn't it been a marvelous day?"

At four o'clock the doors swung open and the crowd began to file in. McKinley, tall and beaming, was his usual genial self, practicing expertly his handshaking skill: a smile, a word, a quick pump of the hand, a pull to the side propelling the citizen on his way. Smiling, smiling, always smiling.

"That's the fastest handshake I ever saw," Hope whispered. "He's got them practically running through."

People were sweating. Some had drawn out handkerchiefs to mop their faces. Five minutes passed. Six. Cortelyou drew out his pocket watch. Howard murmured behind his hand, "Cortelyou doesn't like the setup. I think he's going to close it down early."

Hope was looking toward the open doors.

The shots had a muffled sound, two in quick succession,

like an automobile backfire. A dark young man with a white bandage on his hand stood in front of the President. Smoke curled from the bandage. McKinley stood absolutely still, his face a deathly pallor. For an instant everything seemed as frozen as the statues on the Exposition grounds: the President, tall and gray; the young man, dark and seemingly disinterested; Cortelyou, the Secret Service men, the soldiers, the waiting crowd.

And then a woman screamed.

Soldiers and Secret Service agents leaped upon the dark man and threw him down in a struggling heap, wrenching violently at the bandaged hand. Howard Langden shouted in helpless rage, immobilized in his chair. A small-caliber pistol clattered obscenely across the floor. "Cortelyou!" McKinley said. The secretary helped to lower him onto a line of wooden chairs. "Cortelyou. My wife. Don't let her know."

Someone shouted to close the doors and clear the aisle. Guards pushed and shoved at the crowd, forcing them back out of the building. The gunman was lifted, unresisting, to his feet. An enraged Secret Service man punched him in the face. McKinley mumbled hoarsely, "Don't hurt him. Don't hurt him, boys. Go easy..."

Hope moved to McKinley's side and knelt with a handkerchief. "Are you hit, Mr. President?"

"I don't know... I don't know." He unbuttoned his shirt and put his hand inside. He drew it back and his fingers were covered with blood. He winced from pain and shock. "This wound," he said, "hurts very much."

In years to come, this day would focus on hot flashes of memory for Hope Stewart Langden: the word spreading to the crowd outside, and angry cries of "Lynch the gunman! Lynch him!"; the clanging bell of Buffalo's automobile ambulance as it arrived to carry away its distinguished patient; the frenzy of police shoving the anarchist Leon Czolgosz into a closed carriage and the driver lashing his horses into a gallop, flying across the Triumphal Causeway with an angry mob running in pursuit; and then her own unexpected role, to be with the First Lady when she was told.

Howard Langden telephoned his eyewitness account of the shooting to the *Enterprise*. It was a clear and sensational scoop. In the days that followed, as McKinley revived and grew steadily stronger, Howard went back to New York and it was Hope who followed the questioning of the Polish-born attacker Leon Czolgosz, the former Cleveland millworker, and took down his words for transmission to New York. "I shot President McKinley because I done my duty. I don't believe any man should have so much power and another man should have none."

"The nation is shocked." The voice of the managing editor Jack Slade crackled over a bad telephone connection, shouting to be heard. "Fat John Korpan told J. P. Morgan the news as he came out of his office. Morgan turned pale and went back inside, shaking his head and saying, 'Sad. Sad.' It's been a hell of a beat for us. Our street sales are fantastic. Where is Teddy Roosevelt?"

"He's in Vermont, up in the mountains," Hope shouted. "But he's on his way here, I'm told."

"Stay close to him." Slade hung up.

By September 9, McKinley was sitting up in bed. On the eleventh he asked for a cigar. On the twelfth doctors were proclaiming victory. On the twelfth...

"Jack, he has taken a turn for the worse."

"What do you mean, a turn for the worse?"

"They gave him some toast. His stomach isn't functioning. He's very weak and pale..."

"Oh, Jesus."

At 2:30 A.M. on September 14, Hope made another call to Jack Slade. This time the connection was surprisingly good. "He's dead, Jack. Fifteen minutes ago."

Mark Hanna could not believe it. "Now," the Ohio senator said bitterly, "that cowboy is President of the United States."

And now it was Howard's voice on the telephone, asking for every detail of what she had seen and heard. She described the bizarre swearing-in of Theodore Roosevelt, in the library of the home of Buffalo lawyer Ansley Wilcox, and his promise to continue McKinley's policies.

"Do you think he meant it, Hope?"

"Yes, I think he meant it. Darling, shall I come home now? I miss you terribly."

There was a pause at the other end of the line. Then: "Stay with McKinley, my dear. Cover it all for the *Enterprise,* the funeral, the train journey back to Canton, Ohio, for burial, everything. This is one of the stories of the century."

Hope stayed with McKinley. As the funeral train moved slowly southward to Washington, bearing the body in the black-creped Pullman car *Pacific,* she looked out the window at the crowds of humanity standing at hamlets and crossroads and towns in silent grief. In the fields, farmers removed their hats in respect. Children knelt in advance of the train, to lay pennies on the track. Everywhere, the church bells tolled.

The irony was that she was the second Stewart in history to make such a sad journey with an assassinated President. Her own father Thaddeus had ridden the funeral train bearing Abraham Lincoln back to Springfield, Illinois. As darkness settled over the flatlands of Ohio, a new epoch was gathering and life, for all of them, would never be quite the same again.

VII

The morning came up crisp and fine. Sunshine burned away the ground mists and splashed golden light over fields and woodlands. Along the ridgelines, tree masses displayed autumn colors in splotches of russet, crimson, brown, and gold. Dry grass crunched underfoot. Since dawn, exhilaration had possessed Maurice, and he sensed that it was shared by his hunting companions, Jeffrey Straight and Will Pease, the young owner of Fall River's candy factory.

By midday their game bags were full and the men swung onto their horses for the five-mile ride back to town. Maurice enjoyed the easy handling of his riding mount, a big bay hunter he had named Strolling Jack. As they rode, cloud masses thickened overhead, flicked by lightning. The first heavy drops came down when they were still a mile out of Fall River, so they took shelter in a barn. The downpour ended after half an hour, the sunshine returned, and the horses moved back onto the muddy road, splashing through brown pools of standing water. It was two-thirty by a distant steeple clock as they turned into an unpaved side street near Will Pease's candy factory with their entourage of hunting dogs. Pedestrians kept to wooden sidewalks to avoid the muddy street.

"Damn!" muttered Pease, a member of the Town Council. "Here it is 1901 and half the streets of Fall River still ain't paved."

"Taxes, Will," Straight replied lightly. "Folks don't want to pay the taxes..."

Strolling Jack was picking his way around a large pool of

174

liquid mud. From behind, Maurice heard the unwelcome clatter of a townsman's horseless carriage. The stallion's ears perked up and a nervous shiver coursed through the great body. "Hoah, Jack. Easy, boy!" Muttering a curse, Maurice glanced over his shoulder. The machine was coming up the middle of the street belching noise and exhaust, lurching through ruts and potholes, its wheels caked with mud. The driver, a fat German bakeshop owner named Schiller, sat bolt upright behind the steering tiller. He was encased in white leather motoring coat, gauntlets, and eye goggles. Pedestrians turned to stare. The hunting dogs set up a furious barking, charging at the wheels. The horsemen gave way. Strolling Jack chafed nervously at his bit, eyes rolling.

"Easy, Jack. It's nothing but a..."

The infernal machine backfired, belching a cloud of blue smoke.

The stallion reared, whinnying and backing toward the wooden sidewalk. Maurice heard a splintering as a plank gave way under the heavy hoof. A female voice shouted angrily. He dug his heels into Strolling Jack's flanks and the stallion surged forward on all fours again, cantering sideways and tossing his head.

"Stupid oaf!"

He turned and looked down. An angry female had tumbled face forward into the mud. She pushed herself up on her hands and he gazed into eyes that were the bluest and most furious that he had ever seen. The rest of her—raven hair, dark blue coat with matching gown, handbag, hands, and feet—was drenched in mud. A blue flowered hat lay crushed in the mud.

Maurice Stewart could not contain his laughter.

She came to her feet, glaring. "Oh, you think it is funny, do you?" The words had a distinctively Slavic accent, with a slight rolling of the r's. "I show you what is funny." She swung the handbag at Maurice's boot and delivered a whack that broke the strap of the bag and sent it flying back into the mire. Behind her a crowd had gathered, most of them louts disgorged from a nearby saloon. Jeers and catcalls came from the onlookers.

"Whoooowee, did you ever see a mudbaby the likes o' that?"

"Hit him another lick, sugar!"

"Knock that there horse on his arse, hyah-hyah-hyah!"

Maurice swung the stallion around and dismounted, his

boots squishing in ankle-deep mud. Still smiling, he retrieved the handbag and wiped it against his trousers. "It looks like you took a spill, young lady. Please accept my . . ."

"Took spill, indeed! Your horse back into me, knock me off sidewalk." For the first time, she looked down at the front of her clothes dripping in mud. Even the side of her face was muddy. Maurice Stewart was suddenly aware that it was the loveliest face he had ever seen. "Look at me. Just look what you did!"

"I'm truly sorry, Miss. I couldn't help it. The horseless carriage . . ."

"Oh dear."

Something in her tone caught his attention. Her clothing was cheap but serviceable. The lovely face was devoid of any hint of makeup, even face powder. There was about her an air of working-class respectability. He no longer smiled, but stood there feeling helpless and foolish.

"What do I do now?" she said.

"I'll see that the gown is properly cleaned. In fact, I'll buy you a whole new outfit." Suddenly it seemed terribly important that she think well of him. "I'm really sorry."

"Idiot! It is not dress." The eyes still blazed; the jaw was set. She recovered the hat and clamped it to her head, where it sat like a battered symbol of defiance. "I was going to be interviewed for job. I am sure that mean nothing to you, but job is very important to me!"

Now he was truly contrite. As the crowd dispersed, Maurice was joined by Will Pease and Jeffrey Straight. The two men also expressed strong apologies, each obviously admiring this beauty from the mud puddle.

Maurice came to a decision. "We can't stand here arguing all afternoon. I'll get a cab to take you to the nearest ready-to-wear shop, tell them to provide a new outfit, and escort you to wherever it is you intended to seek employment. We'll simply explain the circumstances. Surely any decent employer . . ."

"I want to go home," she said.

The finality of the statement disrupted Maurice's little speech. As he stood, momentarily wordless, she turned from them, sloshed through the mud puddle to the sidewalk, and began walking away.

"Hey!"

She did not look back.

Maurice threw up his hands and shot a glance at his

companions. "Gentlemen, I'll see you later." Leading Strolling Jack and followed by the Blue Tick hound, he sloshed hurriedly along the muddy street until he caught up with her. "This is ridiculous. I never saw anybody make such a fuss over nothing."

"Good day to you, Mister . . . whatever your name is."

"Maurice Stewart."

"Mister Stewart."

"Delighted to make your acquaintance, Miss . . ."

"I do not speak to strangers."

"I want to make amends. Damn it, woman, I said I was sorry!"

"Being sorry is not enough."

Her heels banged resolutely along the boardwalk. The mud was beginning to dry on her clothing. The ridiculous hat rode on its bed of luxuriant black hair. Passersby turned in amusement as the odd group—woman, man, horse, and dog—proceeded north to Hickory and west on Hickory toward Market.

"Do we have to run a footrace?" Maurice shouted. "This animal trailing along behind me is called a horse. The least that two sane people can do is get on his back and ride."

She slowed her pace, as if to consider the option. After a moment's thought, she came to a decision. "Very well, Mister Stewart. We ride."

Maurice brought Strolling Jack to the edge of the boardwalk. He considered lifting her up in front of the saddle, to a ladylike sidesaddle position. But she elbowed him aside, grabbed the pommel of the saddle, and swung astride the stallion, showing a flash of petticoats. Maurice, grinning, mounted behind her and took the reins.

"Giddyap, Jack."

The ride did not abate her anger. She neither responded to his attempts at conversation nor gave her name. But the feel of her body as they rode was a heady delight to his senses. He could not take his eyes off the mass of raven hair nor the creamy whiteness of the unmuddied side of her face. Finally they stopped before a modest white clapboard house in a working-class neighborhood at the edge of town. At a glance Maurice saw that the yard was scrupulously well tended. The place was surrounded by a neat white picket fence. There were several fruit trees on the property, each showing signs of careful pruning and upkeep. He dismounted and helped her down, feeling the trimness of her waist in his hands.

177

"Good-bye, then," she said, and walked briskly up the walk.

He trotted to catch up. "But your clothes. I must replace..."

"Don't worry about it." Already she had opened the front door. "I will manage, thank you."

His heart sank. In an instant the door would close, an impenetrable barrier. "But your name. At least you could tell me your name!"

"Rachel Birnham," she said.

The door closed in his face.

Rachel Birnham. Rachel Birnham. Rachel Birnham. As the name echoed in his mind, Maurice rode Strolling Jack slowly back down Market Street to Main and on to the boarding-house on the other side of town. Rachel Birnham. A groom from the livery stable was waiting to take the stallion. Maurice handed him the reins, unstrapped the game bag and shotgun, and trudged wearily up the stairs. Mrs. Blessing, the house-keeper, took charge of the quail and pheasant and disappeared into the kitchen. Maurice left the shotgun for cleaning, went up to the bedroom, and unlaced his boots.

Helen emerged from her rooms wearing a dressing gown. "Darling, I'm so happy you're back!" Kneeling quickly, she pulled off his boots and massaged his feet. Then she came up, put her arms around his neck, and softly kissed his mouth. "I love you so much. I'm even jealous of quail and hunting dogs."

Maurice thought, Rachel Birnham. Helen pushed him back on the bed, kissing and whispering. Her hands undid him and freed the swelling mass there.

Rachel Birnham...

"Oh, Maurice," Helen DeMare said. Her gown came open and his hands stroked the velvety smoothness of her skin. She trembled at his touch and moaned softly. "Maurice, Maurice, Maurice."

His mind stopped thinking.

"Here are the week's figures, Mr. Stewart. Three hundred eighty units from the subcontractors. That includes two hundred Continentals. It's a shade short, but Thanksgiving is coming up and you said to let everybody off work."

"Very well, Harrison." Maurice took the paper from the clerk and turned to the window again. He removed the heavy gold watch from his vest pocket and snapped open the cover. Two o'clock. It had been raining steadily since dawn. The sky

178

outside was slate-gray and rain drooled down the window glass, distorting the outside world.

Helen? Loyal, unstinting, loving him to a fault, she had launched this business with a simple expression of faith and now supported him with every fiber of her being. Her loyalty, if anything, was too steadfast, too dependable. There was no mystery about Helen DeMare's love; she plainly adored Maurice Stewart and would walk through fire for him. She was also a physically ravishing creature.

Or Rachel? She was the mystery, the intriguing, beautiful, challenging mystery. Five days had gone by since their meeting. In that time, he had made inquiries around Fall River about Rachel Birnham. "Birnham? Birnham?" came the reply. "Oh, yes. That's the Jewish family in the north end. Lovely girl. They came from Poland, you know, but she speaks very good English. They keep pretty much to themselves. The father is a pushcart peddler and tutors part-time in mathematics."

Was she married?

"No, Mr. Stewart, she ain't married."

He left the office at four o'clock, drove his leather-topped buggy through the pouring rain to the dressmaker's, picked up the package, and then went straight to the house with the picket fence. The rain had stopped by the time he stepped down and tethered his gelding to a linden tree. He walked up to the front door and knocked.

The door swung open and he found himself looking into cool blue eyes.

"Miss Birnham, I . . ." He swallowed and held out the box. "I brought you something."

She did not take the box nor did she smile. "Thank you."

"The things might not be exactly the right size. I had to go by guesswork. But Miss Brinkman, the seamstress, knows you and said she thought this was about right. Anyhow, if they don't fit you can take them back to her shop on Main Street for alterations."

"Yes, I know Miss Brinkman."

There was a pause. He felt foolish, standing there holding the box, under scrutiny of those blue eyes. Today she was twice as stunning as before, wearing a dark skirt and simple shirtwaist with a cameo brooch at the throat. Her hair was upswept and caught with a pair of small ivory combs.

"Did you find a job? That is, were you able to make another appointment for your interview?"

"No."

"I see. Uh, just what kind of skills do you have, Miss Birnham? Perhaps I can help. Of course, it is sometimes difficult for a female to find a position, since so few have any skills..."

The eyes blazed again and a flush of anger spread across the lovely face. "You are offensive and stupid man. Why do you always say wrong thing? I happen to be high school graduate. I am also excellent at typing and filing. I can hold job. Please not to bother me again!"

The door closed in his face.

Again Maurice found himself standing, speechless and dumbfounded.

Rachel Birnham reopened the door, snatched the box from his hands, and closed it again, this time with a slam.

"Well, I'll be..."

"Headstrong girl." It was a man's voice behind him, pleasant and lightly accented. "Just like her mother."

Maurice walked down the steps, weary and deflated. "She has a right to be angry."

The man was smallish and gray with a kindly face. He had come up from the street, and behind him there stood a pushcart laden with odds and ends of merchandise. He wore an old topcoat and heavy shoes. "She is not as angry as she pretends. Women have their ways."

Maurice's eyebrows lifted. "You know her?"

"She is my daughter Rachel." The man put out his hand. "I am Jacob Birnham, the peddler. I also tutor children in mathematics, science, and the Talmud. Unfortunately there is little demand for that in Fall River. But..."—he shrugged lightly and gestured toward his pushcart—"this is good living, and my brother helps. He is Bernard Brinsky, the merchant."

"I know Mr. Brinsky."

"He is generous to us. This house belongs to him, and he lets us live in it. He is kindly man, my brother, and shrewd in business. You are?..."

"Maurice Stewart."

The older man's face lifted in recognition. He touched his spectacles and peered at Maurice. "Mr. Stewart, the buggy-maker. Of course! But you are so young!"

"I have been lucky."

"I was not aware. Rachel mentioned she had met young man who... Well, I won't go into what she said. But I never suspect..."

"It doesn't matter. We must see about finding her a job. I
180

would like to talk with her about it. I think she can work for me. But every time I say something, she gets angry and slams the door in my face." He smiled ruefully. "She is, as you say, a headstrong girl."

Jacob Birnham nodded. "I talk with her. I see what I can do, Mr. Stewart. Please be patient." He offered a slight bow. "She is very proud. But pride, I fear, is luxury of the young. By the way"—the eyes, Maurice noticed, were very blue, like his daughter's, and now took on a speculative glimmer—"do you by chance play chess?"

"Chess?" Maurice smiled. What an odd question. "A little."

"Excellent. Excellent." The hands rubbed briskly; the face radiated warmth. "Well, well, well." Jacob Birnham turned back to his pushcart and began wheeling it around toward the back of the house. "It is very nice to meet you, Mr. Stewart. Yes, very nice." And then he was gone.

Maurice climbed into his carriage and gathered up the reins of the gelding. Curious people, the Birnhams.

But my God, she was beautiful...

It was Will Pease who provided the job for Rachel. The candymaker needed a young woman for filing and typing in his office, and sent word to the house of Jacob Birnham that she would indeed be welcome, at a wage of a dollar twenty-five per day. Maurice was disappointed, having hoped to employ her himself. But his mood quickly lifted when the invitation came to join the Birnhams for dinner on a Friday evening. He arrived at nightfall, bearing a box of chocolates and a potted plant from Slade's Greenhouse.

"I want to thank you for helping me find job, Mr. Stewart." She was stunning in the new clothes he had given her, a pale blue one-piece dress set off by a narrow choker of black velvet. The choker accentuated the dark depths of her eyes. "Mr. Pease is excellent employer who seems to appreciate efficiency."

The comment gave him a twinge of envy. He almost blurted out, for no reason at all, that Will Pease was a married man with two children, but refrained. "I'm glad you like it," he said.

The house was quite small, its furnishings old and shabby, but spotlessly clean. There was no electricity and so they made do with oil lamps. A log fire crackled in the fireplace, providing cheery warmth. The bare floor, though carpetless, had been thoroughly cleaned and waxed and there was about the house an odor of pine scent and soap. Dinner plates were mismatched and chipped, set on an ancient table with three kinds of chairs. The house provided an atmosphere of genteel poverty, but the Birnhams themselves seemed not to notice.

Sara Birnham was a spare, quiet woman with a face of brooding dignity. As they exchanged self-conscious small talk in the parlor, she made frequent trips to the kitchen, from whence came marvelous cooking odors. Rachel sat quietly with her father, who uncorked a bottle of sweet red wine and poured it into china cups. "*L'chaim!*" Jacob Birnham said. "To your health." They drank.

Maurice could not keep his eyes from Rachel. Even when conversation lapsed—they had run through discussions of the weather, the high level of the river, the prospects for an early snow—he found himself gazing at her. The blue eyes, unflinching, gazed back.

Dinner was chicken stuffed with cheese, with small side dishes of vegetables. The meal was hearty if not abundant, and they finished with black coffee. "My customers not all pay in cash, especially country people," Jacob Birnham was saying. "So we barter, as in old country. This way we have canned goods for winter, and cheeses, coffee, and tea, sometimes chicken. This is wonderful country. There is always way for a man to make living."

"I have done the same thing you do, but not with a pushcart," Maurice said. He told them of his travels through the small towns and farming areas selling his first Stewart buggy.

Jacob Birnham listened intently, and was especially interested in how Maurice had extended long-term financing to buyers of his vehicles. "Don't you take chance on bad debt? Do you not worry?"

"Most people want to pay, and pay on time. It is different in large cities. But out in the small towns and countryside, a man's word is his bond. I've seen contracts secured with nothing more than a handshake. If you make it easy for people to buy, you increase the volume of your sales. And people want the better things of life now. Look at the tremendous success of the new Sears and Roebuck company. They're built on a mail order business from a catalog . . ."

As the women cleared the table, Jacob Birnham brought out a chess set. The board was of wood, its painted squares well-worn from use. The men, however, were of carved marble, in black and gray, each piece elegantly wrought by hand. "It belonged to my grandfather," Birnham said lovingly. "These pieces were among the few things we were able to bring from Poland." He placed the chessmen, lit an ancient briar pipe with a wooden match, and smiled across the table at Maurice. "Do you care to open?"

Maurice had played chess well at Harvard, so well in fact that few opponents cared to challenge him. He opened with his usual confidence, and in four moves was on the attack with his queen bishop and both knights. Jacob Birnham smoked and studied, his defense seemingly weak and without plan. On his side of the board, Birnham lost a knight, a bishop, and two pawns in such rapid succession that Maurice already could see a possible checkmate and concentrated his power for the attack.

What child's play. Jacob Birnham advanced his rook into dangerous position, seemed to blunder with a diagonal move of his queen, and did not even bother to protect his king with a castle move when the opportunity presented itself. Maurice smiled, seeing a critical opening about to jeapordize Birnham's queen.

Then, a deft move of Birnham's king bishop, an unexpected thrust of his queen down the now-undefended side of Maurice's board.

"Check," Birnham said gently.

Momentarily confused, Maurice looked to his threatened king and, with a flash of irritation, tried to patch up his defense with a pawn block move.

Birnham drew the pipe from his mouth, brought up a bishop from his back rank, and smiled.

". . . and mate."

Checkmate! Maurice was thunderstruck. He swallowed hard, suddenly thwarted and humiliated. He had been suckered, drawn in, fooled. He looked across the chessboard at the benign blue eyes behind the spectacles and recognized, for the first time, the keen intelligence there. He extended his hand. "Masterful," he said.

"Play again?"

They played three more games. Jacob Birnham alternately displayed commanding power of the center squares, or attacked down one side and then the other, or bottled up Maurice's men until he could not move at all without perilous sacrifice. So casual did it seem on Birnham's part that he soon gave up being outraged and instead studied each new lesson in tactics as it unfolded on the squares.

Finally Jacob Birnham put away the pieces and board and leaned back in his chair. "Do not feel badly, young friend. You play very well for an American. My father was master of the game, as was his father before him. There are men who make me feel as angry and helpless as you. Chess is good lesson in life, I think. It teaches us to be humble. It reminds us that many things are won by correct strategy. Do you agree?"

Maurice felt a rush of affection for this mild-mannered pushcart peddler. He smiled and nodded. "I agree."

Sara Birnham brought out little cakes and served a sweetened herbal tea. Conversation again turned to commonplace things. Rachel's mother gave him the impression of having once been a beauty, but now bore the stamp of a deep and abiding disenchantment with life. It seemed to lay upon the family as an invisible cloud.

Mrs. Birnham put down her teacup. "Do you have religion, Mr. Stewart?"

"Mother," Rachel whispered.

"Dear, it is not appropriate . . ." said Jacob.

"On the contrary"—Sara Birnham sat stiffly upright in her chair, both hands gripping the teacup—"is very appropriate, I think. Young man must have religion. It is part of character. Is this not so, Mr. Stewart?"

Maurice sensed the discomfort of Rachel and her father. "Most of my family is of the Protestant faith," he said easily. "Methodists and Presbyterians, mainly. I do not personally belong to a church, though . . ."

"It is not necessary," Rachel said. "Religion is personal thing. This is free country, yes? Free religion is very basic here."

"Our son Solomon would have become a rabbi," Sara Birnham said.

"Sara . . ."

"Too many young people forget about religion. They forget heritage and tradition. But tradition is what you are, what you belong to. Our Solomon could have been a *tzaddick*. You know what is the *tzaddick*? A true man of God, a wonder worker. In the ancient Chaddism . . ."

"Sara, Mr. Stewart is not interested in those things." Jacob Birnham exchanged glances with Rachel. "Perhaps you young people would like to take a walk?"

Rachel looked at her mother with an expression of deep concern. Maurice sensed that it was time for him to go. He made as if to rise, but Jacob Birnham stayed him with a light touch on the arm. Wordlessly Rachel went to the closet and brought out their coats.

"Mr. Stewart?"

And then they were putting on their coats, while Jacob bustled about the room, poking up the fire and rubbing his hands briskly together. "Don't stay out too long. Your mother worries."

As they went out the front door, Maurice saw that Sara Birnham had not moved but still sat rigidly in her place, staring into the teacup.

The evening was still and cold, with a tang of woodsmoke on the air. They walked in the empty unpaved street past silent, shuttered houses and glowing windows. Bright moonlight filtered down through trees becoming barren of leaf. The air of late fall had a hint of wistful melancholy.

"My brother Solomon died on boat coming to America," she said softly. "He was eleven years old. Mother wanted desperately for him to become rabbi. It was her entire life's ambition. She grieves for him and is even more strong in religion. Do you understand?"

"It must have been terrible, to lose a son like that."

"Father work hard, make life for us. He is fine husband, fine man. But Mother cannot forget Solomon. Do you know the words *messiras nefesh*? In Hebrew, it means 'devotion unto death,' or handing over one's very soul to the memory of another. That is what my mother has done. The memory of Solomon will burn within her until she dies. *Messiras nefesh*."

"Are you glad you came to America?"

"Yes. This is wonderful country. In Poland, there were pogroms. The Poles have always hated us Jews. Anti-Semitism is deep within Polish soul. Life was hard there. It was not much better in England, where we lived for two years. Here, people can be free, make good living, be happy."

They walked. He felt her nearness, the touch of her arm against his, the thrill of breathing the same air she breathed. Everything had a strange enchantment for him at this moment: the night, the cold, the moonlight. It seemed to take his breath, make him almost giddy with delight. What in God's name was happening to him?

"Are you happy, Rachel?" he said.

She sighed, looking up at the trees and the moonlight, her face suddenly glowing with an almost unearthly radiance. "I think so."

"I want you to be happy," he said. "It is becoming very important to me."

They stopped walking. Later, he would go over that moment again and again in his mind, trying to recall the one word, the one movement that drew them together. But it was beyond rational remembrance. All at once, she was in his arms, their mouths meeting, their whispers blending. And as he pressed fiercely against her, and the fullness of desire inflamed his loins, Maurice Stewart felt a joyous surge of life beyond anything he had ever experienced or hoped to experience.

"No."

She pushed free of him, totally composed.

"Rachel."

"Take me back now."

"*Rachel!*"

"Please . . ."

She did not kiss him again. Their hands touched on the front porch, and then—like the fleeting shred of a dream— she was gone. He climbed into his buggy in a state of numbing aftershock. His mind whirled and his testicles ached. And as the brown gelding took them instinctively home, Maurice Stewart knew from the depths of his being. . .

He must have her.

He must have her for his own.

The blizzards and numbing cold of the winter of 1902 was one of the worst in memory. Old-timers in Fall River nursed aching bones and joints. Snowstorm after snowstorm raked down from Canada; streets and roads were choked with drifts; electric power went off; the river froze into a block of ice. Housewives heated snow in buckets for water, and farm families were marooned in snowy isolation and despair. Cattle froze to death in the fields, and cows suffered because farmers could not get to the barns for milking. Three elderly people died from the cold when they ran out of firewood. In separate incidents, a man and a woman living alone committed suicide. An outbreak of diptheria took five children in one family, all within nine days.

Pease's Candy Factory shut down, throwing its people out of work. Rachel Birnham had been forced to remain home even before that to care for her mother, who had become ill. Maurice carried groceries to the little house and did what he could to help, but there was no time for him and Rachel to be together. He and Moneypenny worked long hours in the machine shop, putting together a new buggy model for the spring. It was to be called the Stewart Continental IV. Advertising brochures would hail it as the triumph of the buggymaker's art!

Helen DeMare was starring in a new play in Chicago, and was away from Fall River from early January through the first week in March. Impassioned love letters arrived weekly; the burden of impending confrontation weighed upon him more heavily as the time for her return drew near. And at last, as March brought an unexpected thaw and a welcome break in the grip of icy cold, the evening train brought Helen with a mountain of baggage and a retinue of friends, home to Fall River.

That evening, when they were alone after dinner, he told her what he planned to do.

The fury of Helen DeMare was beyond anything he had anticipated.

"Who do you think you are, Maurice Stewart? God? You're not going to abuse me like this. You will not make me the laughingstock of Fall River. How proud you must be of yourself! While I'm away in Chicago, so much in love I can't even look at another man, you're playing fast and loose with that . . . that little Jewish bitch! Oh, I've heard about it. Several friends tried to break the news to me, after seeing the two of you ice-skating together, taking long walks, and making goo-goo eyes.

"Why, Maurice? What's she got that little Helen hasn't got, eh? Look at me. Don't turn away like that. Look at me! This is yours, Maurice. All yours. I've worshiped the ground you walk on. I've given you something scores of men have desperately wanted, the most precious possession I own: me. My pride, my dignity, my self!

"I've warmed your bed and never asked for marriage, because I knew you didn't want that. I tried not to be too possessive, to give you freedom and respect. And now . . . this!"

Her eyes blazed; her cheeks flamed; the pretty face contorted in rage. Maurice attempted to calm her, but his words were futile. "I don't think less of you, Helen. My feelings are the same. I haven't changed. It's just that . . ."

"That you *love* Rachel what's-her-name!"

"Rachel Birnham."

"You've betrayed me, Maurice."

"I never promised anything, Helen. You know that. It has

always been right up front between us. How can you accuse me of betrayal when there was nothing to betray?"

He should have avoided this. How much easier it would have been simply to ignore her, simply to turn away, shut her out, leave. But that was not the Stewart way. He had to be a damned noble fool and let her know the truth.

"I can sue you for breach of promise," Helen said. "There are laws against this kind of thing. I'll see a lawyer..."

So there it came, the possibility that he dreaded most: a public scandal, dragging Rachel into the mess. Breach of promise, indeed! "Go ahead, then. Get a lawyer if you wish. There was no promise to breach, but get a lawyer if you like. We'll fight it all out in public. Or I'll simply pay you and bail my way out. But one way or the other, this is it. Helen, I have no choice..."

She was silent for a moment, as if holding her breath. And then abruptly her expression changed. Something inside seemed to collapse. Helen DeMare sank to her knees before him, tears pouring down her face. "No," she whispered, "I can't do that, Maurice. I wish to God I had never met you. But I love you. I hate you and I love you at the same time, and that's my cross to bear, not yours. It isn't your fault that I love you."

He left her there, curled up on the floor of her apartment. But the image of that last glimpse of her, alone and bereft, would remain burned into his mind.

Helen DeMare left Fall River for Chicago on the next morning's train, and was heard to say that she would never return.

On a windy, slushy evening in the second week of March, Maurice bought a ring of white gold bearing a single large diamond at Finch's Jewelry Store, slipped it into his vest pocket in a purple velvet box, and went to the little house on Maple Street to ask Rachel to marry him.

She was not at home.

Jacob Birnham met him at the front door. The little man was in distress. "I am sorry, Mr. Stewart, but Rachel has gone to visit cousin in New York. It was"—he seemed to grope for words—"quite quickly that she made up her mind."

"New York? She didn't mention it. When will she be back, Mr. Birnham?"

"I cannot say. I don't know." Jacob Birnham started to close the door.

"Wait! Wait, Mr. Birnham. I want to see her, write to her. What is her address? Where can I find her?"

Now the door swung wide open. Sara Birnham stepped in front of her husband. Rachel's mother was even more grim-faced than usual, eyes hooded and mouth set in a thin line. "Our daughter no longer wishes to see you, Mr. Stewart. She is gone away and won't be back for some time, maybe never. Do you understand? Rachel no longer wants to see you. Now go."

The door closed.

His heart sank.

He went back to his lodgings, opened a quart of bourbon, and drank far into the night.

The weeks passed in a torment. Will Pease could give him no information. He contacted Rachel's few personal acquaintances, but they knew nothing. One day he saw Jacob Birnham with his pushcart on the street and tried to talk with him, but the man was evasive and refused to answer questions. As Maurice turned away, however, Birnham plucked at his sleeve and said, "I'm sorry, Mr. Stewart. I'm truly sorry."

Her letter arrived the second week in April. Heart pounding, he ripped it open.

> *Dear Maurice. I am sorry about leaving. I stay with cousin in Brooklyn, New York, and go to night school to improve my English reading and writing. I miss you. If I never see you again, please know that I regard you as good friend. Love, Rachel.*

The letter bore a Brooklyn address. He caught the next morning train.

It had been five years since he had last seen New York. Enormous changes had taken place. New buildings were rising everywhere; the streets teemed with trolley cars, horse-drawn vehicles, and occasional horseless carriages. An elevated train was under construction through the heart of the city. He had wired ahead, and Hope met him at Grand Central depot. Maturity sat well with this lovely cousin, giving her a remarkable air of self-possession. They rode along Fifth Avenue in a chauffeur-driven horseless carriage to the graystone townhouse where she lived with her ailing husband. Howard Langden was pale and thin, greeting Maurice from a wheelchair. As they drank excellent bourbon and exchanged small talk, Maurice was impressed by the obvious depths of affection between the two.

"Your cousin is doing a man's job nowadays, Stewart. You can be proud of her. Hope Stewart Langden holds her own in the jungles of bigtime journalism. She runs a good newspaper, and a profitable one, too."

Hope smiled. "Howard, you've taught me everything I know."

"Do all Stewart women have so much grit?" Langden asked.

Maurice chuckled. "Well, our great-aunt Catherine built up a steamboat empire. Aunt Francesca still runs her Hudson River shipping operations and is over eighty. And then there's Maybelle, another great-aunt..."

"Maybelle?"

"She used to run the biggest whorehouse in San Francisco. As a matter-of-fact, it was the biggest west of the Mississippi."

Their laughter filled the parlor.

The following morning he declined Hope's offer of the horseless carriage and traveled to Brooklyn by train, trolley, and hansom cab. Rachel's cousin lived in a sprawling working-class block of narrow brick tenements with look-alike front stoops. It was a neighborhood of crying babies, street vendors calling their wares, and housewives quarreling from open windows festooned with drying laundry. He rang the doorbell, removed his black derby hat, and waited. The door was opened by a middle-aged woman with stringy hair, smelling of laundry soap. She eyed him suspiciously.

"If you're a salesman, Mister, we don't want any."

When he asked for Rachel, her eyebrows lifted sharply. "You want Rachel? Your name wouldn't be..."

"Maurice Stewart, from Fall River."

The woman threw up her hands and went running back into the apartment. "Rachel! Rachel! He's here! Mr. Stewart's at the front door. Rachel!..."

She came running. "It can't be. But it is!" Rachel Birnham's face beamed in a joyous smile of welcome. She flung her arms about his neck with such fervor that he almost toppled backward down the steps. "Oh, it's you! It *is* you! I'm so happy. I thought I would never..." She covered his face with kisses.

They were a long time settling down. He was ushered into the apartment to be introduced to the middle-aged woman, who was Rachel's cousin Ruth. There were two shy children, a boy and girl, who studied him with dark eyes. Her husband Frederick, a trolley car driver, had gone to work. Rachel sat holding onto his arm as—at Ruth's insistence—he ate a snack of cheese blintzes washed down with black coffee. And then Ruth took the children and disappeared, leaving them alone in the parlor to talk.

"Why did you leave me? I've been going out of my mind. Your parents would give me no information, so I thought..."

"It was Mother. She insisted that I stop seeing you. She said she would not have me marry *goyum*. They talked with matchmaker in Detroit, and he has picked out good Jewish young man for me. He owns clothing store and comes from good family."

"But you can't marry someone you don't even know. It's out of the question!"

"It is tradition. Mother says we must go by tradition, especially in blessed memory of my brother Solomon."

"Impossible. I'll not stand for it."

"You have no say. Neither do I."

"Marry me!"

"Marry you? You are gentile. I cannot marry you. You probably haven't even been circumcised."

"I've been circumcised."

"Not by a rabbi. Not in a religious way. A gentile man is unclean."

"Marry me. It doesn't matter. Love is all that matters. Religion can't dictate love and marriage. That is a terrible waste..."

"I should never have met you."

"You do love me, then."

"Yes."

"There is no doubt in your mind?"

"I have been miserable without you. You are all I could think about. My poor cousin Ruth and her husband, I almost drove them crazy talking about my gentile love."

"Marry me. We will have a civil ceremony. A judge. A justice of the peace. My cousin Hope will be a witness."

"And my cousin Ruth."

"You will? You will marry me?"

"Yes."

"You really will?"

"Yes! Oh, yes!"

A week later, in the chambers of Magistrate Harry P. Tolliver of the Borough of Brooklyn, Maurice Stewart and

Rachel Birnham were married in a civil ceremony witnessed by a dozen relatives and friends. The magistrate, a sentimental man, wept. At a champagne reception afterward, he told the assembled guests that this was the most handsome groom and beautiful bride that he had ever been privileged to marry in more than thirty years. He was paid twenty-five dollars, and again burst into tears.

Late in the night, they lay entwined in the soft, warm sweetness of first love. She had seemed only mildly responsive. And yet his own ecstasy filled him until he was frantic for more. By the dim moonlight filtering in through massive windows overlooking the Hudson, he watched her sleep. Softly, then, he kissed her again, nuzzling the sweet scent of her, stroking the silken hair and silken flesh.

She stirred but did not return his kisses. He saw that her eyes were open in the moonlight.

"I will love you forever," he said. "You are my life. You are as close as my skin. I will love you with all my heart and soul, forever and ever."

"Don't say forever." Her voice sounded oddly detached, almost cold. "Forever is such a long time, and we don't know what life holds. We have now, and that's what matters."

"Rachel . . ."

"No," she said, turning her back to him. "I'm tired now."

He lay awake until dawn, tormented by desire.

VIII

Autumn blazed along the Potomac. The trees around the Capitol had turned to russet, gold, and scarlet. The bench-sitters of Lafayette Square whiled away the hours beneath stately limbs of magnolia, elm, and beech. The flower beds were clipped and raked for winter, pathways neatly edged and swept. Tourists wandered about the broad sweep of Capitol Mall, past the curious fortlike hulk of the Smithsonian Institution. Pretty young women were fashionably chic in broad-brimmed straw hats, dark ankle-length gowns, and starched white shirtwaists. Every feminine eye turned to the tall, handsome man in the dark business suit and soft hat who bore himself like a soldier and outdoorsman. Casey Stewart, tanned and fit, contemplated the traffic flow along Pennsylvania Avenue and reflected upon the changes taking place. Trolleys and occasional horseless carriages—square, ugly things clattering and honking—shared the road with bicycles, buggies, four-in-hands, and victorias. They were already nearly two years into the new century, an era of electric lights, telephones, great dynamos, and other untold technical wonders. And now at last he felt distinctly a part of it.

He walked past the Arlington Hotel and the Cosmos Club toward the White House, glancing at his watch. Five minutes until two. It was time. He turned up the walkway, glanced across the green sweep of yard, was conscious of the majesty of the presidency as reflected in this official residence...

Something thudded on the ground to his left, bounced twice, and came to rest. Running feet pounded around a corner of the building and two white-clad boys appeared, followed by a pretty young girl. "The football!" they shouted. "Kick the football, Mister!" He scooped up the ball, balanced it on one hand, and kicked. The ball lofted high into the air, wobbled toward the building, was caught by a wind gust, and struck a window. Glass shattered.

"Uh-oh!" shouted the girl. "I told you, Kermit. Now we're in trouble. You've broken a window! Father's going to be upset."

"Don't blame me, Alice. It wasn't my fault. He kicked it!" The boy pointed an accusing finger at Casey.

More running feet. A man's voice, high-pitched and imperious. "Children, children. Bring the ball. It's third down. We get another down!" The stocky figure came rushing around the corner, coattails flying, face ruddy from exertion. He stopped short. The mustachioed face widened in a familiar toothy smile. "Casey Stewart! Upon my word!"

Casey could not believe his eyes. "Colonel! I mean, Mister President!"

"I didn't break the window, Father," Kermit said. "He did."

"Well, now. Well, now." Theodore Roosevelt frowned. "That's very serious. Can't go around destroying government property. We'll just have to reprimand Mr. Stewart."

"You called Father 'Colonel,'" Alice said. "Are you a Rough Rider?"

"Sure he's a Rough Rider," Kermit said. "He looks like a Rough Rider."

"I didn't ask you, Kermit."

"Of course he's a Rough Rider." The President, grinning

193

again, took Casey by the arm. "This is Sergeant Casey Stewart, the hero of San Juan Hill."

Kermit's eyes widened. "Gee!"

More children appeared and more and more. Crowded around Roosevelt and Casey, they all walked to a makeshift football field outlined in white chalk on the White House lawn.

"We were having a little game," Roosevelt said. "Some of these children are mine and some belong to the staff, but I don't remember which is which. Now, children, you continue without me. Mr. Stewart and I have business to discuss. Come along, Casey. We'll retire to the house."

Briskly they crossed the lawn and entered by a side door. The cool elegance of the White House enveloped them as Roosevelt led the way to the Executive Office. He ordered a servant to bring iced lemonade.

Less than two months ago the assassination of William McKinley had catapulted this man into the presidency, Casey reflected, and already he had put his stamp upon the place. Roosevelt brimmed with energy. At age forty-two, he was the youngest President the nation had ever had. Detractors, even within his own Republican party, had seized upon Senator Mark Hanna's phrase, "that damned cowboy." Pictures of hunting scenes and mounted trophies lined the walls of the presidential office. There were stag horns and a brace of pistols in a case, manly knickknacks strewn about, leather armchairs, and a huge desk of polished mahogany by the window. Roosevelt drew a bandanna from his back pocket, mopped his face, adjusted his pince-nez, and sat down in a leather easy chair.

"Casey, it's good to see you. I appreciate your coming all the way from Chicago on such short notice. I know you're busy building Great Northern's new spur line. Incidentally, I hear great things about you as a railroad engineer. Chip off the block. Your uncle Thaddeus would be proud. Your new track-laying process is working splendidly, I hear."

Casey smiled. The breadth of the man's knowledge never failed to impress him. It was the mark of the energetic mind and the consummate politician. "I won't even ask how you knew, Mister President..."

"I've got friends in railroad circles, of course. Word gets around. Your two years as construction chief at Great Northern has caused considerable talk. It's said that you've got a brilliant future there."

"Thank you, sir."

Roosevelt engaged in more small talk. He missed the regiment, spoke wistfully of the fine men who had served with them in Cuba, mentioned the losses—not only in combat but due to yellow fever and malaria as well. And in this personal, roundabout way he came to the point:

"Casey, I asked you to come because I need your help. I always seem to need the most from those who have least time to spare. You've made a name for yourself very quickly as a crackerjack railroad builder. But you've also got unique insights on the old Panama Canal. You'll remember that we talked about this back in '97 in New York, after your cousin Hope's wedding. You gave me some very interesting information at the time . . ."

"I've severed all my ties with Panama, Mister President," he said tightly.

"Yes, yes, I'm aware of that. Terrible thing, the French disaster. That business with your father-in-law must have caused you great travail."

"Yes, sir."

"But the point is, the Panama project might still be worth pursuing. I'm not saying it would; I'm saying it might. As you know, Casey, my administration is committed to a United States Canal across Central America. I consider it vital to our national interest, vital to our extension of naval power, vital to our trade and development as a nation of world stature. In Congress it's almost a foregone conclusion that our Canal will be dug across Nicaragua. Even now Rear Admiral John G. Walker and his Isthmian Canal Commission are completing a study ordered by President McKinley two years ago. I've seen an advance copy of the report. Confidentially, it recommends the Nicaraguan route. However, that report also makes a very strong case for Panama. Very strong indeed. Even I was surprised. The route, for all the French disaster, still has distinct advantages. Knowing politicians on the Hill, this part is likely to be ignored. But Admiral Walker tells me that the only major obstacle to a recommendation for the Panama route is the cost. The French have put an impossible figure of one hundred nine million dollars on their holdings in Panama. That's what it would cost us to take over."

The eyes behind the spectacles shrewdly searched Casey's face for a response. Casey kept his expression noncommittal. The President blinked, hesitated for a second, and pushed on.

"You've still got a lot of contacts in Paris. Henri LaVelle, your former father-in-law, was a director of the original Panama Canal company bankrupted in '89. Now he is president of the Compagnie Nouvelle. It's a new company formed to pursue the Canal business to some final conclusion. They want to recoup what they can. Our commission has had negotiations with them in Paris. Their price holds firm. But even on the chance that Congress did switch to a Panama project, we wouldn't pay a penny over forty million dollars."

Roosevelt hesitated again, breathed deeply, and put his hands together.

"Casey, I want you to go to Paris and talk them into dropping the price. It's the only way we can sell Panama to Congress, and even this won't provide any guarantee. Tell me you'll do it."

Casey Stewart was stunned. Paris? Henri LaVelle? Paulette? His mind said no; he would never do it. This was asking too much. Surely there was some other way. No. Absolutely not.

"It's in the national interest, Casey. You're the man who can pull this off. I see it as an act of courage, the same sort of courage that took us up San Juan Hill. No trooper in the regiment rose so admirably to the task that day. This is why I know you've got the stuff to do this job. Say yes, Casey." Roosevelt leaned forward intently, touching him on the arm. "Say you'll do it. This will mean an awful lot to me, and to the country."

Time. He needed time. Time to gather his thoughts. Time to sort it out. It would require a leave of absence from the railroad and possible disruption of a flourishing career. But more than anything, it would jerk him out from the comfortable hideaway he found in relentless, driving work and total absorption, force him to face Henri LaVelle again, force him to face himself.

"Say you'll do this for me, Casey."

He heard his own voice in reply, as if disembodied from his own mind and body. "All right, Mister President. I'll do it."

God, what a fool! What an idiot he was! Voluble and beaming, Roosevelt escorted him arm-in-arm out of the office, through an anteroom crowded with hushed groups of men and women waiting to see the President, out into the portico area. The world outside was luxuriant with fall, the sky high and milky, the trees ablaze, the air crisp and stunningly clear. But he seemed to move like a puppet, nodding and smiling on cue, taking the firm handshake, accepting the manly clap on the shoulder, his strings pulled by a master manipulator.

Theodore Roosevelt's eyes crinkled behind the spectacles. "About that broken window, Casey . . ."

The broken window? He had forgotten. He had kicked a football and broken a White House window!

"I was going to send you a bill for repairs, Sergeant. But we'll forget it now. Call it even-Steven, right? Bully! Bully for you!" The smiling President turned and quick-marched back into the White House.

Casey Stewart walked back to Pennsylvania Avenue in shock.

Paris was lovely, a city of women and perfumes. Since his student days, he had been enthralled by the sights and sounds and smells of Paris. Every street, every bookstall, every café, had its special memories, haunting and bittersweet. The finest years of his life had been spent here, as the only American in his class at the select École Polytechnique. It was the elite of engineering academies, producer of brilliant young men. They had triumphed at the Suez long before Casey's time; they had built, in the colonies of France from Africa to southeast Asia and the Caribbean, roads and viaducts, water systems, canals, dams. Theirs was a proud heritage even now, in the lingering aftermath of Panama.

To Casey's delight, he found that he still had friends here, among those who had survived. The lighthearted Paul Defey greeted him enthusiastically, embracing and backslapping and shouting, "Casey! Casey, *mon ami!*" Intense Lupin Monet, the mathematical genius, joined them, along with his brother Philippe. And as word filtered through the ministries and offices, more came to join them in a bistro on the Left Bank. Everyone spoke at once, trying to be heard over everybody else. The wine flowed; the smoke thickened; Casey Stewart basked in an unexpected flush of reunion. But they were older than before. They wore spectacles; their bellies tended to paunch and their hair was dusted with gray. The light of conviviality dimmed somewhat when the talk turned to the purpose of Casey's mission to Paris.

"Henri LaVelle! Surely you're not going to see him, Casey."

"I would not advise it, if I were you."

"Is he still that angry?"

"He refuses to speak your name. His associates in Panama

turned their bitterness upon you, for forcing his hand. Henri LaVelle is a haunted man."

"We are all haunted. All France is haunted."

"Casey is a victim too. His wife, his father-in-law, his career..."

"We know that. Of course, of course. But there are those whose eyes can see no farther than their hatreds."

"You did the honorable thing, *mon ami*. You had no choice."

He was grateful. They understood his motives. These were technical men, builders and not schemers. They had no part in the political conniving behind-the-scenes, no hand in the lush private payoffs as contractors had rushed to skim huge profits on promises of kickbacks to their friends. They shared Casey's hostility toward those who had profiteered so hugely at public expense.

"But there is a fervid wish to resolve the Canal question. It is said that Henri LaVelle has even talked to the Russian czar, trying to get financial backing."

"In desperation, men will deal with anybody."

"Hah-hah-hah. Even with Casey Stewart?"

"With the devil himself!"

"What can we do for you, Casey?" It was Monet speaking, his mind functioning as usual with mathematical precision. "What do you need from us?"

Casey lowered his drink and drew smoke from a cigarette. "I need information, gentlemen. Knowledge is power. I need all the power I can get..."

Two mornings later, on a crisp sunny day in Indian Summer, Casey Stewart stepped out of a huge motor-driven Mors taxicab in front of a palatial graystone *hôtel particulier* on the Avenue d'Iena near the Arc de Triomphe. Tall, lean, and superbly fit, he was turned out in an impeccably tailored gray suit, dark vest with gold watchchain, and boots of soft polished cowhide. His soft black hat was downbrimmed on one side in the Paris fashion. As the taxi drove away with a clash of gears, Casey read the small brass plate by the door: Compagnie Nouvelle, and rang the bell.

Two minutes later he stood before a massive oaken desk studden with brass, before banks of narrow leaded windows overlooking the Arc de Triomphe, looking into the ice-blue eyes of Henri LaVelle. The old man had not changed. He still exuded elegance, his patrician features offset by grayish-white hair and a finely trimmed goatee. The nose was a blade, the eyebrows a wild tangle, the manner imperious. Henri LaVelle came to his feet behind the desk, ramrod straight as always, his tailored black morning coat and winged collar framing a handsome gray silk cravat with a diamond stickpin.

"So," he said in that silky voice which masked all feeling, "you have come back to Paris."

"Yes."

"I must say, I'm surprised. Your arrival has created quite a stir. I hope you've brought your dueling pistols."

Casey smiled. "I have given up dueling."

In the first rush of disclosure and recrimination, the word had flashed across the Isthmus of Panama that Henri LaVelle had challenged his son-in-law to a duel. No such thing had happened, of course; but the fiction had fueled the tension gripping that jungle community during those terrible days of collapse.

"Perhaps it is just as well," Henri LaVelle said. He walked to a crystal decanter and glasses on a silver tray by the window. "Cognac?"

"No, thank you."

"I'll have one, then."

Casey watched the elegant hand lift and pour. It was the act of a superbly confident individual. Only one small flaw betrayed Henri LaVelle. As the amber liquid flowed into the sparkling glass, the hand trembled slightly.

LaVelle sipped and returned to his chair. "So you're now the emissary of the American President. Those are weighty credentials. I suppose I'll have to listen to you, however distasteful that might be. What have you got to tell me, Mr. Stewart?"

Casey repeated what Theodore Roosevelt had said. As he spoke, the ice-blue eyes locked onto his face. When he had finished, LaVelle remained impassive and silent. A clock tolled the hour; in the silence it sounded unnaturally loud.

"Impossible," LaVelle said.

"Quite the contrary." Casey kept his tone tightly controlled. "As I understand it, you really have no options left. This new company of yours, despite"—his glance swept the expensive room—"all this costly window dressing, is on very shaky ground financially. In league with the court liquidator, you have gone to every contractor who's still solvent and told him to invest or to be exposed for fraud and breach of contract."

"You are out of your mind." The goateed features did not flinch.

Casey smiled. "Paris has no secrets. It is the talk of the cafés. You are capitalized for the equivalent of eight million dollars, two thirds of it from these blackmailed stockholders. Gustave Eiffel himself put in the equivalent of two million dollars. What you propose to do is persuade the Americans— or anybody else who'll listen—to buy out the company and its Panama interests at top dollar, pay the bankruptcy court as little as you can get away with, and pocket a handsome profit for yourself and your associates. Just like the good old days, eh, LaVelle?"

LaVelle was turning pale. Casey recognized the characteristic blood-draining from past confrontations. It could not be helped. He hurried on.

"Actually, your motives and personal profits are of no interest to me. France's treasury has been bled so much already that a little more hardly matters. As I've said before, LaVelle, you have to face yourself in the mirror; no one can do it for you..."

"Your morality is of no concern to me, Stewart. Get on with it."

"Very well, then. I propose that you reduce the selling price to forty million as Roosevelt proposes. Failing that, I intend to unmask this little scheme in the same way that I unmasked the others; only this time I shall expose your blackmail to the newspapers in both France and the United States. If that happens, LaVelle, you wind up with nothing. Except, perhaps, a few years in prison."

He stood up, suddenly queasy in his stomach. The ice-blue eyes gazed at him from a face now white as chalk. When Henri LaVelle spoke again, there was no longer any pretense at control.

"I will see you dead first."

For a heart-stopping instant they stood glaring at each other across the massive desk. And then, with studied calm, Casey picked up his hat and walked out.

But as he stepped onto the Avenue d'Iena once more and flagged a passing taxicab, he felt that his knees were ready to buckle.

"Why did you come back to Paris? Why? Is it not enough that you've already destroyed my father? Must you hound him into his grave?"

The fury of Paulette LaVelle was complete. Her magnificent face contorted as she stood on the flowered veranda berating him afresh. Casey's mind was a tangle of emotions. My God, she was every bit as beautiful as before, tall and lithe, a picture of classic Gallic poise. One part of him wanted to strangle her and the other wanted to take her into his arms.

"Your father is far from destroyed. His disgrace remains incomplete, and you know it damn well. Besides, he fashioned his own difficulties; I didn't do it for him. Hell, Paulette, my choice was clear. The thing that appalled me, and still does, was your choice. Your loyalty to a father was greater than your loyalty to a husband and a son and, yes, even to France..."

"Don't talk to me of France. Don't say those things to me! What do you know of loyalty? At least my father did not consider me unfit for my birthright, deprive me of my place..."

They were at it again, all the old bitter recriminations. In wrath, they raked them over one by one like long-smoldering coals which, once disturbed, flamed up anew.

He left her, wishing he had never come. He went to the American embassy and wrote a note to the President, to be delivered by diplomatic courier. Then he returned to his hotel, vaguely conscious of being followed. A message awaited him.

Be careful. You are in danger.

It was from Paul Defey. He remembered the words of Henri LaVelle, "I will see you dead." So the threat was real. He remained in his suite for the rest of the afternoon. But evening found him restless and out of sorts. He could not stay here, locked up like a rat in a cage. He made a telephone call. It was raining by the time he arrived at the café on the Rue Beranger. Lupin Monet was waiting. The engineer carried a handsome silver walking stick. They drank Pernod and conversed like conspirators. Even the usually imperturbable Monet was ill at ease.

"The word is out. He has sworn to kill you. The man is dangerous, Casey."

"He's mad."

"That won't help you."

Casey eyed the walking stick. "Is that for me?"

"Yes." Monet handed over the stick. It was fashioned of solid hardwood and the head was surprisingly heavy. "I did the best I could with it. You didn't give me much time. As you can tell, I drilled out the top and poured in plenty of lead."

Casey felt the reassuring heft of the stick. The engineer had done a fine job. It was handsome, dressy, lethal.

"I'm sorry I couldn't get the pistol you wanted. They are very difficult to obtain in Paris."

"This might be even better."

"I hope you won't need it."

"We'll see. Now tell me, Lupin, just how does he intend to get the job done?"

Two days went by. Casey booked passage by ocean liner from Le Havre but would have to wait a week. The beauty of Paris held him, even as the autumn deepened and with it a spell of cold rain. The sidewalk cafés emptied as patrons carried their newspapers and wineglasses indoors. Paris donned smart coats and high-fashion fall dresses and suits. Dead leaves spilled from the trees.

There were two of them, burly nondescript men in black cloth coats and cloth caps. They might have passed for working-class idlers but for the muscular way they carried themselves, hand-heavy and moving on the balls of their feet. He had shared life with such men with the Rough Riders and recognized them for what they were. Casey paused, drawing up his coat collar and watching their reflections in the glass of a store window. They had followed him for three days. Finally he had formulated a plan.

Dusk lowered over the Boulevard Saint Germain. Two blocks away stood the rising hulk of Notre Dame. How much fury and bloodletting had those vast buttresses and bell towers witnessed in this city of revolution? How many mortal sins had been whispered to priests in the dank anonymity of its confession booths? Two blocks to the east of him was the École Polytechnique. He knew the area well. And all around, he was conscious of the aged grandeur that was Paris.

They would not take him here. It was too exposed. Thus, the advantage—what there was of it—was temporarily his. He thought of Blanchet and their chess games. "If you can't defend," the lean former padre had said with an evil grin, "then attack."

Casey turned from the window and walked briskly toward the Seine along the Rue LaGrange. A light breeze spanked off the river, cutting through his clothes. He clutched the cane in his right hand, working it in rhythm to his walk. He wore a gray suit, polished boots, a soft black hat, every inch a gentleman.

All this kept forcing him to a fresh self-evaluation. One could not hide from life. The events of his recent past proved as much. In the ruins of Panama he had tried to hide, first in a blur of alcohol and then with Lollie DeRange. But Lollie, for all her devotion and nubile lovemaking, was not his kind of woman. Her death had sent him fleeing to New York, to Hope's wedding, to a brief interval at loose ends. And then had come the Rough Riders, the war, the aftermath. He had found a new Casey Stewart, ironically, on the bloody slope of San Juan Hill. After that nasty little war, and the terrible deaths of his friends, he had known that life was too precious to waste.

The name Stewart still had a magic power to open the doors of railroad presidents. And so he had plunged himself into a new career on the Great Northern Railroad. Who would have thought it possible? Casey Stewart, railroad builder. But even in that process, he had been hiding; he had avoided the company of women and intimacy and romance of any kind. Not until the other day, looking into the angry face of his former beloved Paulette LaVelle, had he become aware again of the powerful depths of his need. He wondered if she knew that her father had hired assassins to stalk him in the streets of Paris. Probably not. He smiled at the bitter irony.

He walked briskly across the Seine in the gathering darkness. Already the soft streetlights were reflected in the black waters.

In the distance he could see two gendarmes pacing the quay, their police uniforms just distinguishable as they passed beneath a streetlight.

He moved along the walkway in the shadows of Notre Dame. He turned around the building, feeling a fresh gust of chill air off the river. He stepped behind a buttress and stood looking toward the north, across the river, at the city of lights.

He waited.

They came quietly, heavily, unspeaking, hands in their pockets.

Step. Step. Step.

Casey stood poised with the lead-filled stick.

He was sweating and the small hairs stirred on the back of his neck.

He took the nearest man first, throat high just as he passed the stone buttress, swinging the stick with a short, savage chop. The lead weight crunched into the thick throat and the man went down, gurgling and struggling to free his hands. Casey leaped clear of him, dropping into a crouch as if for a bayonet attack. In the interval of a heartbeat, the second man stood stunned and wide-eyed, his brain trying to comprehend. And even as his reflexes began to move, catlike, it was too late. With both hands, like a bayonet thrust, Casey Stewart drove the heavy head of the cane straight into his midsection just beneath the breastbone.

"Help!" Casey shouted. "Police! Help, police!"

The man was doubled over, hands free, instincts ready to charge. His heavy body hurtled forward. Casey sidestepped and brought down the stick on the back of the thick neck. He felt the neck break.

"Help! Robbers! Police!"

He heard the whistles. From the corner of his eye, he glimpsed the gendarmes running back under the streetlight toward him. They ran clumsily, undoing their nightsticks and blowing their whistles.

The first man was coughing blood onto the walkway. He looked up at Casey, ashen-faced. A hand came out of his pocket and Casey saw the metallic gleam of the pistol. He swung the stick one more time. The pistol clattered over the stones.

The gendarmes pounded up to him, breathing hard.

"Thank God you're here, officers," Casey Stewart said in French. "These men tried to rob me!"

Paris newspapers headlined the story of the brave American who had fought off two strong-arm robbers at the Cathedral of Notre Dame. Both attackers had criminal records. One was not expected to live. Excitement surged even higher in subsequent editions when it was learned that the American, Casey Stewart, was a graduate of the École Polytechnique and the former son-in-law of Henri LaVelle, president of the Compagnie Nouvelle and once a leading prosecution witness against Charles de Lesseps in the Panama Canal scandals. LaVelle refused to comment on the episode. His daughter the beautiful Paulette LaVelle unaccountably burst into tears and slammed the door when a reporter attempted to question her at her residence near the Palais Royale.

Casey's friends saw him off at Gare du Nord, the huge railroad terminal. They had partied late the night before and even the usually abstentious Lupin Monet was red-eyed and unsteady. "It is unfortunate that you're leaving us, Casey. You really ought to stay in Paris. We haven't had such a good time in years." Monet belched softly.

"Lupin, you're too kind. Frankly, I don't know if I could survive. The climate seems to disagree with me."

There was a ripple of laughter.

"That's a handsome walking stick you carry, Casey," someone said.

"Ah, I almost forgot. It belongs to Lupin."

"Keep it, my friend," the mathematician said quietly. "A memento of Paris in the autumn."

He boarded the train for Le Havre. With a strangely heavy heart, he stood on the rear platform watching his friends until they vanished.

A cold wind swept off the Potomac; the best leaves were gone. Four days before Christmas, Casey would observe the formalities, tender his report, then catch the night train back to Chicago in order to resume his career at Great Northern. Casey Stewart had done his best, even risked his life; once committed, he had wanted desperately to succeed on this mission. But success was not to be. As if to put a final period to his efforts, a House bill for the Nicaragua Canal had swept through committee without dissent. The bill would surely go to the House floor in January.

"Casey Stewart! Welcome! Welcome!" Roosevelt, a study in perpetual motion, bounded across the office and gripped his hand. He ushered Casey to a visitor's chair, ordered a servant to bring hot chocolate, engaged in a stream of hearty small talk, poked up the cheery fire, rubbed his hands, snapped his fingers, and paced. As usual, the chief executive seemed barely able to contain his own energy. "Tell me about it. Tell me everything!"

There was not much to tell. Casey recounted his visit to LaVelle, the thrust of the conversation, the chilly response. "I'm sorry to say, Mister President, that I didn't persuade him."

Roosevelt smiled broadly. "Then obviously you haven't heard the news."

"What news?"

"From Paris. We got it by cable. Henri LaVelle abruptly resigned as president of the Compagnie Nouvelle. He made his announcement at a meeting of stockholders last evening.

There was a near riot. Police had to restore order. The new leadership has agreed to reopen negotiations on the price for French equity in Panama—equipment, land, excavations, everything. I've already instructed Admiral Walker to tender our offer of forty million dollars."

"But how? . . . What happened?"

The servant arrived with the hot chocolate. Roosevelt stirred his steaming cup. "Officially, Henri LaVelle is suffering from extreme fatigue and desires a quieter life, retirement to the country. Unofficially, our embassy people heard that there was a terrible row between him and his daughter. This occurred, according to our sources, after the Paris press reported that you were set upon by two rogues while walking by Notre Dame. We have no evidence linking the attack to LaVelle, you understand, and see no cause to investigate further. But the gossip is that Pauline LaVelle demanded his complete withdrawal from everything having to do with the Panama Canal. And you know how Parisians love to gossip."

Casey Stewart laughed heartily. "Indeed they do, Mister President. Indeed they do."

"I wouldn't believe a word of it." Grinning, Theodore Roosevelt noisily slurped hot chocolate.

His visit was brief. They were saying good-bye when Casey received his next presidential bombshell. He mentioned to Roosevelt that he was on his way back to Chicago. "I'll have a cold winter of outdoor work for Great Northern."

Roosevelt adjusted his pince-nez spectacles. "Oh, that reminds me, Casey. I'm requesting your help in coming to a decision on the Central America Canal project. I need a seasoned technical man to study both sides of the question, someone I can trust. There's a huge emotional commitment in this country to the Nicaragua route. But as I've indicated to you before, I'm not certain that Panama isn't our best way to go. I want to be certain. I very much need your special expertise."

"My expertise? . . ."

"That means you'll be stationed here in Washington for a good part of the winter, with at least one field trip to Nicaragua. I've already contacted the Great Northern people. They say your leave of absence is assured. Provided, of course, you accept my appointment."

"L-leave of absence? . . ."

"Yes." The handclasp. The clap on the shoulder. The toothy smile. "I knew you'd want to do your part."

The President of the United States cheerily waved good-bye and closed the door.

It was late February. Ice crystals still encrusted the windows of the nation's Capitol building. Casey Stewart's mouth was dry; nervous perspiration glazed his forehead. The ornate hearing room was filling rapidly. He recognized military officers, engineers, politicians, journalists. His cousin Hope Langden arrived, looking stunning in a severe dark suit, her hair the color of spun gold. Politicians bowed and scraped. Casey grinned. If only they knew in what low esteem Hope held Washington politicians.

Already ten days of hearings by the Morgan Committee had transpired under the gavel of old Senator John Tyler Morgan. He was a grayish, hawk-eyed man with a droning voice and a deep commitment to cut the Canal through Nicaragua. Day after day, geologists, Canal-builders, and members of the Walker Canal Commission had thrashed over the pros and cons of the separate routes: Panama versus Nicaragua, a lock Canal versus a sea level route. The latter, envisaged for Nicaragua, inspired visions of great ships sailing over a broad and sparkling lake. Emotions ran high for Nicaragua. And now it was Casey's turn to take the chair, perhaps to burst the bubble. He drummed his fingers restlessly on the witness table.

Casey read rapidly from his prepared report. No one paid attention. There was a stirring and rustling in the hearing room. Journalists came and went. Staff men conversed in low tones. His report was a technical analysis of soil samples across the Isthmus of Panama, as well as a preliminary report of his recent field survey in Nicaragua. The survey had reinforced his opinion that Panama was the most desirable route.

Finally the questions began.

"Isn't it true, Mr. Stewart, that the President of the United States personally retained you as a lobbyist in behalf of the Panama Canal route?" The questioner was a Democratic senator from Virginia, hostile to both Roosevelt and Panama.

"Mr. Chairman, I don't think that's an appropriate question for this witness," snapped a pro-Roosevelt committeeman.

Casey managed to defuse things by replying that as an engineer, it was first his obligation to analyze facts and then, if necessary, to take a position.

"And have you analyzed the facts, Mr. Stewart?"

He had done so, yes. He had read all the available reports, studied the French engineering plans while in Paris, made a field trip to Nicaragua, and interviewed eminent technical men on both sides of the Canal question.

"And what conclusions have you reached, Mr. Stewart?" It was the friendly senator again.

"That the Panama Canal is without question the most feasible route," Casey replied.

A murmur coursed through the committee room. Journalists were listening now, scribbling in their notebooks. There were angry shouts. The gavel banged for order.

Later, Casey would not know what precise point of debate caused him to unleash his impassioned burst of oratory. But suddenly he was on his feet speaking above the tumult. "Gentlemen, we are talking about the most far-reaching public works project in modern times. I have been to Nicaragua. It is a jungle, barely explored. In most places we could not see fifty feet in any direction. For all the talk of Nicaragua, not one series of soil samples and core drillings have been made there..."

The angry voices subsided; the room fell still; even the chairman's gavel no longer sounded.

"The French suffered disaster in Panama. The toll in human life and the drain on national wealth was incredible. But I submit to you, ladies and gentlemen, that that was not the fault of Panama. It was the fault of those making the critical decisions. There were gross human errors involved. I speak as an engineer, not a politician. Venal and ignorant men corrupted the Canal project at the very highest levels of French government."

The listeners stirred in their chairs. Murmurs of acknowledgment rippled around the room. Casey felt exposed and vulnerable, now that he was again overstepping the bounds of a technical man—just as he had done in exposing the behavior of his own father-in-law in Panama. But right was right, and there was no turning back now.

"Panama is the place to build this Canal. It has been a crossing point of the Isthmus for three hundred years. It already has an excellent railroad. The route is known, the trail blazed. But to my mind, the final analysis is this: Panama is favored by the engineers, the technical men. They see it as the most feasible route, the most practical and efficient. And so do I, my friends. So do I."

Casey stood in silence. From the audience, someone started

to applaud. More joined in. The applauders came to their feet, shouting, "Hear! Hear!" The nonapplauders remained in their seats. There were far more on their feet than seated.

Reaction to the Morgan Committee hearings astonished him. Backlash, pro and con, swept Washington and, by news wire, the nation. Casey found himself praised and vilified, sought after and shunned. Invitations poured in as hostesses vied for the handsome engineer's presence at social events. He rejected the letters and cards, and sought the company of known and trusted friends, of which there were growing numbers in Washington.

Spring came to the capital city as the grass greened, the trees blossomed, and the days warmed.

"Really, Casey, you must get out more and enjoy the company of your many admirers." Socialite Marcia Morse was unyielding in her pursuit. Elegant and shapely, she was the wife of Peter Morse, architect and civil engineer. She gazed at Casey with friendly hazel eyes. "You are absolutely the most interesting man in Washington. Even married women are mad about you."

"I've been preoccupied, Marcia."

Her voluptuous mouth turned downward in a pout. "Fiddlesticks." It was time, she said, to get unpreoccupied. They were all planning to spend a weekend at Cunningham Farm in Virginia, for the foxhunting. He simply must come. Marcia would not take no for an answer.

And so he went.

It was a vigorous weekend. This was Washington society, a mixture of ambassadors, senators, upper-level bureaucrats, military brass, Virginia and Maryland well-to-do. Casey joined the foxhunt wearing a black riding habit with scarlet coat, astride a powerful chestnut hunter named Warrior. They pounded after the baying hounds, pouring over hills and valleys, splashing through creeks, spilling over rock walls, crashing through wooded copses in full leaf. In the evening they drank, talked, danced, dined. The rambling farmhouse, on a hilltop commanding a panorama of Virginia hills, was filled with sounds of ragtime and two-step dance tunes from one of Mr. Edison's new electric talking machines.

Marcia Morse took Casey by the arm. "There is a young lady who's dying to meet you. She's my niece Willow Luray. Give her a few minutes, Casey. You know how young people are, so impressionable." She escorted him to the front parlor.

"Willow, may I present Mr. Casey Stewart, your latest heartthrob."

She was not over sixteen. She was tall and willowy, like her name, but with merry brown eyes and a soft spill of auburn hair that caught the light. Her handclasp was strong. "Aunt Marcia is teasing me again, Mr. Stewart." The brown eyes looked boldly into his. "But I really did want to meet you. I was fascinated by your Panama Canal speech."

"My speech? But . . ."

"Willow's father is a major with the Army Corps of Engineers," Marcia Morse explained. "She's a military brat, been on Army posts all over the country. I shall"—she smiled and released Casey's arm—"leave you two to your conversation."

Casey was flustered. What did he known about teenagers? He started to call Marcia Morse back. Willow put her hand lightly on his arm. "Don't worry, Mr. Stewart. I won't bite."

They made small talk. She was now attending a private school, Mary Baldwin at Staunton, Virginia. She had gone to Washington to visit the Morses and just happened to be in the hearing room with her uncle on the day of the speech. She was fascinated by the Panama Canal, had read all about the French efforts there, and hoped that someday her father would be assigned to the Isthmus. "I think it would be fascinating, Mr. Stewart. I really do."

He frowned. "It's hot. It's dangerous. It's uncomfortable. It's ridden with mosquitoes, yellow jack, malaria, typhoid, snakes, spiders, and God knows what else. The two major towns, Panama City and Colón, are pestholes of vermin and poverty and mud and filth. It's a place of death. I have bad memories associated with the place, and if I never go back there it will be too soon."

"But I thought you were a Canal man."

"I once was, Miss Luray. But that was a long time ago. Now I prefer to build railroads here in the States. I have a son Nathan, who's almost your age. He's finishing at Briars Preparatory School. He has a mechanical and scientific bent, and eventually I'd like for him to study engineering . . ."

"And your wife, Mr. Stewart?"

Her eyebrows lifted. She had a fetching way of tilting her head. Willow Luray was the loveliest teenage girl he had ever seen. Casey thought: If only Nathan were two years older. "I no longer have a wife, Miss Luray. We are divorced."

"Oh." She pursed her lips. Was that a hint of a smile in her eyes? She clasped her hands together. "I see."

They strolled onto the porch. She talked of a childhood spent on military posts in Kansas and Missouri. "You might say that I grew up early, Mr. Stewart. I've already been with adults." She had even lived briefly in the Indian Territory, and had known two of the rugged westerners with whom Casey had served in the Rough Riders. Her mother was dead, her father stationed in Washington with the War Department. "He could not be here this evening. The truth is, Father is not comfortable in a social setting."

Evening drew over the Virginia countryside. Stars came out. There were odors of new-mown grass and honeysuckle. Marcia Morse finally found them, sitting and talking quietly in the company of several other guests.

"My goodness, Casey. I didn't mean for Willow to monopolize your entire evening. Young people do lose track of time."

He came to his feet, startled. "Time? Marcia, your niece is delightful. It was I who lost track of the time."

Casey returned to Washington the following morning, remembering the strange interlude with that lovely young girl. How wonderful, indeed, if Nathan were two years older. Or—the thought made him strangely uncomfortable—if he himself were twenty years younger.

Summer heat came to Washington. Humidity wafted up from the Potomac. Men changed to light linen suits and women to cotton dresses and shirtwaists. In Congress, the temperatures were rising in a different way. Both sides geared for a floor battle.

After fourteen days of debate, the Senate voted for Panama. A week later, the bill passed the House. "Make way for the Canal!" shouted a jubilant congressman. "Make way for the Canal!"

A small celebration followed at the White House. To Casey's surprise, even Peter Morse came, his dislike for administration politics outweighed by his desire to obtain design contracts. "The merriment is premature," Morse grumbled. "There's still a lot of hard bargaining to do. It'll be another year and a half before the dirt flies."

"That won't matter to me," Casey said happily. "I'm going back to the Great Northern Railroad. At long last, my work with the Panama Canal is finished!"

"That's not what I hear," Morse said.

Casey had a sinking feeling. "What do you mean by that?"

"I hear that the damned cowboy has got you singled out for a job in Panama."

"Absolutely not." Casey shook his head vigorously. "I'm never going back to Panama. I'll see hell freeze over first."

He really believed it.

This time, he would stand firm.

The rain. It was raining again. Rain pelted the corrugated iron roofs of Colón. Rain pelted the streets and filled the filthy gutters, turning the land into mud. Rain brought a sultry, cloying heat to Panama. Mosquitoes swarmed.

It was June 1904.

Casey Stewart stood on the dock in the rain holding a black umbrella. His white linen suit was soggy; the brim of his straw Panama sagged; his shoes were wet, his socks damp. Rain drummed upon the umbrella. It was stupid. He should not be here. He should be back in Illinois, building railroads. And here he stood on this accursed dock on this accursed Isthmus waiting for a doctor to arrive in an unhospitable place with an unhospitable administration, to do the impossible.

A small coastal steamer nosed out of the rain, riding a dirty gray sea. Casey checked his watch. Water flecked the crystal face. Two hours late!

He stood in his wet shoes beneath his streaming umbrella.

And so William C. Gorgas arrived in Panama. He strode off the steamer in a rumpled linen suit, trailed by a clutch of nervous aides. He was tall, handsome, courtly, white-haired, with smiling eyes, and the languid accent of Alabama on his tongue. The best tropical disease man in the nation, they said. He had the look of an outdoorsman.

"Colonel Gorgas?"

"Yes?"

Casey walked up to him in the rain. He lifted his umbrella to accommodate Gorgas. He said, "I'm Casey Stewart. Welcome to Panama."

"Stewart? Stewart?"

"Casey Stewart."

The eyes widened. The handsome face lifted in recognition. "By God. Siboney. We met at Siboney! You were a corporal. By God!"

They whooped and shook hands and slapped each other's backs. From the docks around them, Indians, blacks, and idlers watched in silent amusement.

"Remember? Listen, Stewart, do you remember?"

"I remember! The coconut grove. We were moving out and you were coming in."

"Sure you remember!"

212

"Sure I do. And later, much later—hell, it was after San Juan Hill—you burned Siboney, burned the damned place to the ground. 'Only way to get rid of yellow jack,' you said. 'Burn out the sonofabitch.'"

"Stewart!"

"Gorgas!"

"I'll be goddamned!"

Three ancient black victoria carriages glistened in the rain. They carried Gorgas, his six male assistants, one plain British nurse, and Casey Stewart. The horses clip-clopped through the downpour. Casey and Gorgas shouted at each other over the noise of drumming rain.

"Where will we be headquartered?"

"Ancon Hospital, in Panama City," Casey replied. "It isn't much, but it's the best we can provide right now."

"Is the chief engineer settled in yet?"

Casey shook his head. "He's still in Washington."

Gorgas stared out at the rain. Colón was a teeming mass of run-down buildings, trash-strewn streets, and naked children playing in gutters. The heat was suffocating, the odors sickening. "Well, that shouldn't concern us right now. My job as sanitary officer is clear-cut. I've got to control mosquitoes."

A heavy gust of rain lashed at the carriages.

"I'm glad somebody knows what he's doing," Casey said.

They boarded the train to Panama City. Locomotive and coaches, once painted a sprightly yellow but now showing years of neglect, rattled through the rain-tossed jungle. It was late afternoon when they finally chuffed into Panama City.

Gorgas did not go direct to the hospital. Trailed by the staff, he wanted to see something of the town. They wandered through streets and alleys, poked around between buildings as the heat bore down; it was like a steam bath. "Phew!" Gorgas said. "This whole Isthmus is a mosquito's paradise. They must breed year-round."

"Indeed they do."

He poked and peered. "What's in those red earthenware jars sitting in every house?"

"Drinking water."

"Hmmph."

Finally they went to Ancon Hospital. The place smelled of mold, disinfectant, and neglect. The windows were without screens. Legs of hospital beds stood in freshwater receptacles, to keep ants off the occupants. There were few patients in the wards. The staff consisted of two French physicians and several Sisters of Charity who served as nurses.

"Any yellow fever?" Gorgas asked.

"No, sir," a nun replied. "Only malaria."

Night fell. From out of the humid darkness came swarms of mosquitoes, singing and biting. The staff ate in the dining hall, slapping their attackers. "Panama is going to be more difficult than Havana." Gorgas spoke to his assistant, an entomologist. He speared a piece of meat into his mouth and chewed rapidly. "Our work is cut out for us."

Casey left them at nine o'clock. An hour later he sat in a café drinking beer with Robert Randolph, a dour and skeptical Canal Commission aide who had done the background study on Gorgas for Admiral Walker.

"Good man, Billy Gorgas," Randolph said.

"Will he get the support he needs to do this job?"

Randolph took a swig of warm beer and belched. "I doubt it."

It was ironic. Neither Casey nor Randolph were impressed by the President's top Canal appointments. The chief engineer, John Wallace of Chicago, had been general manager of the Illinois Central Railroad. Retired Navy Admiral John Walker would serve as the Canal Commission chairman with overall authority.

"Penny for your thoughts, Stewart."

"I was thinking that Roosevelt made a hasty decision."

"Well, what the hell"—Randolph lit a cigarette and shook out the match—"if it doesn't work out, you can always go back to railroading."

"Sure," Casey Stewart said. "Sure."

A busy week went by before he returned to Ancon Hospital. Already Gorgas had set up a laboratory. The water crocks and receptacles had been removed; window screens were being installed. Casey found the doctor peering into a microscope.

Gorgas looked up, smiled, and beckoned him to his side. "Take a look. Here's one of our enemies."

The lens focused onto a delicate creature, strikingly marked in shades of gray, silver, and white.

"Elegant," Casey said.

"Stegomyia," Gorgas said. "The bearer of yellow fever."

"Right now there's not a single case on the Isthmus," Casey mused, peering into the microscope. "How do you account for that?"

"The disease comes in waves. It feeds on large masses of nonimmune people. Bring in new blood and stegomyia does her evil work. It's like piling kindling onto a fire that's burned down. Yellow fever blazes up in a fury. If we don't check it, we'll have real trouble."

"How many cases?"

"If conditions remain as they are, and if twenty or thirty thousand men are brought to work in Panama, the yearly death toll will be three or four thousand."

Casey whistled softly. "And what about malaria?"

"Much more difficult to control," Gorgas said. "Malaria is borne by the anopheles mosquito. She's a bush dweller: dirty water, slimy pools, ditches, wet jungle. Proliferates in incredible numbers."

"What's your first priority?"

"Malaria, by all means. That's what caused the French their worst death toll. If we can control malaria, I don't have any qualms about the other diseases. But if we fail there, our mortality rate will be very heavy."

Gorgas's words gave Casey a chill.

Summer came. The heat worsened. One sweated day and night. Each boat brought a fresh contingent of personnel—carpenters, file clerks, mechanics, engineers, laborers.

The chief engineer John Wallace arrived and established residence in the old Dingler House, once occupied by his French counterpart.

"You've done good work, Stewart. I want you to stay on as my assistant. But be sure that every item is properly accounted for. Yes, every item. That means every dollar of wage, every nut and bolt and fixture. We want no slipups, understand, no room for criticism. This is going to be a clean operation. Clean. Everything requisitioned, and every requisition form in triplicate. Beyond that, our mission here is to make the dirt fly."

The fester and humanity of Colón and Panama City were offensive to the chief engineer, son of a Presbyterian minister, the noises vexing to the spirit, the drinking and gambling unwholesome. Wallace himself seemed out of place. Round-faced and fastidious, he wore little round spectacles, a dark mustache, and combed his hair slightly forward to hide a receding hairline. He kept his suit coat buttoned at all times; torrid climate seemed not to faze him. The man, Casey noticed, did not seem to sweat. But neither did he interact with others. And, most notable of all, he made no offer to begin discussing his plan for construction of the Panama Canal.

"I wonder," said Randolph moodily, "if he has a plan."

One day Wallace said, "Well, Stewart, let's go have a look at it." This meant that it was time for the guided tour.

They rode a special train car reserved for the chief engineer. Casey had been back and forth over the fifty-mile corridor so many times that he knew it all by heart. But to John Wallace, a man whose prior experience involved building railroads and designing impressive terminals for the Illinois Central, the journey was an unpleasant revelation.

Wreckage of the French equipment was spilled everywhere along the corridor: scrap heaps, rusted and vine-grown locomotives, discarded rails, pipes, axles, gears. In mucky shallows near Cristobal they counted eighty huge dredging machines, lying on their sides or sunk in mire. Everywhere buildings were rotting. With a pang of remembrance Casey looked up from the passing train and saw the house he had shared with Lollie, its roof now caved in and one wall collapsed. Abandoned work camps were buried beneath tangles of vines and scrub. The Panama Railroad was worn out, its engines and cars broken down, bridges ready to collapse, signals unworkable.

"Dreadful," John Wallace said, holding his nose as they poked through a rotting warehouse building. "Jungle and chaos, jungle and chaos."

They climbed to the brink of Culebra Cut, a yawning dig more than a hundred sixty feet deep slashing through the spine of hills overlooking the Pacific coastal plain. From this point he could see the hill where he had buried Lollie, now overgrown with weeds and brush. Several locomotive-drawn dump cars were still at work, fed by two French excavators. Half a dozen machine shops and a power plant remained operative; tools, machines, engines, and spare parts had been safely stored.

"Culebra," Wallace muttered, his interest quickened. "By golly, aren't those more excavating machines down there? And I see a lot of dump cars still in pretty fair shape, and locomotives too . . ."

"A hundred locomotives," Casey said. "A thousand dump cars. We've got dredges and tugboats waiting to be refurbished and returned to service."

Wallace was busy scribbling in a notepad.

"Culbra," he said. "We'll make the dirt fly!"

Three weeks later, Gorgas invited the chief engineer for an inspection tour of health facilities. Wallace, Casey, and several members of the Canal Commission arrived at Ancon Hospital. "Gentlemen, we need men and supplies," the doctor told them. "Our first priority ought to be the eradication of yellow fever and the control of malaria. And the key to that, of course, is the mosquito."

Wallace and his men were glum-faced and noncommittal. They mopped their faces with handkerchiefs and asked about expenses, and winced when Gorgas spelled out how much the effort would cost.

Weeks passed. Wallace said nothing about Gorgas's request for men and supplies. It was Casey who asked. "What about those requests from Dr. Gorgas?"

Wallace seemed disinterested. "You will have to speak with Admiral Walker about that."

"Admiral Walker? But you're the chief engin . . ."

"Speak with Admiral Walker."

The admiral, chairman of the Canal Commission, received Casey amiably. He listened with a smile as Casey explained the need to get started on mosquito control before great numbers of laborers, even now being recruited in Jamaica and Barbados, arrived on the Isthmus. The admiral offered an indulgent chuckle. "The truth of the matter, Stewart, is that neither I nor any member of this Canal Commission seriously believes that mosquitoes cause yellow fever or malaria. It would be irresponsible of us to squander time and money chasing all over Panama after mosquitoes. It would look especially ridiculous in Washington. Learned scientists will tell you that these diseases are caused by the miasmas, foul fumes wafting up from the poisonous landscape."

"But Admiral, the mosquito theory is proven. The findings of Dr. Walter Reed have been thoroughly reviewed and pronounced as fact."

"Balderdash, Stewart. Sheer balderdash."

Afterward, Gorgas was thunderstruck. "You can't be serious."

"I'm serious."

"I don't believe you."

"Shall I make an appointment for you to see the admiral?"

"By all means!"

They were kept waiting for an hour outside the admiral's office. When they did get a chance to speak, Walker drummed his fingers impatiently. Finally the commission chairman had heard enough.

"Gorgas, let me give you a piece of advice. The way to get rid of yellow fever is to clean up the garbage and dead cats; paint these houses; pave the streets. It's filth that spreads yellow fever, gentlemen. Filth. Besides, I don't want those fellows in Washington getting the idea that we're throwing away tax money down here."

That was the key to it, of course. It was the shrewd Randolph who said as much. "They've all got a maniacal dedication to playing it safe, avoiding any hint of impropriety. Why do you think it takes six months to requisition a screen door from the States? Everybody's covering his ass . . ."

Casey accompanied Gorgas back to Ancon Hospital. "I'll go to Roosevelt personally. This is too much."

The doctor put up his hand in mild protest. "I've been an Army man for a long time, Casey. I learned early not to rock the boat, not to make enemies in the wrong places. You never know when you might meet them again. In the long run, we shall prevail. You'll see." Tall, gray-haired, handsome, William Gorgas looked out over a harbor glowing in sunset. "We shall prevail."

Casey Stewart wished he were as confident.

IX

"Mommy! Mommy! Look at the funny man!"

The child had golden hair and laughing eyes. She pointed a chubby finger at Isaiah Stewart. He hesitated in the aisle of the coach, laboring with his valise and overcoat. His eyes caught the round blue eyes and saw the mirth fade. The woman with the child scowled, as if to say, "Don't speak to her, you deformed wretch." The child stuck her thumb in her mouth and lay her head upon her mother's breast, staring at him.

Isaiah resumed his struggle through the aisle and made it out of the car and down the steps into the blowing cold. He looked toward the end of the train, to the boxcar. Workmen were wheeling the canvas-shrouded machine down a ramp onto the platform. When it was done, the ramp was removed, the door closed, and the foreman waved.

A voice called, "All aboard!"

It was the afternoon of New Year's Eve. The station was

sheathed in ice and snowdrifts piled high along the tracks. The train chuffed into motion again, blowing great billows of steam. Isaiah found the stationmaster and made arrangements for the machine. Then a redcap appeared and Isaiah gratefully handed him the valise. They went to a hansom cab and he tipped the redcap a quarter.

The man's eyes widened at such a handsome sum. "Yes, suh. Thank you, suh!" A bowing, smiling, tipping of the cap.

Isaiah said to the cabdriver, "The Stewart Continental plant, please."

The man nodded and gathered up his reins. Isaiah settled back against the cold leather seat and gazed out through frosted windows as the cab lurched along behind a plodding mare blowing heavily in the cold. Houses and brick buildings huddled behind snowy drifts. Trees were encrusted with ice and overhead wires dripped icicles. Unexpectedly the sun slipped out from behind a cloud, bathing Fall River in sparkling white.

A good omen, Isaiah thought.

His misshapen body rocked with the motion of the cab.

Tomorrow would begin another year. He thought: How quickly time passes. It was stupid to have come to Fall River on New Year's Eve. He would have been smarter to wait a few days and spend the holiday in Chicago, enjoying the warmth and cuisine of the Palmer House. But the thought of another New Year's alone depressed him. What conceit, though, to think that busy Maurice Stewart would even see him, much less listen to his crazy idea. Maurice's views on the horseless carriage were well-known. An article in the Chicago *Tribune* had said as much.

With a fortune being made in buggies and carriages, Mr. Stewart told this correspondent that he saw no reason to change. He called the horseless carriage a "fad" and "plaything of the rich." The young marketing genius whose Stewart Continental is becoming the fastest-selling buggy in America went on to say, "The American consumer wants a conveyance that is dependable, cheap, and easily repaired. He is not interested in noisy metal monstrosities that raise havoc on our roads and are prohibitively expensive to own and operate."

Isaiah's spirits sank. He missed his workshop in Aunt Francesca's carriage house in New York. He was at home

219

there, in the company of his beloved machines. This he had never spoken out loud, lest people think him mad, but he regarded machines as having life and personality. Engines especially could be capricious and unpredictable, just like people, but they were made of metal, not flesh and blood. The imperfections of a machine were never ugly. It operated by laws of physics, not emotion. One could love a machine such as Number Four, which now awaited its critical test beneath the hood of the horseless carriage back there at the depot, the car he called a Stewart Traveler. Number Four neither laughed at a man nor rejected him for his infirmities. Number Four did not care; it simply functioned as the instrument of its creator Isaiah Stewart. And as the creator of Number Four, Isaiah was special among men. A creator of machines was a little like God.

Stewart Continental. The large rooftop sign topped a rambling brick building, part old and part new, spread along the river south of town. The cab drew up before the main entrance. The driver, having seen Isaiah's tip to the porter at the station, solicitously helped him down and carried the valise up the steps. Rewarded in kind, he went off tugging gratefully at his hat. As the cab moved away, Isaiah reflected ruefully upon the equalizing power of money. He picked up the valise and pushed through a set of double brass doors.

A middle-aged receptionist looked up, saw the clubfoot and drawn figure, and frowned. "May I help you?"

"Mr. Stewart, please."

"I'm afraid Mr. Stewart is very busy."

"I'll wait."

The frown deepened. "May I tell him who? . . ."

"Just tell him that his cousin Isaiah is here, from New York."

She was gone in an instant. When she returned, a bright smile lifted her plain features. With genial ceremony, she ushered Isaiah into a large office. The room was carpeted and impressively furnished. Sunlight streamed through a bank of windows overlooking the ice-choked river.

"Isaiah!" Maurice Stewart came around from behind a massive mahogany desk. His tall athletic body had filled out and he wore a black vested suit with a gold watchchain across his middle. His full black hair was combed straight back and, in defiance of clean-shaven male fashion, he wore a full but neatly trimmed mustache. The only flaw was a slight break and thickening of his nose, such as a prizefighter might have.

The overall effect was that of a substantial young business-man, strikingly handsome and brimming with confidence. Isaiah felt a touch of envy.

"This is a wonderful surprise!" Maurice said. "You should have told me you were coming."

Isaiah smiled. "A whim of the moment. I was in Chicago, and..."

Maurice took the valise, waved him to a brass-studded leather armchair, poured bourbon from a side cabinet, and gave him a fresh Havana cigar. "It's been so damn long since I've seen the family. Tell me about everybody, Isaiah. How is Hope? And Aunt Francesca? Casey is back in Panama, I hear. What's the news from Pittsburgh?"

He told him all that he knew, including tidbits of family gossip. Van Harrison was in Europe, a one-legged terror racing automobiles and raising hell. Maurice's nephew Nathan was still in boarding school in Virginia. Hope was deeply involved in running Howard Langden's newspaper in New York, and fighting journalistic battles.

Maurice's laughter interrupted his narrative. "That's the Stewart clan for you, always squabbling!"

Isaiah did not smile. "I stopped in Pittsburgh. Your father" —he saw pain flick across the handsome face and hurried on—"has not changed his attitude, I'm afraid. You remain disinherited. He refuses even to discuss your success."

Maurice stared out the window, drawing thoughtfully on his cigar. "Bradley Stewart is the most stubborn man alive."

Isaiah smiled thinly. "Like father, like son."

Abruptly Maurice came to his feet. His pent-up energy seemed to fill the room. Summoning a secretary, he fired off a stream of orders cancelling or postponing activities for the rest of the day. Then he was on the telephone to tell someone that there would be an extra guest for New Year's Eve dinner. He made a series of calls, some of them personal and others giving instructions on production and accounting matters. Finally he banged the receiver back into its cradle and turned to Isaiah. "Now I want to take you on a tour of the plant."

For the next half hour they walked through the refurbished mill that now was the assembly plant and shipping center for Stewart Continental. They were accompanied by a wizened ancient named Moneypenny, whom Maurice introduced as his partner. The old man wore ordinary working clothes flecked with paint and sawdust and his hands were as tough as old leather. "We're building ten thousand carriages and runabouts a year, Isaiah. Moneypenny here has got a genius for coming out with new designs, each an improvement on the one that went before. This"—he stopped briefly at a fully assembled carriage with bright tassles and see-through weather curtains—"is our Century model for the new year. Each year we try to come up with a new model. The public likes that, something different, a touch of status. In marketing, you've got to give the public what it wants." They moved past a line of workers busily putting together parts of Stewart vehicles. "As you can see, the units are partly assembled here and shipped out by rail. The actual manufacture is jobbed out to other buggymakers, every last piece of it. That was Moneypenny's idea. It cuts tooling and production costs, keeps our prices low..."

It was late afternoon when the three of them climbed into a handsome Stewart phaeton drawn by matched brown geldings and Maurice drove them to his home. The house was a rambling new three-story structure of fieldstone crowning a wooded slope overlooking the river. A servant took their wraps and Maurice led Isaiah and Moneypenny into the living room to warm themselves at a cheery fire over snifters of Napoleon brandy. A Christmas tree stood in the corner, gleaming with decorations.

Rachel Stewart came down from upstairs as the clock tolled six. Isaiah caught his breath. He had never seen a more beautiful woman. Her dark brown hair was upsweat in the Gibson style. Her eyes were wide and lustrous, her face a perfect oval, her mouth generous and smiling. She wore a pale blue gown with a single diamond brooch. She radiated warmth and gentility. Isaiah, sensitive to the subtleties of human reaction to his appearance, saw only loving warmth. When he extended his hand, she embraced him and kissed his cheek. "Welcome, Isaiah. I shall consider you my cousin, too. And I am extremely fond of your first name."

"My name?"

"Yes. It is very Jewish, even though I know that you are not. How unfortunate. You've got the face of a rabbi. All that's missing is a beard."

Their laughter was punctuated by the clink of glasses. "*L'chaim!*"

Isaiah was shown to a pleasant room where he deposited his things and bathed. Dinner was served at seven, and several other guests—all friends of Maurice's—arrived early to join them.

The subject of automobiles did not come up until coffee had been served.

"Maurice, a lot of folks are saying they're here to stay." The speaker was young Jeffrey Straight, the barbershop owner and Stewart stockholder. "I was in Detroit a few weeks ago and ran into young Ransom Olds. His whole plant burned down a year and a half ago. The only thing that was saved was one little runabout, the Curved Dash model. It steers with a tiller and has pneumatic tires and brass gas-fired headlamps. Very nifty. Last year Roy Chapin drove one all the way to New York for the horseless carriage show. It was a big success. Ransom tells me he has the most popular motor car in America right now. He built over two thousand of 'em this past year."

"Personally, I'm betting on the steam car. The Stanley Twins are building a very good model over in Newton, Massachusetts."

"The thought of sitting on top of a steam boiler makes me uncomfortable."

"Ransom Olds says there's two hundred companies making horseless carriages already—gasoline models, steam, electrics."

"Yes, and most of them going broke."

"I heard a good joke the other day. This fellow says, 'I really enjoy my automobile immensely.' His friend says, 'But I never see you out driving.' The first fellow says, 'Oh, I haven't started driving yet. I'm still learning how to make repairs!'"

Maurice laughed and shook his head. "It's all a flash in the pan. Let those damn fools take risks if they want to. In the long run, the public's going to tire of it. We don't have the roads, you can't get gasoline, and the ordinary person doesn't know how to make repairs. The contraption is smelly and noisy and impractical. There's all sorts of trouble over patents, with carmakers fighting lawsuits over infringements. In another year or two it'll be a thing of the past."

Isaiah spoke up. "Don't be too sure, Maurice. Remember what you said earlier about giving the public what it wants. I've done a lot of work with these machines. You might remember my old Winton from a few years ago. Now I drive a much newer machine with many modifications of my own. I've been in Europe again, and there are horseless carriages running all over Paris and Berlin. The Europeans are putting on road races, and there's a lot of racing interest in this country, too."

"Europe is different. Travel distances are not nearly so great between towns. Road surfaces are a lot better," Maurice said. "Can you see driving a horseless carriage between Fall River and Chicago in a driving rainstorm? You wouldn't get forty miles before you were stuck in the mud."

"Henry Ford claims he's come up with a new design..." Someone snorted. "Ford's a crackpot. His own father said he should have stayed on the farm. He's already launched three companies to make cars and not one of them a success. Last spring a new set of backers kicked him out because Ford was spending all their money tinkering with his damn fool racing cars."

"His latest racer is a monster. The Nine-Ninety-Nine, he calls it. Biggest damn machine you ever saw, nearly ten feet long with four exhausts shooting flame and thunder. He talked Barney Oldfield, the bicycle champ, into driving it against Alexander Winton's big Bullet and several others at Grosse Pointe two months ago. Any doubts I had about speed and power were pretty well scotched with that one. Oldfield did nearly a mile a minute."

"Haw! A man can't breathe, going that fast."

"Anyhow, Henry told me he sold the Nine-Ninety-Nine and now he plans to start up another plant at Dearborn. Call it the Ford Motor Company. He's got an idea for a car called the Model T. He says he's going to put a Model T in every front yard and barn lot in America. You'll be able to repair it with a screwdriver and pliers. And when you're not driving it to town, you can jack up the back end as a power unit and run a sawmill."

Maurice turned to Isaiah. "If you're so sold on that infernal machine, Isaiah, why haven't you tried your hand at a commercial model?"

"I'm a machinist, not a businessman. I have no head for business."

"Well, then, find yourself somebody who does have a head for business, pool your resources, and start a company."

"I have found somebody."

"Wonderful. Who?" Maurice took a sip of wine.

"You."

Isaiah was not prepared for the effect of this. Maurice, caught in mid-swallow, choked and went into a coughing seizure. Others burst into laughter. Jeff Straight pounded his breathless friend on the back.

"Attaboy, Isaiah!" shouted a flush-faced dinner guest.

"Stewart Continental!" roared another. "Drive your next buggy without a horse!"

Maurice recovered, grinning and dabbing at his mouth with a napkin. "Good joke, Isaiah."

"It's no joke, Maurice." Isaiah drew from his breast pocket a small pamphlet and spread it open so that the others could see. It bore a drawing and specifications for his new engine, Number Four. "I've got just the motor to do the job. Look at this, it's lightweight, produces more than fifty horsepower, and is of simple valve-in-head design. I call it Number Four, because it's the fourth in a line of designs that I've been fooling around with for several years. As you may remember, Maurice, I started with a Daimler-Benz engine that I brought back from Germany in '96. This is the logical extension of that. It has a very sturdy design and incorporates features of several other European makes, including the Panhard and the Renault."

He noticed that the others had fallen silent as he spoke. Jeff Straight leaned intently across the table, listening. Even old Moneypenny, who had professed earlier to know nothing about internal combustion engines, seemed fascinated. Maurice's expression, however, was noncommittal.

"You've got a great basic buggy, a first-class design," Isaiah continued. "It's strong, lightweight, well sprung. Marry this engine with your Stewart Continental and you've got a better runabout that can be produced cheaper than anything Ransom Olds, Winton, Ford, Duryea, or anybody else has yet come up with. Best of all, you can do it cheaply, with a chassis works already producing..."

But Maurice was smiling and shaking his head. Isaiah stopped talking and looked at his cousin with chagrin. The others, seeing the skepticism with which the proposal was received, murmured dubiously among themselves.

"Maurice," Isaiah said, "we're three years into the twentieth century. We're on the threshold of the most incredible explosion of technology in the history of man. I wouldn't be at all surprised to see man even develop a practical flying machine within the next twenty years. The automobile, that infernal machine as you call it, is going to become a way of life in this country, and all over the world. People want it, Maurice. They want it not only because it's new and different, they want the speed, the mobility, and freedom it can provide."

"I'm sorry, cousin," Maurice said. "I really am. What you say, of course, does make a lot of sense. The logic is splendid. On your basic presumption, I'd have to say that you're one hundred percent on the money. There's just one small flaw."

"And what's that?"

"The basic presumption is dead wrong. The horseless carriage—or the automobile or whatever you want to call it—is not a valid form of public transportation for the reasons I've already stated. Nor do I see it ever becoming valid, except perhaps over another century of trial and error in which an awful lot of entrepreneurs will go bankrupt. What you're talking about here is more than just a fad; you're talking about a revolution in transportation in this country, and that just isn't going to happen." He reached across the table and touched Isaiah's hand. "You're talking about an entire network of roads, fuel stations, repair depots. You're talking about the creation of a public nuisance—already many towns have got speed limits against these contraptions—with its danger, its noise, and its smoke. People are being killed and injured by these things. No, Isaiah. The public is not going to stand for it, and people are not going to pay the bills for everything this horseless carriage would require. As for Stewart Continental, this is a company built on trust, a solid, conservative organization. We must answer to our stockholders. We've got a proven product. In a few more years, this is going to be the biggest carriage company in America. Our sights are set on precise production goals, and we cannot allow ourselves to be deterred..."

Isaiah's spirits sank. Maurice poured another glass of wine and lit a cigar.

Talk turned to other matters. The drinks flowed and spirits lifted as the hour of the New Year approached. More and more people were arriving, coming in out of the snow stamping their feet and boisterously exchanging greetings. Isaiah was impressed by the diversity of the assorted guests, a colorful mixture of investors and farmers, of actors and circus folk, and everyday townspeople. Maurice and Rachel were the center of attention.

As the last minute ticked away, one of the entertainers struck a chord at the piano. The shout went up, "Happy New Year!" The crowd burst into song. *"Should olde acquaintance be forgot..."* Several of the women, including Rachel, hugged and kissed Isaiah and men pumped his hand and drank to his health.

"Happy New Year! Happy New Year, one and all!"

Isaiah had never felt more at ease in his life.

He waited until the following day to spring his surprise.

Tom Moneypenny drove him to the train depot in the phaeton. The weather was slightly warmer. Fall River lay wrapped in the silence of the holiday. The matched geldings danced along snowy sunlit streets, harness bells jingling. The old carriagemaker lit a battered briar pipe with a wooden match and watched the passing winter splendors. Moneypenny seemed anxious to explain Maurice's strong feelings about the business. "Isaiah, Maurice almost lost this here company when it was bein' born. Thugs from the Pover works come in one night and busted our shop to pieces. Maurice was hurt bad, too: broken leg, broken arm, broken jaw, broken nose. It took him months to heal up. All that time he was settin' his mind on what he was a 'goin' to do. He told me, 'Moneypenny, I'm goin' to rebuild this here company. And when I do, it'll be solid as a rock. We'll build us a reputation for dependability, with a money-back guarantee on what we make. The customer will know that he can believe in Stewart Continental.' And that's exactly what Maurice Stewart done. Your cousin's a millionaire in his own right already, and he's just twenty-six years old. Folks around here believe in him. They know Maurice Stewart's word is as good as gold. So maybe you can understand, Isaiah, why Maurice don't like to take chances. Like he told me, 'Moneypenny, from now on we bet on a sure thin'.'"

The station came into view. Moneypenny reined in the geldings and sprang down with surprising alacrity. "Now what is this big surprise you've been so secretive about?"

At Isaiah's instructions, the stationmaster had moved the Traveler into the depot's storage area to keep the engine from freezing. Now Isaiah removed the canvas covering and stood back proudly as Moneypenny's eyes widened to the size of saucers. "Well, I'll be . . ."

It was a splendid motor car, lovingly modified and refitted from the basic Winton design. Isaiah had toiled for months in Aunt Francesca's carriage house, tooling and polishing, fitting and refitting. The hood ornament was the Stewart design, a triangle in a circle fashioned from gleaming brass. The car was high-gloss black metal with brass radiator, brass carriage lamps, brass wheel spokes, black leather upholstery, black convertible top, a glass windshield that could be cranked open, and a steering wheel. The crowning touch was displayed in metal script across the front of the gleaming radiator: *Stewart*.

"The prototype model," Isaiah announced.

Moneypenny stood openmouthed. "Good God!"

Number Four started on the third crank. Isaiah listened with a satisfied smile as pistons, valves, rocker arms, and crankshaft muttered in harmonious power. The sound kept to its deep-throated tone as they drove out of the depot and turned onto the snowy Main Street of Fall River. The town was no stranger to horseless carriages. And yet the journey of the jaunty Stewart Traveler brought spectators out of nowhere to ogle and point. They followed along in a steadily expanding troupe as Isaiah turned up the hill and came over the winding crest to Maurice's house.

Maurice emerged wearing a dressing robe and smoking a cigar. "What the devil? . . ."

Isaiah let the engine idle as he climbed down and stood in the snow. He seemed even more grotesquely misshapen beside the shining perfection of the machine. "I've brought you a New Year's present, cousin. Happy 1903!"

It was not the best weather for a test drive. In fact, Isaiah thought grimly, he could not have picked a more unpleasant time of year to put an automobile through its paces. One made do, however, with time and circumstances; and if the time were not of the best, the circumstances dictated that it be now.

And so they rolled over the slushy streets of Fall River, Isaiah at the wheel and Maurice slumped on the seat beside him, glum and preoccupied. Isaiah had not the faintest idea of the layout of the town, and soon they were lurching over snowy country roads following the tracks of horse-drawn sleds that had preceded them earlier in the day. The sun had slipped behind a bank of snow clouds; the temperature was dropping and watery ruts freezing again, causing the wheels to spin. Isaiah stopped the car, rummaged in the trunk, and drew out his latest invention, a kind of knobby rubber boot that fitted over the back wheels to increase traction. He then gave the reluctant Maurice a quick summary of driving instructions and took his seat on the passenger's side.

"You don't expect me to drive this thing," Maurice said.

"As a matter-of-fact, I do."

"You're insane. I'll go into a ditch."

"Then into the ditch we go, cousin."

Maurice, grim-faced, put the car in gear and worked the clutch. The machine lurched forward, internal parts complaining noisily. But then the lurching subsided and they were rolling along at the persistent rate of five miles per hour.

"You can go faster, if you like," Isaiah said.

"I'm going too fast already."

"At least you can try shifting into a higher gear."

Maurice slid the gasoline lever foward, the machine responded with a fresh surge of power and—with a jerk and a clank—he duly shifted the gears. Isaiah listened to the engine's rumble. He glanced at Maurice and his spirits lifted slightly. A smile played at the corner of his cousin's mouth.

"By God, she runs good," Maurice said.

"I thought you'd be pleased."

"The Stewart Traveler, you say?"

"Yep. Complete with spring suspension, water-cooled radiator and overhead valve engine, and four cylinders producing eighty horsepower. The engine is built up from a Daimler-Benz configuration, made in Germany."

"You don't say?"

Snowy fields and forest slid past them. Wind spanked at the glass shield and tugged at their clothing. Isaiah's exhilaration took another surge as Maurice increased speed. They went barreling down a curving slope flanked by split rail fences, snow flying in their wake, the rising clatter of the engine echoing over silent, white-browed hills, and treeless forests.

Too late, Isaiah saw the boulder jutting in the road ahead.

"Look out!"

They hit it at full speed. The car leaped clear of the road surface, all four wheels airborne at once. It slewed madly as one wheel touched down and then another, pitching to the side with a grinding crunch of metal and exploding of tires. Both men vaulted clear, tumbling into soft snow. Isaiah winced as he heard the final crash into the fencerow. Then there was silence and the soft moan of wind over the hills.

He rolled over, spitting snow. From beyond a drifted mound he heard a sputtering, choking sound. A stab of fear went through him.

"Cousin! Cousin, are you all right?"

Painfully Isaiah straightened his twisted body and stood up to look for Maurice. There, beyond the mound, he saw him, shoulders shuddering, face contorted in the cold.

He was laughing.

The man sat spread-legged in the snow, laughing.

"Damn!" Maurice Stewart shouted, "that was more fun than a toboggan ride!"

Four hours later, as night settled over the snowy town, they returned to Fall River at a walking pace, riding in a bent-wheeled Stewart Traveler drawn by a team of mules.

At Maurice's house, over cigars and a bottle of bourbon whiskey, the cousins discussed the significance of this strange New Year's—the one twisted and bent, his features bulging-eyed and slacklipped in the play of firelight, the other muscular, tall, and handsome. For the first time in his life, Isaiah Stewart found himself speaking with an intensity of passionate belief, all shyness and reserve aside. This was his ground, his compelling interest; this was what he *knew*.

"I've got to come to a decision, Maurice. Number Four is far and away the best engine in America today. It is packed with my own secrets, everything I've learned in nearly ten years of fooling around with the internal combustion concept. You heard and saw for yourself. Even after that spill we took, Number Four is still running like a top. There's never been a tighter, more durable engine made. I'd like to see her in a Stewart production car. But I can't wait. Every dime I own is tied up in Number Four. I've borrowed to the hilt from Hope and Aunt Francesca to complete this prototype car. I've had three offers for my patents and designs. Tom Jeffrey over at Kenosha, Wisconsin, claims to have financial backing to make it a real success. He's building a machine called the Rambler. Henry Leland, who runs one of the best machine shops in the country, is converting Henry Ford's latest organizational failure into a company called Cadillac. Leland is drooling to get his hands on Number Four. Alexander Winton has already drawn up a contract, just waiting for my signature."

"Why haven't you taken them up on it, Isaiah?"

"Because I want to keep it in the family. Stewarts have always been pioneers in transportation. Think about it. Our great-grandfather, the first Isaiah Stewart, built the boats that took early settlers downriver from Pittsburgh. Remember Nathan Stewart and the Erie Canal? Remember Catherine and Stephen with their steamboat empire, and my own"—Isaiah hesitated, as if touched by an old pain—"and my own father Thaddeus, with the transcontinental railroad? It's heritage, Maurice. Our heritage. But if you look back, you'll find an interesting phenomenon. Not one of those Stewarts was truly a technological innovator. They were systems people; they adapted to rivers, canals, and rails, but they didn't really develop the technology to do it. Times have changed. Today the innovators are technical people, the producers and manufacturers. The great fortunes of tomorrow will be made in the production of vehicles to provide people with mass mobility. And no vehicle in the history of the world has ever lent itself so uniquely to mass production, on a virtually unlimited scale, as the automobile..."

He talked on, and Maurice Stewart listened. At last the clock struck two in the morning. The bourbon bottle stood empty. They climbed the stairs wearily and went to their separate rooms, Isaiah to fall into bed from exhaustion, Maurice to pace the floor of the bedroom he shared with Rachel, stopping occasionally to stare through frost-fringed windows into the snowy moonlit night.

"What is it, darling?" she asked from the darkness. "What is on your mind?"

"I've got to make a decision."

"Is it about Isaiah and the motor car?"

"Yes."

"Do you have any doubt that Isaiah is right?"

"I doubted when I woke up this morning. I don't now."

"Then why do you hesitate?"

"Because it means converting everything, our entire production capacity, our complete product output, to a machine that is still untried, a machine that people make jokes about, a device that I myself have been in the forefront of ridiculing..."

"Some things must be done, no matter the risk," she said. "If you know that Isaiah is right, and you are convinced in your own mind, then it must be done. If it is of any help to you, I agree with Isaiah completely. We are in new century and a new era. The horse and buggy are things of the past. Tomorrow is the future, and only those of vision and courage will seize it."

She stopped speaking. The silence of the night settled in. "Thank you, my love," he whispered.

Maurice made his announcement over lunch at the house. Several of the directors had been summoned, including Jeff Straight and Will Pease. The banker Ruggles had come on the early train from Detroit. Old Moneypenny fingered a water goblet, visibly disconcerted by white table linen and fine silverware and dishes. Isaiah fidgeted, not knowing what to expect.

"Stewart Continental will cease the manufacture of horse-drawn vehicles," Maurice said quietly. "We will begin planning to convert entirely by spring to the production of the automobile and liquidating our buggy stock by the end of the year."

Around the table there was an intake of breath.

"It's a hell of a risk, Maurice."

"We'll be putting everything on the line."

"I am well aware of the risks. It will be all or nothing, as far as I'm concerned. No halfway measures. I can't see, for example, trying to produce both kinds of vehicles. That won't work. So what I'm talking about is quitting entirely the manufacture of horse-drawn vehicles, staking everything on the motor car. The more I've thought about it, the more convinced I am that either way is a gamble. The horse, gentlemen, is on its way out. If we do not act, and act soon, in a few years Stewart Continental will find itself producing obsolete equipment that fewer and fewer people want to buy."

He looked into their faces, and the faces of people who had believed in him, supported him. A company was built on trust, and his error of judgment could spell ruin for them all.

He turned his attention to Isaiah. "There are several conditions that I wish to have understood. First, the corporation takes over every patent and design, every nut and bolt of the Stewart Traveler. Its creator, moreover, joins the corporation as chief of production, under general supervision of Tom Moneypenny."

Isaiah nodded vigorously, beaming with pleasure.

Maurice turned back to the others. "Second, I wish to expand our capital and pool of innovative thinking by bringing the Stewart family in on the creation of a whole new production enterprise. What I have in mind is a national organization on a scale far too large for the financial backing we can now muster. To this end, then, I intend to call a meeting of the entire Stewart clan here in Fall River..."

The discussions went on for more than three hours. At last the preliminaries were concluded, the directors and principal investors of Stewart Continental went away to spread the momentous news, and Maurice Stewart stood alone in his study staring into the fire. Voices crowded his mind.

The voice of Isaiah: "*Stewarts have always been pioneers.*"

The voice of Rachel: "*Some things must be done, no matter the risk.*"

232

The voice of Bradley Stewart: *"You'll fail, by God. And when you do, don't come crawling back to me."*

He turned away, strode to the sideboard, and poured himself a drink.

They came into Paris as conquering heroes. Crowds flocked to the railroad stations to see the daring men and their automobiles. Crowds followed them down the Avenue des Champs Elysée in triumphant procession, cheering, throwing flowers, and drinking toasts from bottles of wine. So tumultuous was the outpouring that gendarmes had to clear a path to the hotel with a flying wedge.

They shouted for the tall, handsome American, Van Harrison Stewart, as he stepped into the sunshine leaning upon his silver-headed cane. Paris newspapers were filled with stories about the half-breed Indian, educated at Oxford and at the United States Naval Academy, who had lost his leg as an American officer on board the battleship *Maine* only to become one of the greatest racing drivers in all Europe. "Hurrah! Hurrah for the Indian!" At Montmartre, francs changed hands in a frenzied shower as gamblers backed their favorites.

"I going with the American. His Panhard is seventy horsepower, *mon ami*. I saw the car being towed from the depot. It is magnificent!"

"You are a fool, Claude, but I will gladly take your money. The American does not stand a chance against the Renaults."

"Hah-hah-hah. You are blinded by your own Gallic loyalties. Done!"

"Done!"

Van Harrison Stewart basked in the adulation of the crowd. People flocked in the street beside the open-air cafés, ogling the drivers and their guests.

The Renault brothers, Marcel, Louis, and Fernand, occupied a huge table mobbed by their friends. Marcel caught Van's eye across the crowd and lifted his wineglass joyously. "To the Spotted Deer!" he called in French. "And may the best driver win!"

Van responded in kind. He like the Renaults, big, hearty men whose automobile factory was producing a dynasty of European cars. It would be a fierce race against them, with no quarter given. Marcel, especially, was a competitor who would run you off the road if it meant taking the lead on a curve. But then, this was the essence of competition, and gave it zest.

"Here!" shouted a young hero-worshiper, waving a newspaper. "Here is a late edition of the *Corriere della Sera*, from Italy. They have a correspondent in Paris. He is calling it the greatest race ever run.

Three hundred drivers, risking life and limb for the glory of sport!

Isn't that something?"

Paulette came unexpectedly out of the street crowd. She was stunning in a picture hat and tightly fitting dress of the latest Paris fashion. The French designers had provided a daring exposure of ankle. Her hair was dark, full, and worn short. Her eyes were like two pools of liquid. She said, "Hello, Van."

He lurched to his feet, blood coursing from Pernod and pleasure. "Paulette!"

The others recognized her, of course. All Paris recognized Paulette DeFresgne. Several men rose to touch their lips to her hand. She accepted their homage, Van thought, as a queen might. She declined a chair and stood before him, eyes challenging. "Behold," she said, "the conqueror."

"Not yet, *chéri*." He lit a cigarette and shook out the match. "We still have a race to run." His smoke curled in the balmy air. "You are looking splendid, as usual. And how is life?"

She shrugged, "Father is well. Prison, I'm happy to say, did not destroy him. But he will never be the same again."

"I see." Van kept his tone noncommittal. "And you?"

"Come and take a ride with me. I have a car and driver here."

Van looked around at his friends. Deliberately, they busied themselves in conversation. "Of course," he said. They made their departure amid the scraping of chairs and bows of courtesy.

"My career flourishes," she said in an offhand way. "I have offers for parts in three new plays, all at the same time." She gave the familiar, throaty laugh that he had always found so intriguing. "If you read the gossip sheets, you will suspect that I am trysting with half the men of Paris." She shrugged. "But in reality, my life is rather virginal."

The smile was only half convincing. The liquid eyes found his. "And Casey? What do you hear from him?"

"He is in Panama. Now that our government has made its commitment to the Canal, I doubt if he ever comes out again until it's dug. Casey Stewart is a very resolute man."

She took a breath. "That is an understatement."

Van sensed the old strain developing between them. He could not abandon his family loyalties, even now. "Casey had to do what he did, Paulette. He could not close his eyes to the payoffs and bribes, even at the cost of his marriage. Surely you can see that by now."

Paulette swallowed quickly. "Casey Stewart's testimony implicated his own father-in-law," she said. Van recognized that the bitterness was still there, the outrage still smoldering beneath that veneer of beauty and composure. "He put my father in prison. I shall never forgive him."

Van put his hands together and studied them carefully. "Each of you made a choice. Your father. Casey. Yourself. It is the way of the world."

Paris flowed past the gleaming windows of the saloon car. They passed the Arc de Triomphe and came into the Avenue de la Grande Armée, which brought them into the magnificent green sweeps of the Bois de Boulogne. The driver stopped at one of the great fountains near l'Allée de Longchamp. The two of them got out and walked. Van moved slowly, shifting his weight upon the cane. The view of lakes and sky and greenery was magnificent. Paulette took his free hand and held it tightly. "But for all my anger, I am torn, Van. You Stewart men have a virility and independence that I find irresistible. People think that your incredible dash comes from being part Indian. I know better. It is because you are a Stewart. Where Casey was concerned, my pride cost me the only man who ever made me tremble and weep like a child. That is a terribly expensive kind of pride, but it is mine and I cannot change it. And now I suppose that"—she hesitated, as if from a flicker of pain—"that Nathan will be the same."

The mention of the boy took Van by surprise. He gave it a moment's quiet thought. Then: "It is not my business, Paulette, but why do you not fight to regain custody of Nathan? No French court would deny you. Surely living in Paris with you would be preferable to that boarding school in Virginia."

Paulette seemed to undergo some quick inner struggle. He knew that he had touched a nerve. "Nathan is better off as an American than he would be as a Frenchman, Van. I am convinced of that. I want him to have all the advantages of his American birthright. And I don't wish for him to be torn between his father and me. What happened to us happened. But Nathan's future is his own."

"You are a rare woman, Paulette."

"And perhaps a foolish one." She moistened her lips. "Will you . . . tell Nathan that I love him?"

"Yes."

She grew even more thoughtful. "Are you happy, Van?"

"Happy? Of course, I'm happy? This is the life, Paulette. Excitement, glamour, women. I've got friends all over Europe. I've got money to burn, thanks to a grandmother who owned the biggest whorehouse in San Francisco. Women find me devastating, and I sleep alone only by choice. I have no responsibilities, nothing to tie me down . . ."

"You thrive on danger. It is not normal. I think you're running away from something. We're all running away from something. Reality, perhaps."

He laughed. "Reality? What is reality? I'm a crippled one-legged Indian. I had a career once, and lost it when a ship went down and this"—he touched the artificial leg with the point of his cane—"this piece of me came off. I was no longer acceptable for the Navy. That's reality, Paulette."

Paulette pursed her lips and shook her head. "Being a vagabond racing driver is not my idea of stability. A man like you . . ."

They stepped into the shadow of an alcove. Abruptly she came to him, kissing him fully and openmouthed. She trembled as he stroked the small of her back. His own desire surged. This woman had always inflamed him. And now she pressed her body frantically against his rising hardness and moaned. The heat of her caused his senses to reel.

"I need you, Van." Her voice was a husky whisper. "Come with me. Let me be the one to sleep with you tonight."

Van pushed away. His mind was a turmoil of wanting and rejecting. It was not to be; it could not be. Casey Stewart was blood kin. But more than that, Van was thinking of the boy Nathan. "I'm sorry, Paulette," he said.

They returned to the car in silence.

She took him back to the café. He opened the door to step out into the sunshine. She touched his arm and he turned back. Her eyes looked deeply into his. "I will pray for you tomorrow," she said.

*   *   *

"It is time, *mon ami*. And a fitting way to go, eh?" Van Harrison Stewart chuckled, pulling on a helmet, goggles, and gauntlets. A cigar jutted from between his teeth. His mouth was dry from last night's champagne debauch. He was a bit lightheaded. There was a taste of perfume upon his lips. He patted the hood of the big Panhard racing car and turned to Roullard, his scruffy machinist from Nantes, for the final word. "What do you say, Roullard?"

They stood in the thunder and smoke of engines. It was a huge field of two hundred seventy-five racing cars gathering in the darkness at Versailles. It was a run to Madrid, with the first leg alone—to Bordeaux—covering a distance of three hundred forty-two miles. Out there along the lamp-lit road southwest of Paris, half of Europe seemed to be gathering to watch. All night they had packed the boulevards of the city with bicycles, motorcycles, horse-drawn carriages and motor cars. One could hardly move in the crush, as platoons of gendarmes and militia attempted to keep order. From the Bastille to the Madeleine, every café was brilliantly lit, every table filled. *"Mon Dieu!"* a waiter had exclaimed, "it is the most excitement since the return of Napoleon!" Van, of course, had a rollicking good time, a Parisienne on each arm, friends and admirers in tow, the champagne and the champagne and the champagne. And now the throngs had advanced, boisterous and celebrating, to mass along both sides of the road to Bordeaux, singing "Le Marseillaise" as the clock dipped toward 3:30 A.M.

"Hey, Roullard!" he called.

Roullard was on his knees with an ear to the tailpipe listening intently to the sound of the Panhard. The man was squat and greasy in a suit of ancient coveralls. His breath reeked perpetually of wine and garlic. He rarely knew a sober hour but he was an absolute genius with automobiles. A fluttering sound from the bowels of the Panhard could tell him more secrets than the most intimate whispers of a Montmartre madame.

It was a monster machine compared to anything Van had ever driven before. For months he and Roullard had worked at enhancing the engine's power by reducing the weight of the car. And so they had drilled out piston walls, chipped and filed bolts, and slotted the frame and levers to mere networks of steel. The Panhard could blast along at speeds of eighty miles an hour on the straightaway. Manufacturers were engaged in a mad competition to build cars bigger, faster, deadlier. To complicate matters, there was no corresponding improvement in braking power or road control, a fact that particularly troubled men of technical mind. Even the officials were inexperienced in managing races of such speed, such magnitude.

But, hell, that was their worry, not his.

"Roullard, the world is waiting!"

Van moved around the car to the driver's side, trying not to favor the artificial left leg. He swung his good leg aboard and settled into the driver's seat, gunning the engine slightly.

Painted on the snout of Van's vehicle was the name Spotted Deer. Every car he had ever driven bore that name, even the big Mors with which he had made the nearly disastrous Paris-to-Berlin run two years earlier, with his car a flaming wreck. Spectators had pulled him from the inferno without a hair being singed; how ironic was fate, when one did not give a damn.

"Van! Van, *mon chéri!*" A female presence rushed to his side. Arms encircled him and kisses rained upon his neck and face. The scent was familiar. Nicole. "Oh, my love," she murmured. "Oh, my black-maned stallion. Be careful. Come back to Nicole."

He kissed her passionately, patted her bottom, promised champagne and flowers when he returned from Madrid. She wept and gave him a golden locket for luck. And then she was gone, swallowed up by the crowd, returning no doubt to her husband Pierre.

The judges came along to each car, fussy, pensive men. "We are concerned, Monsieur Stewart, with safety. Let me repeat the procedure. Each car will receive an individual starting flag, precisely timed at short intervals. You are racing the clock. Upon arriving at the outskirts of a town, you will be stopped and escorted through, following a bicyclist. Your times of arrival and departure will be registered. Our purpose, of course, is to avoid accidents in congested communities. Is that understood?"

Van nodded and gave his chin strap a final tug.

"Roullard! It is almost three-thirty. Get on board, my man! There is nothing more that you can do for the car now."

The mechanic tumbled into the seat to Van's left, wiping his hands on the coveralls and grinning like a mischievous monkey. Roullard had donned a billed leather cap, heavily soiled and turned backward. A pair of oil-smeared goggles were pushed up onto his forehead. "She is singing like a bird!" he cried.

The official starter of the race stepped into the glare of electric lights on a high platform. He wore a gray silk top hat and squinted down at the smoky, guttering ranks of racing cars. He raised the flag and stared at a watch in his other hand. Van had drawn twentieth place as his starting position. One by one the first nineteen cars moved forward. Van's sweaty hands tightened on the wheel. The starter raised his flag, looked at his watch, waited...waited...

Van whispered to himself, "This one is for the *Maine*."

The flag snapped down.

They were off!

The Panhard's seventy-horsepower engine gave them a quick getaway. Van's excitement surged as the wind buffeted his face and the roadway rushed toward them. He gave throttle to the Panhard, dimly conscious of densely packed cheering spectators lining the route. Fumes gushed from the Panhard engine as they hurtled onto a long sweeping turn.

Leading cars had already churned up a fine, sifting cloud that invaded mouth, nostrils, and ears. Dust quickly covered the goggles, blinding one to dips and curves in the road. It clogged engines and hastened breakdowns. Van sympathized with the poor devils fifty and a hundred cars behind, for he had been in such positions in prior races. Now he drew a large bandanna over the bottom of his face to filter out the worst of it and hunched over the steering wheel, squinting through the haze.

He had two alternatives. He either suffered it out or tried to pass as many leaders as possible. Certainly the closer to the front, the better the conditions. The Panhard zoomed along the dirt road south of Paris, flanked by flicking poplar trees in the ghostly gray mists of a sunless sunrise. Van increased speed. He overtook a Mors racer, and then two others. One of the drivers shook his fist as the Panhard zoomed by raising its own choking dust cloud. He knew he was averaging more than sixty-five miles per hour.

The crowds had thinned but this was only temporary. Each village and crossroads hamlet would have its blob of cheering, wildly excited Frenchmen. It was daylight as they neared the first major town, Chartres, dominated by the cathedral. Ahead he could see another large crowd and a band playing lustily. Van's heart came into his throat. The damned fools were surging into the road! Cursing, he twisted the Panhard past a bulge of humanity, slewing in the dust, and barreled ahead into a straightaway. At the entrance to Chartres he slowed for the first official checkpoint.

As they followed the bicycle escort through Chartres, he was trembling from the near-miss back there. The government had posted gendarmes and French soldiers everywhere in an effort to contain the spectactors, but to little avail. People knew nothing of the dangers of these hurtling machines.

The pace had been brutal.

They had told him of the accident at the village of Ablis. Bad news travels fast. A spectator had leaned too far into the road and was struck by a car, but not fatally. Unless the people would stay out of the road, he sensed there was bloody business ahead.

It was more than an hour's run from Chartres to Tours along a fairly decent road with few bends. Another forty minutes brought them to Poitiers. Just twenty miles south of there, the first calamity occurred.

Roullard had a premonition. Marcel Renault had passed them intent on catching his brother who was far ahead. The big Renault racer came perilously close, on the inside of a curve. Roullard leaned over and shouted to Van: "Careful, *mon ami*, this Renault is a madman."

Van grinned. "We are all mad, my friend," he shouted back.

Barely were the words out of his mouth when he saw the trouble ahead. Renault was barreling along the road hub-to-hub with another car driven by an equally aggressive driver named Thery. The two vehicles, hurtling along at nearly seventy, raised a huge cloud of dust. Instinctively Van reduced his speed in order to see. At high speed, the two cars ahead approached the village of Couhe-Verac. It was Roullard who cried the warning. "There is a right-angle bend going into the village!" Thery, who had forged into the lead, saw the turn in time and slowed his machine. Renault, momentarily blinded by dust, was not so lucky. His big machine shot off the road, catapulted into the air, and flipped over repeatedly, landing upside down in a ditch.

"Sacré nom de Dieu!"

Van pulled over and stopped. Ripping off goggles and gloves, he and Roullard leaped out of their car and ran down the embankment. Marcel Renault was wedged into the wreckage, blood pouring from his mouth and ears. His mechanic Vauthier lay near the machine in deep shock and in obvious pain. On the road above them, other racers braked to a halt and men came down to help. As they pushed the Renault upright and lifted Marcel's body free, his eyelids fluttered and he made a sign of the cross.

"Don't bother with us, Stewart," he whispered. "Get back in the race."

"He's hurt bad, poor devil," someone said.

One driver ran back to his car and went for help in the village. Several others, seeing that they could do nothing for the injured men, returned to the race; many cars zoomed past without stopping. Roullard fidgeted. "You are losing time," the mechanic said flatly.

Van held a wet cloth to the forehead of Marcel Renault. The man's face was gray and he had lost consciousness. "It doesn't matter, Roullard."

A voice shouted from atop the embankment. "You men go on. We will take over from here." An official from the town of Couhe-Verac descended with a group of volunteer rescuers.

Marcel's crash seemed to trigger chaos. Only later, as the bloody reality of the race shocked all France, did Van grasp the enormity of it.

Even as a priest was being summoned to the clinic at Couhe-Verac, Thery lost control of his car as he tried to overtake the veteran driver Porter, at the wheel of a Wolseley. Thery caromed into a ditch, his fuel tank exploded, and both he and his mechanic were engulfed in fire. Both, miraculously, would survive. But then Porter, blinded by the dust of a car ahead of him at the village of Bonneval, crashed into a train-crossing barrier and his mechanic was killed. Moments later the driver Tourand swerved his car to miss a little girl who had wandered onto the road. His vehicle smashed into a crowd, hurling bodies like broken dolls. A woman and two soldiers lost their lives. The shock caused Tourand to lose his sanity, a condition from which he would never recover.

On and on it went, on a floodtide of incredible slaughter.

At Angoulême, a teenage girl tried to cross the road in the path of a car doing eighty miles per hour. A soldier rushing out tried to save her; he was struck and injured. The driver wrenched the steering wheel and crashed into a tree, killing a spectator and his mechanic and injuring another onlooker.

Another driver Lorraine-Barrow swerved to avoid a dog, smacked into a tree, and was mortally injured. Gras struck a train-crossing barrier and his car burst into flames, but both he and his mechanic were saved. Stead, running his De

Dietrich racer at top speed in a fierce battle with a Mors, ran off the road and flipped upside down.

Van slowed the Panhard, squinting into the afternoon glare. A crowd of officials was gathered at the outskirts of Bordeaux displaying a large hand-lettered sign: Stop! All the cars which now led him were pulled off the road into a field. Even from a distance he recognized the tall, slope-shouldered figure of Louis Renault in a group of men.

"Now what's wrong, Roullard? This is where we make a tire-change. But there's no scheduled stop this far out."

Roullard had been anxiously studying the right front tire. "We must change it in Bordeaux if we intend to make it to Madrid."

"All right, then . . ."

A warning flag waved him down. He slowed the Panhard and drew up to the officials. "What's the trouble?"

"The race is halted at this point, monsieur."

"Halted? What the devil for?"

"By orders of the prime minister himself. There has been one horrible accident after another. Already, there are several dead. We know of five, and the number is expected to go much higher."

Van parked the Panhard and climbed out stiffly. The afternoon was still cloudy and cool. He walked over to where Louis Renault stood talking his brother Fernand and several friends. Renault's face was covered with grime, except for the great white orbs around the eyes where his goggles had been. His eyes were red and puffy. Van extended his hand.

"How is Marcel?"

"He is dead, Monsieur Stewart," one of the men said. "He died in the clinic at Couhe-Verac. They called ahead by telephone."

Behind them, cars were being flagged to the side, times recorded, and drivers informed. An hour later, a large crowd of drivers gathered glumly around an official standing on a wooden chair. "By orders of the prime minister, this race is terminated. You are not to restart your engines. Each car will be towed to the railroad station. We will load all cars onto the train and return to Paris . . ."

Night settled over Bordeaux. The death toll for the day had risen to eight, with at least two more persons mortally injured. Scores of drivers, mechanics, and spectators had been hurt. Newsboys shouted the headlines in the streets. All France was said to be stunned.

Van Harrison Stewart sat in the slow-moving Panhard drinking from a bottle of Pernod. They were being towed to the station by a dray horse. Beside him, Roullard already was passed out from drinking. Along the cobbled streets, silent crowds stood watching the bizarre parade of immobile machines as they lurched along behind draft animals. So much for the conquering hero, Van brooded. Now he was merely an oil-smeared survivor of another bloody slaughter.

He belched softly, tossed the empty bottle into a weedpatch, and heard it clink. Maybe Paulette was right. Maybe he was running away. What kind of a life was this?

X

Parson Bob Anders stood in Maurice Stewart's office with his hat in his hand.

"Folks asked me to come and speak with you, Mr. Stewart. They're real concerned, and they hoped maybe I could talk to you about it man-to-man."

"What's on your mind, Parson?"

"It's the factory, Mr. Stewart. We're all worried about the factory."

"In what way?"

"Well, we don't mean to be interfering in your business. A man's business is his own. But a factory like Stewart's is something else," he said, clearing his throat uncomfortably as his Adam's apple bobbed. "You see, a factory represents more than the private enterprise of its owners and directors. For those who depend on it, Stewart Continental means paychecks, food on the table, homes, savings, and aspirations. Its successes and failures affect us all."

"I understand that, Parson."

Parson Anders stood quietly, shifting from one foot to the other. Maurice spoke gently, offering reassurance. He had given this a great deal of thought, and was convinced that they actually had no choice. The horseless carriage was becoming a reality. The day would come when they would face a failing market for buggies and carriages. The preacher listened politely. They shook hands. "Thanks for talking with me, Mr. Stewart." He put on his hat and went away.

The word that Stewart Continental would abandon the manufacture of buggies and start mass-producing horseless carriages indeed had struck Fall River like a thunderclap.

"He's a damn fool. Mark my words, Maurice Stewart is going to bring ruin down on his own head and ours too. I say he's taking a terrible gamble. Terrible."

"Well, it's his gamble. It's his company."

"Bullshit. This whole town is involved. Look at the jobs in that factory. If Stewart fails, everybody who works for him fails."

"You're too set in your ways, Fred. You've got to change with the times."

"The horseless carriage ain't nothin' but a rich man's toy, and you and I both know it. It's noisy and smelly and unreliable. Besides, the good Lord never intended for common folks to be thinkin' about such foolishness. Times is hard enough without addin' to our troubles."

"Mr. Stewart says the horseless carriage is the wave of the future, and Fall River's got to go with it."

"Neither one of us will live to see that."

As winter passed, anxiety subsided. But spring brought a new spate of rumors. There was going to be a gathering of the Stewart clan in Fall River in mid-June; young Maurice Stewart was going to try to sell his vision to the family.

As the weather grew warmer and the great elm trees along Main Street came into full leaf, ripples of anticipation coursed through Fall River.

"Stewarts? What makes them so special?"

"Oh, quite a few things. Iron, steel, steamboats, locomotives, publishing, heavy freight business, shipbuilding, and money."

"Money?"

"More money than you and me together could count."

"I didn't know that boy was rich. If he's so rich, how come he went around begging folks to invest in the buggy works? Hell, I remember when Maurice Stewart used to charge his haircuts."

"Family money ain't necessarily his money. Your brother owns a hundred acres of bottomland, but that don't make it your'n. Besides, I heard his father in Pittsburgh cut him off without a penny."

"Is that so?"

"That's what I heard."

Nothing like it had ever happened in Fall River.

Each incoming train brought one or two of them, stepping down from Pullman cars into the clouds of steam, bringing piles of baggage, trailed by servants and friends. They hired the finest carriages, filled every available hotel and rooming house, and converged like visiting royalty toward the big hilltop house of Maurice Stewart.

Wealth and power had its own mystique.

"The rich look different," observed the schoolteacher Pierce as he waited for a haircut in Jeff Straight's barbershop. "They talk different. They even smell different."

"What makes 'em that way?"

"Darned if I know. But it's so."

The eyes of Fall River watched from behind their blinds and fans. Lips pursed and voices murmured.

"Look at them clothes! And all those people who come with her. Why, there must be a dozen of 'em."

"Which Stewart is that, Clara?"

"Francesca Carp. They say she owns nearly every boat on the Hudson River."

The arrival of Hope Stewart Langden and her partially paralyzed husband Howard created another stir. "At the station, she wouldn't let nobody push her husband's wheelchair but herself."

"Imagine. A beautiful woman like that!"

"So that's Hope Stewart. Why, I read her stories about the assassination of Mr. McKinley . . ."

Who could have anticipated such a thing? A few years before, this same Maurice Stewart had arrived in Fall River riding a freight train. He had worked as a common laborer at Pover's buggy factory, side by side with the big Swede Swenson, who now worked for him. Already all that had become part of the folklore of Fall River, along with the torrid gossip about Maurice and Priscilla Pover, Maurice and Helen DeMare, and finally Maurice and his marriage to the beautiful Jewish girl Rachel Birnham.

Rachel Birnham Stewart awaited each new arrival with restless anticipation. For weeks she had seen personally to the preparation of the house, had every window cleaned, every corner dusted, all the woodwork waxed. The place sparkled, and so did she. It was her fulfillment as a woman and as a hostess. "Best housekeeper and hostess in Fall River is Rachel Stewart." She would be content to see to Maurice's home, his entertainment, his social standing as a pillar of the community. If only . . .

She thought of the lovemaking and shuddered. It made her feel used and unclean. But this, too, was her function, and she would endure it. She sometimes wondered if her mother had felt the same way. She intended to be the dutiful wife, however, and bear Maurice a son and a daughter. Then she would devote herself to mothering them properly. Already the process was beginning, for Rachel suspected that she had just become pregnant. Pregnancy would relieve her of the unpleasantness of the marriage bed. After the children were born . . . Well, she would worry about that later.

And so the Stewarts arrived. Each fresh arrival brought bursts of loud talk, hugs, kisses. Rachel greeted all, the perfect hostess. She had fixed her hair just so, put on her most fetching pale blue gown with the single pearl strand. She stood elegantly beside her husband, nodding, smiling. She committed to memory names, faces, mannerisms. The widowed aunt Colette, distinguished, white-haired, a strong woman with a penetrating gaze; it was said that she had taken her late husband's suicide without flinching and had gone on living almost as if he had not existed at all. Such strength. Cousin Vanessa, a seventy-year-old socialite with hair the color of a sunburst, was magnetic and brassy. Her husband Claude Harding, a manufacturer of electrical equipment, obviously adored her. Aunt Francesca was a regal dynamo, constantly holding court with her traveling companions. ("My word, Maurice, does she always travel with all these people?" He chuckled. "Francesca collects people. She loves being admired.") Maurice's brother Casey, lean and deeply tanned from years in Panama, arrived accompanied by his son Nathan, a handsome boy with a grave, preoccupied expression who promptly fell into a spirited technical conversation with his hunchbacked cousin Isaiah. Rachel regarded Nathan fondly. How she would love for her own son, when he came, to be like that.

But there were surprises as well, and not all of them pleasant for her.

"Rachel, allow me to introduce my cousin from the shipbuilding side of the family, Ward Stewart of Boston."

She blinked, smiled, and tried not to appear startled. Ward

Stewart was a tall, striking man, his clean-cut features unmistakably Stewart. He was accompanied by a beautiful black woman who was introduced as his bride Vivian. Ward Stewart obviously had Negro blood. "I'm delighted," Rachel murmured, kissing Vivian on the cheek. "Our home is your home."

Vanessa Harding's son Van Harrison Stewart, the racecar driver and survivor of the battleship *Maine*, walked with a cane, favoring his artificial leg. He had the high cheekbones and flashing black eyes of an Indian. He radiated inner power. Even the man's handshake gave off a hard maleness and sense of daring. The dark eyes gazed boldly into hers with a challenge that caused her discomfort.

And there was Colby Malcolm Stewart, a tall, gangling individual with ill-fitting clothing. He was pale, shifty-eyed, ill at ease. Rachel's feelings toward him were less than cordial. The man looked and smelled like something from the street, like the smells in the hold of the immigrant ship *Argosy* steaming toward New York. "Welcome to Fall River," she said coolly. She noticed, however, that Colby received a warm welcome from Hope Langden and seemed at ease with Aunt Colette. Later, Rachel drew Maurice aside and asked, "Who is that?" Her husband smiled. "Colby Malcolm? I found him this time in the Tennessee State Prison at Nashville. Had a hell of a job getting him out. He's a forger and a thief."

A black man. An Indian. A hunchbacked cousin. A forger and a thief. Maurice's own father had not responded to the invitation to come to Fall River. There was hatred, bastardy, and divorce among Stewarts, and violent deeds of the past. First cousins married one another. What kind of a family had she come into?

Rachel glanced across the room and found Van Harrison watching her. He smiled roguishly. With a flush of irritation, she hurried to the kitchen.

"Personally, I think it's a dreadful idea," Aunt Francesca said. Nearby, the members of her court nodded in vigorous agreement. "To begin with, Maurice, there are no roads. How can people travel in horseless carriages without roads? And where on earth will they buy fuel?"

"Roads will come." It was Isaiah who replied. The hunchback stood beside Maurice, his mind a storehouse of fact and

247

informed opinion. "And so will gasoline stations, maps, direction signs..."

"This is just the point, Francesca," Maurice said. "What we're talking about here is not just the manufacture of automobiles. We're talking about a whole new way of life. It involves everything from roadbuilding and automobile servicing, to spare parts, tires, batteries, lights, accessories, and repair."

For two days they argued, dined, drank wine and whiskey, partied, slept, and argued some more. Rachel had never seen so much energy unleashed so intently in one confined space. The noise, the smoke, and the alcoholic fumes gave her a throbbing headache. Vigorously resisting a Stewart family commitment to the horseless carriage were Aunt Francesca, Cousin Vanessa, Casey, Ward, and Vivian Stewart. But Maurice found strong support in Isaiah, Van Harrison, and Nathan—the boy was an excellent debater and, to Maurice's delight, had a strong mechanical bent—and Hope and Howard Langden. Colby Malcolm spent most of his time in an alcoholic stupor.

"Why did you invite him?" Rachel wanted to know.

"He's family. He's got the same blood rights as anybody else."

"But he has no money."

"He's a Stewart, and that's what matters. If he wants to work for us, we'll find a place for him."

To Maurice's delight, his father-in-law Jacob Birnham joined them at dinner and developed quickly into a staunch ally. Birnham saw enormous possibilities in sales, with extended credits and time payments to buyers.

Maurice glanced down the long, gleaming dinner table and counted thirty diners, including Jeff Straight, Tom Moneypenny, and other local investors. As servants moved from guest to guest, serving food from heaping silver vessels, the argument raged on.

"The horseless carriage is destined to change the way Americans live as nothing has done since the coming of the railroad. We are an independent people. God knows, this family can attest to that. The motor car will put within reach of every adult complete freedom of mobility. It is going to require engineering on a scale never even dreamed of up to now."

"It's dangerous," said Vanessa. "People are being killed and maimed already. Do you want to contribute to that?"

"Isaiah has a hell of an engine already built. You've all seen the Stewart prototype automobile. I want everyone to take a ride in it."

And they did. The gleaming Stewart, laden with passengers holding their hats, rattled merrily through Fall River. Townspeople waved; dogs barked; horses shied; children pointed and laughed.

Rachel was aware that of this entire gathering, only three family members, Isaiah, Van Harrison, and Nathan, possessed mechanical expertise. One was a socially isolated physical freak devoting himself to engines in the absence of human companionship, the second was a teenager, and the third was a strangely haunted half-breed Cheyenne Indian who hurled himself into European racing cars as an outlet for his inner furies. Unexpectedly she found herself thrown into conversation with Van Harrison.

"My real name is Spotted Deer," he said with a touch of irony to his smile. "I'm the bastard son of Vanessa, over there, and a chief of the Cheyenne. Most white people don't like Indians, so I use a more civilized name. I gather you don't like Indians either, Mrs. Stewart."

The depth of his hostility was a palpable thing. Rachel looked at him squarely and unblinking. "What makes you say that, Mr. Stewart?"

"There's something in your manner that tells me."

"I happen to be Jewish, Mr. Stewart. Are you aware of that?"

The Indian eyes faltered. He suddenly seemed unsure of himself. "No, I didn't know that."

"I thought everyone knew. Whenever anyone mentions me in Fall River, it's within the context of being 'that beautiful Jewess that Maurice Stewart married.'"

"I don't live in Fall River, Mrs. Stewart."

"True. But I thought . . ."

"What's the point?"

"The point is, I can hardly be disapproving of a half-breed Indian, now, can I?"

"Touché."

"Besides, I understand that you were educated at Oxford and that you spend a great deal of your time in Europe. In fact, you've just come back from that disastrous race from Paris to Madrid . . ."

"We didn't make it to Madrid."

"So I understand. Well, Mr. Stewart, were you involved in

any of the horrible accidents? It would be sad if your race were not worthwhile."

"Do you disapprove of motor car races, too?"

The line of conversation was beginning to wear upon her. She disliked verbal dueling, and for some inexplicable reason the two of them were unable to communicate in any other way. "Precisely what is it about me, Mr. Stewart, that bothers you?"

The black eyes flashed again. "I have the feeling, madame, that you are a cold woman in bed."

Van Harrison turned on his heel and walked away.

The group bickering continued through the afternoon tea hour, and again dominated dinner. Still there was no accord. But moods were changing. Aunt Francesca began to inquire if a motor car could be built that was easy for women to drive. Hope replied that she was already a driver, and had been since her brother Isaiah had brought the first Daimler-Benz car from Europe. Colby grew tired of drinking and joined the conversation, saying, "The way I see it, there's two things that's got to be done right. First, we build the right kind of motor car. And then we sell it. Know what people like? They like slogans. You got to create your market; advertise it right. Give 'em the idea it's got value. Don't just call it a Stewart car, call it the Silver Stewart! Generate excitement, see? And don't just say it's quiet. Say it's Whisper Quiet."

"Where did you learn all that, Colby?" Hope asked.

He shrugged. "I served time with a confidence man, one of the best. He could talk you right outta yer underwear. Uh, begging your pardon, Aunt Francesca."

Laughter filled the dining room. And suddenly there was agreement. One by one, prodded by Aunt Colette, they began to find mutual accord. They would subscribe to two million dollars worth of capital investment for the creation of Stewart Motor Company, Inc., with Maurice as board chairman and chief executive officer. Claude Harding discussed the possibility of producing wiring and other electrical equipment. Ward Stewart talked of excellent new enamel paints they were using on boats and wondered if they would be adaptable to motor cars. The papers were signed, the commitments made. Maurice broke out bottles of champagne. Corks popped and the bubbly splashed into glasses.

"To Stewart Motors," he said. "To a new dynasty!"

They all drank, refilled their glasses, and drank some more.

And then it was bedtime. Rachel felt the weariness creeping through her limbs. She rolled her hair, put on her nightgown, and slipped between the sheets. Maurice followed twenty minutes later. He turned out the light and came into bed beside her, nude and smelling of champagne. She turned her back to him, feigning sleep. His hand touched her shoulder. He kissed her neck and drew her to him. His maleness was hard and jutting against her thigh. She did not wish to be touched. The touch of his hands was not pleasant. Tonight she did not wish to perform the usual make-believe.

"No," she said.

His hands stopped. He lay still. "What do you mean, no?"

His tone worried her. Rachel sat up in bed. She smiled and touched his face. "I'm sorry, darling."

"You don't seem to want me anymore."

"I want you all the time. It's just that..."

"That what?"

"I think we're going to have a baby."

"A baby!" His anger turned to excitement, as she knew it would. He hugged her and laughed. "A baby!" He kissed her mouth and tossed his pillow, whooping. "That's wonderful. That's marvelous!"

"Sssh. Dear, people will hear us."

"I don't care. I don't care if the whole damn world hears us. We're going to have a baby. I'm going to be a father! Whoopee!"

He kissed her again. His ardor became stronger, his caresses more insistent. He buried his face in her neck, fondled her breasts. His breathing quickened and his hardness was enormous. He drew up her gown and stroked her there and there and there. He opened her thighs and rolled over, above her.

"Rachel. Rachel, my darling. I want you so badly. Rachel..."

It hurt.

She stared into the darkness and forced her mind to think of other things until it was over.

A cold wind had gusted all night out of the north, slapping tent flaps, and blowing gritty clouds of sand. Nathan was awakened at dawn by Wilbur Wright banging on a tin can, the signal for breakfast. Professor Comstock was already up and out of the tent. Reluctantly rolling free of his warm blankets, Nathan dressed quickly and stumbled into the frigid open air. He was still tired from the long trip from Washington by train, buggy, and boat, and depressed by Professor

Langley's failure at Widewater Bay nine days earlier. The question nagged at his mind: Would he see another dream of man's flying dashed this very day against the unyielding law of gravity?

"Hello, lad!" Professor Comstock stood in the wind, beard flying. "Breakfast is ready."

Nathan yawned and stretched, looking around at the numbing desolation of Kill Devil Hills. The place was aptly named. A cold surf boomed a hundred yards away. Around him spread dreary rolling sand dunes, a restless sea, scrub undergrowth, and piny woods. Seagulls shrieked in the wind, wheeling white shapes against a leaden gray sky. The only signs of human habitation were the canvas-shrouded shape of the flying machine, the Wright brothers' shack, an orderly litter of tools, ropes, and implements, and wooden monorail dismantled into wooden segments, and the tent which Nathan shared with Comstock and an occasional visitor from the hamlet of Manteo or the Kitty Hawk life-saving station a mile away. For sheer monotony, Kill Devil had no equal.

An odor of frying eggs wafted from the shack. Nathan Stewart, suddenly realizing that he was famished, trudged toward it, leaning into the blowing sand.

"What's the wind, Nathan?" Orville Wright, lean and mustachioed, knelt at the homemade stove stirring eggs in a pan. As usual, he was dressed in a dark suit, white shirt, celluloid collar, and black derby hat.

"Twenty-two to twenty-seven miles an hour, Orville. Blustery and unsteady, from the southeast."

Wright looked out toward the surf. "Wilbur will want us to wait a bit, see if it dies down. No need to assemble the track on level beach if we're going to have to move up to Big Hill later on."

"That's right." Wilbur Wright spoke, coming in from behind Nathan. After five years, Nathan Stewart still marveled at the uncanny way in which they seemed to think alike, speak alike, even anticipate each other's actions. "Let's see if she dies down by ten o'clock."

"My thought exactly," Orville said.

Everyone helped to lay out breakfast things. They ate seated cross-legged around a ground cloth which served as a dining surface.

"Is the engine ready?" Orville asked.

"I changed the oil and adjusted the spark," his brother

said. "I hope we don't break another propeller shaft. Will this rod hold?"

"It will hold."

"Trouble with the propeller shaft?" Professor Comstock asked.

"We broke two," Wilbur said. "Orville had to go all the way back to Dayton to find steel rods. He didn't get back here until last Friday."

"You could have stopped off in Washington and watched Langley's latest disaster," Comstock said.

"What happened this time?"

"Hard to say. His aircraft went into the river again. He blames the launch mechanism."

"What's the public's reaction?"

It was Nathan who replied. "The newspapers are having a field day. They're saying Dr. Langley's failure proves that man will never fly. The *Post* calls it a needless waste of a hundred thousand dollars of the public's money. Dr. Langley certainly had the financial and scientific backing. Unlike..." Nathan hesitated, suddenly unsure of his ground.

Professor Comstock smiled. "Unlike two bicycle mechanics named Wright from Dayton, Ohio?"

"Well..." Nathan's mood darkened. He respected the white-whiskered Samuel Langley and had been a guest at his Washington home along with Professor Comstock. Langley, the sixty-nine-year-old mathematician, astronomer, and secretary of the Smithsonian Institution, had encouraged Nathan's interest in the flying machine. Six weeks before this, in a lecture to Professor Comstock's senior science class at Briars Preparatory School, he had expressed confidence in the success of his own efforts. Indeed, the famous scientist's prestige had forced the headmaster to recognize at long last Vernon Comstock's courses in aeronautics. "Human flight," Langley had said, "is possible. I have spent the better part of my adult life trying to make it happen."

Now, in the windswept shack at Kill Devil Hills, Wilbur Wright looked somber. "I feel sorry for Langley. Six years spent building a flying machine and it dunks twice into the Potomac River. Seven years ago, when we were just getting started, he was kind enough to send us books and pamphlets on aeronautics. Do you remember, Orville?"

"I remember."

"He risked his prestige, his fame, everything, on an idea that the public refuses to acknowledge." Wilbur Wright sighed.

"And why should they, when even eminent mathematicians such as Dr. Simon Newcomb write that,

The example of the bird does not prove that man can fly.

The irony is that Langley's mathematical tables are in error. Orville and I discovered this with our wind tunnel experiments. All his tables for calculating wind pressures and drift were inaccurate. It almost caused us to abandon our entire project."

This was true, of course. Later, as he cleaned the breakfast dishes, Nathan looked out toward the beach and recalled all those bitter disappointments the brothers had endured. He was sixteen years old now, and had first met then when he was eleven, visiting their bicycle shop in Dayton, Ohio, along with Professor Comstock. The Wrights, bachelor brothers sharing a compulsive zeal to build a successful flying machine, had accepted him as a fellow advocate. And so, on holidays from Briars Preparatory School, Nathan had accompanied Comstock to meet scientists and tinkerers engaged in the mad pursuit of flight. It astonished him that, considering all the public skepticism, there were so many. His favorites were the Wrights of Dayton, simple men approaching things in a practical way. He had sat for untold hours in the bicycle shop listening to their debates of theory, mathematics, and wind pressures. He had watched, awed, as these men with no more than high school educations, brought out slide rules, logarithm tables, and textbooks on physics to argue some obscure technical point.

"Trial and error," Orville had told him in a quiet moment on a summer's eve. "Remember, Nathan, that every great technical advance came largely from trial and error."

So they had built a glider in the bicycle shop and shipped it to Kitty Hawk in two crates. Twice before he had accompanied them to this windswept place off the coast of North Carolina, Kill Devil Hills, with its hilly dunes and brisk Atlantic winds routinely hitting thirty-six miles per hour.

By devising a fan-driven wind tunnel at Dayton, they had experimented with no less than two hundred wing configurations. At last, thanks to their revisions of mathematical tables, they created a glider capable of bearing a man aloft for distances as great as six hundred feet. During the autumn, they had made nearly a thousand glider flights over these empty dunes, while perfecting their skill at maneuvering the machine. Even then it was a risky business, the craft subject to sudden dives and impromptu landings, spilling its pilot into the sand.

"Persistence," mused Vernon Comstock, "is more important than inventive genius." And persistence it was. For three months now, the Wrights had puttered and assembled and modified their clumsy machine, which resembled a huge box kite with twin forty-foot wings and six hundred pounds of dead weight. "She's a whopper," Orville commented one day. "A whopper flying machine."

They waited until ten o'clock. Nathan's reading of the dynamometer showed the wind velocity steady at about thirty miles per hour. Within an hour, half a dozen leathery, sunblasted men arrived as volunteers.

"You gonna do it today, Wilbur?"

"Yep. We'll lay out the track along the level here. There's plenty of wind, so we won't need the downhill run."

"Who gets first whack?"

Wilbur nodded toward his brother. "Orville does."

Already, the Wrights, Nathan, and Comstock had removed the coverings and untied rope fastenings anchoring the flying machine. Men grabbed lengths of board and bolted them into place end-to-end to fashion a sixty-foot wooden monorail track on which a wheeled dolly was placed amid grunts and curses.

Vernon Comstock could barely contain his excitement. "This will be it, Nathan. I feel it in my bones. Someday we're going to look back on this as an historic event. Man flies! Mark my words . . ."

"All right, boys, let's get her into the wind. Easy now." As they steadied the wings, the crew of volunteers slowly rolled the machine backward to the starting point. At last the craft stood poised, the wind at a steady velocity.

Nathan stepped back and gazed at the brothers' handiwork. It seemed hopeless that this thing would take off. The muslin-covered wings were secured by a network of wires and struts fluttering flimsily in the wind. A horizontal elevator jutted in front and a tall vertical tail in the back; the latter fitted with a hinged rudder. It looked ridiculous. Everything was to be controlled with wires, manipulated by the pilot lying facedown on the middle of the lower wing. The engine was mounted beside the pilot with oversize bicycle chains. Nathan himself had helped to bolt that together. He thought of Dr. Samuel Langley's disaster and was glad that, at least, there were no journalists to witness this one.

Comstock insisted that they take a photograph of everyone standing in front of the flying machine. This done, Orville lay belly-down upon the pilot's cradle like a boy on a sled, looking terribly out-of-place in his dark suit and derby. As the other men steadied the craft, Wilbur Wright stepped to the engine and quickly started it. With a sudden harsh noise the chain drives clanked, the twin pusher-propellers whirled, and the big contraption trembled all over. At a signal, they all let go except for Wilbur Wright, who held firmly to a right-wing strut, preventing the machine from tipping sideways.

"Ready!" Orville shouted over the engine noise.

Wilbur nodded. "Go!"

Orville increased engine power. The staccato noise cut through the sounds of wind and surf as if from some gigantic bumblebee. The craft now shook so violently that it seemed ready to fall apart. Comstock released a wire hooking the machine to the monorail. The whopper flying machine moved forward along the track, quickly gathering speed. Wilbur ran along with it, holding the strut. Nathan saw Orville move his hips, warping the wings, wind blasting into his face. And then suddenly, breathlessly, the craft lifted free of the rolling dolly and the thing rose majestically to a height of ten feet, white wings flashing. Everyone was running down the beach beneath it, and he heard himself shouting, "You're flying! You're flying!"

Wobbling, dipping, and soaring, the craft swept over the sands. And then, abruptly, it descended and skidded onto the sand, settling onto its right wing. They all ran down the slope to where a grinning Orville was climbing off his cradle. Behind them, Vernon Comstock was busy measuring. "Twelve seconds," he announced happily, "and a distance of a hundred twenty feet."

"Not much," Orville said.

"But it flew!"

"Yes, it flew."

It was Wilbur's turn. At 11:20 A.M., he took off, and managed to wobble in the air about a hundred seventy feet before hitting the beach. The third flight, by Orville, covered two hundred feet.

"I think I've got the hang of it now," Wilbur said, setting his derby so firmly upon his head that his ears lopped over.

"Flying is an art, you see. You've got to go with the air currents."

At noon, the whopper flying machine rolled for the fourth time down the monorail track and lifted into the air. Wilbur steered the craft southward over the dunes, gained a bit more altitude, made a graceful curve, and flew on. The seconds ticked off on Nathan's pocket watch as he called them out in the wind: "Fifteen. Twenty-five. Thirty-seven. Forty-two. Fifty-two. Fifty . . . nine!"

He could not believe the distance. Comstock plodded down the beach and back again. "Eight hundred fifty-two feet," he announced. "You've done it, Wilbur! Incredible!"

But except for a front-page banner headline in the nearby Norfolk *Virginian-Pilot,* and a few paragraph-length inside stories carried by skeptical editors, the event was disbelieved and ignored. Not even the Wrights' hometown newspaper in Ohio saw fit to carry a line.

"Why, Professor Comstock?" Nathan Stewart asked as they rode the train back into Virginia, returning to Briars School.

"I'm surprised at you for even asking such a question, Mister Stewart." The professor struck a wooden match with his thumbnail and lit his pipe. "As every sensible American knows, man will never fly."

Their noisy laughter startled other coach passengers.

XI

The man was down in the mud on his back, black as a chunk of coal, eyes yellow and rolling to the heavens. A heave, a shudder, and black vomit spewed from his mouth.

"The yellow fever, mon."

Casey Stewart ran clumsily through the muck to where the laborers clustered over their stricken comrade. A huge Bucyrus power shovel rumbled nearby, belching blue smoke. The sound of work—of shovels, clanking dirtcars, locomotives, and fifteen hundred men—did not cease. Around them yawned the vast brown immensity of Culebra Cut.

"Pick him up. Put him on the cart," Casey said. "We've got to get this man to the clinic."

"It's too late, Mr. Stewart. He gone." It was Tall Man, the

black gang foreman, speaking. A huge man from Jamaica, he stood looking down, a frayed derby in his hands. The sufferer indeed had the look of death upon him. His eyes no longer rolled in their sockets, but were glazing. His hands grew cold.

Casey felt a fresh and bitter sense of defeat. Sickness again swept the Isthmus. The spring of 1905 was a season of fear. A thousand men had been admitted to Canal hospitals suffering assorted ailments—malaria, typhoid, pneumonia, tuberculosis, injuries from blast and train and spade.

One of the workmen began to sing. It was a slow, soulful dirge. Two men then picked up the corpse and carried it to a mule-drawn wagon.

"Take him to the main tracks," Tall Man said. "Leave him for the funeral train."

The funeral train. It reminded Casey of the old days. In the streets of Colón, funeral processions were frequent again. Bells clanged and the mourners gathered. Frightened people clustered at the docks, waiting for the next boat back to the States. Undertaking establishments, in anticipation, bought large stocks of wooden coffins and stacked them in the street outside their places of business.

And now these men gathered around Casey in Culebra Cut. They were black laborers, giving off odors of sweat and chewing tobacco. The gang foreman's face was somber. "There is a lot of sickness, Mr. Stewart. A lot of it. But it ain't just sickness that's got the men upset. It's the conditions. The work is hard, the hours are long, the food is bad, and so's the living. We are living in shacks, with rats and snakes. The pay is low, and you've got to stand for hours in line while the paymaster fills out forms."

"I'll see what I can do," Casey said lamely.

"We had to tell somebody, and you're the only white man who seems to care about us." Tall Man turned and pointed. "Look out there, Mr. Stewart. You got fifteen hundred men workin' in Culebra, but they ain't gettin' nothin' done. Except for them two new shovels the chief engineer got, most of the equipment is old. We ought to be movin' three times the dirt we move. But there ain't enough train cars to haul it, and the cars that are workin' keep jumpin' the track. Our tools ain't right for the job. At this rate, we'll be diggin' this Canal for sixty years . . ."

"You men! What're you standing around wasting time for?"

The voice had the sound of a whiplash. Casey turned to see

the white superintendent Crawford trudging across the muck. He was a burly, potbellied man with hamlike hands and a grizzled lantern jaw. Crawford bullied his way into the group. He planted himself in front of Casey, fists on his hips, face burned beet-red by the sun. Casey caught a whiff of alcohol on the man's breath.

"So it's you again, Stewart. You front office guys think you can come down here and draw my men off the job." Piglike eyes glared a challenge. "If you want to talk to the niggers, do it on their time, not mine."

Casey stifled an urge to respond in kind. The bully would only take out his anger on the men. "All right, Crawford," he said quietly.

The superintendent smirked, spat tobacco juice, and suddenly grabbed the tall foreman by the shirt. "Now get your black ass and them niggers back on the job. Pronto!" The gang foreman's derby fell into the dirt. As he stooped to recover it, Crawford delivered a kick. Tall Man stood erect, swallowing his humiliation. As the group broke up, the superintendent rubbed his hands, glanced at Casey with a gleam of triumph, and sauntered away. Casey stood quietly, containing his fury.

He rode the train back to Panama City, watching the gentle flow of this strange and compelling land.

The great Canal project had started with high hopes but gradually, with the passing months of summer, fall, and winter, sunk into a kind of vexing despondency. There had been meetings and more meetings and more meetings. Members of the Canal Commission had made inspection tours. The chief engineer had marshaled his staff from among bright young railroad men. But there was no plan.

The long bright spot for Casey had been the unexpected arrival of Peter and Marcia Morse. His friends from Washington were crossing the Isthmus on a pleasure cruise to California. Morse had insisted on seeing the Culebra Cut, about which he had read so much in the newspapers back home.

After Peter had retired early, Casey and Marcia strolled through the sultry evening talking. He had forgotten that she was such a striking woman, and her nearness and perfumed scent gave him a deep inner pleasure. Instinctively, they linked hands.

"We've missed the pleasure of your company in Washington," she said. "No sooner had we met, it seems, than you were on your way down here to Panama. Perhaps that's just as well. Is it progressing, Casey?"

"Frankly, Marcia, no. But given time, I'm sure things will work out."

"Forgive me for being a prying woman, but do you have a romantic interest these days?"

"No."

"How sad. You're such a handsome man, so intelligent, and masculine. Even my niece Willow is wild about you. She still hasn't gotten over that weekend of the foxhunt. To tell you the truth, she makes me a little jealous."

"How old is Willow now?"

"She's seventeen."

"Willow is wild about you," Marcia Morse said.

Casey Stewart forced the thought from his mind.

"The following instructions have been forwarded to the appropriate department heads: Six vouchers are now required to obtain a handcart. In order to assure a minimum of waste, carpenters will not saw boards over ten feet long without written permit. Vouchers are to be forwarded in triplicate and quadruplicate for payroll..."

It was two days after the workman had died in Culebra Cut. Casey stood before John Wallace's desk, giving his monthly report. The chief engineer fiddled with his pencil. When Casey had finished, he said, "Well, thank you very much, Stewart. This is...a difficult job, m-most difficult." Wallace spoke with hesitation, as if unsure of what to say next. "I have so much to do, so much to do. The dirt is flying at Culebra, just like we said it would. But this damn...damn sickness is more than I can fathom. It is the foul land, the evil land. Panama is filled with natural pestilence, but the worst pestilence is in men's souls." A stray sunbeam from the side window flashed upon the chief engineer's little round spectacles. Wallace had been reading a gold-leafed New Testament, which now lay at his elbow. "I know the trouble here. The trouble here is sin, Stewart. Sin. All that drinking and whoring and carousing. No wonder they come down with such a loathsome disease."

Casey took a breath. "Sir, with all due respect, our trouble has nothing to do with sin. We are up to our necks in red tape. We can't get supplies out of Washington without filing vouchers by the yard. The paymaster is swamped with paperwork, and the pay process is dreadfully slow . . ."

"This heat," the chief engineer said wearily, "it saps the brain."

"We're hiring people out of the Washington office who don't even know what they're doing." Casey persisted. "They sent us a dozen track hands who've never worked on a railroad. They sent us a surveyor who doesn't know a level from a transit. Dr. Gorgas and his people can't get the equipment and trained manpower they need to do their job. Sickness is becoming a major problem."

"Filth, Stewart. Decay. Rot. Moral turpitude."

"And then there's the Canal itself," Casey persisted. "We arrived here nearly a year ago, Mr. Wallace, and to this day there is no *plan* for the Canal. There is no preparation. You sit with your staff in endless conferences, but nothing comes of them."

"It is all very complicated, Stewart. You just don't know what we go through. The forms. The reports." Wallace fidgeted with a stack of papers on his desk. He stared out the window. "Those people in Washington," he said, "expect us to perform miracles."

"We're losing technical personnel every day," Casey said. "They're pouring back to the States on every boat. Our people need reassuring, sir. They need leadership. But nobody ever sees you. You never go out on the job, never talk to the men in the field. Half of them don't even know what you look like . . ."

"Oh, I know. I know. Everybody's afraid. I don't blame them." The chief engineer was growing agitated. "Let me tell you something, Stewart. I want to tell you a secret. I'm afraid too. Do you know what I brought back here the last time I was in Washington? I brought back two . . ."—he stammered, swallowed hard, lowered his voice to a hoarse whisper—"I brought two stout caskets. Yes, I did. One for me, and one for my wife."

"Caskets?"

"Caskets."

Wallace went away again, back to the United States. A copy of a weekly magazine arrived in Panama City featuring an interview with him.

*   *   *

Everything is proceeding in harmony with a well-defined general plan.

Good health, he insisted, was a matter of clean personal habits. There was no disease in Panama that a clean, healthy, moral American' could not resist.

"We've got yellow fever in the Administration Building," Gorgas announced.

Casey swallowed hard. "How bad?"

"The chief architect Johnson died last night."

"The one who said we didn't need screens on the windows?"

The doctor nodded. "I attended to him personally. But there's nothing we can do, really; keep the patient quiet; hope for the best. He died shortly after midnight. We're burying him in one of the chief engineer's metal caskets."

The weather got hotter. The days passed in unrelieved anxiety. There was a mood of panic. Fever wards were filling at the hospitals. Gorgas ran short of newspapers with which to stuff the cracks in doors and windows so that buildings could be fumigated. He cabled Washington to send two tons of old newspapers immediately. Back came a cabled reply:

Two tons seems an excessive amount of reading matter for patients.

Gorgas threw up his hands and cursed.

Casey's office was a shambles. Even without a specific rank in the bureaucratic hierarchy, his post as Wallace's chief assistant made him the highest official left on the Isthmus. The work load was horrendous, the telephone constantly ringing, each mailboat delivery piled high with fresh paperwork from Washington. To make matters worse, Wallace had cabled demanding that Casey send him daily reports. The chief engineer was vacationing in New York.

"Mr. Stewart, there is a gentleman here to see you."

"Send him away."

"It is one of the laborers from Culebra Cut, Mr. Stewart. He seems very distraught."

He came up from his desk and strode into the outer office. The workman stood self-consciously, clothes caked with mud and grime, ebony face glistening with sweat. He clutched a dirty soft cap in hands that were battered and work-worn. Casey recognized him as one of the Barbados men.

"John Barkus, isn't it?"

"Yes, suh." The black head bobbed in acknowledgment.

"What is it, Barkus? What's wrong?"

"It's Tall Man, suh. The gang foreman. He dead. Mr. Crawford, the superintendent, done killed him with a shovel. There's trouble at the Cut, Mr. Stewart. The men stopped work."

"How did you get here?"

"I shagged the train, suh. I left there a half hour ago."

"All right, let's go."

The mob milled in broiling heat near the superintendent's shack. A heavy silence hovered over the scene. All the engines had stopped; not a train ran; not a power shovel moved.

Clouds boiled overhead. The air was filled with menace.

"What is it? What's happened?"

"He's in there, Mr. Stewart," one of the men said, jerking his head toward the shack.

"Who?"

"Crawford." A burly, tan-skinned man was speaking. He wore a battered straw hat and black trousers cut off at the knees. His big feet splayed on the dirt and his bare upper torso was a sheen of rippling muscle. "We gonna kill him for what he done to Tall Man."

"What is your name?"

"Marfot Johnson. I'm Second Man on the Cut."

"Where is First Man?"

"He gone back to the camp. He don't want no part of this. He told us we asking for trouble. But we don't care, Mr. Stewart. Tall Man, he was a good gang foreman."

"Tell me about it."

They told him. There had been a dispute over the break for the midday meal. Crawford, who had been drinking heavily all morning, decided to dock the men for the time taken a few weeks earlier when they had met with Casey during working hours. Tall Man protested. Crawford, in a sudden fury, had picked up a shovel and swung the blade against the side of the gang foreman's head. Tall Man had fallen like a stone, dead in the dirt of Culebra Cut.

"Where is Tall Man's body?"

"We took it to the train siding. He's already gone to Monkey Hill."

Casey's outrage boiled up from deep within. Detaching himself from the workmen, he walked slowly toward the shack. The heat bore down. The sun slipped behind a ragged cloudbank, absorbing his shadow in gray light. Ten feet from the shack, he stopped walking.

"Crawford!" he called.

There was no answer.

"Crawford, it's time you came out. I'm taking you to Panama City to stand charges for murder."

"Go to hell, office man!" The voice came muffled from the shack.

"Come out, Crawford!"

"You want me to come out so's them niggers can kill me. Ain't that right, Stewart? You're a nigger-lover, Stewart. Well, I'm no fool. Besides, it's my word against theirs, and I say they're a bunch of damn liars. That big black attacked me, tried to kill me. I hit him in self-defense."

"We'll let the court decide."

In the distance behind him, Casey was aware of the workmen, clustered and watching. In the distance, more men appeared and more. Black splotches and masses they were, clotted upon the two giant Bucyrus shovels, sprawled atop locomotives and dirt cars, standing on the brown humps and ridges of the cut. Fifteen hundred black men watched and listened.

"Come out, Crawford."

The door burst open. He came out slowly, a shotgun cradled in his arm. He wore a slouch hat low over his eyes, old faded trousers, and a faded shirt crossed by suspenders. His meaty, sunburned face was creased by a mirthless smile. "Here I am, office man."

"Put down the shotgun. We're going to the constable's office in Panama City."

"You're just gonna have to take me, office man."

"Crawford . . ."

Casey stepped forward. The shotgun came off the superintendent's arm and was suddenly poised in both hands. Crawford cocked the weapon. It was loaded and ready.

Casey's stomach was tight. He remembered San Juan Hill. Deliberately he walked forward. He held out his hand for the weapon.

"Crawford . . ."

The gun came down. The snout pointed at his midsection. He was five paces away. Four. Three. The finger drifted to the trigger, tightened. The mouth of his adversary lifted in a broken-toothed smile.

Two...

"Crawford. You don't want two killings on your head. One is enough. One you might get away with. But two? You wouldn't get away with two. They'd hang you, Crawford."

There was a hint of indecision in the big face. Just a hint. There was no stopping Casey.

One...

He made his move without stopping. In the space of a heartbeat, he knew that Crawford expected him to stop. Casey didn't give him the time. He left his feet and sprang directly at the rifle, aiming at the gleam of metal and the beefy midsection behind it. He struck with his shoulder and body, driving the man backward. An explosion went off at his ear. His head rang from the blast. The shotgun had fired, missing him and blasting harmlessly at the ragged sky.

Thunder rolled.

Lightning crackled.

The rain came in a sudden deluge, a wall of water.

They grappled in the mire, slipping and sliding. They were a tangle of arms, legs, blows, and curses. Crawford tried to use the gun as a club. But this encumbered his hands. Casey smashed the heel of his hand into the base of Crawford's nose. He brought his knee up in a sudden, vicious blow to the testicles. The knee struck home. Crawford grunted and gagged. In the driving rain, Casey struggled to his feet, grabbed his man by the shirt front, pulled him up, and drove his fist into the meaty face.

Crawford collapsed like an empty sack.

Desk work. He hated desk work. The routine was stultifying, the demands irrational and relentless. He looked up from the pile of papers on his desk and thought: Christ, Wallace, when are you coming back?

The door opened. It was the secretary again. "I'm sorry, Mr. Stewart, but there's a gentleman..."

"I know," he said wearily, "it's 'urgent and personal.'"

A familiar voice cried, *"Mon ami!* Surely you have a moment for an old friend!"

Blanchet stood in the doorway, looking around at the shambles of the office. The former priest cocked an ear to the ringing telephone. He studied Casey's face. "Things are not going well, eh?"

"It's a disaster around here."

They talked. It was the candid talk of old friends. And finally the talk turned to the crisis of the Canal.

"I have never seen a man so immobilized by fear as the chief engineer," Casey said. "It is no wonder that nothing gets done. And nobody, it seems, dares to rock the boat."

"All of us have our fears, *mon ami*," Blanchet said.

"Thanks," Casey said wryly.

"My chief concern is for you. Such stress, such anxiety and," he paused, "you have made bitter enemies in the Crawford affair. There are those who regard you as a traitor to the white race. Crawford has powerful friends. He was employed at the behest of the chief engineer himself. It is said that this matter has been reported to Admiral Walker, the chairman of the commission."

"So?"

"The chief constable is very uncomfortable, keeping the man in jail. There are strong demands that he be released on bail. And if that happens, he has sworn to kill you."

Casey smiled thinly. "It goes with the territory."

"The word is that the chief engineer Wallace will be pressured to fire you as soon as he returns to Panama."

"The possibility has occurred to me, Blanchet. But it probably won't matter, considering all the other problems besetting us."

Casey Stewart lit a cigar. "One psychopathic strawboss such as Crawford is the least of my concerns. The fact is, we can lose the whole thing. We can lose this whole damn Canal."

Blanchet sipped wine. He seemed heavy of spirit, a man grappling with concepts more formidable than his mind was prepared to handle. "What are you going to do?"

Casey turned in his chair and gazed out the window. Hot afternoon sunshine slanted in through the screens. From the street came the sounds and odors of Panama City. The air had a fetid smell, of putrefaction and despair. "I suppose I'll have to go to Washington," he said, "and see Roosevelt."

"You'll be rocking the boat."

"Hell, better to rock it than sink with it."

Blanchet left him. Casey finished his work, ordered passage on tomorrow's steamer to Washington, and went home to pack. He had just locked his suitcase when there was a knock at his door. He opened it and found Dr. Gorgas standing in the rain.

"Now what's wrong?" Casey said.

"It's Wallace, the chief engineer," Gorgas said.

"He's vacationing in the States. What about him?"

Gorgas held out a cablegram from one of his Army sources in Washington. "John Wallace has just resigned!"

"Damn it, a sea-level Canal is out of the question! It's ridiculous even to discuss such a thing this late in the game." Casey Stewart stood at an open double window of his suite in Washington's Arlington Hotel, chewing furiously at the butt of a dead cigar. He turned abruptly from the window and faced his visitors, an assortment of engineers, lobbyists, politicians, and Canal officials. "It's the Suez mentality all over again. But gentlemen, this isn't Suez. This is Panama, a hilly jungle slashed by the Chagres."

"Easy, Casey." The voice of big John Stevens rumbled from the back of the room. "You'll have a stroke."

Casey shook his head. It was unseasonably warm in Washington. An overhead ceiling fan stirred humid air. The open window did not help. But Casey knew that his real discomfort was not the heat—Panama was much hotter—it was frustration.

"We'll hit Congress with everything we've got," Stevens said.

"Thank God you've got a forum," a lobbyist said.

"And we'll damn well use it."

John Stevens meant business. This much Casey knew. If any man could dissuade Congress from committing them to the folly of trying to dig a sea-level Canal, it was this muscular, fifty-two-year-old chief engineer who had replaced John Wallace in Panama.

To Casey, it was a needless replay of the past. Again, he sat in a crowded hearing room with his maps and charts, talking about fundamentals.

"We propose, gentlemen, to build a bridge across the Isthmus with locks at both ends that will raise the ship to the level of the Canal so that it can float across, and then lower it to sea level again. The Canal will have two unique features. One feature is the creation of a huge freshwater lake, Gatun Lake. The lake will provide twenty-three miles of unobstructed ship channel. The other feature is Culebra Cut, a colossal man-made waterway running nine miles through the Continental Divide on the Pacific side of the Isthmus. Culebra will be the biggest dig in history, providing ample fill for the dam with a mountain or two left over."

"How long will it take to build a lock-type Canal?" a committeeman asked.

Casey turned to John Stevens. "Perhaps, gentlemen, the chief engineer would prefer to answer that question."

Stevens stood up. Already he had become popular in Washington for the changes taking place on the Isthmus. "Construction will take about eight years," he said. "The first ships will pass through in the year 1914."

A murmur of surprise went through the room.

"And if we build a sea-level Canal?"

Stevens frowned. "In my opinion, there isn't enough money in America to build a sea-level Canal. If it could be accomplished at all, the job would take at least eighteen years."

Formal debate came to an end. But informal discussions continued in the parlors and salons of unofficial Washington, where clever hostesses brought subtle pressures to bear on members of Congress or on their key staff people. As the heat of June wore on, and the critical Senate vote became imminent, Marcia Morse arranged a series of small, intimate dinner parties at which Casey and John Stevens talked face-to-face with senators. The socializing left Stevens restless and out of sorts. "I'm an engineer, not a politician in a monkey suit."

Casey smiled and clapped him on the shoulder. "Think of all the free meals you're getting."

Willow Luray's unexpected appearance at a party took Casey by surprise. The girl had blossomed astonishingly in less than two years, from a pretty teenager to a stunning young woman. She laughed at his momentary fluster. "Why, Mr. Stewart, whatever has come over you?"

"You've . . . changed!"

"Really? In what way?"

"Well"—he hesitated, face reddening—"you've matured."

His eyes did a quick, involuntary survey. Her figure was magnificent, her hair a luxuriant dark mass, her complexion the consistency of fresh cream, her eyes dark and bold. As they talked, a thickset man appeared at her side. He was middle-aged, slightly bald, and had the leathery skin of an outdoorsman.

Willow seemed suddenly ill at ease. "This is my father," she said.

Arnold Luray was a major in the Army Corps of Engineers.

He wore a civilian tuxedo. His handshake was perfunctory, his manner cool. "Stewart," he said briskly.

Casey groped for conversation. They talked briefly about the weather, about life in Washington, about Teddy Roosevelt's settlement of the Russo-Japanese War. Luray stared at him with ice-blue eyes. Abruptly, then, the major took his daughter's arm and drew her away. Willow glanced back at Casey with an expression of dismay and mute apology.

It was Marcia Morse who later shed some light. "Arnold is my brother and I love him dearly, Casey. But he is also a strange man in many ways, very possessive of Willow. No male is quite good enough for her. Unfortunately, he also has taken a dislike to you on other grounds, it seems."

"I've never even met the man," Casey protested.

"It doesn't matter. Arnold has very strong views on the Canal. He thinks it should have been built through Nicaragua. He did some of the preliminary engineering studies, years ago, and became quite an advocate for Nicaragua. He blames you for helping to defeat that route."

"I wasn't alone. There were others involved. Theodore Roosevelt, for starters."

"No matter. Arnold read about your speech in the newspapers. He has a way of taking things very personally. He is also a brooder."

"I see."

He didn't see, of course. For some reason, this troubled him more deeply than he cared to admit. For the remainder of the evening, he found himself continually glancing across the room at Willow. When the time came to leave, he pushed through the crowd and took her hand. Her face took on a sudden glow.

"It was good to see you again, Miss Luray."

"Oh, yes." Her hand held his. "It was good to see you again too, Mr. Stewart. I had been hoping..."

Behind her, Arnold Luray frowned.

Their hands parted. Casey glanced at her father. "Major," he said.

Casey Stewart and John Stevens rode back to the hotel in the latter's new Reo automobile. Casey stared out at the passing streets of nocturnal Washington, absorbed in his thoughts.

The chief engineer, sensing his mood, did not offer to make conversation.

Willow Luray was still on Casey's mind two hours later as he drifted off to fitful sleep.

Too fast. It happened too fast. At one moment the most important thing in his life was the Canal, and vague dreams of a young woman whose presence profoundly disturbed him. At the next moment he was jarred awake by a bellman knocking on his hotel room door with a telegram. He rolled out of bed, drew on a dressing gown, and shambled through the darkness.

"Mr. Stewart? I have a telegram, sir."

He blinked in the sudden light of the hallway, took the telegram, and rummaged for change. And then he closed the door and switched on the light and tore open the message. He read, blinked, read again:

Your father suffered a heart attack. Can you come? Aunt Colette.

The pain was deeper than he could have imagined it would be. My God, it had been so long. He had not seen Bradley Stewart in fifteen years. He remembered him as a burly man of power with heavy eyebrows. He remembered him saying, "You will go to Paris, go to engineering school, be on your own. I have chosen Maurice to head the family. Maurice has the talent for it." And then he had turned away, and Casey had watched his broad back move into the other room and felt himself deflate, like a balloon.

He hated him then. It did not have to be openly acknowledged, and yet it gave a boy, and later a man, something on which to hang his self-respect. And so he hated Bradley Stewart, and to a lesser degree Maurice, his brother. It was not Maurice's fault, of course. There had been a vindication of sorts when he heard from Aunt Colette that Maurice had refused the position of head of the family, quit Harvard, and went off on his own, to Michigan. And yet Casey's tangled feelings toward Maurice were still there.

Your father suffered a heart attack. Can you come?

Casey came down the steps of the car in the gray wash of daylight, enveloped in steam and the warmth of a humid, gray morning on the verge of July. And then he realized that it wasn't rainclouds that blotted out the sun; it was Pittsburgh.

Good God. Pittsburgh.

"Casey! Goddamnit, Casey!"

His brother came out of an elegant, shiny automobile. His brother was a handsome, tall man, filled out with muscle, his voice heavy and authoritative. Maurice Stewart was not the youth Casey had known but a man now, a man with a slight break in his nose and a masculine presence, a man in a tailored suit of Oxford gray, highly polished shoes, a gray fedora, a white shirt, waistcoat, and a necktie with a diamond stickpin. A man like himself.

"Maurice!"

"Casey!"

They ducked into the automobile. A woman was there, a stunning woman with sculpted features and fine clothes. Maurice said, "My wife Rachel." Casey smiled and took her hand, trying not to stare. Jesus, she was a looker. The rear compartment was enclosed in glass, the driver's seat outside in front. A chauffeur sat at the wheel, a big blond Swede with hands like white hams. "All right, Sven," Maurice said. The car moved away from the curb with a deep whining sound and a clash of gears.

What do brothers talk about after all these years? It was a question neither of them could rightly respond to. They talked of the past, of all things—hunting, their soot-covered elementary school, sleighrides. It was all smaller than Casey had remembered. He said as much, and Maurice agreed. "Home is always smaller than the way you remember it," Maurice said.

There was a pause. Casey rolled down the window and put his head out to peer up the wooded slope. The house was up there, the sight of its white pillars flicking through the trees. His heart lifted. Stewart House. It was always the homeplace of Stewarts. It was boyhood and young manhood and the place from which one had set out into the world.

"Stewart House," Casey said. "Goddamn, it hasn't changed."

"No," Maurice said. "It hasn't changed."

"And Father?"

The question brought another momentary silence between them. Maurice's mouth set in that curious way he had when reflecting deeply. Casey remembered that mouth-set from the day their mother had died. It went with a slight tilt of the head. Finally Maurice said, "He's waiting for you, Casey. He refused to die until you arrived."

Casey swallowed hard. The lump was suddenly in his throat, unbudging. He swallowed again. "Tough old buzzard," he said.

"He wants to see you."

"Did he see you?"

It was a foolish thing to say. He could have bitten his tongue. Maurice stared out the window, tight-mouthed. Then: "No. He did not wish to see me."

He sensed the enveloping intimacy of the house, heard the old clock, and smelled the familiar smells. He reached the top landing. A door opened. A nurse in white stood there. He went past her, taking off his hat, crossed the threshold of his father's room, and stopped. The blinds were drawn. He saw the pale head and white-clad shoulders on the white bed. The great shaggy head lay back, the face drawn, the eyes deep-socketed. My God, how thin he was!

"Father."

"Casey." It was a whispered croak.

The breathing was torturous. The body shuddered with each rise and fall of the chest. The heart seemed to beat with unnatural force. He moved to the bed and silently sat down on the edge of it and looked into his father's face.

"Glad . . . you came," Bradley Stewart said.

"Didn't you think I would?"

"Wasn't sure. Had to . . . see you if I . . . could."

"Don't try to talk now, Father. Later, when you're feeling stronger."

His father's hand lifted lightly from where it lay on the cover. The movement silenced him. "No more time . . ."

He felt the suffering within his own being. How odd that it would be so. Were the bonds of father and son that strong?

"I made mistake many years . . . ago."

Casey felt a strange inner lift, mixed of hope and despair. "A mistake?"

"You were just boys. I picked Maurice to head family . . . It was the wrong thing to . . . do." The breathing was more labored now. The voice lost its strength. Casey had to lean down to hear, his ear almost touching his father's mouth. "Maurice wanted . . . to be own man . . . You could have taken my place . . . built fortune even greater. Is that true?"

Suddenly Casey's throat ached. His eyes brimmed. He

spoke with difficulty. "That was a long time ago, Father. None of us can predict the future. None of us can undo the past. We are what we are, and we do what we do."

"I wanted to tell you . . . I'm sorry. I wanted . . . tell you, Casey . . . you are a fine man. I'm proud. You are building . . . Panama Canal. I'm proud . . . You follow Stewart tradition . . . and so"—there was deep rattling in the chest, a spasm of coughing, a pain in the deep-socketed eyes—"and so . . ."

"Father?"

". . . does your bro-th—er. . . ."

Two breaths followed. They were quite shallow. Casey waited for the third. He waited. The third breath did not come.

"Father?"

The face seemed to set. The chest stopped moving.

"*Father!*"

Bradley Stewart was dead.

They buried him two days later on the hillside where three generations of family lay beneath the great stone Stewart monument hewn of Pennsylvania granite. It was a sweltering sunny day. Half of Pittsburgh seemed to have come to the funeral in the hilltop mansion, spilling over from the parlors onto the porch beneath the great white pillars and into the yard, and then followed the procession in buggies and carriages and automobiles, winding through the hills to this graveyard with its stunning views of the summer hills rolling away into a haze of heat and smoke.

The Lord is my shepherd; I shall not want . . .

The parson, a spare, black-clad man fingering a worn Bible, droned on in the heat of the cemetery. Sweat trickled down Casey's neck. He was aware of all the names on the tombstones and markers. Isaiah. Martha. Stephen. Catherine. John Colby. Thaddeus. Marguerite. There were names as familiar to him as his own and names that he barely knew; there were the graves of old people and young people and children.

He leadeth me beside the still waters . . .

All these Stewarts. All this living, building, conniving, all this triumph and tragedy, all this loving and laughing and fighting and dying. It caused a man to reflect upon who he was. At this moment, Casey Stewart had a powerful sense of identity. He was a Stewart. These were his people.

A woman sobbed. He looked into the crowd. Rose. How odd, he thought, that Rose would sob. Father had never given her great affection. Hope did not sob. His cousin from New York stood rigidly in black, her face veiled, the garb of mourning accentuating the gold of her hair and making her more beautiful than ever. Of all people, Hope had probably loved him best. Aunt Francesca did not sob, standing with regal dignity beneath a black umbrella held by a chauffeur against the burning sun. Aunt Colette was dry-eyed. Nathan stood with manly reserve beside her, holding her arm. And Maurice, once their father's favorite, gave no outward sign of emotion at all; Maurice stood tall and handsome in his black suit and black hat beside the beautiful woman called Rachel. Casey's eye flicked lightly over the faces, committing them and the scene to memory.

Surely goodness and mercy will follow me all the days of my life and I shall dwell in the house of the Lord forever. Amen.

"Amen," they murmured.
And so it was done.

That evening Casey and his son Nathan strolled together in the soft summer darkness beneath the great trees of elm, oak, and sycamore. The boy was tall, broad at the shoulders, and heavy of hand and arm.

"Will you stay here in Pittsburgh for the rest of the summer, Nathan?"

"No, Father. I'm to meet Professor Comstock in Dayton next week. The Wrights are flying their machine almost every day, and I'm going to learn how to pilot it too. I'm enormously excited."

"Flying? You're not serious."

"Oh, but I am. They've been flying since Kitty Hawk, three years ago. I wrote to you about that, several times. Now they use a pasture on the outskirts of Dayton. They've built a hangar there and everything. They've already flown a distance of twenty-four miles. There was quite a bit of technical difficulty at first. It had to do with turning the aircraft. You see, they lacked coordination between the vertical rudder and the warping of the wings. It kept throwing them into a side-slip. Finally they managed to wire it up together, so that the wings automatically warped every time you pushed the rudder, and..."

"Hey!"—laughing, Casey slapped his son on the shoulder—"wait a minute, Nathan. I don't understand a word you're saying. But why haven't I read any of this in the newspapers? What you're telling me is stupendous!"

"But nobody believes it's possible. There's been virtually no publicity on the Wrights. Professor Langley's two crashes in the Potomac killed everybody's enthusiasm. There've been so many failures that people just assume man will never fly, and that's that. Even my schoolmates laugh at me when I talked about it. We'll go back to the house, and I'll show you what I mean."

They returned to the front parlor to find Hope and her husband playing whist with another couple. "Mr. Langden, there's a terrific newspaper story up in Dayton, Ohio."

"Is that so, Nathan?" Langden smiled indulgently, watching his wife's expert play of the hand.

"These two brothers, Orville and Wilbur Wright, built a whopper flying machine. They're out every day in a pasture, flying. It's just eight miles from town. They've flown twenty-four miles in a single hop."

"Do tell."

"Yes, sir. I've been working with them for three years. That's how I know about it. And this summer, the Wrights are going to let me take the machine up by myself. Isn't that wonderful?"

Langden chuckled. "Son, the only whopper I know anything about is the one you're handing me right now. Next you'll be talking about a river that runs uphill." The publisher glanced amiably at Casey. "This boy has some vivid imagination. He'll make a writer of fiction someday." He spun his wheelchair expertly and rolled toward the kitchen, wagging his head. "Flying machine..."

Nathan looked at Casey and shrugged.

XII

"Blast!"

Casey Stewart shouted the word into the blazing afternoon. A whistle shrieked. Men dropped their tools and bolted for cover. Hammer Man squatted behind the great earthmover shovel, waiting. Casey raised his arm, squinted into the glare of sunshine, and snapped it down. Hammer Man pushed the plunger and ducked. A thunderclap burst in the side of the Cut, vomiting tons of earth and rock. A secondary earth slide broke loose from the terraced slope and came thundering down. Clods rained over the ground and bounced off the steel machines. The roaring subsided in a trickle of dirt and stones.

He stood up in the sudden silence, peering into the dust. A glob of powder smoke hung in the still air over the blast center. Casey glanced behind him at the chief engineer. Goethals nodded and growled, "Good shot."

They moved forward warily. Casey's practiced eye took in what remained of the land shelf, scrutinizing each spot where they had buried dynamite sticks in search of an unexploded charge. But with all this rubble, it was impossible to tell. He turned and waved to the gang foreman. "Bring 'em on in."

Black workmen rose slowly from their places of shelter. They picked up shovels, converged on the blast site, and began to dig. Casey joined Goethals and several of the Culebra foremen at the line shack. "I still think we can cut down on the accidents." He looked into the black face of each foreman. "But you've got to have better control of your shots. Make absolutely certain every man is clear; tighten up precautions when you're tamping charges; don't set your blasting caps too early."

George Goethals shook his head gravely. "Too many dead. Too many hurt. Dynamite's tricky."

It was an understatement. Men were forever getting blown to bits. Explosions were touched off by lightning bolts, by a shovelman digging rubble and striking an unexploded cap, by the hand of God. Maimed men were everywhere, lacking arms, legs, eyes, brains. The danger was increased by the sheer abundance of explosives. Even now another million-pound dynamite ship stood at anchor in the harbor at Colón. The concrete underground magazines were full. In the Cut, dynamite was as commonplace as chewing tobacco. Looking into the distance, Casey saw a long line of black men bearing boxes of dynamite on their heads.

"How much are you using now?" Goethals asked.

Casey scratched his jaw. "You won't believe it."

"Try me."

"Four hundred thousand pounds this month. That's eight hundred thousand sticks."

"Good Lord," the chief engineer said.

Around them loomed the immensity of Culebra. It was more than a gigantic hole in the ground now; Culebra was a vast, living brown presence, teeming with machines and men, a constant clanking, moving, shuffling, rumbling phenomenon. The mighty slopes of Culebra rose like a man-made Grand Canyon, reducing men to the size of ants. Hell's Gorge, they called it. Railroad tracks laced the yawning bottom of the gorge; dirt trains chuffed back and forth; mighty power shovels, the biggest man had ever created, scooped up house-size bites of earth and spewed them onto the trains.

"Culebra alone is going to end up costing us ten million dollars a mile," George Goethals said. The chief engineer squinted toward the east bank of the Cut, to a point near Gold Hill. Casey knew what was on his mind. "If Cucaracha lets go again, we lose another two or three months. What do you think, Stewart?"

The Cucaracha Slide. It was a plague upon his existence: a vast poised glacier of mud, rock, and clay which had repeatedly avalanched down to bury men and machines. In the rainy season of late summer and fall, the soil of Cucaracha soaked up water like a sponge. The deeper they dug the Cut, the more tenuous that terrible slope. Casey looked up at Cucaracha with an old familiar grip in the belly. He had almost lost his life four years ago in the great slide of '07. That was seven months after John Stevens's strange mental breakdown had brought his ouster as chief engineer and an angry Theodore Roosevelt had named taciturn, tireless Colonel Goethals to take his place with a team of Army engineers.

They did not get along well, Casey and Goethals. Goethals made little effort to conceal his distaste for retaining a civilian who held a presidential appointment, had been his predecessor's right-hand man, and about whom there were persistent rumors of past drunkenness and debauchery, including divorce. To his credit, however, the chief engineer did not let personal considerations dominate his judgment of talent. It had startled Casey to hear Goethals say, "Stewart, I want you take charge of Culebra Cut." That had occurred in the wake of Cucaracha's devastating slide. Now Casey Stewart inspected suspicious new cracks in the face of the brooding slope and did some mental arithmetic.

"There's a lot of force building, Colonel. I wish to hell I could predict when she'll let go again. I wish to hell I could."

Casey Stewart arrived at his quarters at half past six. As chief of the Culebra project, he occupied an airy government house with screened porches and a close-clipped lawn in the town of Culebra, itself a product of the Canal. His housekeeper Mrs. Obrey, an efficient, middle-aged German woman, met him at the door.

"Any mail, Mrs. Obrey?"

"The usual, sir." She offered a knowing smile.

The usual letter, and it gave him the usual lift. For two years, at least once a week and sometimes more often, these letters had come. They were postmarked Boston, Washington, New York, or various military bases. This one, oddly, was from San Juan, Puerto Rico. The envelope bore its usual lightly perfumed scent and graceful feminine handwriting. He tore it open, aware of his usual anticipation.

I'm traveling with Father and we made a stop here at San Juan. It's a lovely old city and I wish you could see it with me.

She wrote easily and well, describing the sights she had seen, her acquaintances aboard ship, the weather.

I'm continually reading fascinating stories about the Canal and especially Culebra Cut. Did you know that it's becoming one of the most popular tourist spots in the Western Hemisphere? How I wish I could see you. Love. Willow.

And that's how she closed it, always.

How I wish I could see you. Love.

His own replies, by contrast, were stilted and foolish. He had no gift for the chatty phrase. His weekly efforts to Willow always seemed to bog down in some technical description of digging machines or earth slides or new experiments to improve the safety of dynamite tamping and capping.

Putting aside Willow's letter, he bathed, shaved, and dressed in a cream-colored linen suit Mrs. Obrey had laid out for him. The white shirt was immaculately laundered and crisply starched, the shoes freshly whited, the shirt studs and cufflinks polished. Walking out into the warm scented night of Panama, a full moon coasted overhead, bathing the distant jungle hills in its eerie light. In the residential compound of Culebra, trees and underbrush had been cut back aggressively by Dr. Gorgas's mosquito fighters. Lawns were closely cropped, gravel walkways bordered by whitewashed stones. He walked down a curving flight of stone steps to the railroad depot, conscious of the enormous changes that had taken place in four years.

Men, women, and children stood on the station platform awaiting the evening train to Panama City. They wore white suits, flat straw hats, white shoes, summer gowns; they carried walking sticks and parasols. They were freshly scrubbed, gentle, God-fearing. They worked as engineers, technicians, steam-shovel operators; doctors, bookkeepers, clerks, teachers, nurses, nursery school attendants, cooks. They were part of a white paternalistic society. Status was signified by one's living quarters: group living for single males and females, small apartments for lower-income newlyweds, larger cottages for the higher-ranked, spacious government homes like Casey's for top administrators.

"Here she comes!"

The light of the evening train rounded a bend and flared over the platform. Casey stared out at the moonlit jungle and for some reason found himself remembering Paulette and wondering about what his life would have been like if the French disasters had not broken, if they could have lived on untroubled by the scandals that had pulled his marriage down with the rest. Paulette, Casey, Nathan. The boy was twenty now, a junior at the University of Virginia, flying his own aircraft, traveling frequently with the Wright brothers to Paris and Berlin, a handsome young man filled with adventure and derring-do. Nathan's most recent letter intrigued Casey, for the lad had talked with Maurice in Fall River about—of all things—adding the manufacture of flying machines to Stewart Motors Corp. Nathan had written with his usual optimism,

Uncle Maurice didn't say yes, and he didn't say no.

And one of the boy's converts to flying was none other than Van Harrison Stewart, the legendary racing driver.

Van has a wonderful knack for flying, a kind of élan that is natural to the art.

An art. So now flying was an art. Casey grinned to himself. What next?

"Panama City!" the conductor called.

Casey rode a motor taxicab to the hotel. Lights blazed and the sound of ragtime spilled out onto the street. He climbed the steps and pushed through the crowded foyer, acknowledging greetings and smiles, and found the bar. A moment later he savored a bourbon and soda and scanned the room.

"Hello, you handsome devil." The woman stood beside Casey. She was a fetching redhead with flashing green eyes. There was a sparkle of diamond earrings, a breath of French perfume. "Where have you been keeping yourself lately?"

He nodded, smiled, and raised his glass. "Hello, Elodie. I've been right here."

Elodie Green said, "I could use a drink."

"It's not ladylike."

"Who are you calling a lady?"

"I'll get you a drink."

He ordered. Carrying the two glasses, he led her to a small table flanked by potted palms. Male eyes followed her in covert glances. Casey smiled himself, admiring the shining red hair, the green gown, the small waist, and taut rounded hips. They sat down. They touched glasses and drank.

"My God, Casey," she said, "Every woman on the Isthmus is panting for you. What's wrong, sweetheart? Did you get your balls shot off on San Juan Hill? Don't try to tell me something else. I know you like girls. Or at least you *used* to like girls."

"Now, now, Elodie. Be nice."

"I'm serious. I worry about you. Surely you want something more out of life than that damned hole in the ground at Culebra."

"Culebra's not bad. It is the world's biggest . . ."

"I know, I know. The world's biggest ditch. But you go home alone, eat alone, go to bed alone."

"How do you know all that?"

"Nobody can keep secrets in Panama."

Casey grinned. "Elodie, you're hopeless."

She drank off her bourbon. "A word to the wise."

"Where is your husband?"

"Drunk, of course."

Casey was immediately contrite. He liked Jack Green. "How long has it been this time?"

"Three days."

He reached across the table and took her hand. This stunning woman, for all her salty talk, had remained with a drunken husband long after it was sensible to do so. "I'm sorry," he said.

Elodie Green sniffed. "I love the sonofabitch, Casey. Or at least I used to love him. I loved him so much, when we first married, that it still haunts me. He needs me. And I can't leave him."

"Let's go find Jack," he said.

"Oh, God. Do you know where he is?"

"Yes, damn it. I know."

They stood up to leave. Abruptly, the band stopped playing. There was a drumroll. Colonel George Goethals, resplendent in a white suit and dark tie, stood smiling at the bandstand. It was a rare public appearance for the chief engineer. Casey and Elodie waited for Goethals to speak.

"Ladies and gentlemen, as you all know, we are here tonight to welcome some newcomers to the staff. It gives me great pleasure . . ." Goethals spoke at length about the progress of the work, his pride in the personnel and staff. He offered a few pallid jokes. He introduced several fresh-cheeked young Army officers, the lowest-ranking of the newcomers. Casey fidgeted beside Elodie. He turned away to light a cigar. ". . . a man well-experienced to assume this important task," the colonel was saying, "my personal choice as executive officer of the Canal Zone. Let's have a big warm welcome for Lieutenant Colonel Arnold Luray!"

Casey's head jerked around. He stared in surprise at the bandstand. From out of the crowd, wearing civilian clothes, strode muscular, thickset Luray, Willow's father. His bull neck seemed too big for his shirt collar; his partially bald head gleamed in the light. The back of his linen jacket was saturated with sweat.

He began a brief, dull speech as Casey took Elodie Green by the arm.

"Let's get out of here."

"What's wrong, lover? You look like you've seen a ghost."

They found him on the second floor of the Navajo, one of the dozens of whorehouses which flourished in the city. It was a typical, antiseptic bordello room. Jack lay sprawled in the middle of the bed, facedown and fully clothed.

Casey dumped the unconscious form into the carriage. He and Elodie climbed in beside it. The driver snicked his horses forward as they rode through the dark streets without speaking. As the carriage stopped in front of the hotel the crowd from the dance was coming out. Elodie's car, an Oldsmobile runabout, was parked in front of the hotel.

"There's nothing like being conspicuous," Casey said.

"Go ahead, Casey. I'll get him into the car."

"Like hell you will."

He hoisted Jack Green onto his shoulder again, backed out of the carriage, and carried him to the Oldsmobile. As the crowd watched, murmuring, Elodie opened the door and Casey dumped the body onto the seat.

"Casey Stewart, you're a hell of a man." Elodie Green reached up, grabbed the lapels of his suit jacket, and drew him down. Her kiss was lingering and fierce. "I love you, you big bastard," she said.

She got into the Oldsmobile and drove away, waving.

Casey stood in the street, watching until the car disappeared around the corner, and turned toward the crowd on the steps.

He looked up into the startled face of Willow Luray.

The morning heat was suffocating. Sunshine baked the main street of Culebra and bore down upon the ranks of two-story beige buildings forming the administrative compound. In the corner office of the chief engineer Lieutenant Colonel Arnold Luray sat in a wicker chair, sweat trickling down the back of his neck. An overhead ceiling fan stirred the heat. The screened open windows offered not a breath of air.

"You'll get used to it," Colonel George Washington Goethals said. "One's system adapts over time. It happens to all of us."

They passed half an hour, drinking coffee. Luray was somewhat surprised at the clutter of Goethals's desk. Personally, he was a clean-desk man, everything in its place and a place for everything. The chief engineer's desk was piled high with reports, vouchers, studies, and plans, collected in folders and the folders duly annotated.

"What can you tell me about this man Stewart?" Luray said. "You have him in charge at Culebra, I see."

"Casey Stewart?" The chief engineer put his fingers together and studied them. "We have our differences. He's a civilian. His position is, well, vague. There is no listing of him at all on the official table of organization. He was appointed by the President at the outset, as a kind of troubleshooter. John Wallace found him competent enough to run things during his frequent absences, however. My immediate predecessor John Stevens thought the world of him; Stewart had been his subordinate on the Great Northern Railway. He's a Pittsburgh Stewart, incidentally, which also means a lot, and a hero of San Juan Hill . . ."

"What about his competency at Culebra?"

Goethals fixed his new executive officer with a penetrating gaze. "I consider Stewart the best man in Panama for the job."

Luray let out a breath and moistened his lips. "But I understand he drinks, and that he is a trifler with women."

Goethals smiled thinly. "Many men drink here in the Canal Zone, Luray. Many men also have had, shall we say, affairs of the heart. While I don't approve of imbibing strong spirits, if it doesn't interfere with a man's performance I don't let it weigh too heavily on his career."

"I've been going over the production schedules." Luray shifted his point of attack. "I'm not altogether impressed with Stewart's progress. I think it could be improved."

Goethals stroked his chin reflectively. "We can always stand improvement. You're the new executive officer. I leave such things to your judgment."

"By the way," the chief engineer said, "does your daughter plan to remain in Panama with you?"

"Only for the time being. She probably will return to New York in a month or two."

"Stunning girl," Goethals said. "Some of our younger officers were already vying for her attention at the reception and dance. I'm sure you will be receiving quite a lot of gentlemen callers while she's here."

Luray did not smile. He nodded curtly and walked out without another word.

The chief engineer Goethals watched him go, sensing trouble in the air.

"I know we're right on top of the Cucaracha, Mr. Stewart, but Barry and I do love this little house and we'd hate to give it up." She was a bright middle-aged woman, the wife of an assistant power shovel operator. She stood shading her eyes in the sunshine beside her government cottage. From the distance below came the constant rumble of work in Culebra Cut. "It's the nicest place we've ever had, and the noise doesn't bother me and the children at all."

"You're going to have to move out sooner or later, Mrs. Hawthorne," Casey said. "Do you see these cracks in the face of the gorge?" He led her around the house to the edge of Culebra. He pointed to a network of cracks crisscrossing the soil six feet from the brink. "That means that this entire brow of the cliff is gradually detaching from the stone substrata. Each time it rains, the water pours down inside and saturates the soil that much more, adding weight. Very soon, now, it'll go."

Mary Hawthorne pushed back a stray wisp of brown hair turning prematurely gray. "When do you want us to move, Mr. Stewart?"

"Preferably within two weeks, Mrs. Hawthorne. I'm sorry. I'll make certain that you get the best cottage available; but as you know, there aren't that many standing empty these days. We've got thirty thousand employees on the Canal alone, plus their dependents..."

"I know." She sighed. "All right, then. I'll tell Barry."

"Thank you, Mrs. Hawthorne."

At the line shack, he was met by the big black foreman Marfot Johnson.

"We had company while you was gone, Mr. Casey."

"Company?"

"Lieutenant Colonel Luray, the new executive officer. He say he want to speed up the work in Culebra. He say he gonna talk to you about that."

Casey smiled grimly. "I don't see how we can go much faster. The men are already falling out from heat and exhaustion. Did he feel the temperature down here? It must be a hundred ten degrees."

Marfot Johnson shook his head. "Hundred fifteen, suh."

"Is he coming back?"

Johnson looked over Casey's shoulder. "He's here now."

Arnold Luray walked with short, brisk steps across the rough ground of Culebra Cut. He wore high-laced engineering boots, breeches, and a floppy-brimmed hat. Half-moons of sweat spread from his armpits. The costume gave him a squat, stubby look. He carried a swagger stick with which he slapped the side of his boot as he advanced. Finally he stood spread-footed before Casey, thickset, lantern-jawed, and half a head shorter, folding his arms. "Well, Stewart, I see you got back from your afternoon siesta."

"Siesta?"

"Or wherever it is you wander off to when the work gets boring."

"What do you want, Luray?"

"Colonel Luray to you."

Casey nodded to Johnson. "All right, I'll take it from here."

"Yes, suh." The black cast a hard glance at Luray and went to the line shack.

"You were seen leaving the reception the other night in the middle of my remarks. That was rather a gauche way to get started with a new superior officer; don't you think?" Luray smiled thinly. "But then considering your redheaded companion, I suppose you both had more urgent business in mind."

Casey swallowed hard. He felt the flush of anger in his face. This man, he thought, is deliberately baiting me. With an effort of will, he clamped his teeth tightly shut. Silence fell between them. Their eyes locked. Luray's were the first to waver.

"I've been looking over your work performance here in Culebra, Stewart. This is one of the critical phases of the Canal project and certainly the most dramatic. At the present rate of progress, however, I'm afraid it will be another three years to completion, or even more. We can do better than that. You've got six thousand men employed right here. The sooner we complete the work, the sooner they can be deployed elsewhere or discharged entirely."

Luray spun on his heel, flicking the riding crop against the boot. "Never liked working with civilian administrators anyhow. No sense of discipline. No feel for priorities." His eye surveyed the immensity of the gorge.

Suddenly snagging on the looming bulge of the Cucaracha Slide, he said, "What's that?"

"What's what?"

"That!" The swagger stick pointed at Cucaracha. "Why hasn't this area been cleared, Stewart? Look at these tracks;

they're swung out around it. Do you mean to tell me these men are so lazy they dig around an obstacle rather than go through it?"

"Luray, that happens to be . . ."

"By God, we'll see about this. I want you to get some men in here, Stewart. Load up your dynamite charges right along there. It'll take about—one, two, six, eight—about ten tons ought to do it. Blast that bulge right out of there. Get these tracks straightened."

"You don't know what the hell you're talking about!"

"Oh, I know what I'm talking about, all right. I've been an Army engineer for twenty-five years, Stewart. I've forgotten more about dynamite than you'll ever learn . . ."

"Luray, get your butt out of here." The fury consumed him. His fists clenched, his chest tightened, and he wanted nothing more at this instant than to take this idiot by the neck and shake him like a rat.

The lieutenant colonel stepped back, eyes compressed to slits. "I dare you, Stewart. If you strike a superior officer, I'll have you under arrest and in chains so fast it'll make your head swim."

Casey recognized the bluff. Military law did not extend to him. Civilian law did, however. He said, "I'm responsible for Culebra Cut. And as long as I remain responsible, this project will be done my way. Now move out before I lose my temper."

"We'll see who has the real authority," Luray said.

He stalked away, still slapping at his boot.

The following morning he arrived on the grassy hilltop favored by tourists, overlooking Culebra Cut. He had promised one of the tour guides that he would talk with the usual crowd of visitors, well-fed Americans, the men in white suits and straw hats, the women in lightweight ankle-length dresses and carrying frilly parasols against the sunshine. They stood in the grass staring down into the gorge as if mesmerized.

Casey acknowledged the tour guide's introductions, smiled, nodded, and launched into his description. "Ladies and gentlemen, welcome to Culebra. The Panama Canal, as you know, is the largest public works project ever undertaken by man. Gatun Lake, which when filled will cover a hundred and twenty-four square miles of jungle, will be the biggest man-made body of water. Now, Culebra . . ."

As he motioned toward the gorge, a feminine voice from the back of the crowd said, "Are you married, Mr. Stewart?"

Irritated, Casey glanced in the direction of the voice without identifying its owner. "No, ma'am, I'm not. Now, then, Culebra Cut is the largest excavation ever attempted. One writer from New York came down here and figured out that if all the dirt we take out of here were heaped up in one place, it would form a pile nearly nine hundred feet high. That's taller than the Woolworth Building, which is the tallest structure in the world . . ."

"But why aren't you married, Mr. Stewart? I'm sure you have no shortage of women who would be interested."

A ripple of laughter passed through the crowd. Heads turned. Casey flushed. "Ma'am, if you don't mind, I'd like to continue."

"Oh, excuse me," the voice said. "Please continue."

"Thank you. Ladies and gentlemen, to give you a some-what different frame of reference, we have removed as much earth in two years of work as the French did in seventeen years of supreme effort."

"Mr. Stewart?" It was the woman's voice again.

Casey hesitated, containing his frustration. "Yes, ma'am?"

"Would you marry *me*?"

This time the crowd laughed out loud. Their attention had been totally disrupted. Casey grinned and pushed his way through. Everyone was looking at a trim young woman in a white sailor suit, her face hidden behind a fluffy parasol. "All right, Miss," Casey said pleasantly, removing his hat, "what have you got against engineers?"

Willow Luray looked up with an impish smile. "Mr. Stewart, I adore engineers. Especially this engineer."

And there, on the edge of Culebra Cut in the presence of fifty-two witnesses, she put her arms around his neck and kissed him.

They rode together on the green hills overlooking Culebra. The day was wondrous, the sky magnificently clear and blue, the slopes and trails filled with clouds of butterflies. The Isthmus had suddenly become a magical place. Casey wanted to shout it at the jungle, the steep bridle paths, the river, the distant houses, the train chugging though the hills. He led Willow's sorrel away from the Canal, down a slope into the enveloping green of rain forest. He found a grassy place beside a chuckling clear stream and dismounted. And then he reached to bring her down from the sidesaddle, feeling the wonderful taut smallness of her waist, feeling her lightness in his hands.

They stood breathlessly together for a moment. A monkey shrieked overhead. Parakeets burst from the jungle canopy in a riot of color.

"Casey," she whispered. "Oh, Casey."

He let her go, turned away, and busied himself with the picnic things. They spread a white cloth on the grass, opened a basket of cheese, wine, and fruits. They listened to the stream, to the jungle sounds. The horses grazed nearby, mouths tearing at morsels of grass. There was an odor of moss and flowers. "Do you know that I've loved you since I was sixteen years old?" she said.

"Don't talk like that. I'm an old man. I'm as old as your father."

"But it's true, Casey. I've kept every letter that you ever sent me. I've got all the newspaper clippings I could find, about your speeches in Washington, the Canal, stories about Culebra Cut. Isn't that silly? And when I saw you . . . saw you the other night with that woman in front of the hotel, I could have died. When she kissed you, I was jealous. I was so jealous and confused that my stomach ached."

He felt that he should stop her from speaking this way. He felt half ashamed, an eavesdropper overhearing a schoolgirl's secrets. But then he looked at her—at the luxuriant glow of her hair, the huge depths of her eyes, the full curves and swells of woman beneath that summer frock—and knew that she was no longer a schoolgirl. She was twenty-two years old, a woman capable of making her own decisions.

"How long will you be here?" he asked.

The dark eyes came up, searching his. "For as long as you want me to be."

They sat silently together for a long time. As the afternoon waned, he brought the horses and lifted her back onto the sorrel. They rode out of the glen, up the slope, back to the hills, back to the station.

The platform was crowded. People glanced curiously at them. Casey recognized some of the faces. He and Willow stood together, the backs of their hands just brushing, and waited for the train. The other people were strangely remote. It was as if the people weren't there at all; that he and Willow were standing on an island of privacy.

He shook his head as if to break this spell.

She looked up at him and smiled.

The train came. Too soon, too soon. She got on without him. He stood watching it move away, gathering speed. He felt suddenly alone.

The day was gray and rainy. The machines and the dirt trains glistened in the downpour. Laborers toiled on, heedless of the rain, their clothes and bodies soaked.

"Here you are, Mr. Casey." Marfot Johnson reached his hand down from the dirt-filled flatcar. Casey took it and sprang onto the iron step. They had worked together for four years, since the old superintendent Crawford had killed Tall Man with a shovel. The memory invariably troubled Casey, for Crawford had been allowed to return to the States without any penalty for his deed, claiming self-defense.

"I seen that pretty lady you was ridin' with yesterday," Marfot Johnson said. "It's about time you thought about settlin' down."

"Hell, I've been settled for years," Casey said. "I just haven't had a woman of my own, that's all."

"Man without a woman is half a man."

"Are you married, Johnson?"

"Uh-huh. Got me a wife in Bridgetown, Barbados. Got eleven children."

"How did you manage to have all those children? You're here and she's there."

"I goes back from time to time on the shuttle boat. It don't take long to make a woman pregnant. And my woman, all she got to do is turn around three times and say the magic words, and bam! Pregnant again." He laughed.

They rode the work train to the dirt dump at Gatun Dam. The rain had stopped by the time they returned, but the sky remained leaden and threatening. One of the gang foremen came running toward them as the train neared the line shack. Casey and Johnson jumped clear, splashing in the mud. The gang foreman, a very black man from Guadalupe, was wide-eyed and out of breath.

"Mr. Casey! Mr. Casey! They're going to dynamite Cucaracha!"

He was startled. "What? There's to be no dynamite at Cucaracha. I gave orders . . ."

"The new executive officer, Mr. Luray, he told us to do it. They settin' the charges now, Mr. Casey."

Casey started to run, hesitated, and turned to the Cut foreman. "Johnson, do you see those houses up on top?" He gestured wildly to the summit. "Get up there and warn those people! Drag 'em out, if you've got to, but clear those houses!" Another dirt train came rattling by, headed for the Cucaracha Slide area. Casey and the gang foreman swung aboard.

Drillers had already dug their holes in the muddy base. A line of workmen was strung out beneath Cucaracha, frantically setting charges. Back and forth behind them strode Lieutenant Colonel Arnold Luray, knee boots splashed with mud, furiously chomping at a cigar, slapping his boot with the swagger stick and bawling orders. "Move, you lazy buggers! We don't have all day. Get those sticks tamped and capped. You, there, finish laying out that roll of wire!"

Casey Stewart came off the dirt car at a run. "Luray, what the hell is going on here?"

"If you can't do it, Stewart, I will. We're gonna clean this bulge out, straighten these tracks; get some order and discipline on this job."

"You damn fool, that's the Cucaracha Slide. You'll bring down a whole mountainside into this part of the Cut. And worse, you're jeopardizing the lives of women and children up top. Don't you see those houses, man!"

Luray removed the cigar from his mouth and spat. "Them houses ain't nowhere near danger yet, Stewart, and you know it. I'm tired of excuses. We're going to get a little work done around here for a change."

The executive officer turned away just as the last charge was tamped and capped. An assistant foreman stood ready to connect the wires to the plunger, eyeing Casey fearfully. "Drop those wires and move out!" Casey shouted.

The blasting wire dropped into the mud and the man took to his heels.

With a growl of rage, Arnold Luray spun around. "You son of a bitch!" The swagger struck a whistling blow to Casey's face. As he lurched backward, grabbing at his cheek, Luray's heavy boot smashed into his groin. The pain engulfed him. Doubling over like a sack, he fell into the mud, wretching.

A workman sprinted to the line shack and set off the alarm signal. Its frantic siren blast echoed through a mile of Culebra Cut. Laborers dropped their tools and sprinted for cover.

"Casey! Casey!" Someone came pounding through the mud. In the depths of his agony, he recognized Jack Green. Powerful hands gripped him at the armpits and dragged him roughly across rock and mud. "God Almighty," Green shouted, "the bastard's gonna blow Cucaracha! He's out of his mind!"

"Stop him, Jack!" Casey said. The words came out a froglike croak.

Green yanked Casey to his feet. Still bent under the crushing pain and supported by Green, he moved across double sets of tracks, past the line shack and fifty yards beyond to a huge Bucyrus power shovel. The operator had fled, leaving the engine guttering and the stack belching smoke. They climbed into the steel cab. Green manipulated the heavy gears and the great iron treads of the machine began to move away from Cucaracha.

It was starting to rain again. Casey squinted toward the base of the masif. "What's he doing?"

"He's laid out two hundred yards of wire and is fitting the plunger." Green pointed to a rock outcropping. "All hell's about to break loose..."

The blast went off in the murky light, a deep, muffled boom. Before their startled eyes, the face of Cucaracha Slide gave a mighty heave. Ponderously, freed at last from its attachment to the bluff, a million tons of mud, rock, and wet clay began its torrential descent into the chasm.

The first avalanche was followed by another, and then another, as layer after layer made its rushing plunge. Squinting up into the murk, Casey spotted the Hawthorne house suddenly emerging at the brink high above. The mountain kept peeling away beneath the cottage until the little house tilted toward the gorge and began its downward slide. The sight sickened him.

"Jesus Christ!" Jack Green crossed himself.

"I'm going to kill that son of a bitch."

They were engulfed in a cataclysmic, roaring, all-consuming brown hell which now invaded the cab of the power shovel, rising to their hips, their waists. And then it slowed. And then, miraculously, it stopped. A foot of daylight remained beneath the roof of the cab. The rain drummed down on metal and mud.

Jack Green smeared a muddy hand over his face and said, "Whew!"

Painfully they clambered out of the cab and onto the superstructure of the shovel. They stood in a sea of mud. Two locomotives lay on their sides, deep in debris. Dirt cars, sections of track, power machines, and compressor hoses lay tossed about like so much trash. Casey's groin still ached, but he could move. They found several wide lengths of board, lay them out on the mud, and slowly maneuvered them, one by one, to a mound of solid high ground. Casey looked down the gorge and saw men and machines already converging upon the slide area. He looked up at the top of Cucaracha, where the Hawthorne house had stood, and saw only empty sky. But a movement caught the corner of his eye. He shaded his eyes. There on the crest he could just see Mrs. Hawthorne and her two children standing beside Johnson and the brown gelding. His heart lifted.

It was two hours before they could reach Arnold Luray. The executive officer was trapped chest-deep in mud and writhing in pain, both legs crushed between large boulders. Casey and Jack Green organized a massive rescue effort as laborers shoveled him free. They finally managed to release his legs by forcing the boulders apart with hydraulic jacks. He was carried on a litter to the train and taken to the hospital in Panama City.

Fifteen bodies were taken from the mud of the Cucaracha Slide. Thirteen men remained unaccounted for. The cleanup required three months, during which more mud periodically broke loose and thundered into the gorge. Eventually, all the bodies would be retrieved and sent to Monkey Hill for burial. The chief engineer ordered a full-scale inquiry, and charged Lieutenant Colonel Luray with gross negligence.

Six weeks after the disaster, Casey Stewart and Willow Anne Luray were married in the government chapel at Culebra, without her father's consent. The marriage ceremony was performed by Henri Blanchet, the former Catholic priest. Jack Green served as best man. Despite the delicate politics of Canal Zone life, the chief engineer himself surprised everyone by staging a full-dress reception. Champagne flowed. The Canal Zone dance band entertained with several hours of dance music, to which the bride and groom danced and danced and danced and danced. Mrs. Penelope Hines Jacoway, who had been married four times and presently was the wife of Major Herndon Jacoway of the Army engineers, wept openly and pronounced Casey and Willow the most beautiful couple she had ever seen, even if Mr. Stewart was several years older than his bride.

"Several years? My dear, Casey's twenty years older if he's a day."

"It doesn't matter." Penelope Hines Jacoway dabbed at her swollen eyes with a hanky. "Love conquers all."

They were tipsy. It had been her first experience with champagne. They drove up to Casey's house in the Oldsmobile borrowed from the Greens. Still dressed in her wedding gown and yards of white veil, she lay her head back on the seat and giggled. "The bubbles tickled my nose."

"We shall have more. More champagne, and more and"—Casey burped softly—"more."

"Do you know who I am?" She sat upright, gazing at him with those eyes that reminded him of dark pools. "I am Mrs. Casey Stewart, that's who! I am married to the most hanshum . . . handsome man who ever walked upon the whole, wide earth." She hiccupped happily. "Ishn't that something?"

He got out, went around the car, and scooped her up in his arms. He lurched up the steps, fumbled with the doorknob, pushed it open, and stepped across the threshold. The parlor was filled with flowers. Flowers adorned the staircase, the upper landing, the main bedroom.

"Where did they all come from?" he said.

She found a card on the dresser and read,

From Mr. and Mrs. Barry Hawthorne and the Shovel
Operators of Culebra Cut

His bloodshot eyes brimmed.

"You see?" She put her arms around his neck. Her face was wreathed in smiles. "Everybody loves you."

They changed clothes self-consciously in separate rooms. She emerged wearing a clinging green gown, her hair done with a ribbon to match. They went downstairs, where the housekeeper had put out a cold chicken supper. They ate voraciously, giggling and talking, and drank more champagne. He turned on the electric phonograph. They danced some more.

The evening deepened. A lone candle made a pool of light in the room. They sat together on the sofa, holding hands. He could think of no prior experience with which to measure the joy of this.

Willow leaned against him, her fragrance filling his senses, and whispered into his ear.

"Mr. Stewart, do you know what I would like to do?"

"What would you like to do, Mrs. Stewart?"

"I would like to go upstairs and . . ."

"And what?"

"... and make a baby."

He carried her up. She seemed as light as a thistle in his arms.

XIII

"We want the vote! We want the vote! We want the vote!"

A drum throbbed in desultory rhythm, struggling to provide a tuneless martial air. Stalled traffic thickened in the heat along Forty-second Street. Teamsters whistled and cursed; motorists blatted their horns. Hope Stewart Langden joined a clot of spectators on the sidewalk, watching two dozen white-clad women marching past in uneven ranks.

"Haw! Clear the roadway, Mable!" a heavy redfaced man bawled from in front of a saloon. "You'll getcher petticoats dirty. Haw-haw-haw!"

His example inspired several other males to join in, making a chorus of jeers and catcalls. Hope flushed angrily and glared at the hecklers. But then Bernard Chafin touched her arm and said lightly, "Just ignore them. I'd rather not engage in fisticuffs just now."

He was right, of course. She concentrated on closing her ears and bridling her anger. When the demonstration had passed, she and Chafin moved across Forty-second Street with the human tide. "It's ridiculous," she said. "Those women have a right to express themselves."

The table was waiting at Henri's, a small French restaurant off Fifth Avenue. They were joined by five men, all Manhattan business leaders and major advertisers in the *Enterprise*, for a luncheon discussion of upcoming advertising budgets. Chafin demonstrated his usual shrewd mastery of details, and again Hope acknowledged her good fortune at hiring him as general manager. The decision had not been popular with old Bailey, the *Enterprise's* crusty, tightfisted chief accountant. "Hope, we've barely come out from under the latest Wall Street panic. I don't see how we can afford to pay fifteen hundred dollars a year for an executive barely out of Yale." But she had insisted, Howard had given his backing as usual, and that was that.

"... can't help but think President Taft is right in charting his own course." The speaker was Lawrence Morgan, a portly

Broadway merchant who also owned a seat on the Stock Exchange. "I hate to see this deep rift between conservative and progressive Republicans. Roosevelt hasn't helped matters, with his constant sniping at Taft. Personally, I'm damn glad he's out of office. I flatly disagree with Teddy about government supervision of private capital . . ."

"You've always disagreed with him, Morgan."

"The Square Deal has a lot of public appeal," another man said.

"Yes, but Roosevelt's gone too far. He talks about government control of public utilities, railways and corporations doing interstate business. He favors this damn fool graduated income tax, wants government involved in preserving national parks and natural resources. Does that sound like a Republican to you? Gentlemen, this kind of thing is blatant encroachment on private initiative. By God, we won't stand for it."

Several heads turned to Hope. It was touchy ground. The *Enterprise* editorially stood for everything Roosevelt wanted and more. She dabbed at her mouth with a napkin. "Really, gentlemen, should we discuss politics over lunch?"

Morgan glowered. "I've supported you with my advertising, Hope, but only because my wife gives me no choice."

Hope's eyes widened. "Why, Lawrence Morgan, do you mean to tell me Elizabeth actually thinks women ought to have the vote?"

"You know damn well she does. And because of it, I'm thrown in with you and your progressives. Next thing we know, you'll be writing editorials favoring unionists. But when that happens, Hope, I draw the line. I don't care how much trouble I get into at home. The damned anarchists and Wobblies would cut the guts right out of private enterprise."

Hope offered her most disarming smile. "Lawrence, the last thing I want is for my good advertisers to have trouble at home."

A burst of laughter broke the ice.

"And speaking of home, gentlemen, I trust you'll excuse me. We have editorial conferences this afternoon and then tonight I have a very special engagement. Howard and I are celebrating our wedding anniversary."

Lunch thus ended with congratulations and good humor all around. Hope and Bernard Chafin returned to the great sooty pile of nineteenth-century stone that was the New

York *Enterprise*. As she prepared for the afternoon news conference, Hope reflected upon the stresses of daily realities. Lawrence Morgan was a friend, and thus far she had managed by force of personality to preserve important friendships despite political differences. Such small victories had helped the *Enterprise* weather the 1907 panic four years ago and begin the new decade financially solid. But things were changing every day. The new census figures had come out, indicating that the nation had grown to more than ninety-two million. It astonished her that one in ten Americans were immigrants who had arrived during the fourteen years since she and Howard Langden had married. Literacy was increasing. But so were demands for social change. Everybody wanted an automobile. Stewart Motors in Fall River was flourishing, but Ford's Model T threatened to take the country by storm . . .

Hope's secretary Mrs. Lacey knocked softly and entered the office. "It's time."

Picking up a notepad, Hope walked briskly into the conference room next to her office. It was a place of tobacco smoke and newspaper clutter. Editors gathered around a huge table, consulting notes. Most were men, but a few women now occupied key roles at Hope's insistence. Through the glass partitions she could see the busy world of the newsroom, where shirt-sleeved reporters and editors worked against the rush of deadlines.

She sat down at the head of the conference table and nodded. "Go ahead, Jack."

Managing editor Jack Slade, pale and rumpled, wiped his face with a meaty hand. Speaking in a dry monotone, he offered his review of the day's news as it came in over the wires. "Carry Nation, the temperance leader, is dead in Kansas. Age sixty-four. We've got Rafferty on it. He'll do a wrap-up on page one. We've got a triple murder in the Tenderloin. A guy threw himself off the Woolworth Building . . ."

"Anything special about the suicide?"

"Immigrant. Crippled. No job. Korpan's doing a paragraph. We'll run it somewhere inside."

"Okay."

"There's still a lot of bickering over this new Bureau of Mines in the Interior Department. Mine owners are upset, angry at government meddling. They say mandatory mine safety rules will cost them money. One of the big operators is an industrialist named Winthrop Faraday. He's vowing to kick up a conservative ruckus all the way to the White House..."

"Who did you say?" Hope leaned forward abruptly.

"Winthrop Faraday."

"I wonder if?..."

"Anything special?"

"No." She shook her head. "Go on."

The news conference was completed. The editorial page conference followed. There was a discussion about the Bureau of Mines story. The new acting chief editorial writer Conroy had just been hired off the hotly competitive Hearst newspapers. Word had trickled onto the street that he was at odds with his employers, and Hope—in the tradition of bitter infighting and talent raids—had snapped him up. She and Conroy were still working out differences in their points of view, but Hope preferred a spirit of give-and-take to being surrounded by toadying sycophants.

"Slade plans to lead page one with the Bureau of Mines, Conroy," she said. "You'll probably want to make editorial comments on it."

"Right. Any suggestions?"

Hope glanced at the wall clock. She thought of Howard and their anniversary dinner. "Use your judgment," she said.

Half an hour later, she arrived home at the wheel of her new Stewart sedan and found Howard on the terrace overlooking the back garden, reading.

"Happy anniversary, darling."

The butler brought a great vase of long-stem red roses, compliments of Aunt Francesca, and a silver tray piled high with messages of congratulation. Hope and Howard shared a bottle of champagne and held hands as the afternoon waned.

His hair had gone totally gray. The years of ill health had dug deep lines in his face. He was able to walk a bit, but still could not go far without the wheelchair. It sat in the corner even now, a constant reminder of what they had been through together.

"How difficult these years have been for you," he said. "And don't think I'm not aware of it."

She put her finger to his lips, stilling them. "They've been wonderful years. I share my life with the man I love. He has created for me a world that's rich and full. I would not have it any other way."

"You're thirty-four," he said. "You haven't had children. Your husband is half a man, and unable to..."

"My husband is a splendid man. I've loved him from the day I first saw him lock horns with Hearst and old General Gomez. Remember?"

He smiled. "I remember."

"As for children, I can't imagine that they would be any more fulfilling than what I already have."

It was not entirely true, of course. Many times Hope had caught herself looking with envy upon a young mother with a small child. She had dreamed of cuddling her own baby. She tried to reason it away, thinking with cold logic about how the demands of childbirth would interfere enormously with her newspaper career. But the desire defied reasoning. Once she had even broached the subject to Hetty Green, thinking the old woman would manage, in a few crisp words, to help her put aside the notion. But Hetty had merely looked at her shrewdly and said, "You never know what the future will bring."

They celebrated the anniversary that evening by attending one of the new Broadway shows and having dinner afterward with friends at the Waldorf. One couple had just returned from a trip to Europe and spoke vividly of their experiences abroad. "Howard, you should take Hope and make the grand tour. It would do wonders for both of you." They came home glowing from champagne and giggling like children. When they had gone to bed, Howard felt strong enough to make love to her in his limited and gentle way. It was not complete, but it was enough. She sighed happily and drifted off to sleep, thinking that she was the luckiest woman alive.

The following morning, the lead editorial of the *Enterprise* was a stinging critique of government interference in the coal mining industry. Conroy had written,

> *Washington bureaucrats would do well to reexamine this entire matter of usurpation of control over a private industry by the new Bureau of the Mines.*

Such a marked departure from established editorial policy set the telephone ringing and dismayed Hope's critics in and out of the newspaper. Telegrams poured in. At mid-morning, one arrived saying simply:

> *Congratulations. See you soon.*

It was from Winthrop Faraday. Hope angrily called for Conroy, only to find that he had not come to work that day.

"Where is Mr. Conroy?" she said furiously.

"If past experience is any indication, Mr. Conroy's drunk."

"Drunk!"

"Yes, ma'am. He had a drinkin' problem. That's how come the Hearst people let him go."

She had been mousetrapped! She could almost hear the gales of laughter from the Hearst offices. Hope's anger was complete.

At mid-afternoon her secretary came in, looking flustered.

"What is it, Mrs. Lacey?"

"It's Silas Proctor, Mrs. Langden. He demands to see you."

"Who?"

"Silas Proctor, the union man."

Proctor! The man was bad news, forever haranguing street crowds, making trouble, getting himself arrested. Even Hope had finally acknowledged that he was a nuisance. It had been years since she had seen him in person, not since her cub reporter days with Fat John Korpan and that demonstration on the street. But she knew him well from his reputation, and a personal confrontation was not to her liking. She set her mouth grimly. This was one of those days.

"Send him in, Mrs. Lacey."

"I didn't tell him you were here. You could slip out the side door."

"Send him in."

She had forgotten that he was so tall. His tallness and bulk, indeed, almost filled the doorway. He wore rough clothing, an open-necked shirt displaying a mass of black hair at the chest, a gold medallion on a chain at his throat. His body was all muscle, his face a study of planes and angles as if hewn from granite. A wisp of heavy black hair fell over his forehead. His eyes were like two chips of coal. Suddenly it all came back, the memory of more than ten years before: the sweat-smelling crowd, the man on the platform looking like a vagabond king, and his words crashing upon her from some dark depths of the soul. "Demand bread," he had said. "It is your sacred right!"

She kept her voice even. "What can I do for you, Mr. Proctor?"

He produced a folded newspaper and spread it on her desk, open at the editorial page. "I see that you've finally thrown in with the bosses, Mrs. Langden. I figured you might, in time."

"I don't quite get your meaning."

"Well, up to now the *Enterprise* has been the only voice of journalistic sanity around." His words came out in a deep rumble, strangely compelling. He stood at a challenging stance, feet apart. Thick neck muscles moved as he talked. The black eyes seemed to bore into hers. "The others are sensation-mongers, nothing more, no real feel for people. Not that your paper has any abundance of human commitment either, but at least it was fairly consistent. But this"—a meaty hand whacked at Conroy's editorial—"is a disgrace."

"In what way, Mr. Proctor?"

"Do you know anything about life in a coal mine, Mrs. Langden? Have you ever *been* in a coal mine?"

"No, but I . . ."

"As a matter-of-fact, Mrs. Langden, have you ever seen a sweatshop right here in New York, where women toil from dark to dark making clothes for pennies an hour? Have you ever been in a textile mill and seen the kids, ten and eleven years old, working at the machines? Did you know that they cover up the windows so passersby can't see in, and the kids can't waste their time looking out? And there are industrialists, like Mr. Winthrop Faraday, who actually consider that they're doing children a favor by giving them jobs . . ."

Faraday again. If it was the same Faraday, she thought, he had come a long way since his days as Maurice's roommate at Harvard.

"Frankly, Mrs. Langden, I suspect that you're just like all the rest of the progressives nowadays. You live a life of wealth. Your principles are all intellectualized. You talk a fairly good game, but you really don't know a great deal about life beyond your office, your townhouse, your private club."

"What is it that you propose?" she said quietly.

"I don't propose anything, Mrs. Langden. I challenge. I challenge you to come with me and see firsthand what I'm talking about. I'll take you to see the sights and smell the smells. And then if your newspaper can still stomach such reasoning as this"—he poked a heavy finger at the editorial—"then you're not only deaf and blind, you've got veins full of ice water." Later, she would wonder what prompted her to reply so immediately and so decisively. Did she have a flicker of clairvoyance about the future? Or was she simply impelled to do so against her will? "Very well, Mr. Proctor," she snapped, "I accept your challenge."

His mouth dropped open. "You accept?"

"I accept."

They began in New York. It was the Fat John Korpan tour all over again, only worse. Dressed in her plainest clothes and traveling by elevated train, trolley, and bicycle, she accompanied Silas Proctor through a dreary devil's den of human exploitation. In the sprawling slum areas of the city, they visited sweatshops and machine sheds, picked their way through foul and airless factories that made soap and shoes, fur coats and cotton garments. They walked down aisle after aisle of sewing machines where hunchbacked women worked twelve-hour days feeding cloth to the slashing needles, and paying the price in punctured and shattered hands.

"What happens if they're hurt?" She had to shout it over the noise of machines.

"Tough luck," he replied. "They're out of a job."

They saw the children. Everywhere, one saw the children. They labored beside their elders, faces gray and old before their time, earning half the wage that a grown man would earn but working the same hours.

Wherever they went, working people recognized Silas Proctor. They plucked at his shirt as he passed, looking up at him with eyes filled with trust. Hope had never seen such trust. "Mr. Proctor, be careful," they whispered. "There's goons just outside that door. Go the other way." Sometimes they hid them from view until factory guards were out of the way. In one garment shop, Silas and Hope lay concealed in a pile of cotton dresses in a storeroom for half an hour. His nearness gave her an odd sense of warmth and weakness. When a seamstress finally opened the door and they stepped into the light, Hope found herself holding on to Silas's arm, strangely short of breath.

At night she recounted her daily adventures to Howard, who nodded his approval. "Excellent. You're taking complete notes? Good! And where will you be going next week?"

Hope fell asleep thinking of Silas Proctor.

She met Winthrop Faraday for lunch at his private club. Except for a few facial lines and gray hairs, he had not changed outwardly from his student days. Even his voice had the same quiet, diffident quality that she remembered when he was the shy young man on a weekend at Aunt Francesca's house. He moved about the city in a new Rolls-Royce, however, and was said to have built up his family's wealth with vast holdings in land, oil, and industry.

Only when they talked over lunch did Hope sense the ruthlessness of the inner man.

"Faradays have operated coal mines in Pennsylvania for fifty years." He forked a delicate white morsel of fish, put it into his mouth fastidiously, and chewed. "If it wasn't for free enterprise, those seams of coal would never be tapped. Faraday mines have provided employment for thousands of men."

"Who works your mines?"

"Immigrants, mainly. Bohunks. Polaks. Irish. It's all they're good for. But as long as a man works, he won't starve."

"And children?"

Faraday glanced up sharply. "We have boys who work the tipples. Their job is to pick out stones from the coal. Some of them go underground, too. But we only allow the strong boys to go down."

"Why? Because of the danger?"

"No. Danger is a part of mine life. We put the strong boys in the pits to load coal all day. It's a question of production."

"Human life doesn't count, then?"

"Hardly. These people, as I say, aren't good for much else. They're ignorant and slow. Many of them can't read or write or even speak English."

"But the Bureau of Mines..."

"Ah, there you get at the crux of things." Faraday wiped his mouth with a napkin. He wore a gray tailored suit and a gold watchchain across his middle. His face was lean and patrician, dominated by round spectacles. His hands were delicate and very white, almost feminine. "The Bureau of Mines is a deliberate intrusion by the government into private enterprise. It's all Roosevelt's doing. Next thing you know, they'll be piling on all sorts of nonsensical safety standards that will do little but add to our costs of production and make it that much more difficult to turn a profit. As if natural market forces were not enough, now the private investor has got to take on his own government."

It went on for another half hour. They then rode back to the *Enterprise* Building in Faraday's chauffeur-driven Rolls-Royce. Hope was glad to be free of him, for he impressed her as the epitome of selfish wealth, placing profits ahead of human condition. The idea suddenly brought her up short.

302

"Heavens," she thought, "I'm beginning to think just like Silas Proctor!"

Three nights later, she stood in a downpour at the head of a shattered pit at Faraday Mine Number Twelve in the anthracite fields of Pennsylvania. Smoke still wafted from the shaft. A crowd of sobbing women waited behind a barricade manned by derby-hatted Pinkerton men armed with shotguns and wooden clubs. Silas Proctor towered over the scene. He was blackened and work-worn, dressed in miner's clothes and wearing a cap with a sputtering carbide lamp.

"The whole second shift's down there," he said. "Two hundred forty-three men, blasted to bits." He sat down wearily and lit a cigarette. "We'll be bringing up the bodies pretty soon."

The blast had occurred the previous night. On the afternoon before that, ironically, the men of Mine Number Twelve had managed to smuggle Silas and Hope down into the pit. Dressed as a boy, walking at a crouch or crawling on all fours, she had followed Silas through dank, dripping tunnels shored up with timbers, where men toiled in twelve-hour shifts wresting coal from the mountain seams with pickax and sweat, occasionally stopping to blast out new faces with dynamite. It was such a blast apparently that had opened the gas pocket. Hope and Silas had returned to the surface only three hours before the explosion. They had gotten the news while touring the squalid mountain settlement of company-owned workers' shacks, where families lived in perpetual bondage to Faraday Mining Company. Silas had returned immediately to the pit to join the rescue effort.

It was three more days before the last body was brought up.

She watched Silas at work with a rising sense of awe. The man was tireless, magnetic, a born leader. He marshaled people, organized rescue teams, issued commands like a field general. Again, his impact upon the downtrodden and exploited showed in their faces. And then there occurred a bizarre torchlit scene when Silas stood atop a wooden cask speaking to mass meeting near Tipple Number Five in the next valley. "My friends, we've got to band together to fight them. The Faraday Coal Company does not care about you or your loved ones. Human life is cheap in these coal camps. It will remain cheap until we can come together in a mighty union"—his voice had a mesmerizing effect, rising in power as he spoke—"that will show them who we are. A union is our strength. It is the strength of the men in the mines, and of their wives and children. It is the hope of tomorrow, people. Union! Say it with me. Union!"

"Union!" they said.

"Say it. Union!"

"Union!" Stronger now. Louder. "Union!"

"Make it ring out over these hills. Let 'em hear it in town. Let 'em hear it in Washington. Union!"

"Union! Union! Union!"

The Pinkertons came then, down from the offices of the Faraday Coal Company. They rushed the mob of miners at Tipple Number Five, swinging clubs and firing shotguns into the air. The clubs struck flesh and bone, splashing blood and sending the mob screaming down the muddy, coal-dusted road.

"Come on!"

He had her by the arm in an iron grip. They ran together down the road, lost in the crush, fleeing from the Pinkertons. She stumbled, falling, but he swept her up in his arms and pounded down the slope into the darkness.

Later, much later, they sat at a rough table in a miner's shack, sharing the hospitality of the family. They ate boiled beans, cooked greens, and hard bread. Children looked at her in awe, dazzled by the blondness of her hair and the smooth, well-fed texture of her skin. They were thin, woebegone children with runny noses, big eyes, and protruding bellies. There was a stench of poverty and despair. The father, a lean, hardbitten Irishman, bore the black rings of coal dust perpetually about his eyes. Black coal was ground into his fingers and facial pores, into his very soul. He had a deep, wet cough.

"It's in his lungs," Silas said. He sopped up bean juice in the bread and ate.

"His lungs?"

"Silicosis. From coal dust." He finished eating, pushed back from the table, and looked at her. "Do you have a better understanding now?"

"Yes," she said. "I do."

He fell silent again. Then: "Do you know why I really came to your office that day?"

"Because of that editorial," she said.

"Not entirely. What really made me mad was that brief note the *Enterprise* carried about the suicide who threw himself off the Woolworth Building. I knew that man. He was a Hungarian. He had worked as a construction laborer, broke his heel in a fall, was permanently crippled, and couldn't get another job. He had seven children, going hungry. He couldn't stand it any longer, so he committed suicide. Your paper gave him one paragraph, inside."

"It couldn't be helped," she said. "We just can't cover them all."

He nodded. "No, I suppose not."

"Mr. Proctor," the miner said, "please do me a favor."

"Sure, Paddy."

"Don't tell nobody you was here in my house. It would go hard with us."

"I won't, Paddy. I won't tell a soul."

Hope Stewart Langden returned to New York and began to write. Her series, COAL: BLACK GOLD FROM HUMAN MISERY, was spattered across page one day after day and sent out across the nation by the Associated Press. Washington responded with calls for the congressional investigation of mine safety. The Faraday Coal Company became the target of several damage suits.

Howard Langden was jubilant. "What a hell of a newspaper woman! Another clear beat for the *Enterprise*. I'd promote you to star reporter on the spot if you weren't already acting publisher."

Friends poured in for an elaborate dinner party. Guests included Aunt Francesca, leading her usual entourage. It was an evening of champagne, music, and lively talk. Hope accepted the praise of her friends as if it were a heady wine. But in her heart, the evening was strangely incomplete. Someone was missing, and she hardly dared to admit to herself who that someone was.

She was thinking of Silas Proctor, and the power of his arms as he had carried her down that hill at a dead run.

She immersed herself in work. Each day Hope Stewart Langden managed to fill every minute with details of the *Enterprise*. Others noticed and commented on it.

"She's driving herself too hard," Fat John Korpan said. "A woman ought not to work that hard. What's on her mind, you reckon?"

"Mind your own business," Jack Slade grunted.

"Do you know something I don't know?"

"If you've got so much idle time, give me a rewrite on this obituary."

Hope prowled the newsroom in search of sloppy writers and dirty desks. She haunted staff meetings, drove deskmen crazy rewriting their headlines, nagged at her editors, ordered a whole new format for the society pages.

"What the hell is eating the boss?"

"I don't know, but stay out of her way."

She arrived early and stayed late, carried home a briefcase stuffed with work, did not go to sleep until two o'clock in the morning, and was up again at six.

But still Silas Proctor remained very much on her mind. In the midst of a shouting match with the city editor, he would flick across her consciousness: the lock of hair straying over his forehead, the wide-footed stance as he spoke, the sound of his voice ringing across the crowd, the handsome angular face in the firelight.

"What is it, Hope?" Howard asked gently. "Do you want to talk about it?"

She patted his hand. "No. I'll work it out."

The thing to do was to drive him forever out of her mind and keep him out. The very idea of a grown woman thinking this way—and a married woman at that. She must be going through a change of life.

He didn't call. He didn't write. She skimmed the wire stories about union activities—a riot in Chicago, another threatened strike in the Colorado mines, trouble in the steel mills—but found no mention of him. Well, good riddance to bad rubbish.

And then . . .

"Mrs. Langden, you have a visitor."

"A visitor?"

"It's that Mr. Proctor."

She dropped her notebook, poked at her hair with a pencil, fiddled with her glasses. "I'm busy, Mrs. Lacey. Please tell Mr. Proctor that I cannot see him."

"Well, that's too bad." The familiar voice rumbled from behind the secretary. "I was going to offer lunch."

And so they went to lunch in a Chinese restaurant off Mott Street. They talked and laughed and ate shark fin soup and *moo goo gai pan*. They washed down the food with a rice wine, which brought a flush to her cheeks and a fine giddiness to her mood. They took a trolley to Central Park, rented a bicycle built for two, and rode through the pathways in the summer afternoon. Finally, they rested beneath a willow tree beside a lazy brook. She trailed her fingers in the water, aware of her inner excitement.

"Why did you come back?" she asked.

"Oh, I wanted to bring you up-to-date on things." A smile bracketed his mouth in slashlike dimples. "You know, union stuff."

"Is that true?"

"No, it isn't true."

A warning tugged at her mind. They were coming close to things she had no wish to confront. To feel them was one thing, to acknowledge their existence something else again. Acknowledgment, Hope told herself, was unacceptable.

"Don't . . ." she began.

"Don't worry. I won't." He stood up, tall and muscular against the blue sky, smiling down at her in that raffish way that put sparkle in his black eyes. The vagabond king, she thought. She took his big hand and came to her feet. They walked, not touching at all; but even inches apart, she could feel his nearness all over her body.

"What is your background?" she said. "You don't speak like an uneducated working man."

"I'm not, really. That is to say, I've got more education than most union people manage to acquire. My father owned a small furniture factory in upstate Pennsylvania, Proctor Furniture. I went to Columbia and, well, my father made some bad land investments. He went heavily into debt. Along came an outfit called the Delaney Trust. They bought up all my father's debts, took over the business, sucked it dry of assets, and threw away the shell. They put fifty people out of work. My father died three months later. I was so damned angry I vowed to have vengeance. The best way I saw to do it was to declare war on privilege and power. I became a union organizer. I've organized miners, steelworkers, textile hands, you name it. The more I did it, the more I realized how ignorant and helpless most of these working people are. They don't have a damn thing to call their own. They're at the mercy of the robber barons of industry."

She threw back her head and laughed.

"What's so funny?"

"The situation," she said. "My family is basically industrial. Stewarts are involved in river traffic, freight, iron and steel, shipbuilding, locomotives, and automobile manufacturing. We employ thousands of people. I don't think there's a union in the whole Stewart enterprise."

He grew somber. "There will be."

They walked past a large rosebush. Impulsively, she plucked a blood-red rose and pinned it to his shirt. "There," she said. She straightened it with her hand and started to step back.

But his arms came up and caught hers. They stood for a breathless moment, bodies touching. The strength drained from her thighs. Her breathing quickened. There was a rush of blood to her face.

"Hope..."

"No, Silas. Please." Giddy from the sheer power of it, she pushed away. Her head seemed to be swimming.

"Afternoon, Mrs. Stewart." The voice came from behind them on the path.

Hope turned and looked into the somber face of Lawrence Morgan. The merchant's eyes flicked to Silas. He nodded, touched his hat, walked on.

A spasm of guilt almost nauseated her. "I ... I must go back now."

She left Silas standing there with the rose pinned to his shirt.

It was stupid and childish and wrong. This kind of thing destroyed people; it could destroy what she had worked for and what she shared with Howard. The thought of Howard tormented her. Dear, trusting Howard, so lovable and dependent. For two days after the park incident she did not go to the office at all, but remained at home with her husband. Each ring of the telephone caused her heart to jump; each ring of the postman's bell sent her rushing to the mailbox.

This would not do. It was more than torture; it was being the instrument of one's own torment. As for staying home, she could hide from the world but not from herself. She returned to the *Enterprise*. There were three messages from Silas, each written on note paper in his strong, flowing hand.

Missed you. S. Lunch Thursday? S. Call, if you have a chance. S.

The latter bore a telephone number. She wadded up the notes, tossed them into the wastebasket, retrieved them, spread them out, and reread each one. Then she put them into her desk drawer.

Ten days passed. She called him. His voice was strong and clear on the telephone. "I hoped you wouldn't stay angry with me."

"I'm not angry. It's just...Oh, darn, Silas. We've got a problem."

"I know."

"You know?"

"It takes two to make a problem. And my problem is that I'm in love with you."

She did not answer him. The words stuck in her throat. She hung up the telephone.

At home, Howard was pensive. "We should talk," he said.

"All right." She sat beside him, holding his hand.

"I know about Silas Proctor."

It stunned her. "Silas..."

"Don't be concerned. Lawrence Morgan came to see me. He talked about seeing the two of you in Central Park. I suggested to him that he was overstepping the bounds of discretion and that your private life was your own business."

"Howard, I..."

"It is your own business. I know you for what you are. I also know that you have been suffering lately." He did not look at her as he spoke. He stared out from the veranda at the garden. Twilight spread over the scene. There was a scent of roses. They reminded her of the red rose she had pinned to Silas's shirt. Howard said: "Human beings are enormously complex. We love at many levels and in many different ways. Love can steal upon us when we least expect it and entrap us without our really willing it to happen. I have lived for more than half a century and experienced many things. One learns from living."

"I love you very much," she said.

"Of course, you do. You let me know it, every day in a thousand little ways. But knowing that you love me does not change the basic realities of life. Do you remember our wedding vow? You insisted that the wording be changed, and I quite agreed. I still agree. Love is not something one can promise forever and ever. It is not decreed by God. It is like a bird that you hold in your hand, perishable and ready to fly. There is no guarantee of love enduring, or being a total and all-consuming thing."

He stopped talking. They sat in silence. The evening came down. A nightbird called. The dew settled. From inside the house, she heard the muffled tolling of the clock.

She lay her head upon his shoulder. "Let's leave New York for a while. Let's say to hell with the paper; let Slade and the others run things. Let's take a ship for Europe. There's no reason why we can't do that."

"Of course," he said. "We can go any time you like."

She sat upright in her chair. "Oh, can we, Howard? Can we really go?"

"Yes, we can go."

"When? Oh, when?"

"Next week, if you'd like. We can tour England and France. When the weather cools, we'll go to the south of Spain, the Riviera..."

"Do you feel up to it?"

"I feel stronger already."

She hugged him. She kissed him about the face and mouth. "Thank you, darling. Thank you, thank you, thank you!"

Howard Langden chuckled softly. "And thank *you*."

Ten days later, Mr. and Mrs. Howard Langden boarded the luxury liner *Atlantis*, bound for England.

XIV

Hope Stewart Langden felt the bittersweetness of leaving Paris.

"We're ready, Mrs. Langden," the concierge announced. She was a severe woman with iron-gray hair and a black ankle-length uniform trimmed in white lace. A snap of her fingers brought the ancient porter, grabbing at luggage and muttering to himself in French. The concierge stood proudly erect, smiling thinly as the poor man struggled down the narrow stairs. "Is everything satisfactory?"

"Quite satisfactory, thank you." Hope gave a last, wistful look around the suite. The double balcony doors stood closed, the glass panes frosted but commanding stunning views of Paris in early spring. The flower vases were empty now, the overstuffed furnishings awaiting their next tenant. Above the couch hung an Impressionist painting, a great splotch of summery colors.

"Hope?" Howard stood impatiently in the corridor with his cane.

"I'm ready, darling."

They descended in the creaky elevator, which jerked to a stop at each floor and opened with an iron clatter as if by diabolical prearrangement. No one entered or left the machine. Finally they arrived at the marbled lobby with its potted plants, dark wainscoting and odors of furniture wax. The manager, a nervous, dyspeptic man, bowed them to the waiting taxicab, a massive black Renault with a guttering engine and a roof piled high with their belongings.

"*Adieux! Adieux!*"

The taxi lurched away from the curb and down the Champs Elysée toward the train station. An hour later, they were on the train to Le Havre, speeding westward through the cheerless landscape of early April. Another spring rain began to fall, streaking the window glass and darkening the land beyond.

"Ghastly time to travel," Howard grumbled.

"It's been lovely and you know it," she said. "Six months of sheer heaven."

"We can't stay in Europe forever," he said. "Besides, we've seen everything."

It was true. In six months they had crisscrossed the continent, from their Paris base to Spain, Portugal, and North Africa. They had seen Naples, Rome, Florence, and Vienna, drenched their senses in Alpine scenery, taken side trips to Berlin, Stockholm, Oslo, and Copenhagen. They had prowled museums and castles, floated along the great rivers—the Rhine, the Danube, the Thames—and dined in the finest restaurants. Their friendships had multiplied enormously. Hope was refreshed and invigorated, her horizons vastly expanded. She had not thought of Silas Proctor for weeks.

"I could stay in Europe forever," she said, "if you were with me."

He smiled. "We'll come back."

From Le Havre they took a steamer to London, and then finally they took the train from London to their destination, the seaport city of Southampton.

"May I help you, madame?" The policeman stood in the crash of traffic leading to the docks. The April weather was cold, the morning blustery and raw.

"The liner *Titanic*?" she said.

"Are you boarding as passengers?"

"Yes."

"Follow the traffic that way, madame."

Their taxicab advanced slowly with the traffic stream and rounded the corner of a warehouse. Hope peered through the front windshield and gasped.

"Howard, she's huge!"

"Biggest liner ever built."

"Look at that. Look!"

The ship stretched along the busy dock, her sides like cliffs, her great black hull rising to a dazzling white superstructure topped by four mighty smokestacks jutting into the leaden sky. A swarm of workmen loaded mountains of luggage, trunks, bales, and boxes. The dock teemed with a mass of passengers, friends, officials, posters, trucks, and taxicabs.

They cleared customs, bought their tickets, and moved up the gangway onto the ship itself. It was like entering an elegant building, with grand stairways, fine woodwork, lush carpeting, and gleaming brass. A blue-uniformed band played ragtime music among potted palms. White-jacketed stewards and uniformed porters attended to piles of hand luggage.

"B Deck, first class. Right this way, please." Hope followed as the attendant pushed Howard's wheelchair ahead through a bewildering sequence of passages and promenade decks, ever upward and forward. At last they crossed the threshold into a sumptuous two-room suite with large portholes looking out onto the glass-enclosed bridge deck. Hope's eye took in a heavy brass bed, a marble washstand, wicker armchairs, a large sofa, a ceiling fan, electrical fixtures. A latticed doorway opened into a full bathroom and dressing area.

A uniformed steward greeted them, touching his cap. "I am Alfred Crawford," he announced. "Welcome aboard for the maiden voyage of the *Titanic*."

It was splendid. At high noon, with flags flying and sturdy tugboats chuffing about the waterway like smoke-belching waterbugs, the *Titanic* moved away from the dock. Hope and Howard went out onto the forward deck area to watch the departure. So massive was this vessel, and so majestic her progress, that it almost seemed as if they were standing still and the rest of the waterfront passed in slow motion. At one point this turned out to be more than an illusion, as the wash of the great propellers created a suction that drew a smaller liner into a near-collision. A bump was avoided only when the *Titanic* abruptly shut down her engines.

"They're still getting the hang of handling these big liners." The speaker was a distinguished-looking man standing near them, accompanied by a well-groomed Airedale dog.

Howard's face lifted in recognition. "Astor! Fancy meeting you here."

"Langden, upon my word!"

Hope was introduced to John Jacob Astor.

From then on, it was a never-ending round of introductions, parties, dinners in the first-class dining rooms, walks on the sheltered promenade deck, dances to the music of the ship's band, bridge games, even a round of tennis and swimming at the G level, far belowdecks. The *Titanic* made two more stops after Southampton, picking up passengers and mail. In Queenstown harbor at noon on the second day, April 12, Hope was watching a mass of Irish immigrants come on board for their journey to America in the liner's steerage. "Think of the lives ahead of them, Howard," she said thoughtfully. "Who knows, one of their future offspring might become President."

First class abounded with the rich and famous. They dined in abundance and variety. Hope thought of Silas Proctor, the mining camps, the pinched, undernourished faces of children in the shadow of Tipple Number Five at the Faraday Coal Company.

She skipped lunch that day.

The ship plowed westward through the northern latitudes of the gray Atlantic, her massive bulk pushing aside the swells and resisting even the ordinary roll of the sea. Longtime travelers spoke in glowing terms of the comfort of the *Titanic*, and those inclined to seasickness were more than grateful for the difference. The weather was very cold, with temperatures in the thirties and very little sunshine.

On the fourth evening out, a Sunday, Captain Edward J. Smith joined them at the Astors' table for dinner and discussed genially the mechanical wonders of his vessel. Hope took an instant liking to the white-bearded patriarch of the White Star Line, whose *Titanic* command capped thirty-eight years with the company. Resplendent in a blue uniform and a gold braid, Smith lit a fine Havana cigar and talked of his love for ships. "The wonder never leaves me, Mrs. Langden, especially as I stand on a bridge and watch a vessel plunging up and down in the trough of the sea, fighting her way over great waves. A man never outgrows that."

"They say you're retiring after this trip," John Jacob Astor remarked. "A pity, Captain."

"I'm fifty-nine years old, Mr. Astor. It's time to make way for a younger man on the bridge. And I can't think of a finer vessel to pass into competent hands."

"My wife had misgivings about this voyage," another passenger remarked. "I think she felt that such a brand-new ship, untried in Atlantic waters, might be unsafe."

Smith looked at the man with amusement. "I trust that she is reassured now. Quite frankly, I can't imagine any condition that would cause this ship to founder. I can't conceive of any vital disaster happening to it. Modern shipbuilding has gone beyond that. The most marvelous feature is the design of the watertight compartments. The ship is double-hulled and built of sixteen such compartments, formed by watertight bulkheads across the vessel's entire width. In case of trouble, I merely have to touch an electric button on the bridge and the bulkhead doors close off, sealing the compartments."

The captain was intrigued by the discovery that Howard and Hope published the New York *Enterprise*. "One of my favorite newspapers," he said. "My compliments on the quality of your reporting and editing. I've been interviewed many times during my years at sea, but never with greater accuracy and attention to detail. I was especially impressed by your factual treatment of the events in Cuba during the Spanish-American War." He drew out his business card and wrote a note on the back. "If at any time you wish to go about the ship, to the bridge or the engine room or wherever, this will serve as a pass. In fact, I encourage you to visit the bridge. It should prove quite interesting to your readers."

"Thank you, Captain."

Hope slipped the card into her purse.

The night was clear and cold; the sea was a sheen of black velvet. Hope wore the fur coat Howard had bought for her in Paris. She had bundled him in a heavy coat, muffler, and hat. Pushing the wheelchair slowly along the upper A Deck, she was dimly aware of the deep throb of engines and the gentle rush of seawater far below.

"Nathan insists that the airplane will replace the ship for transatlantic travel," Hope said. "He believes the day will come when we'll fly in huge planes, spanning the globe."

Howard chuckled. "That boy is irrepressible."

She smiled and patted him on the shoulder. "Just remember, you doubted him once before."

"I remember."

The night was moonless and ablaze with stars. They could see their breaths in the cold. They stopped at the railing near one of the lifeboats. A ship's officer came by, huddled in a dark topcoat, and touched his cap. "Good evening. I'm Lightoller, second officer. Bracing weather, eh?"

"What is the temperature, Mr. Lightoller?" Howard asked.

"Thirty-two degrees. Right at freezing."

"Brrrr."

The officer stood beside them looking up at the riotous display of stars. "They always seem brighter on a cold night like this."

"Why is that?" Howard asked.

"Atmospheric conditions. It cuts down on the mist, clears the air."

Hope glanced into the darkness off the port quarter. "I thought I saw the light of another ship out there on the horizon. It was just a small bright spot. Maybe my eyes were playing tricks."

"There's another vessel out there, right enough. We raised the *Californian* by wireless in the late afternoon and sent her a batch of radio messages for relay to the States. Her transmitter is a bit more powerful than ours. But the ship's radioman finally shut down his receiver in a pout. She's about ten miles from here. Sometimes the light refracts over the horizon, so that you see a ship that's actually beyond the earth's curvature, and . . ." He stopped talking.

"What is it?"

"Nothin'. Thought I heard one of the lookout bells, that's all."

"What are the lookouts for?"

"Icebergs. We've got six lookouts posted. There were iceberg warnin's on the radio today. We're keepin' a sharp eye out. Nippin' along at twenty-two knots, you could be on top of one in a jiffy." He turned away from them again. "I've never seen the water so still, like a sheet of black glass."

Howard glanced back at the lifeboat. "Just as a matter of curiosity, Officer Lightoller, how many passengers do we have on board?"

"Two thousand, two hundred seven, sir, countin' steerage."

"And what's the ship's lifeboat capacity?"

"Actually, there are boats and collapsible craft for eleven hundred seventy-eight people."

"Enough for slightly more than half the ship's complement." Howard Langden stroked his chin thoughtfully.

"Yes, sir. But according to British maritime rules, we are only obliged to carry life crafts for nine hundred sixty-two. The company put on the extra boats just to be doubly safe."

Howard smoked his cigar and stared out into the blackness of the night.

Hope glanced at her watch. The time was almost 11:40 P.M. "Are you getting cold, darling? Maybe we should..."

The second officer had been staring up at the crow's nest. Abruptly he said, "Excuse me!" and began walking rapidly toward the bridge.

Hope's instincts quickened. Something was not right. She had a sense of a great alien presence bearing out of the darkness, an onrushing weight mightier than the mightiest ship. "Howard..." Barely was the word out of her mouth when it loomed up, a vague gray mass reflecting the lights of the *Titanic* and seeming to give off a deep and menacing cold. It was high, higher than the topmost open deck upon which they stood, almost as high as the four great stacks disgorging their heavy plumes of smoke; high and unbelievably heavy, an immobile ice monster risen up from the deep. And it was bearing down on the starboard side.

The *Titanic* shuddered as if raked deeply along its starboard hull by the finger of God. The sound was heavy and gentle tearing, a rumbling and scraping. Hope watched the ugly gray mass slide past almost close enough to touch. She was aware of a shower of ice scraping off its face and tumbling down onto the lower decks. And then, as silently as it came, the thing was moving away, a massive black shadow on the star-cut sea.

The ship's engines changed pitch. The ship seemed to be veering to the side. Male passengers emerged from the smoking room. Voices shouted into the icy void.

"What was it?"

"A jar. It jarred the whole ship."

"We hit something; that's for sure."

"An iceberg!" someone said. "We hit an iceberg!"

"Where? What iceberg?"

"There it is! Back there! Look!"

"Charlie, come out here. You won't believe this."

"An iceberg!"

Several of the men joined Hope and Howard, firing questions. Hope exchanged instinctive glances with her husband. "The bridge," she said.

"You go."

"Are you all right, Howard? I hate to leave you here."

"Go to the bridge. Find out what the hell happened."

She left him with the men and hurried to the bridge. An officer stepped out of the gloom, barring her way. "I'm sorry, madame, no passengers allowed."

Groping in her handbag, she found the captain's card. "Here. The captain wrote me a pass. I'm with the New York *Enterprise*." The officer inspected the card and stepped aside.

Captain Smith was just arriving in a rush from his quarters, buttoning his uniform coat. He confronted the first officer. "Mr. Murdoch, what was that?"

"An iceberg, sir. Seaman Fleet rang his bell and telephoned from the crow's nest. I asked him what he seen, and he said an iceberg, dead ahead. I hard-a-starboarded and reversed engines, but it was thirty-seven seconds before the ship responded. I was going to hard-a-port around it, but she was too close. I couldn't do any more."

"Close the emergency doors," Smith snapped.

"They're already closed, sir."

Captain Smith saw Hope enter the bridge. He nodded brusquely. "I'm glad you're here, Mrs. Langden. You will see how we handle an emergency." He turned to the speaking tubes. "All divisions, report."

A cockney voice came on the communicator from Boiler Room Number Six. Hope moved nearer in order to hear what was being said. "We seen the red light flashin' over the watertight door, sir," the voice said. "There was a very loud noise, and the starboard side of the ship just seemed to cave in."

"What happened then, Breathwaite?"

"It was . . . It was terrible, sir. Some of us got out, just as the watertight door slammed down. The last thing I seen, the sea was rushin' in, fillin' the whole compartment. There's a lot o' dead men in there, sir."

More ship's personnel were arriving on the bridge. Hope glanced up and saw Bruce Ismay. The president of the White Star Line had thrown on trousers and a suit coat over his pajamas.

"What's the damage, Captain?"

"Can't tell at the moment, Mr. Ismay. We know that Boiler

Room Number Six is flooded. "I'm going to summon Mr. Andrews."

"Very well."

Barely had his name been mentioned when Thomas Andrews appeared, disheveled from sleep and wearing a topcoat over his pajamas. Tucked under his arm was a roll of ship's plans. As managing director of the *Titanic*'s builders, Harland and Wolff Shipyard, Andrews knew every inch of the giant vessel. He spread the plans out on the navigation table and said to Captain Smith, "She's down by the bow a bit already."

Reports continued to come in from stricken areas. Each fresh scrap of news registered itself in the grim faces of Smith, Andrews, and Ismay as they made notations on the plans.

Finally, Andrews sighed wearily and straightened. "That's it."

"What do you think?"

"We've got Numbers One and Two holds flooded, along with the mail room and Boiler Rooms Six and Five. Water is fourteen feet above the level of the keel. As best I can tell, the iceberg sliced a three hundred-foot gash along the starboard side. We've got sixteen watertight compartments in all, from bow to stern. Five are already flooded. The ship will stay afloat with three compartments gone, probably even four. But five?" He shook his head and dropped his pencil. "Impossible."

"You can't be serious, Andrews."

"She's sinking by the bow, Mr. Ismay. As she sinks deeper, successive compartments will flood—Number Six, Number Seven, and so on. It's inevitable."

"How much time do we have?"

"I'd suggest, gentlemen, that you prepare to abandon ship."

Captain Smith grimaced and turned to his first officer. "Mr. Murdoch, start uncovering the lifeboats. Have the crew rouse the passengers and get them on deck. I want lifebelts on everybody." He glanced around at the officers crowded in the bridge. "I know that every man will do his duty. Sparks, get on your radio and start broadcasting our position. Maybe we can reach that other ship that's out on the horizon. The *Californian*, isn't it?"

"Yes, sir. She's a Leyland Liner, six thousand tons, bound from Boston to London."

"What shall I tell them, sir?" the radio operator said.

"Tell them . . . Tell them to come at once; the *Titanic* is sinking."

The captain's gaze found Hope. His eyes filled with an infinite sadness. "I'd suggest, Mrs. Langden, that you rejoin your husband."

Sinking. The *Titanic* was sinking! Hope stepped from the enclosed bridge into the cold open air, her mind grappling with the numbing reality of it. She made her way along B Deck toward the suite where Howard would be waiting, thinking about what she should take in the lifeboat. Should I pack a suitcase? Then she realized the folly of such an idea. The challenge now was simply to survive.

Survive . . .

The time was 12:05 A.M.

"Everybody on deck with lifebelts on. At once, please."

The stewards spoke calmly, politely. There were no bells, no sirens. Hope had always imagined that there would be alarms going off in a stricken ship. It seemed the appropriate thing to do. But here were the uniformed stewards of the *Titanic*, knocking politely at each stateroom door. "We are having a bit of a problem. Dress warmly. Put on your lifebelt. Please hurry."

The people spilled into the corridors, puffy-eyed and disoriented.

"What is it? What's going on?"

"An iceberg, you say?"

"Well, if this isn't the limit, rousting us out of bed in the middle of a cold night. I intend to register a complaint with the White Star Line."

"Move along, please."

Some wore only their woollen pajamas. Others were in tuxedos and evening gowns. Many had thrown on overcoats, fur coats, or simply wrapped themselves in their blankets. Women wore hair curlers, nets, and facial creams. They clutched lifebelts, jewel boxes, and briefcases.

"Howard, we have to go."

"Thank God you're back," he said.

"Take your coat, your gloves, and hat. Put on a sweater under the coat. It will be very cold in the lifeboat."

"Thirty-two degrees . . ."

She slipped out of her furs, put on an extra sweater, and put the fur on over it. They talked quietly as they got ready. Crawford arrived and urged them gently to make haste. There would be no way to get the wheelchair on deck, for the

319

elevators no longer functioned. Crawford and Hope supported Howard as he walked out into the corridor.

They joined the flow of the crowd. "How bad is it?" Howard said, gasping from exertion.

"Very bad," she said.

They stepped onto the open boat deck and recoiled from the cold. The crowd milled about. The first-class people had been brought up amidships. Hope glanced over the side and could see other passengers gathering on the lower decks. She thought of the people in steerage and wondered how they would get to the lifeboats, now uncovered and hanging from their davits at this topmost level.

The ship lay at an odd slant, bow down and tilted slightly to port. It made the footing tricky, especially where patches of ice had formed. Lights glared down upon the deck, reflecting off the white superstructure and casting hard shadows. People smoked, talked, and waited for instructions.

Captain Smith appeared on deck carrying a megaphone. The electric lights gleamed off his brass buttons and white beard. He radiated calm assurance. "Please put your lifebelts on," he said through the megaphone. "They will help keep you warm even if you don't need them." Two crewmen walked by. Hope heard one of them say, "The water is up to F Deck in the mail room." She glanced apprehensively at Howard. His handsome face gave no indication that he had heard, but he reached over and took her hand.

Some of the people went into the card room and the first-class lounge to escape the cold. Hope and Howard remained on deck. The unreality of it all came over her in waves. Forward of where they waited, the bow assembly was submerged and the decks pitched at a slant. Things were beginning to splash overboard. From below she could hear groanings and wrenchings as the pressure intensified.

An officer shouted to the deck crew, "Let's get these lifeboats cleared and start loading." Men sprang to the davits. There were eight boats on each side of the ship, four forward and four aft, making sixteen in all. When these had been lowered, four collapsible Englehardt rafts could then be slung from davits for lowering.

"How are they going to do this?" Howard asked quietly. "There aren't nearly enough boats and rafts for us all. And who is to go in what boat? We haven't been given assignments or any kind of drill." He looked into Hope's eyes and leaned closer, his voice dropping to a murmur. "This deficiency must be corrected. We must crusade for it with the *Enterprise*. If one of us doesn't make it, the other must remember that."

She squeezed his hand fiercely. "Both of us will make it, darling. *Both* of us will go back to New York."

He smiled.

And then the answer to his question about lifeboats got its unintended answer from an officer standing beside boat Number Seven. "Let us commence boarding, please. Women and children. Please board women and children first."

Response was less than enthusiastic. Women stood looking at each other, as if undecided who should go first. Those with husbands did not step forward at all. "Ladies," an officer said, "we're wasting precious time. We must lower the boats. Please, come forward." Several of the single women finally detached themselves from the crowd and climbed into the boat. An argument broke out near Hope, as an officer and one of the male passengers attempted to coax a woman and a little girl into Number Seven.

"I don't want to go without you," the woman said. Hope recognized them as a quiet couple from New Jersey with whom she and Howard had played a game of bridge. She was not a pretty woman, but they had seemed devoted to each other and to their daughter Elizabeth. "I won't go without you, John."

"Take Elizabeth and go," he said firmly. "I'll be along in a little while."

The woman pushed her daughter forward. "Elizabeth, you get into the boat."

"Both of you go," pleaded the husband.

The wife burst into tears, took her daughter's hand, and allowed herself to be lifted into Number Seven. She sat in the boat gazing at him, tears streaming down her face.

One by one, women and children came out of the crowd and got into the boats. There were fervent hugs and kisses as they left their men. Hope watched as if she were detached from it all, making no move to join them. When an elderly woman refused flatly to leave her husband's side, a crewman shrugged. "Don't waste time. Let her go if she won't get in." When no more women would step forward, several couples got into the boat. Howard stood up and grasped the arm of Elizabeth's father. "You're going too." He turned and shouted to an officer. "This is the father of the little girl. Let him into that boat!" The officer nodded. The man joined his wife and daughter, who embraced him joyfully.

From somewhere, the ship's band began to play. Hope looked around, puzzled, until she realized that the music was coming from the first-class lounge. They were playing ragtime tunes, the sprightly music adding yet another touch of the bizarre to the scene.

"All right, lower away!"

Lifeboat Number Seven was not full, but with a creak of turning cranks and pulley ropes it swung free of the ship's side and began to lower into the sea. The occupants stared without expression at the crowd on deck until they descended out of sight.

"It's safer here than in that little boat," someone said. Hope turned to see John Jacob Astor standing in pajamas and overcoat. Astor smiled thinly. "I think I'll go into the smoking room and read a bit." He sauntered away as if on a constitutional stroll.

Hope glanced at her watch again. The time was 12.45 A.M.

From the bridge there came a series of muffled explosions. Rockets arced high into the night sky and burst in showers of bluish-white light. The flares drifted down over the great ship, her lower foredecks now submerged almost to amidships and the stern lifting to expose portions of the mighty triple-screw propellers.

The minutes dragged by. The *Titanic's* decks steepened.

"Ladies, we *must* fill these boats."

Now it was Number Five having difficulty finding boarders. The scenes on deck grew more intense, more scrambled. They tried to separate a woman from her husband and she collapsed, holding onto his knees. "Where you go, I shall go!" she cried. They left her there.

Crowd noises welled up from below. Hope looked over the side again. A horde of the Irish immigrants—men, women, and children—had come onto the lower decks from steerage. They had no boats at all, and were being blocked by armed crew members from ascending the stairways to the boat deck level. "Howard, they're not letting . . ."

"I know," he said. "Make note of it. Remember."

Remember? What did he mean, remember? She had no thought of leaving him here. If they could not board a boat together, they would not board at all. With an astonishing clarity, she now realized the vital importance of Howard Langden in her life. It was as if she had not lived before

Howard; this gentle, understanding man had given meaning to her very existence. She could not imagine life without him. They belonged together, always. They would be together, always.

A group of desperate men rushed boat Number Fourteen. An officer drew a pistol and fired it into the air, driving them back.

Finally, the last lifeboat was gone. Like the others, it had descended onto the sea woefully unfilled. Members of the crew and several male passengers now struggled to free four collapsible boats from the roof of the officers' quarters. It was difficult labor. Working clumsily against the worsening slant of deck, they undid lashings, tore off canvas covers, and managed to drag two collapsibles to the davits. They hooked them to the pulley ropes and swung them out.

The bandsmen had left the first-class lounge and arrived on the boat deck with their violins, tubas, saxophones, and clarinets. Some wore blue uniforms; others still had on the white dinner jackets in which they had played in smaller combos during the evening. As Hope watched incredulously, the bandmaster Wallace Henry Hartley, tapped his bow upon his violin. "Uh-one, uh-two!" Another ragtime tune spilled into the night.

"All right, let's go." Hope recognized the second officer Lightoller, the man who had talked with them as they strolled on deck just prior to the iceberg collision. It seemed to have happened ages ago.

The time was flying. It was 1:40 A.M. The last rockets sizzled upward, burst high above them, and descended in a shower of fire. It illuminated a stern now risen obscenely clear of the Atlantic's frigid surface. Seawater slopped into the *Titanic*'s forward well deck.

The first collapsible went. Men still struggled to free the remaining two, but were unable to push them up the steep slope to the davits. Only one boat remained functional. The ship groaned; the bridge slipped under water; waves washed aft along the boat deck. Loose chairs and equipment slid down the deck into the water.

Passengers swarmed up the stairwells from below, breaking past the posted crewmen. "Let us on that boat!" Damn you, we want on that boat!" Lightoller signaled his deck crew, who locked arms, pushing the mob back. The second officer then stepped clear of the crush and came to where Hope and Howard sat.

"It is time, Mrs. Langden."

"Time? What do you mean, it is time? I'm not going anywhere, Mr. Lightoller."

"Yes you are," Howard said gently. He took her by the arm. "You have a responsibility, Hope. This story must be told by a trained journalist. It must be told in the *Enterprise*. I cannot go. You must go in my place. There is no alternative."

"Howard, I don't . . ."

He turned her to him, stilling her protest with a kiss. "I don't have long to live anyway, my darling. I've known it for some time, now. We've had a wonderful journey together; we've shared a fine, rich life. And now this is the end of it. It is pointless for both of us to die here. From now on, you must live for both of us. I shall expect you to do that, with all the courage that you're capable of."

With a sudden reserve of strength, Howard rose to his feet. Lightoller moved ahead of them, shouting for the crowd to make way. Howard gripped her arm firmly, still speaking in calm, measured tones. "My control of the *Enterprise* passes to you. It is already arranged in my will. It is my hope that you will marry again, have a fine, strong son and name him Howard Langden, after me. I could not give you a son. So I would like that very much."

"Howard, I love you. Howard . . ."

They were at the boat. He kissed her again. He gave her arm to Lightoller and walked away. His back was straight, his step sure, his bearing proud. Hope wanted desperately to stay with him, to shout her protest and break free of Lightoller's hold on her arm. But the will of Howard Langden was too strong, his finality too complete. Overwhelmed, she climbed into the last boat. The davits creaked, laboring at a perilous slant. The loaded craft descended onto the gentle wash of the sea. Crewmen and several women passengers grasped the oars. Hope stared up in disbelief at the vast, stricken hulk, its entire forward section sunk and the stern poised high above them, lights glowing. People clustered like ants along the superstructure and were beginning to drop off the after section. The band played ragtime.

The boats seemed so tiny and so fragile, bobbing on that enormous sea.

Hope gazed at the tiny clot of humanity clinging to the deck. She kept her eyes upon the spot where she and Howard had spent their final hour together, hoping that he was there. He would know her eyes were upon him. He would know. And the knowing would give him strength.

The lights of the ship flickered and went out.

They waited. The sea washed beneath the lifeboats, rushing to the stricken colossus. The sounds of the night filled her senses: creakings and groanings and splashings. Voices called thinly across the abyss between the living and the doomed. The band stopped playing. The bow went deeper, dislodging the forward funnel and sending it toppling into the sea. At last the after section of the *Titanic* stood at a perpendicular, the stilled propellers glistening, a massive jutting hulk poised against the starry sky.

In Hope's boat, a woman sobbed.

And then with a massive sigh, the ship plunged to eternity, raising an angry white boil as if to mark the watery grave of sixteen hundred souls. Automatically, Hope looked at her watch. The time was 2:20 A.M.

Overhead, the night sky filled with shooting stars.

In years to come, the events that followed would merge into a blur. She would remember, at odd times, the devastating silence of the empty sea as they bobbed along in the lifeboats, the hollow cheers from several boats as the rockets of the oncoming rescue ship *Carpathia* were sighted, and the brilliant light of a rosy dawn, with sunlight glistening in myriad colors upon numerous coasting icebergs. A sailor's powerful hand hauled her up from the lifeboat onto the slanting gangplank of the *Carpathia*. A heavy silence pervaded the ship as sodden survivors came to grips with the enormity of what had occurred. All Hope could think about was Howard and their last moments together.

Over and over and over it played across her mind. Howard. Howard . . .

"The *Californian* had shut down her radio and didn't hear our distress call. Can you imagine that?" a woman said. "She ignored our rockets, thinking we was having a party on board. Only ten miles away, and they didn't lift a finger to help."

It was all so fraught with unanswerable questions. What if this had happened? What if that had happened? And above all, why? Why had Captain Smith not reduced speed in waters known to abound in icebergs? Why had the *Californian* first officer assumed that the rocket firings were unimportant, when this was the signal of distress known all over the world?

At last the day came when the *Carpathia*, laden with seven hundred five survivors, steamed in the rain up the North River into New York Harbor, accompanied by an escort of tugboats full of newspaper reporters shouting questions through megaphones. Hope thought she recognized a reporter from the *Enterprise,* but could not be certain. The sight of Manhattan brought her a sickening emptiness. The mood did not lighten as the ship nosed into Pier 54, where thirty thousand people jammed the docks in the rain. As the gangplank descended, Hope stood on deck in the crush of survivors, the rain beating down. Her hair was soaked, her clothing soaked, but she did not care. He was gone. He was gone and would never come back. Nothing mattered now, nothing at all.

She descended the gangplank, holding to the railing.

"Hope!"

It was a man's voice, strong and deep, from the pier below. She looked over the crowd but recognized no one. It was a sea of upturned faces.

"Hope Langden!" There were several voices now, shouting from the right side of the gangplank. She was almost down when she saw him, standing taller than the rest, the black eyes shining and the great cleft of a jaw lifted in a smile. He waved, pushing through the crush toward her and clearing the way for others. Behind him came Aunt Francesca, Isaiah, Hetty Green, Jack Slade, and Fat John Korpan.

Hope stopped, confused. She said, "I . . ."

Silas Proctor wrapped her in his strong arms and she burst into tears.

XV

Isaiah Stewart was uncomfortable under the girl's scrutiny.

Rhoda Monski sat on a straight-backed chair in the family kitchen eating an apple. She ate very slowly, taking deliberate, full-lipped bites; each bite a statement of lascivious pleasure. And as she chewed, she looked him up and down with a lazy, friendly warmth. "Honestly, Mr. Stewart, I think you're as cute as you can be. I don't see nothing wrong with a man having a lame foot and a hump on his shoulder. What difference does that make, as long as he's all man?" Rhoda Monski's eyes were a smoky gray, turned up fetchingly at the corners. She wrinkled her nose and gave her shoulders a little wiggle. The gesture emphasized the magnificence of her bosom, straining to be free of a very tight bodice. Her voice dropped a note and her eyes filled with hidden meaning. "I'll bet you are all man. I have an instinct about men."

He flushed, dry-mouthed. "Miss M-Monski, I don't know what you mean..."

Frowning, she bent over and said, "Help me with with my shoe."

"Your shoe?"

"Yes. It's too tight, or something."

He knelt clumsily at her feet and took the shoe in his hand. Gently she lifted her skirt just a bit, exposing a curve of calf and the hint, merely the hint, of white thigh. Isaiah's breath quickened. He tried to keep his eyes from straying. "This shoe?" he said.

"Do you think you could make it a little looser? Your hands look so strong; I'll bet you could." She took another bite of the apple.

Isaiah did not know what to do. He felt the shoe. It seemed loose enough to him. He tested the laces with his fingers. The foot was petite, rounded, with a high instep. Lovely. "I don't think..."

Abruptly she looked up behind him and pushed down her skirt. Isaiah heard a step and turned. A gray-haired older woman stood in the kitchen doorway with a puzzled expression. "Mr. Stewart?"

"Yes. I was just..."—he struggled to his feet, mentally cursing the clumsy body that refused to respond quickly— "just checking Miss Monski's shoe."

"I see." The woman had an attractive round face and brown eyes. Her body was soft and somewhat stout, her skin very white. "I'm Phyllis Monski, Rhoda's aunt. We're pleased that you could visit us." She shook his hand and gestured toward the parlor. "Mr. Monski has come down and will see you now."

Isaiah looked back toward the girl Rhoda, but she had turned her attention to the apple again and seemed unaware of his presence. He muttered a good-bye and followed Phyllis Monski into the parlor. The shop foreman sat in a large winged chair, his right foot—injured in an accident at the plant—encased in a mass of bandages and propped on a low footstool. He wore baggy brown trousers and suspenders over his underwear top. He smoked a cigar. As Isaiah came into the room, Pyotr Monski leaned over the arm of the chair, spat carefully into a brass cuspidor, and said, "Well."

"Monski, I'm sorry to bother you at home, but you said . . ."

"Quite all right, Mr. Stewart." Isaiah caught a whiff of whiskey on the man's breath. A meaty hand waved him to an adjoining chair. "Take a load off your feet. You brung the drawings, like I said?"

"They're right here." Isaiah unrolled the blueprints for the new production line and spread them across a small table beside the foreman's chair. Carefully avoiding the bandaged foot, he stepped around into the light and ran his finger across the plan. "Now, the way I see it, we run the engine line down this side and the chassis line over here. Your men will have room to move freely in between the two . . ."

The talk went on for an hour. Isaiah disliked the foreman, a brute Slav with cold eyes who smelled of sweat. And yet Monski commanded the respect of rough-hewn workmen, had a technical mind, and ran the assembly line with tough efficiency.

He was preparing to leave when she made her appearance. Rhoda looked at him boldly, almost (was he deluding himself?) with desire. "I hope you will come back and see us, Mr. Stewart. Surely you two have not finished all that business so soon?"

"Well, not really. There are"—he felt Monski's cold eyes upon him, but pushed on lamely—"a number of things we've yet to discuss." He took his hat from Mrs. Monski, nodded, and mumbled good-bye.

That night he was too aroused to sleep soundly.

It was a week before he saw her again. The word came from his secretary, a proper, middle-aged woman, with an expression of distaste. "Mr. Stewart, there is a young . . . female outside who insists on seeing you. A Miss Monski, I believe."

He tried to contain his excitement. "Send her in."

She wore a different costume, but in the same enticing style. This time the bodice had a lower neckline, displaying a fuller cleavage. The secretary sniffed with disapproval as she went out. Rhoda gazed about Isaiah's private office, visibly impressed. "I'd say you've done all right for yourself, Isaiah. You must be very rich."

He was suddenly defensive. "We've had some success, a little luck, and a lot of hard work."

The point seemed lost on her. She had come, she said, for her father's paycheck at the business office. Being in the building, she decided to pay him a visit. She hoped he didn't mind, being a busy man and all. Isaiah stared. She offered a languid smile. "Do you think I'm pretty, Mr. Stewart?"

He invited her to dinner.

They went into Detroit on the evening train. Her nearness sent fingers of delight running up his back. It was a sensation Isaiah Stewart had never known. Rhoda Monski made small talk, preened at her reflection in the store windows, and seemed not to heed his physical afflictions, even as they walked together into one of the finest restaurants in the city.

The menus came. "What would you like?" he asked.

"I don't know. I've never been in a place like this. Whatever you say is all right by me." She stared boldly at a handsome man at another table. The man smiled, lifted his wineglass to her, and drank. Isaiah felt a spasm of jealousy.

He ordered Chateaubriand for two and a good Bordeaux red wine, vintage 1892.

Their table talk was perfunctory, totaling involving herself. It was as if in the mind of Rhoda Monski nothing existed beyond personal gratifications. Isaiah was pained when her gray eyes lingered upon the waiter and the busboy. But at the same time he was accorded a level of service unique in his lifetime. He learned that Rhoda had been orphaned at an early age, was taken in by her father's brother Monski, and his wife. "I really don't like my uncle," she said offhandedly. "He's crude and boring. I like a man"—the eyes lingered upon Isaiah—"who's got class." They went back to Fall River late, after attending a musical comedy. She allowed him to hold her hand.

Only years later did Isaiah learn of the conversations that took place afterward in the Monski house, as Pyotr grumbled to his wife about Rhoda's latest interest.

"I don't like her fooling around with no cripple. What kind of a man is that, for a pretty young woman to be seen with?"

Phyllis Monski, a handsome but neglected woman of fifty-five, did not wish to antagonize her husband. Nevertheless she replied: "He has money. And besides, I think he is quite interesting. He does have a gentle face and is nice to women. It's nothing serious, Pyotr. Did Rhoda ever take any young man seriously?"

Things were busy at the plant. Isaiah Stewart spent long days and evenings in preparations for the new model. In the advertising department, Colby Malcolm pored over his sketches and ate, slept, and dreamed slogans. "Listen to this, Isaiah. 'New for 1912: the smooth, whisper-quiet elegance of a Stewart.'"

"Whisper-quiet compared to what, Colby?"

"You're still bitching about that whine in the transmission? They all whine in the transmission."

"I just wish I could get it out, that's all."

"This is a class automobile."

"Yeah, and that worries me too. Ford is building Everyman's Model T and we're going with class."

"You're a pessimist, Isaiah."

"I'm a realist."

"What d'ya think of this: 'Show her you love her, with a new Stewart'?"

"Aaagh..."

"Okay, okay, I get the message."

But it wasn't bad. Cousin Colby, for all his felonious past, had a shrewd knack for selling cars. They had come to realize that the sales pitch was as vital as the product. As Maurice had put it, in a strong speech to the board of directors in defense of Colby's surging budget: "Damn it, the finest motor car in the world isn't going to sell unless people get excited about it and want to buy. With two hundred companies out there competing with Stewart, we've got to move our butts!" Conservatives on the board such as Colette Marten and, surprisingly, Vanessa Stewart Harding, also fiercely criticized Maurice's expenditures—his plan to build a nationwide sales organization, his Dealers Partners program of direct aid in financing cars for customers, and his overbuilding of inventories. "Listen," Maurice retorted, "when a customer comes into a showroom, he wants cars to be there, a selection of Stewarts, ready to drive off. And damn it, that's what we're going to give him!"

Isaiah worried about Maurice. The man was consumed by a maniacal passion to succeed. He spent days and nights at the plant, and sought relaxation more and more frequently in the company of drinking cronies at the Pontchartrain Bar in Detroit. On one occasion, a brief but noisy confrontation over some technical detail of the new production line, Isaiah had told him: "You're working too hard. Why don't you take some time off, get to know Rachel and the children again?" In part, the comment had been spawned by his own deep envy of a man who had everything and still was not satisfied. Maurice whirled on him, eyes blazing. "Mind your own damn business, cousin. I don't criticize your social life, so you lay off mine."

For all the frantic pace of things, Rhoda Monski was never out of his mind. Rather, she stayed with him as a warm, vaguely frightening presence. Common sense told him to beware; instinct opted for noninvolvement. There were even those who offered well-intended advice. Old Moneypenny touched an icy finger to his heart. "Hear you've been out with the Monski girl, Isaiah. I'd watch my p's and q's. They say she's a real hellcat, that 'un."

It was none of their business. He was his own man, and would control his own life. To hell with Old Moneypenny, or anybody else who tried to snoop. And so thinking, he went back to the little house of Pyotr Monski on Elmwood Avenue, parking the car on the street and dragging his twisted body up the brick walkway bearing a bouquet of tea roses and a pain of anxiety in his belly.

"You came to see my uncle? He isn't here. He's down at the saloon, drinking with his pals. I'll show you"—she stepped out onto the porch, brushing his arm with her breast and pointing down the hill—"it's two blocks that way and turn..."

He pushed the roses at her and tried to clutch her hand all in one clumsy motion. "Well, I didn't really come to see him. That is, it'll wait. I was hoping you'd be home. Maybe we could sit and talk, or something."

The languid smile again, the doe eyes tantalizing him in the darkness. "Sure, Isaiah. I don't mind. I kind of wondered when you were coming back to see me."

"You did?"

"Rhoda gets lonesome sometimes, here in the house with nothing to do."

"She does?"

She traced a forefinger along the side of his face. "You got a nice chin. It's real strong and manly." Her mouth was nearing his, that delicious, warm, full, wet mouth. He felt himself drawn to it, drawn by the wanting and the half-promised delights and the hammering of his heart. And then, at the last instant, she giggled and turned away, burying her face in the tea roses.

"I'll just put these in some water," she said. "They're so fresh and nice."

"Who is it, Rhoda?" A light came on in the parlor. Phyllis Monski peered into the shadows of the front porch.

"Oh, nobody. Just Mr. Stewart, come to see Uncle Pyotr."

"Pyotr's not here." She pushed open the screen door and came out, a large, soft woman. Her gray hair was worn in a pile tonight. She was tying on an apron. "But it's nice to see you again, Mr. Stewart. You're welcome to take supp... My, what pretty roses!"

Supper was leftovers, served in a bewildering array of small dishes, a little of this and a little of that. Phyllis Monski radiated pleasant feminine domesticity, filled with interest and chatty talk. The house smelled of soaps and freshly starched curtains and floor wax. The rooms were small, wallpapered, orderly. His impressions were of tintype family pictures, beaded and tasseled lampshades, dark wood furnishings with antimacassars on the chairs, a waxed upright piano in one corner bearing sheet music, a small gilded statue of "Winged Victory," and a stereopticon with a box of photographic slides.

"Your work must be fascinating, Mr. Stewart. I think men with mechanical gifts are so fortunate. They say you created the Stewart engine. Did you know that, Rhoda?"

"No." Rhoda, suddenly bored, glanced at her reflection in a wall mirror and patted her hair.

Isaiah found himself talking about machines to an attentive Phyllis Monski. When they had finished eating, Rhoda got up restlessly from the table and went outside. Isaiah put down his napkin and Phyllis nodded understandingly. He found the girl on the porch, rocking in the wicker swing. The evening was scented with blossoms—Phyllis Monski's petunia patch beside the porch—and soft light from a streetlamp filtered through the trees.

"That was delicious," he said, lighting a cigar.

"It's all right, I suppose. But I get fidgety, staying home. I like to get out, see people, do things, go dancing. Do you like to dance, Isa..." She caught herself and glanced at his slumped shoulder and his withered foot. "No, I suppose you wouldn't. Anyhow, it's great fun. I like picnics too. All those handsome men, showing off their muscles. Do you like picnics?" She prattled on about picnics she had been to, and how Dexter Quatrain had almost drowned her in the swimming hole last Fourth of July, the big oaf, and how some boys seemed to have their minds on what they could do to a girl, and didn't Isaiah think that was terrible, the way the younger generation was nowadays...

He did not know how they started kissing. It just seemed to happen. One minute Rhoda was talking on about herself and the next she was kissing him. Unexpectedly he was enveloped in warmth and smell of her luscious mouth working against his, her lips opening and a soft moan coming from her throat. His hand accidentally brushed her breast and she seized it and pressed it there, astonishing him by its firm fullness. Her mouth opened wide and he felt lightly, lightly, the flick of her tongue. Isaiah thought he would explode.

She pushed free of him, panting. "Take me...in your...car. Let's go for a ride in...car..." He stood up, embarrassed, his manhood jutting. She knew, pressed against him, hurried ahead of him down the walk. And then they were driving through the dark streets of Fall River and out onto the road to Great Falls. She lay against him, grasping at him, panting. Her scent made his senses reel.

"I have an apartment," he said. "We can go there."

"No!" she said. "I would never go to a man's rooms. What kind of a girl do you think I am?"

So finally they stopped in a grove of trees, kissing and fondling. Her heat raised afresh. Rhoda Monski lay back, opening, as he fought to maneuver his twisted body from behind the steering wheel.

At last he was free.

"Do it to me!" she cried. "Oh sweet Jesus, do it to me!"

He was consumed. Every moment, waking and sleeping, it was Rhoda. She had saturated into the fiber of his being. Rhoda. She was ecstasy and pain, joy and wanting, feasting and hunger. Rhoda. Nothing mattered anymore, not the work nor the increasing deadline pressures nor Maurice's constant badgering, "Get it done, Isaiah! For God's sake, man, what's come over you?" Nothing mattered, nothing could intrude; he had found a wondrous new dimension of life beyond his wildest dreams. Rhoda. Rhoda. Rhoda.

"Rhoda?"

"Ah, Mr. Stewart. How nice to see you again. I'm sorry, but Rhoda isn't at home. She has gone out for the evening."

"Gone out? Uh, did she say, Mrs. Monski, where..."

The eyes were large and brown and suddenly filled with concern for him. She opened the screen door and took his hand. "With some friends, Mr. Stewart. Just with some friends. You know how young people are." She drew him into the parlor. The evening was warm and scented. Phyllis Monski wore an odor of lilacs. A clock chimed. She had been playing the piano when he arrived, and the sheet music was spread open. It was a piece by Mozart. "Let me put your flowers in water," she said. "How lovely. You have exquisite taste, Mr. Stewart."

"Did she say when she'll be back?"

"In a little while. She's with some friends."

"Oh." He just stood there, feeling empty inside and not knowing what to do.

Phyllis Monski found a vase and half filled it with water for the tea roses. She hummed softly to herself as she snipped off the stems. Her hands worked deftly, expertly. "You have excellent taste," she said.

"Did she say when she'd be back?"

Mrs. Monski went to the mantel. "I'll just put the flowers here, where they'll show nicely. There. Isn't that lovely? Now, then, I was just going to fix some tea. Will you join a lonely lady with her tea?"

They had tea in the darkness on the porch. He sat in a white wooden rocking chair and she on a swing. The swing creaked beneath her weight. The odor of lilacs blended with the soft summery night.

"I've lived in Fall River all my life," she said. "It's a pretty little town. I've never been anywhere else, except occasionally into Detroit and once on a trip to Chicago. Mr. Monski doesn't like to travel, and it is expensive. Have you traveled widely, Mr. Stewart?"

"Paris, Rome, Berlin." His eyes kept drifting to the street, hoping to see Rhoda. There was pain in his stomach. He felt almost physically ill. "Switzerland, London, New York, San Francisco." This was ridiculous, to suffer so. What on earth had gotten into him?

Mrs. Monski seemed fascinated. She talked of how this contrasted with her own quiet life, alone much of the time. Monski was rarely at home in the evenings, and besides their interests were different. But she had her piano, her needlepoint, her flowers, her home. If life was less than complete, it wasn't all that empty, either. But her dream was to travel someday, to see Paris and Vienna and Rome. "That, and love, are my fantasies, Mr. Stewart. Do you have a fantasy too?" Isaiah did not reply. He had been only half listening, staring at the street with pain in his stomach.

He said, "Rhoda is out with friends, you say?"

Phyllis Monski put down her cup and studied him thoughtfully. Her voice was very gentle when she spoke again. "You are in love with her, aren't you?"

He looked down at his teacup. He was suddenly conscious of the warped and twisted body in which he was imprisoned, this ridiculous body that made him different from other men, that made him ugly and ridiculous in the eyes of pretty young women. What right had he to love anyone? It was the supreme folly of a foolish man.

"I don't know," he lied.

Lightly, her hand came through the darkness and touched his arm. "It's all right to love, Mr. Stewart. We don't have to reject it. Love is what makes our lives sublime. It is man's most noble instinct, the thing that makes us different from other creatures. Love makes life worthwhile. Don't you agree?"

"I don't know."

"Well, I do. And I'm twenty years older than you."

They sat for a long time in the darkness of the porch. They shared the night sounds of crickets and frogs. Instinctively, Phyllis Monski seemed to sense his need for silence. It was not until the clock struck eleven that he got up to leave.

"Will you tell her that I came by, Mrs. Monski?"

"Of course, Mr. Stewart."

He put on his hat and walked to his car with a heavy heart. Isaiah did not sleep at all that night.

"What do you mean, where did I go? What business is that of yours?" She was filing her nails in the parlor, speaking in low tones so as not to disturb her uncle, who was sleeping in the next room. "I go where I please and when I please. Does that bother you?"

"Your aunt said you were out with friends." He was miserable, tormented by doubt, and had not slept at all the previous night. "I stayed until eleven o'clock and you didn't come home."

She shrugged, inspected her nails, and tossed her head defiantly. "Did somebody hire you as my keeper, Mr. Bigshot?"

The words struck him like a lash. Rhoda had the jugular instinct, the sure knack for causing hurt. He hesitated, groping for words. "I'm . . . sorry. I didn't mean. It's just that . . ."

"Just because you're rich and have a big fine office and employ my uncle, don't think you're got a right to tell Rhoda what to do. That don't give you the right."

Her eyes blazed. Isaiah was crestfallen. He looked at the lovely white hands, working with the sharp file. His inner being was torn between adoration and torment. How he would love to hold those hands this minute, hold them and kiss them. "You are beautiful," he whispered.

He reached for her, but she squirmed away frowning. "Don't manhandle me. I don't want to be handled, just now."

"I'm sorry. Please, know that I'm sorry. I didn't mean to offend you. I won't do it again. I want to be your friend, and be near you. Do you know, I think about you all the time?" Careful, a part of his mind said. Careful. "You are . . . so beautiful, so perfect. I even wrote a poem for you." He reached into his shirt pocket and brought out a folded piece of paper. He spread the paper on his knee. "I wrote this poem last night. Do you want me to read it to you? I'll read it to you." He cleared his throat.

Soft, soft the moonlight upon my bed of pain; cry the gentle spirit . . .

She got up and walked away, not listening. "Aunt Phyllis," she called, "have you seen my blue shirtwaist? The one I wore last night has grass stains."

Her moods were wholly unpredictable. Each swing of them caused him, by turns, ecstasy and agony. When he came to visit one evening, she would be coquettish and flirty, deliberately arousing his lust, and arousing herself to a fever heat, using him insatiably. They made love in his car, behind a dark hedge in the park, in her uncle's toolshed. On another evening, she would be cold, distant, seemingly disinterested in anything he said or did. On other nights, she would not be at home at all; and if Monski was out drinking with his tavern friends, Isaiah would while away a few hours with Phyllis, listening to her play the piano or talking about the places he had been, the concerts he had heard ("Tchaikovsky came to New York in '91. I was just a boy. But Aunt Francesca took me and my sister Hope to see him conduct. It was one of the memorable evenings of my life."), and his fascination with automobiles.

At the plant, Monski was his usual surly self, making no mention of Isaiah's involvement with his niece. But the foreman did not conceal his dislike for Isaiah and made cutting remarks to fellow workmen about "the hunchback." Once he commented sarcastically, "Ain't it amazing what money will buy." Monski's own relationship with his niece was a mystery to Isaiah, but from Rhoda he had the impression that the two were constantly quarreling and that Monski considered her headstrong and promiscuous. Once she startled Isaiah by saying, "The old coot's just mad because he can't get me for himself."

As summer waned, there were violent arguments between Rhoda and Monski. A despairing Phyllis Monski sought Isaiah's advice. "What am I going to do, Mr. Stewart? I'm afraid Monski will come home one night and kill her. Rhoda has no place to go, no one else to turn to. The child is only seventeen . . ."

After a night of deep soul-searching, Isaiah asked Rhoda to marry him. She laughed in his face.

But a week later, at two o'clock in the morning, she turned up at his apartment in a crisis. Her dress was torn, baring her shoulder and part of one breast. A great bruise mottled her cheek. Her hair was disheveled and her eyes filled with fear. "Monski tried to rape me." Isaiah took her in, put a cold compress to her cheek, calmed her, bathed her, put her into his bed, and slept on the sofa.

He confronted Monski at the plant. The foreman angrily called his niece a liar. Nevertheless he signed the paper Isaiah had obtained from a lawyer, consenting—as the girl's legal guardian—to her marriage. "And good riddance," he grumbled.

They were married five days later by a judge of the county court.

Isaiah Stewart's joy was beyond belief.

His passion was Rhoda. Full-breasted, tempestuous Rhoda. If only he could make his wife happy, make her love him. With this goal in mind, for the first time in his life Isaiah Stewart devoted his wealth to something beside automobiles. They went on shopping trips to Chicago, Philadelphia, and New York to buy her gowns, jewels, furs. Rhoda acquired a closet full of shoes, two closets full of dresses, a special drawer for her gold, diamonds, and rubies. Whatever whim possessed her, Isaiah Stewart sought to fulfill it.

Two weeks after the wedding they were off on a two-month tour of Europe, first class. They did London, Paris, Brussels, Rome, Berlin, Vienna. They saw the best shows, dined in the finest restaurants, stayed in Rhine castles and villas by the sea. And then, laden with trunks, boxes, and barrels of new possessions, they returned to Fall River, where fresh surprises awaited Rhoda: a fine stone house on a hill high above the river. A house even grander than that of Harry Pover, the wagonmaker, and his wife Priscilla. A house? A mansion, actually. It had twenty-five rooms, eight bathrooms, a solarium, a great veranda overlooking the river valley, a formal garden, a separate greenhouse, a carriage house, and a guesthouse.

"My darling!" he shouted, standing with her for the first time to gaze at the splendid view from the living room. "It's yours, all yours. A house fit for a queen!"

Rhoda made a face.

"You can redo your bedroom if you like," he said. "Hire decorators. Buy different furnishings..."

"Isaiah, I'm bored. We don't have any friends. We're always going someplace, but we never *do* anything. Why don't we go to parties like other people? Let's go dancing...Oh, hell, you don't dance. I've got it. A picnic! Let's go to the community picnic this Sunday!"

He thought: Well, why not? The poor thing was tired. She seemed preoccupied, uninterested in physical intimacy. Throughout the European trip she had complained of fatigue and headaches. Not once in that entire trip had they slept together. She needed something to perk her up. A picnic might do the trick. "All right, my dearest heart, to the picnic we shall go."

They drove the all-new 1914 Silver Stewart. It had luxury lines and a powerful eight-cylinder engine, with interior appointments of burled walnut and real leather. The body was hand-crafted and shone with twenty coats of rubbed lacquer. Isaiah's monogrammed initials gleamed in silver on the door. The butler put their picnic hamper into the roomy back seat compartment, along with a collapsible table and chairs. Rhoda was stunning in an outfit of pale blue from Paris, complete with an original hat and a bouffant hairdo. But she insisted on a low neckline displaying much more bosom than he thought appropriate, especially for a picnic. "Oh, pooh, Isaiah," she said, "you're nothing but a bluenose fussbudget."

He did not offer further protest.

It was the annual Labor Day Outing and Picnic of the Fall River Volunteer Fire Department, featuring a band concert, horseshoe-pitching, swimming in the river, bag races, canoeing, baseball, dancing, and evening fireworks. As usual, small children stared at Isaiah and teenagers whispered and giggled as he walked by. Rhoda, however, was the center of attention, their area quickly attracting a crowd of admiring young men and some less-admiring wives and girl friends. Isaiah talked with factory hands and local business folk, drinking beer, and enjoying the afternoon more than he had imagined he would. At four o'clock, a double-winged airplane appeared overhead and, to the crowd's delight, performed a series of loops and dives. The pilot waved and tossed down paper streamers.

"That's Nathan," Old Moneypenny said delightedly. "He's been practicing those maneuvers all week. It gives me the willies, just to watch."

"That nephew of mine keeps prattling about his goddamn airplane," grumbled Maurice. "Says it's going to revolutionize travel and warfare." He belched softly, and Isaiah caught a whiff of hard liquor. "Well, who the hell knows? he might be right." Maurice Stewart turned and stared rudely at Rhoda's cleavage. Isaiah tried not to notice.

She was having a good time. She laughed noisily and leaned briefly against one of the young men. Someone suggested they all go canoeing, and Rhoda went off with a crowd of young people leaving Isaiah behind. He watched from the bank as the laden canoes moved upstream, paddles flashing in the sunlight. One of the young men, wearing a straw hat and white flannels, produced a mandolin and they sang songs in chorus, the sound diminishing as they vanished around the bend.

Maurice put a hand heavily upon Isaiah's shoulder. "I know it's none of my business, cousin, but I'm damned if I'd let my woman run around with her tits hanging out. You'll have your hands full of trouble before long." Maurice's eyes were glassy and his face flushed from drinking. The words touched Isaiah like hot irons, but he made no reply. They didn't understand his Rhoda. Across the field, horseshoes clinked and a crowd shouted with excitement.

The evening fell. All the canoes returned but hers. Fireworks lit up the night sky over Fall River; couples strolled in the darkness. Bonfires were lit in the picnic area, and there were odors of roasting meat. Isaiah sat on the riverbank, waiting.

"Good evening, Mr. Stewart. How nice to see you again." Phyllis Monski smiled down at him, her aging features soft and strangely lovely in the glow of lamplight. She wore a white sailor outfit with a calf-length skirt. Isaiah noticed that her legs were very shapely. "I hope," she said, "that you've been well."

He came to his feet painfully. "Rhoda and I just got back from Europe last week. We're settling into the new house."

He smiled a happiness he did not feel. "You know how it is, busy, busy, busy."

The brown eyes studied his face. "Is everything all right?"

He grinned. "Couldn't be better."

"Good." Her hand lightly touched the side of his face. "I'll be thinking of you." She left him and walked alone toward the distant town square. He wanted her go, strangely moved.

It was after nine o'clock when the canoe returned. It bore Rhoda, the young man with the mandolin, and another couple. The couple avoided Isaiah's eyes as they climbed onto the dock and quickly walked away. The young man grinned, nodded to Rhoda, and strolled toward the bandstand, whistling.

"I was worried," he said.

A look of exasperation came to her face. She seemed flushed and in disarray. He noticed that one of her buttons was improperly buttoned. She refused to take his hand and walked beside him as one resentful of being too closely questioned.

"Why should you worry? I can swim."

"Well"—he tried to keep his voice light—"you were gone for several hours."

She stopped, turned, and glared at him. "We were having a good time. Is there something wrong with having a good time?" She put her hands on her hips. "Honestly, I get so tired of being watched. You watch me like a hawk. I can't stand somebody watching every move I make . . ."

The quarrel went on all the way home. When he drove up in front of the mansion, she got out sullenly and slammed the car door. Later, he knocked softly at the locked door of her room. "Rhoda? Darling?" There was no reply. He showered her with gifts, had fresh flowers delivered. He came home to find the flowers in a trash can, the gifts lying unopened. One evening, after a couple of drinks, he became more aggressive, stroking and fondling her. "It's been months since we've . . ."

"I don't feel well."

Isaiah's temper flared. He became insistent. She shrugged, went to the bedroom with him, removed her clothes. She lay naked beside him, bored and unresponsive. He cursed in frustration. His attempts were clumsy and, in the ultimate, futile. He left her, embarrassed and angry. She smirked at his discomfiture. He went to the library, opened a bottle of rum, and got gloriously drunk.

One day she told him, "I'm tired of being married. I don't want to be married anymore."

"That's ridiculous, Rhoda. You don't just tell somebody, 'I don't want to be married anymore.' You're my wife, for better or worse, in sickness and in health, remember?"

"You want a reason? I don't love you; that's the reason. You bore me. Besides, you're crippled and ugly. People stare at you. It's embarrassing."

He felt suddenly cold inside. It was as if ice had formed around his heart. He urged her to give it a chance; one didn't just throw a marriage out as if it were a dirty towel. He argued, pleaded, begged. She went up to her bedroom and closed the door.

The night was hell and the next day and the next night. He stumbled off to the factory. Old Moneypenny eyed him with pity. Workmen avoided his glance. Maurice Stewart came to his office, stood uncomfortably, started to speak, changed his mind, and went away. Isaiah's anger turned on them. Why were they meddling in his life? What business was it of theirs? This was his problem, his and Rhoda's. She was a good girl, a good wife, a little high-strung, that was all. She needed love, caring, understanding.

He would go home and tell her that. He would go home now, right this minute, and tell her how much he loved her. He looked at his watch. It was early, only two o'clock in the afternoon. No matter.

Isaiah drove home in the Silver Stewart. He drove up the hill, on the winding road, and pulled up at the front door. A man's bicycle was parked by the steps. He used his key and went into the foyer, into the dining area, into the kitchen. She wasn't there. He went up the broad stairway, feeling the thick carpet underfoot, sliding his hand along the silky waxen banister. Understanding, that's what she needed; the velvet touch of a man who really loved her. He had not . . .

He heard a voice from her bedroom, a sighing sound, a murmuring, and giggling. He stopped. His heart quickened. The door was slightly ajar. A male voice was speaking quietly. Isaiah heard her cry out. He moved to the door, pushed it silently open.

The bare male buttocks moved up and down in the white V of her thighs. He stood, frozen, watching. The buttocks quickened their rhythm. She shouted in ecstasy. The two forms came together, shuddering . . .

"Rhoda!"

There was a scrambling in the bed, a grabbing of covers. He looked into the swarthy, startled face of a mustachioed man. The man was fighting to untangle the bedclothes. His powerful, sweating body rippled with muscles. Rhoda's face was beneath him, wide-eyed.

Isaiah's legs seemed to drain of their strength. He sat down slowly beside the door. "Rhoda," he whispered. Their voices in reply were frightened at first, and then subdued. The man moved from the bed to a chair, gathered his clothes, quickly drew on trousers and a shirt. His eyes were watchful. There was a strong odor of male sweat.

And then Rhoda spoke, her voice shaky and uncertain. "What are you going to do, Isaiah?" When he did not respond, she asked again. "What are you going to do?"

The man looked intently at Isaiah. When there was no response, the man slowly straightened and smiled contemptuously. "He ain't going to do nothing, doll."

She came to her knees on the bed, naked, white-faced with rising fury. Afternoon daylight streamed through lace curtains, giving her eyes a strange glow. "You aren't going to do anything, Isaiah? You're not going to thrash this man you found ravishing me? You're not going to shoot him?" Her fists clenched beside her body. Already the mustachioed man was laughing as he stuffed his shirt into his trousers. "Goddamn you," Rhoda said, "*do* something, Isaiah!"

He shook his head as if to clear it. He got up from the chair. He looked at them both without expression. He turned and walked down the stairs.

Their laughter came rolling down in waves against his back.

For weeks afterward, the despair raged within him. He drank incessantly, but could not dissolve the pain. He looked at himself in the mirror, thinking: You're a twisted misfit in an ordered world. He contemplated suicide, but found that his sense of self-preservation was too strong. He plunged back into his work, haunting the machine shop, trying to devise a new generation of Stewart Six engines. But loneliness and rejection gave him no peace. He drove back to the hilltop house one evening, only to find the servants gone.

Six weeks went by. One evening, he took a long walk. He felt like an alien in Fall River now, a man out of place and out of time. As twilight settled, he found that he was on a familiar street. Slowly he walked past the house of Pyotr Monski.

His heart pounded. Perhaps she was there. Maybe she missed him. It was not impossible. He had excited her once, and why not again? She was waiting there, waiting for him to come, waiting to beg his forgiveness. And, of course, he would forgive. He would be magnanimous and forgive. She was, after all, only a child...

"Mr. Stewart! What a coincidence. I've been thinking about you, wondering how you've been." Phyllis Monski opened the door. Dusk filled the parlor. He stepped into the familiar surroundings, breathed the familiar smells, saw the shadow of the piano. "Rhoda went to Chicago, you know. She's a flighty girl, doesn't really know what she wants. That's youth for you. She said to tell you there's no hard feelings."

"No hard feelings? Did she say anything else, Mrs. Monski?"

"No, Mr. Stewart. I'm sorry."

She made him comfortable on the sofa. She fixed him tea. She moved about the room, wafting an odor of lilac. Strangely, he felt at home and more at peace than he had felt in months. Phyllis Monski sat down beside him, chatting. He asked about her husband. She sighed. "Pyotr is out every evening. He has his friends at the tavern. I don't like to go there. I'm a homebody." She smiled. She touched his hand lightly. "I've missed you, Mr. Stewart."

They talked, and the room grew darker.

The intimacy filled him with its strange warmth. He began to talk of things he had never talked about before. He spoke of his physical affliction and the pain of rejection it caused. He talked of his acute shyness among ordinary people, something he had never been able to overcome. He felt that he was a failure at the age of thirty-four.

She chuckled, a soft, pleasant sound. "A failure at thirty-four? My goodness, Mr. Stewart, you're only beginning at thirty-four. I'm fifty-five. My husband and I have not had physical contact for ten years. I have few friends, for I've always been a retiring person too. Mr. Monski and I never truly loved each other. We married simply because it was the thing to do. He is a cold man, without genuine affection." She hesitated. "My goodness, why am I telling you these things?" But then she continued. It was as if, like Isaiah, she carried a burden of secrets that needed sharing with a sympathetic ear to listen. He listened, spellbound. "Do you know, Mr. Stewart, that I have never in my life really been in love. Love is so important, in my opinion, and yet I've never experienced it in the way that some people do. Does that make any sense at all? And now I am fifty-five years old, and I'm supposed to be resigned to the fact that this..."—he sensed that she glanced around the darkened parlor—"is all I shall know for the rest of my life. And yet my heart tells me there's more to live for, Mr. Stewart. My heart has so much love to give . . ."

They were quiet then, sitting in the darkness. The clock ticked. He could hear her breathing. He was conscious of the flow of blood in his veins, the workings of his heart and lungs and brain. He thought: I am a man.

From the darkness her hand sought his, found it. "You have something that is priceless, Mr. Stewart. You have youth. How I would love to have youth again! But I shall always be twenty-one years older than you. For as long as we live, that age difference will remain. And youth, Mr. Stewart, is far more enduring than a straight body. Besides, it is the soul that matters, the soul and the sensitivity and the caring. Come. I will show you."

She stood up in the darkness still holding his hand. She led him from the parlor through a hallway and into her bedroom. Here the lilac odor was stronger. She left him standing and moved briefly away from him. There was a rustle of clothing and of bedsheet. When she came back to him, she was naked and breathing heavily. Gently, she undid his clothing. His excitement was a rising, throbbing thing. Her mouth found him, and he shivered from the pure delight of it. And then they lay down together . . .

Afterward, she stroked his body and whispered her secrets. "I never thought that I would have love. Isn't it strange, how things work out?"

Two weeks later, Phyllis Monski packed her things and moved out of her husband's house. It was said about town that she had found employment as a housekeeper for the crippled Isaiah Stewart. Townsfolk nodded sympathetically. "A good thing. The poor devil needs someone." And, of course, what better situation could an older woman find?

Pyotr Monski knew better.

The foreman came to Isaiah's office filled with rage and bluster. "I'm going to get her, cripple, and I'll take her back by force. You won't stop me."

Isaiah stood squarely, face-to-face. Never in his life had been surer of his ground. "Phyllis is not yours to own like a piece of garbage. She has her own mind and her own life, and you won't change that. If you harm her, I'll kill you."

Monski's eyes widened in surprise. His first impulse was to

344

smirk. "And how will you do that, little man? With your fists?"

Isaiah opened his desk drawer and drew out the pistol he had bought a week before in anticipation of trouble. "No. With this."

A taut silence descended between them. Monski looked at the pistol and at the face of this bent cripple. Like all bullies, he knew that another man's resolve radiated from the eyes. What he saw in this man's eyes disturbed him. His own face became a mix of emotions. His bluster crumbled; his tone abruptly changed to entreaty.

"How can you take her from me? Listen, this woman is all I have in the world. We've been together more than twenty years. You, you're rich and young and have power. You can get anything you want. Just snap your fingers. But look at me. I'm a working man, with a working man's wage. This woman makes my home, warms my life. Maybe I ain't the most romantic fellow, but I love her. The house, it just ain't the same without her. I got cold food, and nobody to take care of things. Look at this shirt; it ain't even ironed. What you're doing is taking my life away. Have a little pity. You can't love her. She's old enough to be your mother..."

Isaiah felt contempt. "What do you know about love, Monski? You're a lot like your niece Rhoda. All you care about is yourself, your own creature comforts. Look at you." He opened the desk drawer and put away the pistol, knowing it would no longer be necessary. Abruptly he turned and glared up at his adversary. The Slav was a head taller, but bore his heavily muscled body in a slouch.

"Stand up!" Isaiah Stewart snapped. "Stand up! Don't snivel at me like a dog. Stand up straight like a man!"

Instinctively, Monski stiffened his back and shoulders and drew erect. His meaty face bore a puzzled expression.

Isaiah smiled, turning his head sideways to look up from his bent body and humped shoulder. His eyes bore a luster of triumph. "And you expect me to have pity for you?"

Pyotr Monski went away. Isaiah stood at his office window looking out over the hillsides, splotched with the colors of early autumn. The sky was a milky blue and afternoon sunshine played over wooded slopes of scarlet and russet and gold. He lit a cigar and smiled, thinking of Phyllis. It was a good day to be alive. It was a very good day indeed.

XVI

He was drunk again. Good old gloriously sloppy down-and-out and everloving drunk sitting in his library all by himself, in this big fancy house he built for Rachel and the children, with a bottle of bourbon three quarters empty beside him.

Maurice Stewart belched.

Cigar. He needed a cigar. He got up from the chair and started to take a step but there was something wrong with the floor. The floor wasn't where it was supposed to be when he put his foot down. And so he stopped, got his balance, and started again. Carefully, carefully, he walked across the room and the rocking floor. He walked over to the window and looked out and saw that it was raining. The rain drooled down the windowpanes. The windows went all the way to the ceiling of this tall, tall room. That's how his architect had planned them. "Mr. Stewart, I see you in a big room, like a baronial room, with a very high ceiling and tall, tall windows."

The whole house was built that way, on a hilltop overlooking the valleys and the winding splendor of Fall River. The damn house wasn't a house at all; it was a castle. It looked like something in Germany, above the Rhine. It had cost a fortune. He couldn't even remember how much it cost. Maurice snickered at that. Looking out his huge window, he said, aloud, "I can tell Isaiah how much every fucking part in the Silver Stewart automobile costs, but I don't know how much my own fucking house costs. That's a joke."

He had forgotten something. Standing here, thinking about windows and castles, he had forgotten something very important. Very, very important. And, of course, everything about Maurice Stewart was important. Very, very important. Here was the very important Maurice Stewart, chairman of the board and chief headknocker of Stewart Motors, trying to remember what very important thing he had forgotten.

Oh, yes. Cigar. He had forgotten a cigar, which was the reason for this very important journey across this very important room in the first place. Cigar.

He went to the humidor on the side table. He fumbled with the top of the damn thing and the top of the damn thing slid off and fell to the floor and broke. His foot crunched on the broken ceramic. He drew a fine Havana cigar out of the humidor and unpeeled its wrapper and bit off the end and spat the shred onto the Oriental carpet. He found a wooden match and struck a fire and lit the cigar, taking big blue puffs. And then he looked up and saw the wall mirror and the puffy-eyed sonofabitch in the mirror with his head wreathed in blue smoke, the puffy-eyed sonofabitch with the eyes that bugged out from fleshy folds and the cheeks mottled with small red veins and the nose that was too red. And the sonofabitch was him.

"Ouch!"

The fucking match burned his finger. He shook it out and dropped it on the Oriental rug.

"Maurice? Maurice?" She pushed open the big white door from the main hallway and walked in. Her eyes were large and lustrous, her face beautiful—goddamn what a beautiful face—and her body, even fully clothed from neck to foot in something blue and frilly and feminine and flowery, was a body like a goddess's body, with big firm tits and a tucked-in waist and rounded fine hips like the flanks of a white mare. But cold. Cold as a block of ice.

"Maurice? Oh." She stopped. The eyes filled with disapproval. The eyes looked at the cigar, at the bourbon bottle, at the glass beside the chair. The eyes turned cold with disapproval. "I see," she said.

"What do you see?"

"You won't be going out, then?"

"Do I look like I'm going out?"

"I'm going to Mother's. I'll take the town car."

"Do I look... look like I'm going out?" he repeated.

"Will you be eating dinner here?" she said.

"No. I don't think so. I don't think I'll be eating dinner. I don't want any dinner. I don't think so. I don't feel very good."

She turned to leave him. God, she was beautiful. He said, "Rachel?" She hesitated, not looking at him. She stood with her hands clasped and her fine chin sort of lifted, staring out into the hallway. He said, "Honey, I . . . Rachel, I . . ." He went to her. He remembered the cigar in his mouth. He took the cigar out of his mouth. He said, "Rachel?" He reached for her. He said, "Rachel." He rubbed his hand over her breasts. Something was in his hand. Something left a smear on her frilly blue blouse. The cigar. The goddamn cigar. It left a smear and a big glowing spark. He wiped the smear and spark away, but the smear was still there. He said, "God-damn, I'm sorry. I didn't mean to. Goddamn, lemme, here, lemme wipe it off. Here, lemme wipe it."

But she moved away from him. She said, "I'm going now." Her voice was icy. She walked out into the hallway and closed the door and left him standing there alone, trying to get his eyes into focus.

Maurice said, "Rachel?" He turned away from the door and went back to his chair. He picked up the glass and took another drink. He sat down in the chair and started to cry.

"Is he drinking again?"

"Yes, Mother."

"What's wrong with that man? Why does he drink like that? I don't like a man who drinks. Certainly I don't approve of it in a son-in-law."

"I don't know, Mother. I really couldn't tell you why Maurice drinks."

It was not altogether true, of course. She knew. He drank because his wife was a respectable woman and not a whore in bed, like some of the others he had known. He drank because he needed her, and could not have her totally and completely. She would give no man that.

"Well, I think you ought to do something about it, Rachel. I don't see why you and Jacob and Catherine remain with him. You should take them and leave. Your father will get you a very good lawyer. Abe Fineman's son is a lawyer in Detroit, and I understand he handles divorce cases."

"I have no wish to divorce Maurice, Mother. He is not unkind to me or the children. We have our accommodations with one another. I understand why he drinks. In a way, I am partly responsible."

"That's foolishness. How on earth could you be responsible?"

"I don't wish to discuss that."

"You shouldn't have married him in the first place. Marrying a gentile, it was a terrible thing to do. You did it to defy me, to hurt me."

"I did it because I loved Maurice."

"Hah! You did not love him."

"And I still love him, in a way."

"That's ridiculous."

"Oh, Mother, do we have to go on like this?"

"You should bring the children for the holidays. We will take them to temple."

"The children are not Jewish."

"They should be. They should be Jewish. They could be. We can talk to the rabbi. He is reform. He is a wise man. I'll have your father talk to the rabbi. Jacob and Catherine should be going to temple. Jacob should be preparing for a Bar Mitzvah."

"Mother, he's only four years old."

"It is not too early to begin preparing for a Bar Mitzvah."

"He won't have a Bar Mitzvah. He will make up his own mind about religion. Other people do."

"You have turned away from your people, turned away from your blood; you have forsaken your birth."

"I don't want to argue with you about this."

"You cannot escape it. Listen to your mother. I know what's best for you and the children. You have married this worthless gentile who insists on destroying himself simply because you are a proper young woman and not some kind of a whore. If he had wanted a whore, he should have married a whore."

"Mother, how can you say that?"

"Oh, I know; I know very well what it is with you two. This is why you should be married to a good Jewish man, a religious man, who would be gentle and not demanding."

"Jewish men are as demanding as any others, and sometimes more so."

"How do you know that? You don't know anything."

"Mother, I refuse to discuss it anymore."

"I have told you since you were a little girl of the evils of such a man. Lust is evil, and lust with a gentile is unclean. You have allowed him to violate your body."

"Stop it!"

They glared at each other, white-faced. In the instant of fury, mother and daughter looked remarkably alike. The silence stretched out, measured by the ticking of the wall clock. At last, Sara Birnham looked away. She breathed deeply and smoothed her dress. Her face had an expression of righteous vindication. She stood up and walked across the fine room of the new house Jacob Birnham had bought for her, with its lush carpeting and rich furnishings and pictures on the wall. She went into her new kitchen.

She was a mother and knew what was best for her daughter. Sooner or later, Rachel would realize that. In time, Rachel would come around to her mother's way of thinking.

"I'll fix us some tea," Sara Birnham said.

* * *

The 1913 Silver Stewart was having teething problems. Orders were accumulating nicely enough. The company was financially healthy, and expanding. Isaiah Stewart's plan for subletting parts contracts to company-owned subsidiary manufacturers was proving to be both functional and efficient, allowing for much better quality control. But costs ran high. Customers complained about chassis troubles, frequency of breakdowns and repair. In the hotly competitive world of automobile manufacture, with new companies springing up virtually every day, Stewart's crowning achievement was its engine. Nothing on the market could compete with the Stewart Valve-in-Head Six. Even Henry Ford was said to be complimentary, and would have preferred such a power plant himself if he had gone into a more powerful automobile than the Model T. But a car was more than an engine. A car was chassis, design, suspension, braking. And these were the sources of headaches.

It shouldn't be happening. Maurice Stewart chafed over this. It should not be happening. After all, the heart of Stewart automotive technology was the new plant sprawled along Fall River south of the town. It was a marvel of industrial function, planned down to the smallest detail to allow quick retooling for model changes and a rapid, stream-lined production line. Such a plant could be created only with the massive capitalization of the Stewart family, and to this end Maurice had concentrated his efforts in the nearly eight years since switching over from buggy-making to motor cars. That abrupt switch was, everyone agreed, the smartest move Maurice Stewart had ever made. The nation had gone car-crazy, and hardly anybody bought buggies anymore. Even old Harry Pover's wagon works was having hard times, with frequent layoffs and dwindling production as America turned to the motor truck. Maurice privately relished that, for the assault on him years ago had never been resolved. He enjoyed Pover's getting his comeuppance. Good, he thought. Good.

As for the Stewart phenomenon, it was the stuff of trade magazines and popular journals. Articles and picture stories were constantly appearing in national publications, giving the impression of production marvels by a company absolutely in control of its own destiny. Actually, this was not altogether true. The widespread publicity, along with the highly ener-getic advertising campaigns and marketing techniques of Stewart automobiles, was the work of the family member with a specialized touch, Colby Malcolm Stewart. Only one small published item had ever appeared about Colby, and that was buried in a year-end wrap-up of the automotive industry put out by *McClure's* magazine.

Tall, self-effacing, reticent, Colby Malcolm Stewart is little known outside his own company. His background is not known. He is rarely even recognized on the streets of Detroit. And yet if Stewart Motors truly flourishes in a dog-eat-dog industry of many failures and sudden turn-overs, this strange Stewart deserves more of the credit than he is generally given; for his is the promotional and advertising genius that has put Stewart's in the minds of American automobile buyers with no less prominence than Ford, Winton, Oldsmobile, and Chevrolet.

What the journals did not say was that in the inner sanctum of Stewart Motors, all was not what it appeared to be. In this frenzied model year, the thrust of production lacked focus. There was disagreement as to the direction Stewart's should take: the luxury market, or the low-priced model.

Leading advocate of the quality car approach was the very man who had created the Stewart Valve-in-Head Six engine, Isaiah Stewart.

"We can't compete head-to-head with Ford," Isaiah was saying. "Model T is Everyman's car. That's how Ford designed it: sturdy, high-wheeled, mechanically simple. Model T is the car of the farmer, the small tradesman, the salesman traveling on back roads. You can fix it with a pair of pliers and a screwdriver." He squinted across the conference table through a fog of cigar smoke. "And he's bringing down the price every year. Starting from eight hundred fifty dollars three years ago, the sonofabitch is already down to seven hundred. And do you know what he's saying? He's saying he'll continue to drop prices until people buy enough Model T's to turn him a profit. Then he'll know the price is right."

"The man's crazy," grumbled old Tom Moneypenny.

"Crazy as a fox," said Maurice.

Isaiah gave his cousin a searching look. Maurice did not look well. His face was more florid than usual. He was puffy around the eyes. His hands were swollen. The signs were obvious. He had gone on another bender. How long could the man drink like this and get away with it? And the question that really intrigued Isaiah was: Why?

"Well, what are we going to do about it?" This question was put by Van Harrison Stewart. The tall half-breed Indian sat at the foot of the conference table, his eyes missing nothing. Isaiah felt comfortable with Van and was glad that he had joined the company as a vice-president for production. Not only did they share a mutual concern for finding a surer direction for Stewart's share of the automotive market, but Van's Stewart Special racing teams, and his personal car Spotted Deer, were burning up the dirt tracks across the nation and giving them invaluable data on mechanical advances. From the racer they had patterned the Stewart's new suspension system and routed out interior crossbeams and metal braces for lighter weight.

"We've got to bring down costs," Isaiah grumbled. "At the same time, we need more quality control. Our main objective ought to be the production of a safe, dependable, comfortable automobile. We don't need any more broken axles, broken drive shafts, and cracks in the transmission."

"It's a steel problem," Maurice said. "I've said all along it's a steel problem."

"Then, damn it, let's get Aunt Colette on the ball there in Pittsburgh, check out the castings, see what's wrong."

Van Harrison disagreed. "We've got bugs in the overall design. I can spot 'em, and so can you, Isaiah. I'd give my seat in hell to have a look at some of the stuff in Henry Ford's plans safe."

"His plans safe?"

"Yeah. The word at the Pontchartrain bar is that Ford has got another car model all drawn up and ready for production. It's a bigger car, closer to the Silver Stewart. His only problem is the engine. He doesn't have an engine that will compete with us. If he had our engine, he could blow us right out of the water."

"Do you mean he could produce two Fords, a Model T, and this bigger model?"

"That's exactly what I mean. He calls it his 'supercar.'"

"How do you know all this, Van?" It was Colby Malcolm who spoke. The big man usually sat silently through the technical conferences, absorbing ideas for his advertising campaigns—his "con jobs," as he called them—but contributing little to the conversations. "I ain't heard nothing about no plans safe, no supercar."

Van smiled. "We don't run with the same social set, Colby."

"Sounds to me like pillow talk," one of the production managers said. "There ain't no secret were a woman's concerned. And damned if Van don't share more pillows than any man in Michigan."

"As a matter-of-fact, it does come from such a source," Van said.

"Where does he keep this here plans safe?" Colby wanted to know.

Van swung around in his chair. "In his office, behind his desk. You sure as hell are chatty today, Colby."

"Yeah, well, I was just interested, that's all."

"Ford has got everybody in a box," Maurice muttered. "He's got the mass market locked up with the Model T, and the rest of us are scrapping for what's left. I say we ought to go for a utility model, like Model T, only better."

"And I say," Isaiah snapped, "that we'd be damn fools to try. Go for the upper market, but with real dependability, more luxury features, an electric starter..."

"Hell," said Van with a chuckle, "steal Ford's goddamn plans and go from there."

The meeting broke up in a burst of laughter. But Colby Malcolm did not join in.

He had money now. He had fine clothes, a nice house, a fine car. What man could expect more? It was the family's doing, of course. Maurice had given him another chance. More than a chance, really. Colby's cousin had come to Tennessee and gotten him out of prison—God knows how, but money talks—and brought him up here to Fall River to make a fresh start in life. Who would have suspected that a forger, swindler, and thief would find success in the car business? As Maurice sometimes put it, "It either says a lot for Colby Malcolm or it don't say much for the car business." Either way, Colby had flourished. Hell, why not? Selling cars was pure con. What you did was build it up all out of proportion to what it really was. "The new, all new, whisper-quiet Stewart Six." And, "Now, elegance in the Silver Stewart."

A man used his noodle and got things done. They wanted to sell cars; they had to create a market. And what better way to create a market than to put money in people's pockets? If not cash money, then borrowed money would do. So Colby had dreamed up his EZ Credit Plan. A working man who had a job and a steady income could buy a Stewart on time, with just a little money down and so much a month. He could even trade in an old Stewart on a new Stewart, because the market in new cars had led to a secondary market in used cars. Maurice, expanding on the same system he had used to sell buggies, had set up dealerships in Stewart cars, with franchises in various big cities.

The family had treated Colby well, far better than he expected or deserved. A man could not take such treatment for granted. He had to give Stewart Motors his best efforts, and this he did. Colby Malcolm did not give loyalty lightly, and once given it stuck. And now, the company was not doing as well as it should. There was trouble. They had talked about Ford's plan for a secret supercar. And Van had said, in jest, "Hell, steal the damn thing."

It was midnight. Colby Malcolm Stewart parked his car in the shadows a block from the main building and walked the rest of the way. He knew his route, for he had reconnoitered in the daytime and asked questions. They did not even keep a night watchman on the place. Drawing up his coat collar against the autumn chill, he walked purposefully to the main building and, without hesitation, mounted the steps to the front door. Drawing a wire from his pocket, he expertly slid it into the lock, caught the tip of the tumbler, and turned. With satisfaction, he heard the lock snap open. Old Colby hadn't lost his touch. He opened the door, slipped into the quiet hallway, and closed it. The office was to the left, the one with the frosted glass door. He went in through the anteroom and opened another door.

The safe was behind the desk, they said. He snapped on a flashlight, its beam masked with tape, and found the desk. It was surprisingly small and cluttered to belong to such an important man. He stepped behind the desk. There was no safe. Instead, he found an unlocked cupboard. He opened it, saw a large manila envelope, and quickly inspected the contents. Plans. Car plans. Across the face they bore the legend Ford Motor Co. and a stamped warning, Secret.

Colby tucked the manila envelope inside his topcoat and left the way he came.

Three hours later he sat in the back room of a tattoo parlor in downtown Detroit, watching his old cellmate Gimpy LaBelle flip through the blueprints with practiced fingers. "It don't look like much to me, Colby. There ain't nothing difficult about prints. Easy as pie."

"Okay, Gimp. Here's what I want you to do." Colby unrolled a set of plans for the new Stewart sedan and opened them beside the Ford prints. "See this here hood configuration? I want you to work it in, see. Make it look like a Stewart. And these running boards, here. And that wooden-spoked wheel. And don't forget the trunk lines and brass headlights. What I want is a Stewart outside and a Ford inside. Change everything external that could identify the Ford, including serial numbers. Get me?"

"Hey, I'm a forger, not a draftsman."

"There ain't no better draftsman anywhere, Gimpy. I've seen your work, remember?"

"Aw, gee, Colby. That's nice of you to say."

"I'll pick 'em up in a week, pal."

"Make it ten days, will ya? I gotta go visit my sick mother-in-law in Plymouth next week."

"Ten days it is."

True to his word, Gimpy had the plans ready on time. Colby paid him five thousand dollars out of advertising funds, budgeted as "artist commission." It was such a handsome sum that Gimpy almost wept for joy. Colby then placed the revised plans in the file marked New Material. It consisted of plans coming off the drafting boards and awaiting Maurice's review. Stewart's had become large enough so that work modifications on paper often combined the ideas of several department heads, including Maurice himself.

The response was everything Colby had hoped for. Maurice was enthusiastic over the drawings for the Silver Stewart. "This is handsome work, Isaiah. You've got some tremendous innovations in here!" Isaiah, puzzled, was himself impressed. The most dramatic changes, of course, were in axle weight, balance, and undercarriage framing, creating a markedly sturdier, safer, and more comfortable car.

"The all new Silver Stewart," Colby's new advertising slogan proclaimed, "—a revolution in motoring!"

"Don't be concerned," Phyllis said. "Maurice is a full-grown man. He can take care of himself."

"He's so damned miserable. I see him destroying himself a little more each day." Isaiah pushed his plate aside and sipped a fine Bordeaux red wine. "He sits up in that castle of his drinking like a fish. He won't talk about his problems, keeps it all bottled up inside."

She smiled gently. "Stewarts are proud men. I ought to know; I was lucky enough to catch one."

"A fine catch you made, dear lady."

"The finest I could ever hope to make."

She came around the table and took his plate. Odd, that she always insisted on serving him. They were wealthy now, lacking for nothing. The house had a butler, a cook, a maid, a housekeeper. He had bought Phyllis a grand piano, which sat by the window overlooking the river. Their friends came for recitals and dinner parties. But this heavyset, gray-haired woman treated him as if he were a king, always sitting next to him, seeing to his needs, his plate, his cigars. Isaiah had never dreamed that such contentment was possible. He only wished that Maurice could know life like this. But the man seemed both driven and haunted, driven by his lust to make Stewart Motors first in the automobile market, haunted by a private life of unrequited loves.

"Has he ever loved another woman?" Phyllis asked.

"That's hard to say. He was smitten by Priscilla Pover. That was a long time ago. He was happy for a while with Helen DeMare. Sensational girl, beautiful beyond words. She left Fall River before Maurice married Rachel, and never returned."

"I've read about her. She has so many gentlemen admirers. The glamour of an actress in Chicago..."

"In Helen's eyes, no man would ever take the place of Maurice Stewart. That's probably why she has not married."

"And Rachel?"

"Rachel could make his life complete. He loves the children. I don't know what went wrong with their private life, but I have my suspicions."

"Yes," Phyllis said. "So do I."

Isaiah smiled, stood up, and walked to the window. He envied no man. How extraordinary that he, the least attractive of mortals, a freak of nature, should have found such completeness. And now everything else seemed to be falling together too. At last, after all these years of trial and error, they had found the chassis and body works to combine with his Stewart engine. The car would be slightly larger, slightly heavier, but of finer quality in every respect. He still wondered how it had happened, and why Maurice wanted to give *him* the credit for design. But then, that was Maurice's way. The board chairman of Stewart's had forged a strong management team. If he considered it important not to acknowledge his own design work on a new model, then so be it.

"What are you thinking about?" she said.

"I'm thinking that I love you very much."

"How could you love an old lady like me?"

He lit another cigar and exhaled the smoke luxuriantly. "To tell you the truth, I've lost count of all the ways. But if you'd like to go up to bed with me, I'll try to refresh my memory."

"Isaiah, shame on you!" She laughed, got up from the couch, and headed for the stairs.

Colby was a loner. He had always been a loner. Basically it was a matter of choice. Women found him acceptable enough. Oh, they weren't bowled over by Colby Malcolm Stewart. He was no Silent Flicker idol like some of his cousins. Maurice, he thought: Now there was a man women took a shine to. Even getting bloated, with those little blood vessels around his face and the eyes tending to bulge, Maurice was still a handsome man. He could have virtually any woman he wanted. But Colby? Well, the guys in prison had said he looked like a big, clumsy crane, all knobs and neck. It did not matter, though. You took what God gave you and did your best. And Colby's best, lately, had been about as good as a plain man could possibly attain.

The difference was money. When a man had money, it did not matter overly much what he looked like. He could look like a crane or a moose, and somehow the money made up for it. Colby Malcolm enjoyed money. He spent it well. He wore spiffy tailored suits now, drove the newest model Silver Stewart, lived in a nice house on Water Street, and had a housekeeper and a maid. He owned a nice fishing boat with a gasoline engine, and could go out as often as he pleased with old Tom Moneypenny or Will Pease or some of his other cronies. He liked to go for the big catfish that lay deep in the channels downriver, or for the bass and trout at secret spots he knew upstream. He could hunt when the mood struck him, or ride one of his two Morgan saddle horses. Or he could go get himself a woman.

A woman was something Colby could do without, but not forever. He had no desire to marry—the thought had never crossed his mind—and was restless in the social company of females. In social company, they made prattling small talk and vexed his spirit. But when the need came to him, that basic and animal craving that he could neither fully understand nor possibly ignore, only a woman would serve. Over the years, he had finally come to a system of sorts. The quickest, easiest way to have one's needs fulfilled was to visit a whorehouse. For this purpose, he usually took the train to Detroit. The pickings were much better there; and besides, one went about his business discreetly. He considered this a private matter and did not care to be fodder for the wagging tongues of Fall River.

And so the evening closed, warm and velvety, and Colby Malcolm Stewart went into one of his favorite haunts in Detroit. It was a bordello that served the well-to-do, with good food, nice carpets, potted plants, and brass spittoons. He then proceeded to have himself an evening of entertainment. It began, as always, with the proprietor, Mme. Rose, introducing him to one of her new girls. A new girl was more to Colby's liking, because she would be younger and fresher and give the illusion of not having been manhandled overly much.

"Mr. Jones, this is Tulip Germaine," Mme. Rose said. Colby looked up from his table and saw a young, big-eyed blond with high breasts and creamy skin. She was nicely packaged in a filmy gown of lavender print with a deep-plunging neckline. He liked her smell, which reminded him of flowers. He stood up gravely, towering above her. The blue eyes widened. Mme. Rose said, "Tulip is one of our new girls."

"I am pleased to meet you, Miss Germaine," he said. "Won't you join me for a bite of supper?"

"I'd be delighted, Mr. Jones." The accent was pure Southern, pure magnolia, probably pure hokum. But it did not matter, Colby reflected as she took the cushioned chair beside him in a swirl of lavender and scent. Creamy breasts exposed in twin billows as she leaned toward him. Life was a game. "Charmed."

"I'll send the waiter right around," Mme. Rose said, and was gone. They wined. They ate aged, tender steaks, the best in the house. She chatted about this and that, and he replied in monosyllables. When silences yawned, he made no attempt to fill them. The wine warmed his blood. He stared at her cleavage. A string trio struck up a ragtime tune. A small, secluded dance floor occupied a corner behind a bank of indoor plants. She led him by the hand to the floor and they came together, moving quickly. Colby was a good dancer, but dancing was not what he had in mind. She clutched at him, her head barely to his shoulder, moving expertly. He was quickly aroused. Full-length mirrors upon two walls displayed the superb roundness of her little ass and the sheen of golden hair tumbling down her back. A long slit in her gown exposed a flash of thigh.

"Ooooh," she said. "I just love great big tall men with great big hands an' great big feet an' great big. . ." She came up on tiptoes and whispered the word into his ear.

They went upstairs. She led him into a warmly lit room with red velvet wall covering and a huge brass bed with red covers. She turned down the covers, exposing the whiteness of sheets and pillows. She undid his belt and his trousers and his shirt and his shoes. She reached back, unfastened one hook and stepped out of the lavender gown. She fondled him until he was raging with lust, jutting out like a stallion, and then she took him.

Tulip was good. Tulip was the best he ever had. He knew, from the way she moved and moaned, that she was not a new girl. But it didn't matter. Nothing mattered. He just went and went and went again. And then he slept. And then he woke up, found her there with a bottle of bourbon, and they drank.

He did not see her slip the powder into his glass.

Lord, he was having a fine old time! His head buzzed and his face was numb and he was happy, happy, happy. He told her a coarse joke and laughed some more, laughed until his sides ached and he gasped for breath. The room went around and around like a merry-go-round, and ole Colby went with it, having a hell of a celebration. She folded him into her arms, all white flesh and golden hair and the smell of perfume and woman scent; she enfolded him softly, softly in white-billowing clouds and took him up high, high, high and held him there. And then she unfolded beneath him like a golden-white flower and he drove it in, drove it furiously, looking all the while into the wide blue eyes and the laughing mouth.

"Goddamn," he said, rolling over. "Goddamn, that was good."

He was spent. His body was like rubber, with the stretch gone out. She put out the light beside the bed. In the warm darkness, they lay together and gently she asked him questions. Gently, she whispered to him, prodding into his consciousness. The images came back. The jails. The prisons. The old cellmates. The good times and bad. The coppers, the jobs. "Um. . . used'ta be damn good second-story man. The best. Yeah. I worked in Toledo, second-story. Yeah. Banks, too. Did a bank in Charleston, West Virginia. Ole Colby could torch a safe and never singe a bill . . ." The time drifted by. The images floated past, like leaves on water. "Um . . . my cousin Maurice. Great man. Great. Give me a chance to change myself, Maurice did. Grateful. Goddamn, wonderful bunch of fellas." An infinite gratitude welled up, a love and a sadness. It came up like water from a well, choking off his speech, spilling out of his eyes. Colby wept for the gratitude he felt. He hoped he hadn't done wrong, done a bad thing. He worried. "I stole them plans, knowing I shouldn't have. Gimpy, he done a good job. I tell you, nobody would know. But it's getting to be a big thing, bigger than I thought. It's got all them glinches worked out, and Silv . . . Silver Stewart is on the way into big time. Big time. Big time. But I've got this nagging feeling. Did I do wrong?" He sobbed, strangely relieved. He sobbed and sobbed.

She whispered. The whispers calmed him. They poured into his ear, calming, calming, calming. "You sleep now, honey. Y'hear? You sleep now . . ." Colby rolled onto his side like a baby. He drifted off into a deep and dreamless sleep.

When he awoke, sunlight streamed through the blinds. The room was shabby in daylight, the velvet wall peeling and the bed linen not as clean as it had seemed. He got up, feeling wobbly, and put on his clothes and left the room. There was no one downstairs. The tables were bare and piled up and two black men swept and cleaned. There was an odor of dust and stale tobacco smoke. An old woman with straggling gray hair stood at a cash register with his bill. He paid. There was a stack of envelopes and a hand-lettered sign, For the Girls. He folded a hundred-dollar bill into an envelope and dropped it into a slot marked Tulip. He stepped out into the glare of morning. He had coffee at a small café before taking the train back to Fall River.

Mother finished dressing Catherine and doing her hair. Then Mother went away and Catherine inspected the result in the full-length mirror. She smoothed down the front of the pink party frock. It was new and very pretty. She gave her blond curls a poke and smiled at her reflection. The smile showed the gaps where the tooth fairy had taken two teeth. She thought: darn tooth fairy.

With a quick frown, Catherine went to the big feather bed, where her dolls waited. She arranged the dolls on the bed, imagining that the lumps and folds of the heavy counterpane were hills and valleys. This was important, because Fall River was surrounded by hills and valleys. Mother and Father were a part of that, too. Two of her dolls were Mother and Father.

"Oh, I do wish you wouldn't drink so much." Catherine mimicked the voice for Mother Doll. The doll had dark hair and dark eyes and was very beautiful, but its voice was harsh and accusing. "Whatever am I going to do with you?"

"Don't bother me. Shut up, woman, and stop nagging." This was Father Doll. Catherine had taken her largest doll and dressed it in men's clothing, drawn with crayons on heavy paper. Father Doll had a deep voice and a dark mustache. He was very handsome, and his smile could light up the whole room. But when he and Mother Doll quarreled, he did not smile.

The door opened behind Catherine and Jakey came in. He was dressed in a new suit with a wide white collar. His dark hair was wet and freshly combed. His nose was dusted with freckles. "It's about time," Catherine said. "Jakey, you're so slow."

Her brother ignored the play-acted rebuke. He did not understand, and Catherine realized this. "You're just too little to understand," she said.

"Too little to understand what?" Jakey said.

"It doesn't matter, Jakey."

Jakey was having his fifth birthday, but Catherine was six and a half, going on seven. She feigned impatience with her brother. He was always getting in the way. He was always taking his toys apart to see what made them run and scattering the pieces around his room. He was rough at play. Boys were a problem.

"Father's downstairs," Jakey announced. "So are Grand-mother and Grandfather, Cousin Isaiah, and other people, too."

Catherine jumped up from the bed. "Goody! Let's go!" She grabbed Jakey's hand and they ran out of the room and down the broad, curving stairs. They could smell the cigar smoke and hear the heavy male voices. They burst into the parlor together.

"Father! Father!" Jakey cried.

Maurice Stewart stood up from his chair, smiling broadly. He was pale, and his eyes peered out from dark shells. He spread his arms wide. Catherine and Jakey ran to the arms and were scooped aloft, laughing. He kissed them both, his mustache tickling their faces. He smelled of tobacco and shaving lotion. His hands trembled slightly as he held the two of them.

"Here you are! Now the party can begin!" he said.

Grandmother Birnham, who was seated nearby, pursed her lips with disapproval.

Other children were arriving with their parents. Soon the driveway was crowded with horses and buggies and gleaming motor cars. The afternoon unfolded in a golden rush. The house filled with happy sounds. The yard was warm and sunlit, a sweep of summer green. Jakey was the center of attention. He wore a paper party hat. His eyes were dark and glowing. Catherine looked across the crowded table into the happy face of her brother. Jakey giggled, freckles dancing. "A handsome boy," someone murmured. "Like his father."

"Here, Jakey. Look!" It was Cousin Isaiah. He bent over Jakey and held a gleaming toy train in his hands. Catherine felt a stab of envy. She loved Cousin Isaiah. He was gentle, more gentle than most grown-ups, and always brought her presents. Now the present was for Jakey, a toy train. Jakey's eyes were shining. Jakey and Cousin Isaiah left the table and sat on the floor, putting the train together, while Mother said, "Isaiah, he'll get his new suit soiled." But Mother was laughing. Father was laughing too.

Catherine saw Father put his hand around Mother's waist, and saw her stiffen and draw away.

They all ran outside into the sunshine to play. They played tag and blindman's buff around the big fountain. It was Catherine's turn to be the blind man, and they tied the handkerchief over her eyes. She laughed and laughed, groping in the darkness and feeling the sun upon her face, hearing the sounds of the children running away from her, giggling and shouting. She grabbed a man's leg and held on. "I got you! I got you!"

Someone took the blind off and she looked up, and it was Father. He gathered her into his arms and hugged her, squeezing out her breath. Catherine had never been so happy. "Oh, Father," she cried. "I love you!"

The afternoon passed and the evening came. Jakey was tired and fretful. One of the other boys teased Jakey, making him cry.

"It looks like the party's over," Father said. "The guest of honor is all tuckered out."

Jacob Birnham sighed wistfully. "He's not alone."

"A man doesn't reach the ripe old age of five every day," Cousin Isaiah said. "It takes a lot out of him."

Father carried Jakey upstairs. The other children all left, one by one, leaving a few of the grown-ups. Catherine sat on Cousin Colby's lap, growing sleepy, while they talked around the table. Grandmother Birnham remained in the kitchen, helping the maid finish the dishes. She did not seem to want to be in the same room with Father.

"Jake's bright as a button," Cousin Isaiah said. "He has a quick technical mind. Already he's figured out how to take that toy train apart. I never saw anything like it."

"He'll make a fine automotive engineer someday," one of the other men said.

Mother shook her head. "Oh, I really don't think so, Jeffrey. We've got enough technical people in this family. I think Jacob is cut out for business, like his grandfather Birnham, or for law."

"I just wish he could learn to put it back together," Cousin Isaiah said.

"Put what back together, Isaiah?"

"The toy train. He can take it apart, but he can't put it back together."

"Give him time, Isaiah," Jacob Birnham said proudly. "A fellow can't master everything at age five."

Catherine drifted off to sleep in Cousin Colby's lap.

She awoke to the sound of angry voices. She lay on the davenport in the parlor. Everybody was gone except Father and Mother. The lights were down and there was an odor of stale tobacco smoke. There was also another familiar odor, which had been absent during the afternoon. Father was drinking again.

"You don't have to do that," Mother was saying. "Look what it's doing to you. You're sick, Maurice. Can't you leave it alone for one day?"

"None of your business," Father said. "Go on upstairs and leave me alone."

"It is my business. I make it my business. The very idea, on Jacob's birthday . . ."

"Don't bring the children into this."

Catherine felt her stomach cramp, the way it always did when they argued. She kept her eyes shut tight, trying to blot it out. But the voices went on and on, and Father's voice became louder and angrier.

"You don't want a man; you want a eunuch. You want a

363

money-making machine with all the lah-de-dah social graces and no balls. Why didn't you marry one of those faggot men?"

"Hush. Catherine will hear."

"Let her hear. Maybe it's time she heard. Let the whole damn world hear. A lot I care."

"Hush, Maurice. Please."

The voices fell silent. Mother came to the davenport. Catherine did not open her eyes. Mother slid her hands beneath her and picked her up. Mother bore her past Father—Catherine felt his presence and wanted to reach out and touch him, but didn't—and into the hallway and up the stairs. Mother put her down on the bed with the dolls and murmured, "Catherine?" She opened her eyes then, sleepily, and yawned and stretched.

"Is the party over?"

"Yes, dear," Mother said. "The party's over. You get undressed now and crawl into bed."

Mother kissed her on the forehead, walked out, and gently closed the door. Catherine heard her go to her own room.

Catherine undressed and went to bed. The house was silent after that. Moonlight sifted in from the windows, illuminating the dolls around her. The sightless eyes watched Catherine.

She lay awake for a long time, staring at the ceiling. She did not hear Father come upstairs until after the hall clock had struck two. His footfalls were shuffling and unsteady as he made his way to his solitary room.

"Why can't you be happy?" Catherine whispered to the Mother Doll. "Why can't we all just love each other and be happy?"

The Mother Doll stared mutely into the sifting moonlight.

"Please take your shirt off, Mr. Stewart. Dr. Farr will be with you in a moment."

The nurse's face was noncommittal, her white uniform crisply starched. She left him in the examining room and closed the door. Maurice removed the shirt and sat on a metal stool in the cold silence of the room trying to contain his anxiety. It was his imagination, no doubt, or perhaps a pulled muscle. A man his age was bound to have aches and pains. Besides, he had put on weight. Even now, white belly muscles bulged over his belt. It was nothing to worry about, for all men of substance were portly. My God, President Taft had weighed three hundred pounds. Besides, it wasn't the weight problem that caused his back pains. A skinny man could pull a muscle. But would a pulled muscle cause his urinary pain, too?

Dr. Melvin Farr came in with his genial smile. "Well, well, well, Maurice. Lovely weather we're having. And how is Rachel and the children?" He offered a round-faced smile, washed his hands at the sink, paid no attention to Maurice's replies, mentioned his golf, asked about Maurice's golf ("Oh, you don't golf? Pity. A wonderful game, golf."), said three more well wells and then looked intently into Maurice's eyes. "Now, then, what's the trouble?"

He told him. The back pains. The frequency of urination. The sleepless nights. The headaches. The occasional chills and fever. "I probably pulled a back muscle." He put his hand against his back. "It's down around here."

The doctor examined his eyes, his ears, his nose, his throat. He listened with a stethoscope, probed with fingers, and made small grunting sounds as if communing with some inner counsel. Maurice was obliged to remove all his clothing. The doctor looked at the swellings around his knees and elbows, and made more grunting sounds. Maurice's anxiety increased.

At last he sat fully dressed across the desk while Dr. Farr scribbled a few notes. A grandfather clock ticked in a corner. Maurice looked up at the doctor's framed certificates.

The doctor rocked back in his leather chair. The springs creaked gently. He took off his glasses. "Maurice," he said gravely, "I'm giving you a choice."

"A choice?"

"Between living and not living."

A cold knot formed in Maurice's stomach. "What do you mean?"

"You are drinking yourself to death."

"But I don't drink that much, Mel. Only a little now and th..."

Farr lifted a forefinger and wagged it gently. "We both know better than that, Maurice. Let's be honest with one another. You're drinking like a fish. You're suffering the effects in both the kidney and the liver. These things are very dangerous. You have high blood pressure, the early stages of bloating associated with a bad liver, and the makings of a heart condition. I can, and will, give you medication. But the basic decision is yours to make. You've got to stop drinking, cut down your smoking, eat less, relax more, get into better physical condition..."

"Hey, Doctor. What are you trying to say?"

"I'm saying that if you don't get yourself in hand, right now, you might live one year or two or five. But not much beyond five. And the quality of your life will gradually deteriorate. I don't know any other way to say it. But I might add that you're much too young and vital a man to be in this condition; you've got a grand career, a wonderful family, everything to live for." He sighed and put on his spectacles again. "The choice is yours."

Maurice left the doctor's office in shock. "...*One year or two or five. But not much beyond five.*" He needed a drink, a good, stiff drink at Jerry's Saloon. He needed to sit at the bar and sort out his thoughts. Just the idea of a drink caused his mouth to water. He glanced at his watch. Two o'clock. A bit early, but what the hell. He drove down Main Street, parked near the saloon, and went in. He smelled the familiar smells of old leather, stale cigar smoke, beer, pickled eggs, and pigs' feet. A few other drinkers were there.

He sat at his usual stool. The usual bartender, Jerry himself, came wiping the usual glass, smiling the usual smile. "What'll it be, Mr. Stewart? The usual?"

He started to reply. He hesitated, thinking, "*But not much beyond five...*" He said quietly, "The usual."

Jerry brought the double shot of bourbon and a glass of beer. He put them on the bar in front of Maurice and went away. The beer was foamy and cold, in a stein bearing the name Stewart. The bourbon sat very still in the double shot-glass, still and rich and reddish-brown. The bourbon waited. The usual was half a shot at a gulp, burning his tongue and mouth and throat, catching his breath in that delicious fiery way as it went down, chased by the cold foaming beer, the whole stein at a draught. And then Jerry would snatch up the stein and bring it back full again, foam drooling down the sides. But Maurice would wait awhile, looking at the bourbon and the beer, smoking a cigar, feeling the flush of alcohol as it went to work on his system; and he would take the second drink at a more leisurely pace, while contemplating the rest of the afternoon from the lofty perspective of this bar stool.

It was all crowding in on him too fast and too soon. That very morning he had quarreled again with Rachel. They quarreled bitterly and frequently now. This time it was over, of all things, religion. She wanted to take the children to temple. His children, to temple! There had never been a Jew in the entire Stewart line, never a question of religious choice. They had all gone to Protestant churches or not at all. And here was Rachel talking about preparing Jake for a Bar Mitzvah. Maurice had said cutting things. "Hell, Jake might have a Jewish mother, but that don't make him a Jew. Besides, you're not really Jewish either, my pet. You haven't been to a synagogue since the day we married."

She had screamed at him. Screamed and wept. How did he know what was in her heart? He was a *goy,* and it had been a mistake to marry him. She was isolated in this castle of theirs, isolated from her people and her parents and her heritage, cast among non-Jews. There were many acquaintances but no close friends, for how could women of differing cultures bridge the chasm of religion and background? There was nothing between the two of them, either. And he was drinking himself into an early grave. "Look at yourself, Maurice. Look in the mirror and tell me what you see. You're becoming a drunk!"

"Then give me a divorce!" he had raged.

"Never!" Her eyes had blazed with the fury of determination. He knew why. They had already argued this point time and time again. She was committed, and once committed to this marriage she did not intend to see it collapse in ruins. If they could not keep up the pretense of respectability, at least they would not be exposed to a public scandal in a divorce court. Besides, there were certain distinct social advantages to being the wife of Maurice Stewart. Drunk or sober, he was still the board chairman of Stewart Motors and the father of their children. "Divorce you? I'll never give you that satisfaction!" With that, she had stormed out and slammed the door.

He stared at the bourbon, sensing its aroma and beckoning warmth. He caressed the cold beer stein lovingly with his hand.

"Maurice?"

Her voice was near and warm, behind him. The male talk ceased. Jerry the bartender stared openmouthed, not knowing quite what to do about the presence of a woman in his saloon. Maurice turned on the stool and looked into the face of Helen DeMare.

The years had been kind to her. She had matured superbly, retaining a youthful glow of face and skin. He had seen her pictures in the magazines from time to time as her stage career blossomed. There had been talk of Helen DeMare going into the silent films, talk of her love affairs and break-ups. But the pictures had not done her justice, and the words did not convey the magnetism of the woman who now stood smiling at him in the afternoon depths of Jerry's Saloon.

"Helen . . ."

"You big devil. Haven't changed a bit." She touched his shoulder with a gloved hand, kissed him lightly on the cheek. She wore a pinch-waisted gown at ankle length, a bouffant hairdo, and a large picture hat perched on the side of her head and filled with egret feathers. She smiled, and her beauty kindled his response from deep inside.

"How did you know I was here?"

"I finally got up my courage and came back to Fall River, to visit friends. I've been shopping, and just happened to see you come in here. It took me awhile to get up the grit to follow you, but here I am."

"Helen, my God, you look wonderful."

She smiled and looked down at the glasses on the bar. "Well, are you going to drink them?"

He turned, hesitated, licked his lips. The decision was his. With a flash of resolve, he made it. "I don't think I will." He pushed a couple of dollar bills toward Jerry, slid off the stool, and took Helen by the arm. "Let's get the hell out of here. We've got a lot of talking to do."

Jerry the bartender looked at the untouched liquor and smiled. With a flourish, he picked up the glasses and poured them into the sink.

"She's been waiting to see you for over an hour, Mr. Stewart." The secretary wore an expression of disapproval. "I tried to refer her to somebody else, Van Harrison or maybe young Nathan in engineering. But she insisted on talking to you. Said it was personal and private."

Maurice peeked into the outer office. A bosomy blond with a doll-like face sat rigidly in the chair. She wore a lavender ensemble and clutched a matching parasol. "Never saw her in my life," he grumbled. "Oh, well, tell her to go into my office. I'll be there in a moment."

The secretary conveyed the message to the girl. She watched with distaste as the blond stood up, gave her head a saucy toss, and sauntered into the board chairman's office, undulating her bottom and trailing expensive perfume. The door closed. Two minutes passed. The secretary heard Mr. Stewart enter the office from his side door. There was an interval of quiet.

Three more minutes went by.

Suddenly the quiet of the office was broken by her employer's incredulous voice, shouting: "He *what*? He *stole the plans from Henry Ford*!?"

It was a living nightmare, the most humiliating task Maurice Stewart could imagine having to perform. Flanked by two lawyers, Isaiah, Van Harrison, and a contrite Colby Malcolm, he stood before the desk of Henry Ford groping for words to explain what had been done.

"Mr. Ford, we don't do business that way. Competition is competition, but this"—he shot a dark glance at Colby, who winced and hung his head—"is outright thievery, and I am prepared to make amends."

Ford's lean face showed no expression. His eyes bore into Maurice's. He had no company representatives with him, not even a secretary. Beyond his plain wood-paneled office the busy Dearborn plant of Ford Motor Company hummed and clanked, turning out Model T's in an endless stream. To the astonishment of the entire nation, the man had just announced a guaranteed five-dollar daily minimum wage for his workmen, and dropped the price of Everyman's car to five hundred fifty dollars. A spasm had gone through the automobile industry. In Maurice's plant, Tom Moneypenny had gasped, "The feller's insane. I tell you, he's a menace!"

And now, Maurice Stewart stood at the mercy of this menace, admitting that his own advertising and marketing director—hell, his own cousin!—had filched the chassis design for the new Silver Stewart from Henry Ford's personal files. Coming to this point of confrontation had been an ordeal. After paying the tart named Tulip five hundred dollars for her information, Maurice had suffered a week of agonies. The bombshell struck at the vitals of things. He now confronted the certainty of losing his reputation for business integrity, possibly a fortune in indemnity, even losing Stewart Motors itself. There had been long and noisy scenes with the top staff, a painful standoff with Colby Malcolm—who had confessed all and tendered his resignation this very day—and the added strain of remaining, through it all, personally sober.

"All I can tell you, Mr. Ford, is that I am here to express

my complete apology and my intention to see that things are set to rights, whatever the cost to Stewart Motors."

Henry Ford blinked. He sat back in his chair. To Maurice's surprise, the lean face lifted in a smile. Ford chuckled softly. There was a glint in his eye. Maurice thought: The hunter moves in for the kill.

"Mr. Stewart," Ford said, "it's nice of you to visit me like this. We always like to have company here at the factory, even from our competitors. It shows that we must be doing something right." The smile persisted as he gazed at Maurice and drummed his fingers lightly on the desk. "As for any plans being stolen from this office, I just don't know what you're talking about."

"But your security cabinet. It was right . . ." Maurice pointed to where Colby had told him the cabinet was located. There was no cabinet there. He glanced at Colby, who looked confused.

Ford shook his head. "My eyesight's not what it used to be. But I sure don't see any security cabinet."

It was flustering. Isaiah and Van glared at Colby. Maurice stammered more apologies. The lawyers shifted on their feet. Ford stood up. "Now, if you don't mind, gentlemen . . ." They all shook hands, including Colby. They filed out, with Isaiah in the lead. Maurice, perplexed, turned to go. Ford plucked at his sleeve. "A moment, Mr. Stewart."

The others were gone. The office door closed softly. Henry Ford rummaged in his desk drawer and drew out a box of cigars. "Care for a stogie?" Maurice, still uncomfortable, accepted a cigar and lit it.

"Never did like those plans," Ford said whimsically.

The cigar almost dropped out of Maurice's mouth. "Then there *was* . . ."

"Some of my associates were right fond of them, though," Ford continued, "so I was stuck in the middle. It was like having an old hay baler in the barn; you don't want to keep it and you don't want to throw it away." Ford sat down in his chair again and put his feet up on the desk. Maurice saw a hole worn in the sole of one shoe. The man was a compelling mixture of commoner and powerful intellect. Even the office in which they talked, the heart of Ford Motor Co., was all utility and devoid of ostentation.

"I still don't understand," Maurice said.

"Well, let's just say that there are those right here in my own organization who still don't believe in the Model T. They want us to go on to grander things. They don't like the idea of dropping prices instead of raising them, and paying the help a living wage, and producing a product for the betterment of the common man. But it's the common man who holds the consumer power of this country, Mr. Stewart. My theory, right or wrong, is that if you produce for him a machine that he can afford to buy, that he finds useful—you can jack up the Model T, hitch a drivebelt to the back wheel, and run a sawmill with it—and that makes his life better, then he's going to tell his friends and neighbors to buy that product, too. He'll be loyal, and pass that loyalty on to his children and grandchildren."

"But what's that got to do with?..."

"Excuse me for rambling." The feet came down. Ford leaned on his elbows and looked intently at Maurice. "Those plans were part of the bigger ideas for Ford. That's why they were drawn. It was to be a bigger car, a higher-priced car. And I didn't like it one damn bit. I was not going to abandon the Model T for anything such as that. In the first place, while it had a good chassis design we just don't have the power plant to run it. And by the time we developed a stronger power plant, we'd be up to our ears in expenses, fragmenting our Model T production program and losing sight of who and what this company stands for. So actually, I was delighted when one of my competitors came along and took it off my hands. I was especially delighted that it was Stewart Motors, because I've known for months that you were thinking about coming up with a smaller car in direct competition with me. When you produced the new Silver Stewart instead, hell, I recognized our work right away. It forced you to make a commitment to a bigger car, which suits me just fine. It means from now on you're competing with the boys over at Buick and Oldsmobile, not me. Your man unintentionally did me a favor, and I'm much obliged."

Maurice grinned broadly. "Well, I'll be damned."

Ford stood up and escorted him to the door. "Incidentally, I really appreciate your honesty. That was a brave and noble thing you did a few minutes ago. I could have taken you to the cleaners."

"Yes, and I expected you to do just that."

"Under other circumstances, I wouldn't hesitate."

"I know."

"As for that fellow who filched the plans, I wouldn't be too hard with him, if I were you."

"Why not?"

"You can't buy loyalty like that. A man who'll steal for you, under those circumstances, is pretty rare. I'd give that a little thought before I sacked him."

They shook hands at the door.

"I always knew Stewarts had good stuff in 'em," Henry Ford said.

Maurice walked out into the sunshine of Dearborn. His step was light, the day was suddenly beautiful, and it was great to be alive. The others eyed him guardedly as he joined them in the parking lot. "Let's get back to Fall River, boys. We've got production quotas to meet." He slid into the driver's seat of his Silver Stewart and touched the new electric starter. Isaiah's great engine roared to life. As the others turned to their cars, he rolled down his window and poked his head out. "By the way, Colby . . ."

"Yes, sir?" The big man's somber face was a study in chagrin.

"You've got your job back. And a bonus."

Maurice laughed, shifted into gear, and roared away.

That night, in spasms of pure joy, he made love to Helen DeMare.

No one could say definitely when the New York *Enterprise* surged into the first rank of American newspapers. Those personally involved in journalism, and notably Hope Stewart Langden's competitors, saw the changes begin soon after the sinking of the *Titanic*. Suddenly the newspaper became more aggressive and editorially demanding. It pushed for reforms in safety measures at sea, demanded full disclosures of the *Titanic* tragedy, brooked no political foot-dragging.

But this was only the start. In months to come, Hope Langden went after fresh causes with a vengeance which unsettled the male-dominated fraternity of rival publishers. Reporters for the *Enterprise* dug into milk scandals, white slave traffic, and the meatpacking industry. They ferreted out payoffs in Big Oil and cronyism between Washington and Big Steel. The newspaper's expanding readership was given a steady diet of exposés about child labor, the emerging role of women in public affairs, and the hard lot of immigrant workers in the coal fields.

Hope put in sixteen-hour days, rode herd on her staff, and hired and fired in a constant quest for excellence. Fat John Korpan, the best street reporter in New York, was elevated to city editor; Jack Slade, the tough, longtime managing editor, became Hope's associate publisher. "I want people at the top who know the guts of this town and this newspaper," she declared.

The source of all this energy was apparent to all. They discussed it openly in saloons neighboring the *Enterprise* and in card rooms where reporters and deskmen frittered away hard-earned pay at endless games of stud poker.

"She grieves for Langden. No question about it. The woman's driven."

"I'll never understand it. A fine-looking female like that, living with a ghost."

"Hope lives for both of them. Fat John says she feels guilty for not going down with Langden on the *Titanic*."

"What about Silas Proctor? It's no secret how he feels. The man would go to the moon for Hope Langden."

"Faw! What's he got to offer?"

"Handsome devil. All man."

"Union organizer. Proctor's got no class."

"Don't be too sure about that, Bucko. I hear Proctor's determined to run for Congress this fall. He says the only chance the working man's got is to have a voice on Capitol Hill. And he's got the blue collar vote in his pocket, I'll tell you that. Hell of a good speaker, too."

"A gift of gab won't win the heart of Hope Langden."

"You want to lay a little wager on that?"

"Why don't you guys stop gossiping and play poker. How many cards?"

"Two."

"Here they come, down and dirty..."

Hope Langden heard the whispers and ignored them. Let the louts speculate all they wished; a woman had a right to be single and undominated by any man. For all the charms of Silas Proctor, and they were considerable, she was not going to be arm-twisted into anything.

But time passed. The *Enterprise* was reshaped into its new model. Life went by. Hope whiled away her evenings at the office or carting home piles of unfinished paperwork. The telephone rang, every evening at nine. And it was Silas again, always Silas.

"How are you?"

"Fine. I'm... getting some work done."

"Do you need anything?"

"No. Nothing."

"How about dinner? Have you had dinner?"

"Yes. Thank you."

"Tomorrow, then. Will you dine with me tomorrow?"

"I'm afraid not."

"Next day? Next week? Next month?"

"No. No. No."

He laughed. She laughed too, in spite of herself. "Are you really going to run for Congress?"

"Yes. Will the *Enterprise* back me editorially?"

"I'm already committed to the incumbent Ned Frye. He's a good man."

"Just thought I'd ask." A pause. "Hope..."

"No, Silas."

"I'll call you again tomorrow."

She hung up.

The hot summer waned. The election campaigning began. It was low key at first. She watched closely, insisting that *Enterprise* reporters cover all the candidates fairly and evenly. The incumbent congressman for the Fourth District, Frye, invited her to dinner. "I'm depending on your support, Hope. We can't let labor get into the House. It would be unconscionable."

Hope's eyes widened. "How can you say that, Ned? I didn't know you felt so strongly on the subject."

"Well, now you know. I put my cards on the table. This race is going to get dirty; mark my words."

She went home late, troubled. A card from the butler lay on her nightstand.

Mr. Proctor called at nine o'clock.

The race did get nasty. Silas Proctor became the target of a smear campaign. He was accused of being the tool of anarchist forces threatening to destroy free enterprise and American capitalism. Pictures of Ned Frye were adorned with Old Glory. Vote For a Patriot: Frye, the posters read.

A Proctor rally was scheduled in the Tenderloin District. Hope summoned Fat John Korpan to escort her there. "I want to see things for myself," she said.

It was a large rally, by torchlight. Silas had lost none of his magnetism. He stood shaking his fist, exhorting the working man to wield his most powerful weapon against the capitalist exploiters: his vote. The crowd responded with fervor, cheering his name. Twenty minutes after the speech had begun, police whistles blasted and a blue phalanx came charging into the square. Fat John Korpan hurled his bulk into the crowd, clearing a path for Hope. Swinging clubs thudded against heads and bodies.

"Unbelievable," she said. "It's the coal fields all over again, but this time in New York City!"

She found Silas the next day, lying in a hospital bed. His great head was swathed in bandage. The sight of him, suddenly injured and vulnerable, caused an inner response for which she was not prepared.

Hope Langden's eyes brimmed. "What did they do to you?"

He smiled. "Frye's people warned me to pull out of the race. I refused."

"But why this?"

"You were there. They said we were unlawfully assembled."

Hope called in her personal physician. The examination disclosed a hairline skull fracture and concussion. Silas was moved to a private room, attended by full-time nurses.

In the editorial offices of the *Enterprise*, Hope Langden's announcement fell like a thunderclap.

"Say that again!" exclaimed Jack Slade.

"We are withdrawing our support from Ned Frye and giving it to Silas Proctor."

Two weeks later, riding the crest of an unprecedented blue collar vote in the Tenderloin and neighboring districts, labor oganizer Silas Proctor scored a surprise upset victory over the entrenched incumbent Ned Frye for Congress of the United States. The victor, smiling and leaning on a cane, his head still bandaged, received a tumultuous ovation at a mass rally of supporters.

He telephoned at nine, as usual.

"Will you have dinner with me?"

"Yes."

"Today? Tomorrow? Next week?"

"Yes. Yes. Yes."

Silence. Then: "You *will*?"

"After all, you are a congressman now, and . . ."

It was as if some great inner blockage had been released. They would be friends, she resolved, and nothing more. Nothing beyond that. But suddenly, as she waited for Silas to arrive to take her to dinner, Hope Stewart Langden was as excited as a young woman going out on her first date.

Later, she would remember the evening as a whirl of fresh

impressions. He brought her flowers; he was impeccably dressed in a tasteful dark suit and tie, complete with walking stick; he drove a new Winton town car. They dined at the Waldorf. Well-wishers kept dropping by the table to greet them. Champagne corks popped. Then, giddy from wine and celebration, they took a carriage ride through Central Park. He deposited her in the foyer of her town house at 1:00 A.M., brushed his lips to her hand, and departed.

In the days and weeks that followed, they were out regularly together, strolling, horseback riding, bicycling. They motored up the Hudson to meet some of Howard's old friends. Silas's social composure surprised her, for he had the knack for convivial talk and popular appeal. "A lovely time," their hostess murmured as they departed. "Hope, please do bring Silas back again." It was sincere.

On one of their walks, he talked about children. It had always been his wish, Silas said, to have children. "But I always felt that I should be older, more mature. Children are a great responsibility. They need love and caring; and I think to bring them up properly, we need to have our own feet on the ground. Don't you agree?" The gentle warmth of his words surprised her. This big, muscular man, who reminded her of a vagabond king, had a wistful quality that belied his appearance.

"Yes," she said. "Yes, I agree."

She went home that night with butterflies in her stomach, but refused to acknowledge why.

And then it was time for him to leave for Washington to prepare to take his seat in Congress. The thought of being separated lay heavily upon her mind. Already, of course, she was planning to immerse herself in work. That was always an appropriate therapy; indeed, it had helped to keep Silas out of her mind once before.

"You can go with me, you know," he said quietly.

"With you?"

"To Washington. As my wife."

"Silas, I . . ."

"Don't say anything right now. Think about it. There's no rush."

Time went by. The subject was not mentioned again. Four days later he stood on the platform at Grand Central Station, holding his luggage. "Well," he said, "it's time to go."

They embraced in a cloud of gushing steam. The power of his arms took her breath away. The parting brought an ache to her heart. He stepped back, smiled, and touched the brim of his hat. "Write to me," he said.

He climbed the steps of the Pullman car and was gone.

"It's out of the question, my dear," an old friend said that evening. "After all, what is he? A common labor organizer. Oh, handsome as the devil, I'll grant you. I don't mind saying that women have certainly begun to notice Silas Proctor since he ran for Congress. But you would be stepping out of your class. I mean, he's so far beneath you. Hope Stewart Langden and Silas Proctor. Oh, my..."

Long after midnight, Hope lay in bed staring up into the darkness. Voices whispered in her mind, from out of the past.

"Be yourself," Aunt Francesca had told her. *"Make your own decisions, and blast convention. It is the only way."*

"It is my hope that you will marry again," Howard had said on the slanting deck of the *Titanic, "have a fine, strong son and name him Howard Langden, after me."*

"It is out of the question, my dear . . . out of the question, my dear . . . out of the question . . ."

"Don't say anything right now. There's no rush . . ."

Three weeks later, with no word to anyone, Hope took the train to Washington. She checked into the Willard Hotel and, the following day, sat in the press gallery of the House of Representatives listening to the debate. The freshman congressman from New York, the Honorable Silas Proctor, gave a low-key but effective speech on behalf of tariffs in the fur trade. Tall, handsome, and commanding, he made his points with such skill that three members of the House changed their votes. The bill lost anyhow. Congressman Proctor, engrossed, did not look up at the gallery.

That evening the congressman dined alone, as was his habit, at a table by the window of his hotel dining room. He was reading the evening newspaper, which contained a small paragraph about his speech on fur tariffs.

"Congressman Proctor?" Hope stood in shadow slightly behind him, hands clasped tightly to help calm the pounding of her heart.

The handsome head lifted. He looked around and half rose from his chair. Hope smiled and stepped into the light.

His mouth dropped open. He seemed momentarily unable to speak.

"I'd like very much to have children too," Hope said.

* * *

"Clear for takeoff! Get those men off the flight platform!" Van Harrison Stewart squinted into the sunlight across the converted battle cruiser *Natchez*. A twenty-knot breeze spanked the prow. But the cruiser no longer resembled a cruiser. Her decks had been torn out and rebuilt, the bridge and superstructure altered, and a great platform of wooden beams and steel fitted onto the ship, jutted slightly forward of the bow. Now the morning was filled with the clatter of engines and whirring propeller noises from the two-winged flying machine poised on the platform. Seated in twin cockpits were a frightened Navy lieutenant, junior grade, and behind him— watching Van through aviator's goggles—twenty-five-year-old Nathan Stewart.

A large crowd of naval officers watched from the bridge. Enlisted men massed upon the afterdeck. A dubious Navy captain joined Van at his post beside the leading edge of the makeshift platform. "Are you ready, Mr. Stewart?"

"Yes, sir. We're ready."

"I still say it's a damn fool thing to try. You fliers seem to have a death wish. But go to it."

Van grinned. "Aye, aye, sir." He thrust his hand into the air, waited for Nathan's signal of response, and abruptly dropped his arm.

Nathan opened the throttle. The engine noise became a roar, causing an intense vibration of the cloth-covered fuselage. Nathan signaled thumbs up. Two sailors darted forward and yanked chocks from beneath the front wheels. The plane rolled forward along the platform, picking up speed. Wind from the propeller blew upon the crowd of sailors, causing them instinctively to shield their eyes and turn away.

Van watched the moving airplane, fists clenched. He heard himself shouting, "Go! Go!" The momentum increased. The frail craft rushed toward the lip of the platform and seemingly certain disaster. It hurtled off the platform, sank toward the glistening sea, steadied, wobbled, and slowly began to rise.

Cheers broke out on the deck of the *Natchez*.

Engine noise throbbing in his ears, Nathan Stewart felt the familiar lift of flight. The old elation surged over him as the aircraft soared skyward, its propeller blast sweeping his goggled face. Below, the sea was a sparkling sweep of sunlit blue. Reaching forward from his cockpit he poked the shoulder of young Lieutenant Tasker, who glanced back at him with a white-faced grin. Nathan jerked his thumb upward and Tasker replied with a vigorous nod that he clearly did not feel.

Poor devil, Nathan thought. The worst is yet to come.

Easing down his left rudder while sliding the control stick to the side, he put the Wright biplane into a banking turn and flew slowly back over the *Natchez*. The cruiser looked small in the distance as it began its own swing into the wind, laying a plume of coal smoke and cutting a white wake. What a strange-looking vessel she was, Nathan thought, but how functionally beautiful. Cousin Ward and his shipwrights in Boston had done a splendid job reconstructing the *Natchez* in a very short time. As he brought the plane back to level flight, Nathan remembered with a smile Ward's astonished reaction when he and Van had first presented the idea: "An *airplane carrier*! Big enough for takeoffs and landings? You're out of your minds!"

And so Van, the former Navy lieutenant commander with powerful Washington contacts and a brilliant technical mind, had joined Nathan and Ward Stewart in Boston for seven months of intensive labor, translating blueprints into reality under the eyes of doubting naval engineers who were plainly aghast to see such liberties taken with a capital ship, contract or no contract. The team had done well. Now it was up to him to prove that ships and planes were made for each other. But just before takeoff, even the usually daredevil Cousin Van had suffered a twinge of doubt.

"Take off and land on a ship at sea? It's not too late to back out, Nathan."

"The takeoff is nothing new, Van," he had replied, masking his own nervous tension. "Eugene Ely did it three years ago in a Curtiss biplane. But we can't always depend on a ship being close enough to shore for a normal landing. And coming down on pontoons presents problems of landing gear design. It's also time-consuming hoisting the aircraft back out of water. Besides, I want to do this in a Wright plane. I want to do it in Wilbur's memory..."

In Wilbur's memory. One year ago, on May 30, 1912, his friend Wilbur Wright had died in Dayton, Ohio. Nathan drew back on the stick and gained altitude, thinking how much Orville and Wilbur had meant to him, and how their dream had charted the direction of his own life. Even now he could look back eight years and sense the extraordinary elation of his own first flight alone in the Whopper Flying Machine. Lying prone amidships, not sitting upright in a cockpit as they did today, and operating rudder and ailerons by instinct, he had experienced that unbelievable sensation of being one with the birds. After that, their invention still ignored at home, the Wrights had taken him abroad, to Berlin and Paris; and it was Nathan who did much of the demonstration flying which thrilled crowds across Europe and at last brought the brothers from Ohio the fame so long denied them.

It was time. He made his last circle over the *Natchez*, lining up for his approach. How small the ship appeared from up here!—a floating postage stamp on a sea of infinite blue. The ocean merged into a horizon softened by heat haze. Nathan gave the young Navy pilot in the front cockpit another reassuring pat on the shoulder, lined up with the platform, and gradually settled the Wright machine along its glidepath. As the wind sang in the wire rigging, he could almost imagine the quiet voice of Wilbur Wright murmuring instructions. "Gently, boy, gently. You're flying, not wrestling. Use your fingertips on that control. Feel your way down, floating like a thistle. Gently, gently..."

The biplane settled. The *Natchez* gradually enlarged. The image of the complex landing mechanism came to his mind: the big hook, implanted in the rear of the fuselage, the cables stretched across the ship's landing platform, ready to be sprung up manually in the path of the hook. They had fashioned it all in the shipyard at Boston, toiling through the night to make final adjustments. Would it work? Would it hold?

"Gently, boy. Gently. Down. Down. Down..."

The prow of the *Natchez* began to loom massively in front of him. The ship rocked gently with the action of the sea. The wings of the biplane wobbled as Nathan fingertipped the controls. Suddenly he sensed the wind, gusting and tearing at the wing wires as if to blow him off course. His eyes stared through the goggles; his face broke into a sweat. The great steel ship grew larger and larger. He could pick out broken paint spots on the hull, see the spikes in the timbers of the platform, see Van Harrison Stewart facing him in a half crouch, mouth open, arms outstretched and moving up and down with the motion of his own wings. And beyond Van, the sailors of the *Natchez* massed along upper decks and lined ladders and bulkheads. The prow flashed beneath him. The platform came up. The right wing tipped. He drew the control stick all the way back and switched off the engine. His wheels struck the platform with a teeth-rattling jar. The plane hurtled forward. He was conscious of a mighty metallic grinding. Abruptly a mighty hand seemed to grab the tail of the aircraft and bring it to a head-snapping halt.

A mighty human roar erupted over the *Natchez* as the ship's company welcomed its two fliers home.

XVII

Willow lay drenched in sweat. For two days she had suffered the ravages of fever. The doctors came, checked her pulse, felt her brow, and placed stethoscopes to her pregnant abdomen. They shook their heads and advised aspirin and plenty of liquids. "It is the malaria, Mr. Stewart. As for the baby's prognosis, we cannot say." They went away again.

He sat in the darkening room beside the bed, watching her face. The pale features were implanted upon his mind, each line and plane.

"We will make it, love," he said. "You'll see."

The Barbados midwife Marjory Crown came into the room with worry in her eyes. "Is there any change?"

Casey shook his head. "No change."

"You must eat something," she said. "I shall cook it for you. I brought groceries from the store. Some ham, some tea, some beans and carrots."

"I'm not hungry, Marjory."

"I fix it anyhow. You must eat."

And so she fixed it. And, reluctantly, he ate. It was nearly midnight when Blanchet arrived.

"I brought you a bottle of wine, *mon ami*. We will drink, eh?"

"You know I no longer drink, Blanchet."

"Well, then, I will drink for both of us."

Casey watched the Frenchman remove the cork from the bottle and pour the red wine into a glass. How old Blanchet had become, his hair shot through with gray, his face deeply seamed, his shoulders stooped. He wondered if he also looked that old. He was an aging man with a young wife he

381

adored, a young woman more than eight months pregnant and ill with malaria.

"I was thinking, Blanchet..."

"Yes?"

"Has it really been seventeen years since Lollie left us?"

Blanchet drank wine and put down his glass. "Indeed it has been, my friend. Seventeen years."

Leaning toward the bed, Casey dampened a towel and placed it upon Willow's forehead. The lamplight fell softly over her features. "We both want this baby very much, Blanchet," he said.

"I know."

"She has lost two already. A little boy and a little girl."

"It is God's will."

"Surely God would not be so cruel."

Blanchet shook his head gravely and drank more wine. "The older I get the less I am inclined to discuss such things. Death comes to us all in time." He lit a cigarette. "Life is cruel."

Willow stirred. Her eyes fluttered and opened. Sweat bathed her face, which glistened in the lamplight. "Casey?" she said.

"I'm here, my darling."

"Casey, will I die?"

He glanced at Blanchet, busied himself with the towel and basin of cold water, and dabbed at her face with it. "You are not going to die and neither is the baby. I promise you that. The doctors are very optimistic."

"No, they're not. I heard them."

"You will not die. I will not let you die. Or the baby either."

She smiled weakly. "I love you, Casey."

"And I love you."

She slept again. The midwife returned. "You men must leave us alone for a few minutes." Casey and Blanchet went out onto the screened veranda. They smoked and stared into the night. Below, the great Canal shimmered in the moonlight.

"I can't believe that it's all over," Casey said.

"The construction, you mean?"

"Yes, the construction."

"I can't believe it either. But then, I've been at this much longer than you, *mon ami*."

They were silent again.

"Everything has come together splendidly," Blanchet said, looking at the Canal.

And indeed it had, Casey thought. What was it Goethals had said in response to the journalist's question about the secret of success? Oh, yes: "The pride everyone feels in the work." The pride of completion would be more apt. Casey himself had felt it in rising stages, first with the completion of the great locks at Pedro Miguel and Miraflores, and then with the final shovelful of earth dug from the Culebra Cut at forty feet above sea level, and then with the slow rise of water in Gatun Lake, and finally—relentlessly, stage by stage—the filling of the whole Canal to a level of readiness.

"It looks like it's always been there," he said.

There was an unbelievable finality to it all. By the thousands, hands were paid off and engineers and technicians discharged. Every outbound steamer to the States was loaded. The cleanup crews took charge. Houses and buildings were dismantled. Whole villages simply disappeared as if struck from a stage set. Now it was August 1, 1914. In two more days, the first oceangoing vessel, the cement boat *Cristobal*, was due to be locked through from sea to sea. He considered the irony of that.

"We have spent more than three hundred fifty million dollars in ten years and lost five thousand six hundred lives. Add the French deaths to that and you've got five hundred lives for every mile of the Canal. And the first vessel to be locked through is a damned cement boat."

"More will come," Blanchet said. "Many more will come."

"And now Willow and the baby fight for their lives."

"You're still torturing yourself."

Casey sighed. "I've expected too much from life, Blanchet. Already I've had more to be grateful for than any ten ordinary men. Who could have imagined that an old reprobate like me would have such a love in his life? She has enriched me far beyond my worth. But having this baby has been so important to both of us. She was doing well until this damned malaria."

He slept fitfully that night on a cot beside her bed. The August heat was even more intense than usual. He dreamed of Gorgas and his mosquito brigades, and how they had waged seven years of intense warfare against the anopheles mosquito. In the dream, it was Casey who fought the mosquitoes, monstrous things whirring and spinning around the room over Willow's bed. He doused them with kerosene and beat at them with brooms, and still they came on, descending lower and lower to where she lay. If one touched her, she would die . . .

Something touched his shoulder. A voice said, "Mr. Casey, wake up!" He opened his eyes and saw the midwife standing over him. "She has started going into labor."

The doctor arrived at dawn. Casey and Blanchet paced the parlor. The sun burst over the eastern horizon, beating down on Panama like a great solar furnace. Out beyond them, and beyond the shining new waterway, the jungle steeped and steamed. Beneath the great canopy of the rain forest, creatures crept and crawled and walked and flew, creatures that were microscopic and gigantic, aggressive and passive.

The doctor was a pensive Englishman with pale blue eyes in a white round face. His manner was cordially noncommittal. He placed his hand on Casey's shoulder. "We can't be sure, Mr. Stewart. We'll do all we can. But I suggest that if she has any next of kin, they be summoned."

"Would it help if we took her to the hospital?"

"I wouldn't recommend moving her at this time."

Dr. Gorgas came. He looked at he patient, felt her abdomen. "The baby is kicking nicely," he said, "but the fever is too high."

"How can we bring down the fever?"

"Ice," the English doctor said.

Blanchet brought ice. They packed it around her body in a blanket. She shivered so severely that her teeth chattered. "C-C-Casey, what are they d-d-doing to me?" And in between, she thrashed with the pains of labor.

It was late afternoon when Arnold Luray arrived. He came up the walk at his labored, swinging gait, using two heavy canes. The shattered legs were braced in steel and the once-muscled body reduced to skin and bones. He was bald except for a fringe of white hair, tufting about the ears.

He looked at Casey as one would inspect a rat. "I have come to see my daughter."

Luray stumped into the bedroom and stood over her, tightlipped and dour. She opened her eyes and smiled. "Father." They had not spoken for years. His mouth worked but no sound came out. He turned and labored back to the parlor.

"She will die?" he said.

Casey shook his head. "She will not die."

"You've done this to her," Luray said. "And you did this to me."

"You're insane," Casey said. His voice was toneless.

Luray's eyes had a strange glitter. He straightened himself proudly on the canes. "You caused this injury to me, caused me to lose my Army career, took my daughter away, and now you're killing her. What more do you want?"

"I want you to see reality," Casey said.

"Reality?" Luray offered a hollow laugh. "What is reality?"

"You caused your own injury. You tried to entrap your daughter into a life of your making. It was like entrapping a bird. She refused, and came to me. Oh, I understand more than you think I do, Luray. I understand her attraction for me, an older man. I have you to thank for that too, as a kind of surrogate father. But I never tried to be a father to Willow. The most important thing in my life is that Willow loves me. I wish . . . I even wish that we could be friends, you and me." He put out his hand. "Past is past, Luray. Let's bury it with all the other dead. You need your daughter. You need me. You need a grandchild."

Luray looked at the hand. Conflicting emotions flicked across his face. Casey kept his hand outstretched. In the corner, the clock ticked.

Blanchet muttered, "Take the man's hand, Luray. You may never get another chance."

"I have suffered the torment of the damned," Luray said. He seemed to sag on the canes. "It is not the physical agony I've minded so much, it's the mental."

"We've all suffered. It's time to stop."

Luray stiffened his back again. He did not speak further. He turned and walked out of the house and down the walkway to his waiting automobile. A driver opened the back door and he got in. The doors slammed, the driver took his place behind the wheel, and drove away.

The hours passed. She worsened. By midnight, her fever was raging again and the labor pains continued at a steady rate. There was a look of death upon her, a hollowness of the eyes and a pinching of the nose and face. He had seen that look before and dreaded it. Willow, he thought; Willow, don't leave me.

He knelt at the side of the bed and for the first time in his life, Casey Stewart silently prayed.

Lord, I don't know if you're up there, he prayed. *I don't know if you even exist. But if you do, if you are up there and you do exist, please hear me. I'm worthless, as worthless as the clay of the Cucaracha. If I die tonight, nothing will be changed. But I ask you, Lord, please don't take her away. I ask you, Lord, to spare Willow and spare our baby.* He opened his eyes and looked at her in the lamplight. A fresh spasm of labor pain struck and she writhed with it. The sweat poured from her face and body and saturated the bedclothes. *That's all I have to say, Lord. Amen.*

He sat beside her for the rest of the night. He gave her water, bathed her face with a damp cloth, listened to her labored breathing, and watched. Toward morning, he fell asleep in the chair.

Someone spoke his name. It was daylight again. He sat half awake, conscious of the sunlight in his eyes. He yawned, stretched, and looked at Willow. Her eyes were open and watching him. She sat half erect in the bed. She smiled. She said, "Casey?"

"Willow!"

"You shouldn't try to sleep in a chair like that. You'll get a crick in your back."

He jumped to his feet. "Willow, you're awake!"

"Yes."

"You're all right, you're awake."

"Well"—the pain hit her again—"I'm about to have our baby. But I'm awake."

"Oh, my God," he said. He rushed around the room. "Jesus, this is great!" He went to her, felt her forehead. Cool. "It's cool. The fever's broken. You're cool!"

"Casey, where is Marjory?"

"I'll get her. Wait right there. I'll get Marjory." He hurried from the room, shouting, "Marjory! Marjory!"

The midwife appeared, wearing a gown and slippers. "Yes?"

"Marjory, we're going to have a baby. Willow's all right, and we're going to have a baby! She needs you! She needs you right now!"

He pushed the midwife into the room. There was a great whooping and laughing. Blanchet came in, sleep-rumpled and alarmed. "What is it?"

"She's okay! She's going to be okay!"

The men were banished from the room. Marjory Crown took charge. Casey paced, smoked, paced. Blanchet fell into a chair and slept for an hour. When he awoke, Casey was still pacing.

"Really, *mon ami*, don't you think we ought to?..."

Casey stopped pacing. From behind the closed door came the sound of a sharp slap, followed by a baby's cry. Five minutes later Marjory Crown came out of the bedroom.

"Mr. Stewart, you have a fine son!"

He hurried past her into the room and was greeted by Willow's wan smile from the bed. Beside her lay a wiggling form bundled in a light coverlet. He leaned over and kissed her. "Congratulations, Mrs. Stewart."

"What shall we name your son?" she whispered.

"Stephen Luray Stewart," he said.

"Stephen?"

"From my grandfather, one of the true pioneers of this family."

"All right, then"—she pushed aside a corner of the coverlet and exposed a tiny, puckered face still flushed from the rigors of birth—"...Stephen."

The morning passed into afternoon. Happiness filled the house overlooking the Canal. At three o'clock, a sound brought Casey bolting from his chair.

"What is it, *mon ami*?"

"A boat whistle! Blanchet, that's a boat whistle!"

He rushed to the window and looked out upon the waterway. She came around a bend in the Canal, stubby and ugly and old, her sides streaked with rust and her superstructure badly in need of paint. Grabbing binoculars, Casey focused on the name at the bow. It was the cement boat *Cristobal*, making her maiden journey from ocean to ocean.

"Willow. Willow, you've got to see this! Look, darling." He got her up from the bed and walked her to a chair by the window. The four of them, Casey and Willow, Blanchet and Marjory Crown, waved eagerly at the vessel and were rewarded with a series of whistle blasts that echoed off the surrounding hills.

"She's a rustbucket and ready for the scrap heap. But she's beautiful!"

The *Cristobal* moved along on a steady beat of engines and blasts of whistle. The ringing telephone kept Casey informed of her progress, down through the final locking and departure from the port at Panama City. They celebrated with champagne and a chicken supper.

It was nightfall when Arnold Luray returned. They fell silent as the car door slammed and the sound of his canes came thumping up to the door. Blanchet answered the knock. Luray made his entrance gravely, removing his hat as he stood in the doorway of the dining room. From behind him, the driver appeared holding a spray of fresh flowers.

"May I see my grandson?"

"You certainly may, Father." Willow stood up in her robe and walked weakly toward him. Blanchet rose to steady her, but Casey motioned him to sit down. Willow put her arms around Luray and held on while he patted her clumsily on the shoulder.

"Well, well, well," he said. "Here, now, let's not have tears."

"I'll cry if I want to." She sniffed.

Casey stood up and pulled his chair back from the table. "Please. Sit here, Mr. Luray."

"Thank you, Mr. Stewart." The canes thumped on the dining room floor as he made his way to the chair and sat down.

They brought the baby and placed him in a basket by the old man's side. Blanchet poured a glass of wine and pushed it across the table. Luray picked up the glass in the manner of a toast. "To my grandson. By the way, what is his name?"

"Stephen Luray Stewart," Willow said.

"Stephen Luray Stewart. A splendid name." He drank off the wine with a flourish. "A very splendid name indeed."

They talked amiably for an hour. The telephone rang again. Blanchet answered. He came back looking pale.

"What is it, Blanchet? What's wrong?"

"It's war," he said quietly.

"War?"

"The Germans have declared war in Europe."

Casey sat back in his chair in disbelief.

"Oh, my God," he said.

Three days later a telegram arrived designating Casey Stewart as the first superintendent of the Panama Canal.

XVIII

"Nathan, this is going to be a hell of a Fourth of July. You've got to come with me to the big Cincinnati race. Damn it, I know you're not interested in running cars around a track, but at least you can work in my pit crew."

"Van, you're too old to be racing cars, especially against the likes of Rickenbacker and his team. It's time to give it over to younger men."

Nathan spoke in jest, of course. Van Harrison Stewart, the legendary half-breed Indian, one-legged survivor of the battleship *Maine*, had become one of the most famous names in automobile racing. In this blazing summer of 1916, despite his fifty years of age, Stewart was idolized by car-crazy Americans. Running the supercharged Stewart Special, powered by Cousin Isaiah's mighty Valve-in-Head Eight and bearing the name Spotted Deer across the hood, Van had rocketed to fame two years earlier by winning the grueling Indianapolis 500 and then following it up with the Vanderbilt Cup. He drove as Nathan flew, with a reckless élan that took no heed of danger. If men dashed themselves to pieces in flaming wrecks, or perished in a spiraling fall from the sky, then so be it. The winds of fate blew upon the lucky and the luckless alike.

It was this sharing of danger, even if in different machines, that forged the cousins' powerful friendship. From their first meeting years ago during one of Maurice's family get-togethers here in Fall River, the two had sensed their mutuality of interests. The successful work on the airplane carrier *Natchez* had further strengthened the bond. Since then, they had hunted together, womanized together, hurled their technological energies into Stewart Motors—and earned Maurice Stewart's grudging respect—together. Not since Comstock had taken Nathan under his wing as a boy, and inspired him to look to the sky, had he had such a loyal friend. Now Comstock was dead, himself the victim of an automobile accident in Virginia. Nathan Stewart, who had never felt close to his father Casey, found in the tempestuous and brilliant Van the support he needed.

"I'm flying on the Fourth, right here in Fall River."

"For Christ's sake, you'll kill yourself one of these days, stunting for a bunch of yokels at a picnic. These people are so stupid they might shoot you down with a skyrocket."

"That's my worry." He shook Van's hand and chuckled. "A word of advice, though. Take it easy on curves."

It was a standing joke. Neither had seen fit to marry. They were of the breed that attracted so many women that marriage seemed unnecessary. A wife would tie a man down, or worse, ground him. "The most dangerous curve known to man," Van quipped, "is hidden in a dress."

Van left for Cincinnati on the same train that carried his crew and two Stewart Specials. Nathan saw him off and then drove through Fall River's crowded streets to the automobile plant. God, how the town had grown! It was hard to conceive of Fall River as the sleepy little place Maurice described eighteen years before this. And the growth, of course, was due entirely to Stewart Motors. Half the families in town worked for Stewart and the other half depended on the company for financial sufficiency. Nathan had argued long and hard trying to persuade Maurice to expand into airplane manufacture as well, but thus far without success. "Don't push us, boy," Maurice would grumble. "Everything in its own good time." But Nathan's pride and joy, an airplane hangar and runway, now occupied property adjoining the automobile works. He parked his car beside the hangar and found Cousin Isaiah, as usual, deep in the new engine he had developed for Nathan's Burger-Wright biplane.

"What now?" Nathan said.

"I've been working on these mountings. If you're going to wring her out on the Fourth, as I know you will, I want to be sure"—the hunchback reached up, fitted a wrench to a bolt and turned it, grunting from the strain—"that everything's nice and tight."

Nathan grinned, climbed the stepladder, and gazed down into the gleaming new power plant. "The Stewart Thunderbolt," he said admiringly.

"That's right." Isaiah wiped sweat from his face with a greasy sleeve. "She'll give you three hundred horsepower, maybe a little more. I've done some more carburetor adjustments, allowing for variations in altitude. Wouldn't do to have her hiccup in the middle of a power dive."

"I've got more engine than airplane here. This fuselage

construction just doesn't seem to match your mechanical standards."

Isaiah chuckled. "Be patient, boy. It'll all come together in time."

He sounded like Maurice.

Nathan frowned. "I wish I could take one of those engines with me."

"You're really going to do it, then?" Isaiah wiped his hands on an oily rag. "You're going to France?"

"I've got a commission waiting in the Lafayette Escadrille. I'll be a captain, if you please."

"Lah-te-dah. And maybe a corpse, too."

"I feel a strong kinship to France. After all, my mother and grandfather live in Paris. Father went to school there. I've visited from time to time."

"But the war . . . do you have to sign up for a war? They're shooting real bullets over there."

"Yes," Nathan said quietly, "so I've heard."

The Stewart Thunderbolt was a masterpiece of engineering. As Nathan opened the throttle, climbing high into the sunshine, he marveled at Isaiah's genius with engines. This one gave him more power than he thought possible in an aircraft. Kicking the left rudder, he went into a quick sideslip followed by a slow roll and came out of that with a shallow dive ending in a loop-the-loop. Coming back to level flight, he looked down upon the silvery bend of the river, the town and the park, a colorful tableau of holiday crowds, flags, and the town brass band, its instruments gleaming in tiny pinpoints of golden light. With the white steeple of the Methodist Church as his aiming point, Nathan pushed the nose over into a power dive. Gathering airspeed, he flipped a switch that sent streams of red, white, and blue smoke gushing from wing tips and tail. As the Thunderbolt roared, he watched the ground and the awed massed faces of the spectators come swooping toward him. With a split second to spare, he pulled back the stick and did a series of low loops, making a spiral of the colored smoke. Banking and reducing throttle, he came in for his landing on the broad grassy sweep of the athletic field beside Fall River College.

"Beautiful, Nathan. What a thrilling show!"

"Spectacular, old man!"

They crowded around the biplane as he climbed out of the

cockpit and nimbly jumped down. Young women rushed in with hugs and kisses and young men wrung his hand. Happily animated, they escorted him to the bandstand where top officials of Stewart Motors now gathered for a speech by Maurice Stewart. Someone grabbed Nathan's arm and held on. He looked down into the laughing green eyes of a stunning redhead.

"Who are you?" he said. "I thought I knew all the beauties of Fall River."

"I'm Julie Straight, Jeffrey's cousin. And I'd just love to take an airplane ride."

"You'll get airsick."

"Try me."

The ceremony began with a medley of patriotic tunes, rendered with more enthusiasm than musical fidelity by the Fall River Marching Brass Band. Tom Moneypenny awarded prizes for winners in various competitors of the day—horseshoe pitching, sack races, apple-bobbing, the canoe race—after which votes were tabulated for Queen of the Picnic. The calling of Julie Straight's name brought a burst of applause. Nathan watched her with admiration as she ran up the steps and accepted a cardboard crown and a spray of red roses.

"And now, folks"—Tom Moneypenny put up his hands for quiet—"it's my pleasure to present a young feller we all know and love. I brought him here ridin' a freight train eighteen years ago, and we stopped off in jail for a few days in a little town in Ohio. Sometimes, I think they oughta kept him." Laughter coursed through the crowd. "I remember when he was so pore that Jeff Straight had to cut his hair on credit. But he made his way, and we're all mighty proud. Here he is, folks, the top man at Stewart's, my friend and yours, Maurice Stewart!"

As applause rose around the bandstand, someone touched Nathan's arm. Julie Straight was back, wearing her cardboard crown at a fetching angle.

"I never went to a picnic with a queen before," Nathan said.

Maurice looked healthier than he had in years. A murmur went through the crowd as the applause died down. "Sobriety," Nathan said quietly, "seems to agree with him."

"That," Julie replied, "and Helen DeMare."

It was no secret, of course. The bond between Maurice Stewart and Helen DeMare since her return to Fall River was such common knowledge that even the gossips tired of discussing it. There were those who said that Helen was good for Maurice, had stopped him from drinking, and probably saved his life. And what was good for Maurice Stewart and Stewart Motors was good for Fall River. The fact that Rachel Birnham Stewart saw fit to ignore the relationship and live on as Maurice's wife stirred mixed feelings. ("How on earth can Rachel stay with him, having Helen DeMare flaunted in her face?" "My dear, with all that wealth you'd stay with the Devil himself.")

Maurice acknowledged the applause, smiling and waving. When it subsided, he spoke of Fall River, its people, and its growth. He touched upon the community's aspirations. It was the kind of speech that appealed to pocketbooks and parochial pride. Nathan listened spellbound, aware for the first time that his cousin was a superb orator. Finally Maurice gave them his surprise message of the day, one that he described as highly significant for this Fourth of July.

"My friends, it pleases me to announce that on July the eleventh, President Wilson intends to sign into law the Federal Aid Road Act. This is something for which we in the automobile industry have lobbied long and hard. The act will provide five million dollars for road-building programs. It marks a new era of federal subsidies for the automobile in America. It also creates a system of highway classification, federal, state, and local, creating a basis for further government funding. Needless to say, this is a tremendous breakthrough for the nation's automobile industry. It promises a booming growth of fantastic proportions. Today, there are three million private cars and a quarter of a million commercial vehicles registered to use public roads. Within the next decade, America will easily double this figure. And that, my friends, means jobs and undreamed of prosperity for those of us engaged in this fantastic industry, expanding man's horizons beyond his wildest dreams. For you and me here in Fall River, it promises a continuation of prosperity on an historic scale. I predict a flourishing of this city beyond anything we could have imagined a few short years ago. And what finer tribute for a great community on this Fourth of July!"

Maurice Stewart stepped back and thrust both arms aloft, waving.

On cue, the band broke into Sousa's march, The Stars

and Stripes Forever. The crowd burst into a spontaneous cheering.

Hours later, the darkness settled, the temperature cooled, and night sounds filled the gentle air over Fall River. Nathan and Julie Straight lay on the grass beside the biplane, watching lightning bugs and holding hands. They had spent the afternoon and evening together, caught up in the rising magic of something for which neither was quite prepared.

"Are you really going to France?" she said.

"Yes. I've made a commitment."

"To whom?"

"To my mother, to my surrogate country, to myself."

"I don't want you to go."

Silence.

"Did you hear me?"

"Yes, I heard you."

Crickets called from the grass. Frogs raised a discordant chorus from the river. A full moon stood high overhead, casting in silhouette the wings of the biplane. Nathan thought: What an ungodly time for this to happen.

"Nathan."

"Yes."

"I will wait for you."

"You don't even know how long that will be. The war in Europe could go on for years."

"I will wait for you."

Nathan Stewart grappled with his feelings. One part of him wanted to break free of this unexpected snag, another part rushed to accept it. At last he simply surrendered himself to whatever the fates might offer, remembering with a half-smile his own warning to Van Harrison: "Just be careful on the curves."

He took Julie in his arms.

The night deepened. The dew came down. The moon rushed upon its timeless course.

Johnny get your gun, get your gun, get your gun . . .

The dogs of war were loosed. President Wilson pledged the nation's manpower and resources, declaring, "The world must be made safe for democracy." America was committed. Young men appeared in uniform on the streets of Fall River. There were bond rallies in the park and prayer vigils for Our Boys. Every outgoing train was the cause of another tearful scene of parting at the railroad depot. American flags appeared in the windows of homes whose sons had gone to war, and the newspapers carried their pictures from the camps, young and smiling and eager. Everyone was seized with a patriotic fervor. Marshal's Music Store sold out of George M. Cohan's new song, "Over There," and ordered more. Children played soldier with broomstick guns and young women wept over the pictures of uniformed men, reading and rereading the letters headed "Camp Dix" and "Somewhere at Sea" and finally, "Allied Expeditionary Force, Europe."

"Black Jack Pershing will make hash of the bloody Boche, you'll see," grumbled the late drinkers in Jerry's Saloon. "My nephew, he's in the Seventy-seventh Division and they're ready to go any day."

"That Stewart boy's a major now in the Lafayette Escadrille. Got six German planes to his credit, I hear."

"Seven."

"No, it's six. Isaiah said six, and he knows."

"Seven, I tell you!"

"Six, goddamn it!"

At the Stewart Motors plant, the lights burned late and workmen went on double shifts as production changed from civilian automobiles to Army ambulances and trucks. A top secret memo from Washington requested that Maurice assign a research team to develop an American heavy tank.

"Isaiah, we're going to have to change the gear ratio on this ambulance. She's geared too high for six cylinders on a heavy-duty vehicle. What do you think?"

"You're right, Maurice. The ambulances will be operating over very rough terrain. I'll see to it."

"What about your Thunderbolt engine? Can it power the tank?"

"It'll need modification. But at three hundred horsepower, the Thunderbolt can handle just about anything. By the way, Nathan writes that they could use the Thunderbolt in the French Nieuport aircraft. I've ordered a dozen shipped to his squadron at Toul, France."

"What else does he say?"

"He says Stewart Motors ought to start developing an American bomber aircraft, similar to the German Gotha, with long-range capabilities. Because the Gothas bombed London, he thinks the Allies should also carry the air war to the enemy's homeland. I've checked with Silas Proctor in Washington, and he's positive we can get a government contract. The War Department is excited about the idea."

"And what do you think?"

"You know that already, Maurice. I think we ought to do it."

"We'll have to present it to the Executive Committee, but I don't see any obstacles. Hell, we're building every weapon of war that exists. Ward Stewart's shipyard is turning out Navy gunboats and cutters. Aunt Colette is making howitzers in the locomotive works and armor plate at the rolling mill. We might as well build airplanes too."

Isaiah scratched his head. "I told Nathan not to get his hopes too high. With this crazy family, you never know."

"I'll call a committee meeting."

I miss you so terribly, dear Nathan. It is as if the time had stopped . . .

She wrote with a flowing hand on pink paper, scenting it lightly with her favorite wildflower cologne. Three times a week and sometimes four, the letters went out. Julie tried to keep them chatty and newsy, but her emptiness crept into the pages. He had been gone for more than a year, and it seemed an eternity.

More and more of the young men are leaving for war. I read in the papers that 24 million are signed up for Selective Service and nearly 3 million of these are expected to be drafted by the end of this year. There was an article in the Detroit papers about your exploits over the Western Front. I am so proud, but longing for you to come back home. I am sending, in a separate package, the fur-lined gloves and heavy scarf that you requested. I pray for your safety, my love . . .

The hot summer of 1917 dragged by interminably. Julie was employed in an armament factory near Detroit and commuted daily by train. Life thus settled into a humdrum pattern, broken only on weekends when she sometimes visited her parents at the village of Battle Creek. Loving Nathan—there was no question about what she felt for him, and never had been—had changed her from the Julie of old. No longer did she flirt with young men, even though they constantly asked her out. Friends accused her of being standoffish and foolish. She tossed her head and let them have their say. Nathan was on her mind, and nothing else mattered. She lived for the arrival of his weekly letters.

He wrote,

The word is that our old outfit will no longer serve the flag of France but be shifted over to American command. I have a strange duality of loyalties now, having flown for the French for eight months and speaking the language to my ground crew every day. The squadron is changing over to the Spad, a fine little aircraft, but I prefer my old Nieuport with Isaiah's big engine. The German pilots are very good. They have reaped a bitter harvest of fine French and British pilots this year. Our losses in aerial combat against their Albatros and Fokker triplanes are four to one. All of us are tired. We are constantly on sortie. One loses his touch at times; the fine movements and instincts are no longer there when you need them. A doctor came up to the squadron and used a fancy new term for what ails us. Battle fatigue. It's just another way of saying we're worn out . . .

Such a heavy tone was unusual for him and filled her with a nagging dread. She awoke before daybreak to stare at the ceiling, the words tumbling in her mind. *"One loses his touch at times . . ."* Oh, this war. This damn, damn war.

"I don't like this idea of Isaiah's," Aunt Francesca said. "It really bothers me. Conventional armaments is one thing, because we are at war. But I don't want to see the Stewart name identified with a bomber that will kill help-less civilians."

"Neither do I," Hope said grimly. "We will simply have to convince Maurice that it's unconscionable. I think we have the votes on the board."

"I wouldn't be too sure about that."

Hope looked out the train window. They were somewhere in Ohio, passing through another dreary factory town. The weather was cold and gray with flurries of snow. It seemed that January would never end. Smoke belched from a line of chimneys at a glass works, and a tattered sign flicked past, Buy Liberty Bonds.

"I hate traveling to Fall River," she said.

Aunt Francesca sniffed. "It's so boring."

The woman was amazing. Tall, white-haired, and erect, she still reminded Hope of an aged queen attended by her court. As usual, they had taken a series of compartments as well as a private drawing room to accommodate their self-contained crowd. Half a dozen of Francesca's friends surrounded them, murmuring among themselves or nodding off, mesmerized by the eternal rocking of the coach. They had grown old with their sovereign and several had died. Hope reflected upon the cruelty of time's passing, and wondered what these men and women would do when Francesca was no longer there to light their lives. The old woman was over ninety now. She could not live forever.

"Mommy," a small voice said at Hope's side, "I'm cold."

"All right, Howard. Let's put on your jacket. Here, let me help you. And what about you, Marguerite?"

"I want to sit on your lap," Marguerite said.

"All right. Let me fix Howard first."

"I'm afraid you spoil them," Francesca said.

"*I* spoil them? You should see Silas. They could ask for the moon and he'd try to get it for them."

"Children shouldn't be spoiled like that."

"You were always good to me and Isaiah."

"That was different. You were practically foundlings. Besides, they're growing up. Howard is four and Margie is three. They need to do more for themselves."

Hope smiled. "Silas says love is the only thing that multiplies as you give it away."

Francesca smiled and looked out the window. "I wish Silas could have come with us."

"He had to be in the House for the President's speech and to assure passage of the women's suffrage bill. There wasn't any choice."

"Yes, I suppose not. He does take being a congressman so seriously. Everything is complicated nowadays. Sometimes I wonder if all this fuss is really worth it."

Hope finished with Howard and lifted Marguerite to her lap. The child had Silas's dark eyes and Hope's blond hair. In time, she thought, it would be a fascinating combination. "Aunt Francesca, I think you're forgetting something."

"Oh?" The eyebrows arched and the patrician face looked amused. "And what is that?"

"In this family, things are always complicated."

The meeting of the Executive Committee to decide the question of whether Stewart Motors, Inc., would begin preliminary design work for a long-range American bomber was to be held in the main conference room of the new Administration Building. It was a setting of power and wealth. Isaiah Stewart had difficulty relating the scope of today's giant company with their small beginnings fifteen years ago. In this cheerless January of 1918, as the nation remained locked in a bloody war, Stewart was a household word across America. The Silver Stewart had become the most popular mid-size sedan on the ever-expanding network of streets and highways. Subsidiary companies produced Stewart parts, batteries, carburetors, and accessories. There was even a plan to begin making Stewart tires when the war was won, although God only knew when that might be.

"Isaiah, what is your position on the bomber?"

His sister Hope, still beautiful in maturity, fixed him with a blue-eyed gaze filled with intensity of purpose.

"I don't want to debate it here in the hallway, Hope."

"You're still favoring it, then. Frankly, I'm surprised at you, Isaiah. I thought you had more sense than that."

He resented the effrontery, but did not respond in kind. "Since when do we get personal over something that's strictly business?"

The blue eyes smoldered. "Isaiah, surely you don't intend..."

"I'm not going to debate it here."

Theirs obviously had not been the only personal confrontation. The eight executive committee members were in a somber mood as they took their seats around the polished mahogany table. Even Aunt Colette, normally vivacious and outgoing, was subdued as she spoke quietly with Hope, Francesca, and Ward Stewart. From Isaiah's talks with them individually, he already knew that they were the opposition bloc. Favoring the project were Van Harrison, whose energy and leadership had catapulted him to the presidency of Stewart Motors, second in command to Maurice; Casey Stewart, who had come up from Panama accompanied by his lovely wife Willow and their sons, Luray and Henri; old Tom Moneypenny and Isaiah himself. And so, as Maurice rose to gavel the meeting to order, the eight were equally divided.

Under the bylaws of Executive Board meetings, this meant that unless there was a change, the chairman of the board would cast the deciding vote. The air was charged with expectancy.

"You all know why we're here," Maurice said. "It has been proposed that the Stewart corporation create a subsidiary company to engage in the manufacture of a long-range bomber for use in the American war effort. The original idea came from Major Nathan Stewart, now serving with an American air squadron on the Western Front. Most of the aircraft in his unit, incidentally, are powered by the Stewart Thunderbolt engine, developed by Isaiah Stewart. Four such engines would be used on the bomber. I don't have to remind you that our enemy, the Germans, have bombed London in air raids with both the zeppelin lighter-than-air craft and the Gotha heavy bombers. Strategically, the Stewart bomber..."

As Maurice spoke, Isaiah reflected on the changes in the man in recent years. It troubled him to see a once-strong and vital kinsman now in persistent frail health. But clearly, Helen DeMare had given Maurice a reason for living, and this made all the difference. It had even triggered a fresh zeal for corporate leadership, especially as it related to the war effort. The board chairman of Stewart Motors pushed himself unmercifully on the job and expected his subordinates to do the same, a fact that caused its share of muttered complaints. One common comment in the shops was, "What's he trying to do, win the war all by himself?" Only Maurice Stewart's close associates and relatives were aware of his passionate devotion to his country's cause, borne of four generations of Stewart enterprise in America. "By God, Stewarts helped wrest this country from the wilderness," Maurice once grumbled to Isaiah in a discussion of the war effort, "and we're damn sure not going to let her down now."

Isaiah's reverie was broken as Maurice came to the end of his opening statement, saying, "... now entertain comments from the members of the committee."

"Mr. Chairman"—it was Colette who spoke—"I wish to make a brief statement."

Maurice nodded. "Proceed."

Colette came to her feet. Now in her eighties, she continued to oversee the Stewart enterprises in Pittsburgh with an energy exceeding even that of her late brother Bradley. Isaiah marveled at the strength of these Stewart women—Colette,

Francesca, Hope—who had risen individually to take their places in a business world dominated by men. But then, theirs was a family legacy of strong females, from Great-Grandmother Martha to the late aunt Maybelle, and Great-Aunt Catherine and, yes, even his own mother Marguerite.

"I will not be a party to the creation of a machine designed for the purpose of bombing cities and terrorizing, maiming and killing helpless noncombatants," Colette said. She stood ramrod straight, hands clasped, her tone icy, and her manner imperious. "War on the battlefield is horrible enough, and God knows I wish we were free of it; but to carry that bloody madness to innocent civilians is utterly barbaric."

Colette sat down. She was followed, with equal brevity and passion, by Hope, Francesca, and Ward Stewart. The latter, a handsome, very light-skinned man with flecks of gray in his brown kinky hair, startled even his kinsmen with the intensity of his feelings. "As you all know, I am your black cousin. In my veins runs the blood of Stewarts and of slaves. My grandmother was the black concubine of my grandfather and namesake Captain Ward Stewart, who had been the white commander of a slave ship. I, and my father before me, have lived as half-Negro men in a white man's world. We have prospered beyond a black man's wildest dreams. As a Stewart, I have a white man's education from Princeton. I own one of the biggest shipyards on the East Coast. I'm making weapons of war under contract to the U.S. Navy. My relationship toward this country is one of love and of hate; love for the opportunity it has given me, the grandson of a slave, and hatred for continuing to enslave black people in a nation divided. Nevertheless, I am a Stewart. I am proud to be a Stewart. I will not besmirch that name, nor stain it with the blood of innocents. I oppose this bomber with all my heart and soul."

It was Isaiah's turn. He had heard them, respected their feelings, and weighed their points against his own convictions. He came clumsily to his feet, conscious—as always, when he stood before an audience of normally shaped people—of his grotesqueness. The hump on his shoulder seemed heavier, the twisted body more stooped, the drawn hand more twisted. Even his self-identity defied clear definition. He was Isaiah Stewart, a freak, inwardly shy, vulnerable; but he was also Isaiah Stewart the mechanical genius whose vision and creativity had brought this company, and much of America with it, into the twentieth century. Isaiah Stewart's engines

401

not only powered automobiles all over America, they now hurled combat aircraft through the skies over Europe. And who could envision what the future might bring?

"Why are we kidding ourselves?" As he spoke, their eyes turned to him and the room became hushed. "We are discussing the war in Europe as if it were some kind of a parlor game. The parlor game mentality says that we will keep all the fighting men in their place and the civilians in their place, keep it neat and tidy, and let them fight by prescribed rules with prescribed weapons, confident that righteousness will prevail. The fact is, my friends, our troops are up against a vicious, highly resourceful foe who thinks nothing of dropping bombs on cities and committing other crimes against civilians in order to triumph. We are fighting the Hun. We are fighting a people who send their submarines to prowl the seas, sinking helpless merchant and passenger ships, and who were the first to use poison gas on the battlefield. We are fighting to preserve the great principles upon which our country was founded, principles of human dignity and worth."

Isaiah paused. He took a sip of water. He looked around the table, into their eyes. He continued. "If the Hun prevails, he will bring down upon Western civilization a new Dark Age. I have heard it said that this is the war to end all wars. I'm not so certain of that. I submit to you that the Hun is a cruel and persistent enemy. He will not be stopped until the whole structure of his militaristic society is brought down and dismantled, and even his great cities lie in ruins. And even then, he could rise from the ashes to smite us again. We did not start this war. We were not the first to bomb cities or sink ships. And God knows, I wish it were not happening at all. But the monster of technology is unleashed. The world has been launched into a new era of warfare, the potential for which I shudder even to contemplate. I guarantee you that long-range bombers will be built, if not now then in the not-too-distant future. But I also guarantee you that aviation, as a peacetime servant of man, will shrink this globe in ways that we can't even dream of happening right now. And thus, the bomber we make today will become the great transport plane of tomorrow, carrying passengers, cargo, and mail to distant parts of the nation and even the globe. So what we propose to do now is develop, with the help of government funding, a plane that can serve in war and also serve in peace;

402

a weapon for the defense of democracy as we know it, and a servant of enormous potential to all mankind."

Finally, it was all said. Each, in turn, had expressed his point of view. Only Maurice Stewart had not spoken. To everyone's astonishment, he did not speak now. He simple called for the vote.

Not one mind had been changed. The vote was four-four, a tie.

Maurice looked tired. He stood and faced them again. "There are some things that must take priority," he said. "I've already given this matter considerable thought on the chance that we might come to just such a dilemma as this, which it is my uncomfortable duty to resolve. The unity of the family, in my opinion, is more important than the issue at hand. I will not let this family be torn apart in dispute over a weapon of war."

He set his jaw, placed his fingertips on the table, and looked straight at Isaiah. "I therefore vote no."

Everyone in the room let out a breath.

It had rained for two days. Heavy clouds lay at treetop level, drooling wisps of mist to the ground. The weather made it impossible to fly. The squadron pilots lay in their soggy tents while mechanics worked under canvas, making repairs and fine-tuning engines. Major Nathan Stewart's Nieuport was being worked over by Roullard, the ancient Frenchman and former automobile mechanic whom he had insisted on bringing into the American unit from the old Lafayette Escadrille he had flown for France prior to the U.S. entry into the war. The Nieuport was fitted with the big Thunderbolt engine, which Stewart and nearly every other pilot in the squadron now swore by. In the late afternoon, the major walked through the downpour to the special working tent where Roullard still labored, smeared with dirt and grease.

"She took a bullet in the manifold, monsieur." The Frenchman stepped down from his ladder, wiping his hands on an oily rag. "I am not pleased with this at all. I need to open her up for a complete overhaul."

"How long will that take, Roullard?"

"Two days."

Nathan paced the wet ground impatiently, heedless of the downpour. He was taut and lean; two years of war had etched his handsome face in lines of chronic fatigue. His eyes had lost their boyish wonder. They were flat and cold now, the eyes of a man who killed other men. When he had first come to France, one of the adventure-seeking American youths eager to take to the skies against the Boche, life was a lark and war a frolic. Even in late 1916 they had still fought with a certain gentlemanly élan, the knights of the sky. But that had passed as men became aces with their kills and comrade after comrade had spun to earth on a curling stream of fire and smoke.

He spun on his heel. "If the weather lets up, I fly tomorrow."

"Then I suggest you take another plane. I will roll out the spare eSpad that belonged to Lieutenant Tremaine. It was designed after Guynemer's great fighter, with the Hispano-Suiza engine. Two hundred horsepower, but on a very light frame..."

"Have you tried a run-up on this engine?"

"I'm about to try one now."

"Good. Then do it."

Roullard removed the canvas and closed the cowling as Nathan swung into the cockpit and switched on the magneto. The mechanic swung the propeller once, twice, three times before the engine barked to life with a sputtering roar. Despite the difficulty in starting, probably a result of the wet weather, the Thunderbolt sounded strong to him. At his shouted command, Roullard removed the wheel chocks and Nathan taxied the Nieuport past the line of squadron planes and up and down the rain-drenched runway. He returned to where the dour mechanic waited, shut off the engine, and sprang down from the cockpit.

"It'll do."

The mechanic looked chagrined. "But, monsieur..."

"Have it ready, Roullard." He turned and walked briskly to the squadron canteen.

"Here we go again," muttered Crandon, a former Philadelphia lawyer now flying as Nathan's new wingman.

"And here's to Major Stewart begging his Boche Number Twelve!" said a young lieutenant, hoisting a glass of warm beer. "To the ace!"

"To the ace!" they shouted.

Nathan offered a noncommittal grin, drank off a beer, and went to his tent.

Julie's latest letter was waiting. The sight of the pink envelope with its flowing handwriting and delicate scent lifted his spirits from the strange malaise which now seemed to afflict him constantly.

She wrote,

> My darling, the newspapers are full of the big push along the Meuse, and there is talk that the Germans will sue for peace. My heart leaps just to think of it, for such a thing is almost too fanciful to contemplate . . .

His eye skimmed down the page, searching for bits of hometown news as one would search for nuggets. She had bought a new dress, pale blue with a trimmed bodice that she intended to wear when he came home. Young Sandy Tillman had caught a thirty-five-pound channel catfish in Fall River. Hope's husband Silas Proctor, the congressman, was thinking about running for the Senate from New York, but powerful antilabor interests were vowing to stop him.

> And as if I hadn't written this a million times already, I love you; I love you; I love you.

He went to sleep with the letter under his pillow, trying not to think about tomorrow.

The wake-up bell clanged at four o'clock in the morning, and by first light they were breakfasted, suited up, and on their way to the planes. Roullard stomped about morosely, unshaven, and covered with grease.

"You look terrible, Roullard."

"I worked all night on that engine, monsieur. Now, if you get into a fight and she sputters, don't take chances. Dive for the deck and let your wingman cover you. I can't guarantee..."

"You're an old woman, Roullard."

"And you, monsieur, are the image of your wild cousin Van Harrison, who also thumbed his nose at death in the great race of 1903."

"He survived, too."

"Yes. He survived."

It was a sparkling morning. The squadron took off at sunup and flew stairstepped formation high over the valley of the Meuse. Wind spanking his goggled face, Nathan scanned a turquoise and rose-tinted sky flecked with purple cloud banks. Some of the old elation returned. God, he thought, what a glorious adventure.

Far below, men slogged in the no-man's-land of the Meuse,

battling in a world of mud, slime, and barbed wire, cowering beneath thunderous shellfire and scythed down by machine guns. Even now he could see light flickers and tiny bursts of dirty gray smoke flecking a tortured landscape. The once-green fields of France were plowed, shell-pocked, and slashed with trenches.

He scanned the sky, eyes shifting and probing in the way that they had done millions of times. Evil blooms of antiaircraft fire gushed off to their left. And then his eye caught something, a blob of specks glinting in the sunshine. He waggled the wings of his Nieuport and gestured, then started to climb.

They were Fokker Triplanes, multicolored and gleaming. Their rate of climb was very fast, and by the time the two formations came together the altitudes were about equal. Nathan concentrated on the lead aircraft. Black crosses loomed as the enemy advanced in a ragged bank of v's. And then, in an explosion of engines and flashing wings, both formations broke.

The Fokker offered him a tempting target, seeming to slow and fall away. Nathan, tense and eager, gave the Nieuport full throttle and dove, firing a long burst from his nose gun. *Tatatatatatatatatat!* Rapid recoil shook the plane as he adjusted for a slight deflection and prepared for the Triplane to cross into his bullet stream. But the German did not cross. With an abrupt flip and sweeping turn, the Fokker caught Nathan off-balance. Too late, he realized that he had been suckered! Now he was the hunted, and the German lined him up for the kill. He kicked right rudder and dove, but his adversary stuck on his tail. Bullets stitched through his wing fabric.

A Spad came out of the sun to his right. Flashing across his line of vision, American decals gleaming, it loosed a long burst into the Fokker. As Nathan flipped his Nieuport and came over in a fast roll, he saw the big three-winged aircraft falter in flight like a wounded bird. Then, as if in lazy slow motion, the stricken plane winged over and swept into the blue void, spitting black smoke.

The dogfight spilled all over the sky. Planes were burning and falling everywhere, and the air filled with the grinding, spitting roar of combat. Nathan lined up on his second big Fokker, a camouflaged-painted brute with silver slashes on the wings. "Here goes Number Twelve," he murmured, peering through his gunsight.

It was an easy burst, an easy kill. The Fokker made a sluggish attempt at evasion, but too late. Flames licked from the shattered cowling and one of the wing sections collapsed as the plane nosed over in its fatal dive. Nathan followed him down, making certain of the kill, still hammering bullets into the camouflaged fuselage as the Fokker hit the ground and exploded.

He was now an ace. But there was no joy in it, no feeling of triumph. He felt no emotion at all. A man had died down there. Twelve men had died, in fact, under the guns of Nathan Stewart. Only a madman could celebrate such a thing. He started his climb back up to the fight.

The engine sputtered. He let the stick go forward, dropping the nose a bit to gain speed but the engine continued to cough and sputter. There was a clanking that began to shake the entire plane, and he realized that he had broken a piston. Roullard's warnings came back to him, but it was too late to heed them now. He had been a pigheaded fool.

He was alone; the dogfight had swirled away. In the distance a plane spiraled lazily down on a plume of smoke, but he could not tell whether it was German or American. The clanking worsened. He manipulated the throttle, but to no avail. The Nieuport shook and coughed and finally died.

The silence was profound. Wind whistled through the wing struts. From below came the sound of the constant rumble and rattle of war. He made a turn back toward the Allied lines and looked down. He had about two thousand feet of altitude left and nothing below but water-filled shellholes and stobs of shattered trees.

He managed to hold the Nieuport in a shallow glide.

Something flicked at his wings, chewing out bits of fabric, and thudded into the framing of the fuselage. A shock of awareness went through him. Rifle fire. The bastards were shooting! He looked down again as the aircraft coasted across a trench. The trench was filled with helmeted men, some of them aiming their rifles at the plane. He crossed into no-man's-land.

He thought, Well, this is it.

The ground came rushing up. Instinctively he tried to lift the nose a bit, but the big Thunderbolt engine was too heavy. He would just have to ride her in, shellholes, tree trunks, and all.

The Nieuport hit with a bone-jarring impact, plowing across rough ground toward a shattered concrete bunker. As it hit the bunker, Nathan's body rocketed forward, tearing loose the seatbelt, and his face smashed into the top of the instrument panel.

Flames licked at a pine log in the fireplace, driving off the November chill. The dancing light glowed about the room, illuminating crystal glassware, deeply textured carpeting, and Chippendale woods. Shadows played over papered walls of tiny rosebud print. There was an odor of Parisian perfume. The walls displayed good pieces of French art. The room had a contrived clutter, intimate but uncrowded, blending the exotic and commonplace. It was all Helen's doing. She had the knack for creating a mood, reminding him that life was part reality and part illusion. It was the actress in her. This, he supposed, was the major source of his fascination. In a world of technical materialism, she gave him pleasant diversion, made him happy.

Maurice Stewart was happy. In the warmth of the moment, he felt vigorous and youthful. Talk about illusions. This was the autumn of 1918. Hell, he was forty-one years old. His black hair was dusted with gray, his brown eyes bracketed in thin lines. But at this moment, in this place and time, he could relax and let the mood flow. He settled back on the Chippendale divan in his dressing gown, looking into the fireplace across the rim of a bone china coffee cup and waiting for Helen to come to him. He thought: How priceless are the small pleasures of life.

She came in from the boudoir, her movements a whisper of silk, a green body sheath buttoned loosely down the front. Her hair was a tumbling mass of auburn waves, accentuating creamy white skin, lustrous dark eyes, the soft and radiant face. He knew that beneath the sheath she was nude. His desire was strengthened by the fact that they shared life in stolen moments. The decision was hers, of course. It had always been hers. He would have left Rachel—and the children too, for all his love for them—but Helen would not hear of it. She would put her finger to his lips. "Let's not talk about it anymore, darling." And so, time passed. She would not even accept a stipend from him for support, and so he made do with expensive gifts—a mink coat here, a roomful of furniture there, this very cottage in which she lived when in Fall River.

Helen sensed the overriding complexity of Maurice Stewart's life, even to the massive clutter of detail forever demanding his attention. Even now it dogged him. The new blueprints would be there in the morning, awaiting his approval. He would have to attend to the revised tooling schedules. The union business demanded decision. And then there was the persistent bickering going on in the family. Stewarts! Either they adored one another or fought like tigers. And now that the war in Europe seemed almost over he thought of young Nathan, horribly wounded.

"My dear," Helen DeMare murmured, "I will endure anything but being ignored."

He chuckled. "Impossible. I might as well ignore breathing. I was watching the fire. There is something hypnotic about a fire."

She smiled, took his arm, and lay her head upon his shoulder. He breathed the scent of her hair. His senses quickened. As always, in these moments of intimacy, Helen was magnetic. It was a trick of atmosphere and timing, of course, but she seemed suddenly to exude passion.

He slipped his hand beneath her sheath, to stroke her breast as one would stroke velvet. She stirred with sensual pleasure, whispering, "Oh. Yes." He found her mouth, full and wanting, and covered it with his own. Lightly, her tongue caressed his.

Her hands played at his robe, undoing it, finding him. So expertly did they move, those hands, fondling just the right places. The old jealousy flickered in his mind. She was an actress. How many other men had she loved? In times past he had almost uttered it aloud, but refrained. Some mysteries one did not dare to explore.

"Darling..." she whispered.

There came a sudden unfolding, a nearing nakedness. His lust surged, a powerful force generated partly from an inner rage he could never understand. He wanted to overwhelm her, consume her. His senses reeled in the firelight. Blood-gorged and jutting, he mounted her.

Giant shadows writhed upon the walls, over the tiny patterns of rosebuds.

When it was done, they lay quietly intertwined on the floor. She turned her face to the fire and sighed.

"Happy birthday," he said.

"I don't like birthdays anymore. I'm thirty-five years old. You'll be looking for a younger mistress."

"Don't use that word."

"Paramour, then. You'll want a younger paramour. Somebody very chic, very smart. You're so devilishly handsome. I know that other women throw themselves at you. They always have. Remember Priscilla Pover? I still think of her and turn green."

He wanted to say, "Then why don't you marry me?" but did not. It would do no good. Once upon a time, before Rachel, it would have been appropriate. But something irrevocable had taken place on the day he had left Helen, so long ago. They would share excitement, touching, breathing, complete intimacy, but never marry.

She lay quietly. The fire warmed their naked bodies and gave her eyes a glow. "How strange it all is. Here we are, together again. But I have the feeling that we're running short of time. Isn't that peculiar?"

"We have a lot more living to do," he said.

"How did you feel when the doctor said that you would not live if you didn't stop drinking? Were you frightened?"

He sighed. "Not really. I didn't especially care to live. That was before you came back into my life. Besides, it wasn't something all that abrupt. A liver condition, he said. I still had a choice. Having a choice makes a difference. It removes the urgency."

"Yes, I suppose it does," she said.

Then, for no reason at all, she flung her arms about his neck and whispered fiercely, "Hold me, Maurice."

Later he would remember thinking: What an excellent performance.

Finally they dressed, self-consciously gathering up discarded clothing. She had finished brushing her hair when the car arrived. Maurice pretended not to hear the sound of the motor.

The rest of it would haunt his memory.

Helen put down her hairbrush. "There's a car in the driveway."

"Oh?"

"Who could that be?" She went to the window, drew aside the lace curtain, and peered into the frosty night. The headlights bathed her face. "Somebody's here. I'm not expecting company."

"Let's go out and see."

They shrugged into coats and stepped out into the cold. Maurice flicked on the outside electric light. He recognized the humpbacked figure of his cousin Isaiah emerging from behind the steering wheel. The car was a gleaming new

Stewart Runabout Six, fresh off the assembly line and painted in Helen's favorite shade of green. Isaiah limped toward them through the glare of headlights, his lean face lifted in a foxy smile. "Here it is, Maurice. And a real beauty, too."

It was several minutes before the truth dawned on her. They had finished an inspection of the runabout and were talking about oil changes when Helen clapped her hands to her face. "For me? Is it for me?" The two men smiled. She jumped up and down in the cold, clapping her hands and laughing like a child. She hugged Maurice, hugged Isaiah, and planted a kiss upon the great Stewart hood ornament. "Beautiful! It's just beautiful!"

"Happy birthday, Helen."

"I *love* birthdays!"

An hour later, as Isaiah drove Maurice's car back to Fall River, the cousins shared the afterglow of the evening's elation. "I've never seen her so excited over anything I gave her," Maurice said.

A misting rain was falling. The windshield wipers of the Silver Stewart thumped as the headlights picked out patches of fog. "Miserable driving weather," Isaiah said. "Do you think she'll take the car out again tonight?"

"Hell, no. I warned her not to."

"She drives like a bat out of hell."

"I know. She's a menace. I think she'd like to be the world's first female racing driver."

They entered the city limits of Fall River. The town was cloaked in early darkness and lashed by the November weather.

"Here we are." Isaiah pulled into the gravel driveway of Stewart House, stopped at the double iron gates and got out, a grotesque humpbacked figure limping through the rain. The gates swung open and Maurice drove through, waited for Isaiah to get in on the passenger side, and then proceeded up the winding drive. Headlights picked out the dun-colored brick mansion with its fluted columns, Gothic arches, and slate-roofed gables. He despised the place; too pretentious, and it harbored too many bad memories. He drove under the porte cochere. "Take the car, Isaiah. I'll see you at the board meeting in the morning."

As Isaiah drove away, the front door was opened by Jacobson, the butler. Maurice acknowledged the servant's greetings and quickly mounted the broad, red-carpeted staircase to his room in the east wing. He had changed into a robe and pajamas when Rachel came in from her adjoining room.

"So you decided to come home after all."

411

Her beauty was the same, porcelainlike and unchanging, although maturity had added a few fine lines to those regal features. Even the black hair remained luxuriant, loose-brushed, and shining in the light. The features were finely chiseled; the eyes a stunning shade of ice-blue. She wore a white negligee with a pale blue satin ribbon at the waist. "You've seen the DeMare woman again, I presume."

"That is not your business, Rachel."

"I merely would hope that you'd be more discreet. I know that discretion is not a Stewart strong point, but in this instance . . ."

"Don't bring my family background into the discussion."

"You could consider me and the children for once. They do have a share in this. Fall River is a small town, and when its most prominent citizen and employer flaunts himself with a common whore, tongues will wag."

He stared at her, fighting down waves of outrage that ripped him like nausea. No human being had a right to speak to him in this manner. In times past, he would have said so. He would have said, "For God's sake, woman! All you care about is money and this . . . this fucking mausoleum and your precious social position." But that was in times past. He saw no need to open all the old wounds again. Jesus, how many years must they both endure this?

"Please go to bed, Rachel." He turned his back, ignoring her fight for self-control. "Let's not quarrel. You'll feel better in the morning."

He removed his robe, slipped into bed, and put out the light while she stood there. The silence was broken only by the whisper of the rain at the windows. A moment later, she returned to her room and softly closed the door. Maurice got out of bed, then, and put on his robe. He moved softly down the hallway to Jacob's room. As he slipped inside, he heard the boy's measured breathing. He sat down on the bed in the darkness and remained there, not moving. The boy awoke gradually, aware of his presence.

"Is it you, Father?"

"Yes. How are you, Jake?"

"Fine." The boy rubbed his eyes, sat up and switched on the light. He was ten now, and Maurice was astonished at how rapidly he had grown. Around them, the room was a clutter of books and mechanical models, a ship in a bottle that Jake had just finished building, a football, a baseball poster.

"What time is it?" Jacob asked.

"I don't know. It's late. I shouldn't disturb you. I just wanted to say hello."

They spoke in whispers.

"I'm glad you came in. I was going to try to stay awake. I wanted to show you the new model airplane."

"A model airplane?"

"Yep. A Spad, just like the British fighter. Isaiah got me the plans."

They went over to the worktable by the window. Something was always in construction there. This time the paper blueprint for the British biplane was attached to the workboard. Already, balsa wood ribbing for the fuselage was pinned in place, ready for gluing. Maurice was conscious of how tall the ten-year-old was growing; already Jake was up to his shoulder.

"Will it fly?"

"Isaiah says it will." Jacob grinned. "And you know Isaiah."

There was a movement behind them. Catherine stood sleepy-eyed in the doorway, her golden hair in disarray. She wore a white robe and slippers of rabbit fur. "What are you two talking about at this time of night?"

"Hello, Puddin'." Maurice hugged his daughter and kissed her cheek. She was eleven, and on the verge of adolescence. "You sleep like a cat."

"What are you doing, Jakey?" she whispered.

"Aw, I'm just showing Father the new Spad. Go back to bed, Catherine."

"Hey!" Maurice chuckled. "I wanted to see both of you." He hugged them again. "Jake's right, though. Let's all go to bed."

Catherine grinned and turned away. "'Night, Father."

"'Night."

"'Night, Jakey."

"'Night."

"Gooooood night."

Morning dawned gray and misty. The chauffeur Patterson drove him to the plant in the Rolls. Maurice watched the dreary passing scene of the workers' neighborhoods, thinking of the savage strikes that had rocked the steel mills of the East and wondering how long they could hold out here. Ford was to blame for all this unrest in the automobile industry, Maurice was convinced of that. For four long years, first in peace and then in war, they had lived with Ford's guaranteed daily wage. If only . . .

"The front entrance, sir?"

"What? Uh, yes, Patterson. The front will do nicely."

The Rolls braked in front of the great brick main building, dominated by its gigantic sign, Stewart Motor Car Company. Maurice walked quickly into the building and took his private elevator to the third floor. As he moved through the reception room, he recognized a rumpled figure dozing on a chair. Isaiah. Maurice touched his cousin on the shoulder. "Don't you have a home to go to?"

The hunchback came awake. His face was drawn and unshaven, the eyes filled with torment and peering out from dark shells. Isaiah got to his feet clumsily, stammering, "I . . . I . . ." He groped in his pocket for a cigarette, drew one from a crumpled pack, and lit it. "Maurice, I . . ."

"Come into the office. You're a wreck."

Isaiah did not accept the invitation to sit down. He stood before Maurice's desk and spoke rapidly, like a man describing a nightmare. As the words tumbled out, Maurice stared at his cousin in disbelief. And then came his own numbing response, like a blow to the stomach.

"She died instantly, Maurice. They said she couldn't have felt anything. It was the damned road, slick as grease. She must have been doing ninety going into the big curve. They came for me at four o'clock this morning. The sheriff, he didn't want to come to your house. It would only cause more talk. I . . . I'm sorry, Maurice."

No. It could not be. It was not happening. It was a dream. He was in his own bed having a nightmare. The thing lashed and snapped at him, echoing in his mind. " . . . died instantly. The damned road, slick as grease . . ." He got up from his chair somehow, moved in a dreamlike state through a fog of shock. He would remember later Isaiah plucking at his sleeve, asking where he was going; he would remember Isaiah's voice shouting at him to come back, and the gray light of morning with the rain upon his face. And so he walked, drenched. People stared from the workers' houses. Voices murmured, "It's him. It's Mister Stewart, the big boss." "What's wrong with him?" "Don't know. Mister Stewart? Are you all right?"

Fuck them. What did they care? What did anybody care? " . . . died instantly. The damned road, slick as grease . . ."

And at last he came to a saloon from the old days, Jerry's.

He pushed open the sagging glass door and moved into a close, oddly familiar world of smoke and heavy male laughter and the odor of whiskey. It was the morning crowd, working men, and hangers-on fortifying themselves for another day in Fall River. The talk abruptly subsided, but he gave them no heed. There were whispers and a scraping of some chairs. He moved through the smoke to the bar and put his foot upon the railing and his elbows upon the worn, polished wood. The talk resumed, more quietly than before. A heavy, white-aproned figure came into view. "What'll it be, Mister Stewart?"

"A bourbon, if you please. Neat. Water on the side."

"Is that really what you want, Mister Stewart? Don't you think . . ."

"I said a bourbon. Now give me a bourbon, please."

"But Mister Stewart . . ."

He glared at the man through the fog of his misery. Behind him, all around him, echoed the sighs and whispers. ". . . *died instantly. The damned road, slick as grease . . .*" The saloon-keeper's eyes surrendered. He lowered his head. His hand reached for a polished glass and a bottle. The amber liquid poured out in the sifting morning light. It filled the glass with a life all its own. And then it sat there on the polished wood, waiting. A droplet oozed down the side of the glass and made a small wet spot on the bar. Maurice stared into the amber without touching the glass. It was like the old days, making a ritual of it, holding off the first heavy bite of bourbon on his tongue, delaying the sweet, sweet hell.

And then, very slowly and very deliberately, he picked up the glass, put it to his mouth, and knocked back his first drink in years.

Two hours later, someone barged into Jerry's from the street shouting the news. "The war's over. By damn, the Armistice is on! I just heard it down at the depot. The news come over the wire. It's over!" There was great shouting, handshaking, and backslapping. From the back of the saloon, a whiskey tenor began to sing, *"Over there! Over there! Send the word, send the word, over there . . ."* Crowds were massing in the street. In the distance, churchbells began to ring.

Maurice Stewart did not hear the din of celebration.

The most prominent citizen of Fall River was unconscious at the bar.

The night vomited flame and thunder. Engines snarled. A machine gun spoke with a flat, tearing sound. As he twisted the Spad away from the Boche gunner, Nathan could see the fire spitting at him through a sky of velvety black. *Tatatatatatat!* The gun stitched a seam of death across his wing surfaces and gouged great chunks of fabric from the fuselage. *Tatatatatatat!* The bullet stream thudded into his cockpit, shattering glass from the instrument panel. He spun away, falling, falling. His Spad trailed a smear of fiery oil smoke, plunging into the abyss while his executioner leered from above . . .

He awoke in the darkness, sweat-drenched, and sat bolt upright in bed trying to control the trembling that had seized him. He switched on the bedside light and looked at the time. Five o'clock in the morning. This was not another combat patrol. He was not in a hospital room, either. This was Fall River. He rolled out of bed, lit his last cigarette, and crumpled the empty pack. He went into the kitchen, fixed black coffee, and sat with the steaming mug at a white ceramic table, smoking.

So much for sleep. So much for peace. His hand trembled as he lifted the mug.

It was his first morning back in Fall River, his first morning as a bona fide human being again. He would neither fly out to kill other men over a war-torn land, drenched from four years of bloodletting, nor spend another day recuperating in St. John's Military Hospital from the head wound that had almost killed him. He was a civilian again, but he had sneaked back to this town like a thief, insisting that his cousin Van keep his arrival secret. He was a war hero, but everything frightened him. Even the thought of seeing Julie again frightened him. He wanted to hibernate, to dig a hole and crawl into it. Would she be revolted when she saw him? Worse, would she pity him?

"The war is over, Nathan." Van Harrison had said it, driving him to this house from the railroad depot last night. The big man's voice had been gentle. Only later when Van carried his luggage into the house, walking with a limp, did Nathan remember that this cousin with the partial artificial leg had also been marked for life by war. "You've got to get hold of yourself, Nathan. Start living again. Get busy. We've got a place for you here in the management team. There's going to be a real car boom, you watch, and Stewart Motors will be in the lead. We'll take the postwar market by storm."

The market. The postwar sales. It was as if a war had not occurred, as if all that death and devastation was for nothing. Nathan Stewart, former combat pilot, was back in the good old U.S.A., a genuine bloody hero with medals and newspaper clippings to prove it. He held the Distinguished Service Cross, the Silver Star, the Air Medal, the Purple Heart with Cluster, the Croix de Guerre. And for what? To get back into production? Back into the market? Back into the swing of things?

He finished the coffee and paced. His slippers scuffed over the carpet, back and forth, back and forth. Daylight streaked the eastern sky beyond the river and the range of summer hills. An hour passed. Two. The sun came over the ridge, lighting the windows with its warm glow.

Nathan dressed in the new gray suit he had bought after being released from the hospital. He combed his hair neatly and studied his face in the hallway mirror. It was leaner, older, etched in fine lines; a Stewart face of precise lines and planes, but slashed up the right side by an angry red scar terminating in a black patch where his right eye should have been.

In a world of peace, the face of war was a shock.

Turning angrily from the mirror, Nathan stalked out of the house, got into the new Silver Stewart Runabout which Van had provided, and sped down the hill into Fall Creek, tires screaming. He raced all the way through town to the main plant of Stewart Motors.

"Here he is!" Van Harrison Stewart came out from behind the desk and wrung Nathan's hand. "Lo, the conquering hero!"

They were alone. It was a huge office, done with massive furnishings and commanding a splendid view of the river and the rolling hills. A brass name plate on the mahogany desk read, Spotted Deer, Chairman of the Board.

"I'm delighted to see you, Nathan."

Nathan grinned at the name plate. "Where did that come from?"

"It was Isaiah's idea." Van put his arm around his cousin's

shoulder and they strode to the window. "He said it was in honor of the first half-breed Cheyenne Indian to take over a major American company. Nifty, eh?"

"Nifty."

Van opened a box of cigars and offered one to his cousin. They smoked. "Julie doesn't know you're back. She's coming here at ten o'clock."

"Do you think? . . ."

"You've got to face it sooner or later. It might as well be now."

Nathan hesitated. "Yes, I suppose you're right." He changed the subject. "And how is Rachel holding up?"

"Rachel? Quite well, actually. She has the children and her own interests. The last six months of being widowed were rough on her. Maurice rarely drew a sober breath, and then he just went out like a candle. He didn't want to live anymore. When Helen died, there was nothing left for him. I think Rachel reminded him of his personal failings." Van set his jaw grimly. "But I have no sympathy for that woman, never did."

"I don't think Maurice failed."

"Neither do I. I've always suspected that it went back to his father, and being disinherited. It hurt him that Bradley refused to relent even on his deathbed. But then"—Van shrugged—"how the hell do I known what goes on in a man's mind? At the last, Maurice kept muttering about a Mexican whose only crime was that he couldn't speak the language that everybody else spoke."

"What was that all about?"

"Old Tom Moneypenny said he was remembering a Mexican drifter who hanged himself in their jail cell long ago at Fostoria. It was the first dead man Maurice had ever seen. The sheer pointlessness of it made a profound impression on him. He had never realized that human life could be so cheap."

"Maurice was never in a war," Nathan muttered.

"On the contrary, cousin, he was in a war with himself."

Nathan drew on his cigar and blew smoke, looking out at the panorama of river and hills, and said nothing.

They came in one by one, as if on cue. Old Moneypenny, garrulous and effusive, overdoing it in his folksy way; Isaiah, quiet, sensitive, seeming to perceive the unspoken depths of Nathan's restless discomfort; Colby Malcolm, visibly ill at ease in the presence of a war hero but anxious to be accommodating; Jeffrey Straight, carefully avoiding the subject that he obviously wanted to talk about, his cousin Julie. Other members of the firm trailed in with the top brass. They shook hands, stood around self-consciously, drank coffee.

"Lot of changes since you been gone, Nathan. Maurice's death. Van here elected chairman of the board. We had a big fight over aircraft production. But I guess you know that. The board refused to go into producing warplanes. Your aunt Francesca..."

"Yes, he knows about that," Van said quickly. "There was a difference of philosophy, that's all." He turned, put down his coffee cup, took command. Nathan sensed a new depth and power in Van Harrison Stewart. The man exerted a natural leadership that made its presence felt. How remarkable that he had taken control so quickly. "We want to make changes as we go into peacetime production." It was a cryptic comment, quickly made and quickly passed. Nathan looked into the level eyes of his cousin but read no meaning there.

"Changes?" Nathan said.

Van seemed not to have heard. "Nathan will be rejoining us in a very special capacity, gentlemen. I know you will all be pleased when the announcement is made."

It did not last. They trickled away in the same way they had come, almost in a defined peck order: the least important first, the higher-ranked later. Finally even Isaiah and Moneypenny were gone. Van looked at his watch. "It's almost ten," he began. "She will be..."

There was a soft knock at the side door. Van smiled, stepped across the room, opened the door. Julie Straight stood there, sunbeams playing over her flaming hair. Nathan caught his breath, seeing her beauty for the first time in three years.

She said, "Van, I..." The words caught in her mouth. The green eyes widened in astonishment. She gazed at Nathan as if frozen in shock.

Van smiled. "I'll be leaving you two alone now." He nodded and walked out.

Julie moved into the room. The door closed gently behind her. She did not speak. Nathan did not speak. They stood ten feet apart in utter silence. The eyes of Julie Straight seemed to devour him. He felt a strange tightness in his chest, a weakness of the stomach and knees. Good God, what was happening to him?

He was the first to find his voice. "Aren't you going to say hello?"

With a choked sob, she ran across the room and flung herself into his arms.

Isaiah maneuvered the wheel of the new Silver Stewart Town Sedan, grinning impishly. Nathan rode beside him and wondered what all the secrecy was about. Van Harrison had gone ahead of them, accompanied by several members of the executive group. The chairman's insistent manner had done nothing to sweeten Nathan's mood.

"Frankly, Isaiah, I've got better things to do than go rushing out here on some damn fool project of Van's. Julie and I are supposed to go shopping in Detroit this afternoon."

"Fine, fine." The hunchback glanced at him with the maddening half smile. "This won't take long. Besides, you two haven't been separated since you got back to Fall River."

It was true. The week had been idyllic. Nathan was amazed at how the presence of Julie Straight stabilized him. It was almost as if there had never been a war. Even this damned eye patch and scar no longer seemed worth worrying about. Julie Straight had simply accepted it as the price of his survival and that was that. "Besides, it gives you a touch of derring-do. I rather like it." And so from the moment she had arrived in the office of the board chairman Van Harrison Stewart, they had been apart only to sleep. Nathan protested even this separation, but Julie insisted that they avoid creating a scandal. "Really, Major Stewart, I'm a respectable woman."

"I want you," he had insisted. "I'm miserable when we're apart. We've already been separated for nearly three years. Isn't that enough?"

She would smile and squeeze his hand. It warmed him to remember her words even now: "You never left my mind, Nathan. All the time you were gone, I was thinking about you, worrying and praying that you'd be safe. Some of your old friends said I was a fool, that Nathan Stewart was foot-loose and fancy free and always would be that way. But I knew better..."

"Nathan, my boy"—the voice of Cousin Isaiah jarred him back to reality—"you're daydreaming."

"What?"

"I asked you a question." Isaiah spoke over the noise of the car and the rushing wind.

"I'm sorry."

"I asked, 'When are you going to pop the question?'"

Nathan glared at Isaiah. "Of all the damned impertinence!"

"Perfectly logical thing to ask. If you and Julie aren't aware of how moonstruck you both are, then you're the only people in Fall River who don't know."

"Damn it, Isaiah..."

"Ah-ah! You wouldn't hit a cripple. Especially when he's driving."

They both laughed.

"I haven't thanked you for shipping over the Thunderbolt engines, Isaiah," Nathan said. "I had it installed in my fighter aircraft. My whole wing converted to the Stewart. It gave us a tremendous advantage."

"Glad to oblige." Isaiah had been following the main highway south of town. Now he turned off onto a side road newly paved with blacktop. There was an odor of tar paving as warm summer air flowed into the big sedan. "Anything for the war effort, you know."

"Too bad the rest of the family didn't see things that way."

"They meant well, Nathan. Some of them were afraid of creating a monster if we went into military aviation production. They saw the airplane as the ultimate weapon of destruction."

Nathan started to reply, but thought better of it. There was no point in dredging up old family hostilities. Besides, the war was over.

It was as if Isaiah had read his mind. "The war, Nathan, is over."

The road terminated in an open field. A large square building with double doors rose up ahead of them, surrounded by automobiles. A crowd gathered beside the structure. Nathan recognized Colby Malcolm, towering over the others. His spirits lifted as he saw Julie. She came running as Isaiah drew up and parked in the shade.

"What is it?" Nathan said. "What's all the fuss?"

"Come on." She took his hand and they joined Van Harrison at a makeshift speaker's platform draped in red, white, and blue bunting.

Above the building's double doors, a sign was masked in white muslin, ready for unveiling at the proper moment. Photographers fiddled with their cumbersome press cameras. Nathan smiled ruefully. When it came to publicizing a new Stewart model, old Colby Malcolm didn't miss a trick.

A whistle blew and the Fall River Brass Band struck up a ragged medley of martial tunes. Nathan felt a surge of nostalgia. It reminded him of the Fourth of July celebration of 1916. But so much had happened since then; the world had changed, and nothing would be the same again. In the crowd, he recognized the faces of old friends and acquaintances. The band struggled through the medley and came to a straggling halt.

Van Harrison faced the crowd. The Indian was still tall and spare. In the glare of sunlight Nathan noticed for the first time that his black hair was dusted with gray and the handsome face etched with fine lines. "My friends," Van said, "we are gathered here today to honor the return of one of our own. Fall River is proud to be the hometown of this hero of the skies, Major Nathan Stewart, an ace who wears a chestful of medals for valor. In the spirit of courage and faith in the future which Nathan so nobly represents, we are launching today a bold new era of Stewart endeavor..."

"What's he talking about?"

"Shhh!" Julie replied.

The speech was mercifully brief. The crowd applauded. The band played another tune. At a nod from Van, a pushcart of champagne was rolled out from the building and white-aproned waiters began popping corks and filling glasses. When every hand held a glass, Van smiled broadly and turned to Nathan. "And now, it is my great pleasure to announce the creation of a new Stewart subsidiary company. As its president, I am designating the man best qualified to carry the dream to a resounding success, Nathan Stewart!"

Nathan gave Julie a puzzled look.

Van nodded. A workman yanked at a rope. The muslin cover fell away from the sign over the double doors.

Nathan looked up and read, *Stewart Aviation Company*. "Well, I'll be a sonofabitch," he said.

The crowd cheered, the band blared again, and they all drank champagne.

Isaiah appeared at his side and lifted his glass, shouting to be heard over the din. "As your vice-president in charge of research and development, I propose a toast. Here's to a new dynasty!"

Nathan laughed. "To a new dynasty!"

They drained their glasses and smashed them against the double doors.

ABOUT THE AUTHOR

CHARLES WHITED was born in West Virginia, attended the University of Virginia and was a paratrooper sergeant during the Korean War. He has been a journalist for twenty-five years and now writes a daily commentary column for the *Miami Herald*.

He ghostwrote Mrs. Elliott Roosevelt's autobiography *I Love a Roosevelt* for Doubleday. He later collaborated with treasure hunter Martin Meylach to write *Diving to a Flash of Gold*. His book about the true adventures of Dan Chiodo as a NYC decoy cop, *The Decoy Man*, was published in hard and soft cover by Playboy Press. He has published several paperback novels.

"MICHAEL KORDA HAS FASHIONED AN IN-TRIGUING TALE AROUND A WORLD OF WEALTH AND POWER—A WORLD HE KNOWS BETTER THAN ANYONE ELSE . . . MESMERIZ-ING."
—Robert Ludlum

WORLDLY GOODS
by Michael Korda

Paul Foster is the enigmatic billionaire with a dangerous thirst for power. Nicholas Greenwood is the ruthless, un-imaginably wealthy master of Foster's rival empire. Clash-ing in the dollar-mad world of high finance, Foster feeds the fire of their explosive rivalry when he plunges into a burning international romance with Greenwood's dynamic mistress.

But the obsessive hatred between these two giants has its roots in something far more profound than love or money —a terrible crime of passion and greed that reaches back to the horror days of the Third Reich . . . a crime that could now claim Foster's fortune, the woman he loves, and his very life . . . a crime that can be laid to rest only by an act of equally terrible vengeance.

Buy WORLDLY GOODS, on sale June 15, 1983, wher-ever Bantam paperbacks are sold or use this handy cou-pon for ordering:

Bantam Books, Inc., Dept. WG, 414 East Golf Road, Des Plaines, Ill. 60016

Mr/Ms_____

Address_____

City/State_____ Zip_____

WG—5/83

Please allow four to six weeks for delivery. This of-fer expires 11/83.

SAVE $2.00 ON YOUR NEXT BOOK ORDER!

BANTAM BOOKS 🐓

Shop-at-Home
Catalog

Now you can have a complete, up-to-date catalog of Bantam's
inventory of over 1,600 titles—including hard-to-find books.
And, you can save $2.00 on your next order by taking advantage of
the money-saving coupon you'll find in this illustrated catalog.
Choose from fiction and non-fiction titles, including mysteries,
historical novels, westerns, cookbooks, romances, biographies,
family living, health, and more. You'll find a description of most
titles. Arranged by categoreis, the catalog makes it easy to find
your favorite books and authors and to discover new ones.

So don't delay—send for this shop-at-home catalog and save money
on your next book order.

Just send us your name and address and 50¢ to defray postage and
handling costs.

BANTAM BOOKS, INC.
Dept. FC, 414 East Golf Road, Des Plaines, Ill. 60016

Mr./Mrs./Miss _____
(please print)

Address _____

City _____ State _____ Zip _____

Do you know someone who enjoys books? Just give us their names and
addresses and we'll send them a catalog too at no extra cost!

Mr./Mrs./Miss _____

Address _____

City _____ State _____ Zip _____

Mr./Mrs./Miss _____

Address _____

City _____ State _____ Zip _____

FC—2/83